# the Friends Forever Collection

*Secret Meeting* first published in Great Britain by HarperCollins *Children's Books* in 2004
*Is Anybody There?* first published in Great Britain by HarperCollins *Children's Books* in 2004
*Sugar and Spice* first published in Great Britain by HarperCollins *Children's Books* in 2005

First published in this three-in-one edition by HarperCollins *Children's Books* 2007
HarperCollins *Children's Books* is a division of HarperCollins*Publishers* Ltd,
77-85 Fulham Palace Road, Hammersmith, London W6 8JB

The HarperCollins *Children's Books* website address is
www.harpercollinschildrensbooks.co.uk

1 3 5 7 9 8 6 4 2

Text © Jean Ure 2004, 2004, 2005
Illustrations © Karen Donnelly 2004, 2004, 2005

The author and illustrator assert the moral right to be
identified as the author and illustrator of this work.

ISBN-13   978 0 00 724820 9
ISBN-10   0 00 724820 2

Printed and bound in England by
Clays Ltd, St Ives plc

# Secret Meeting

## JEAN URE

Illustrated by Karen Donnelly

HarperCollins *Children's Books*

*For Chris and Joan,*
*with love and respect*

# one

MY FRIEND ANNIE is completely bonkers. Loopy, wacko. Seriously *doo*lally, as my nan would say. She does the craziest things! Like in biology, one time, we were supposed to be dissecting plums, and when Miss Andrews said, "Annabel Watson, where is your plum?" Annie said, "Oops, sorry, miss! I ate it."

"*Ate* it?" said Miss Andrews. "Ate your *plum*?"

She couldn't believe it! I could, 'cos I know Annie. She drank some paint water once, when we were in juniors. She said it looked so pretty, like pink lemonade.

Some people think she does it to show off, but it's not that at all. She just happens to be a very zany sort of person. I, on the other hand, am desperately sensible and boring. I would never do anything silly, if it weren't for Annie. She is always getting us into hot water! The only times I ever have my name in the order mark book are when Annie's told me to do something and I've gone and done it, even though I know it means trouble. Like, for instance, hiding ourselves in the stationery cupboard when we should have been outside playing hockey. I knew it would end in disaster. I only did it 'cos I hate hockey – well, and because Annie said it would be fun. What she didn't realise was that Mrs Gibson, our head teacher, was due to take a special sixth form study group in our classroom. With us still in the cupboard!!!

Mrs Gibson was quite surprised when someone opened the cupboard door and we fell out. We were quite surprised, ourselves.

That was *two* order marks. One for missing hockey, and one for damaging school property (trampling on the stationery).

Then there was the time she decided – Annie, I mean – that we should go to school wearing birds' nests in our hair. She'd found these old nests in her garden and she said, "Think how cool it would look! We could start a new fashion." She perched one on her head and it sat there like a little cap, really sweet, with tiny bits of twig and feather sticking out, so

I did the same, and we went into assembly like it, and people kept looking at us and giggling, until all of a sudden this *thing*, this horrible maggoty *thing*, started to crawl out of Annie's nest and slither down the side of her face, and the girl next to her screeched out, really loud, like she was being attacked by a herd of man-eating slugs.

I screeched, too, but in a more strangulated way, and tore my nest off and threw it on the floor, which started a kind of mini stampede and brought the assembly to a standstill.

We didn't actually get order marks for that, but Mrs Gibson told us that we were behaving childishly and irresponsibly, adding, "I'm surprised at *you*, Megan." Later on, at Parents' Evening, she told Mum that I was too easily influenced.

"She lets herself be led astray."

She meant, of course, by Annie. If it weren't for Annie I'd probably be the goodest person in the whole of our class! I might even win prizes for "Best Behaviour" or "Hardest Working". To which all I can say is *yuck*. I'd rather have order marks and be led astray! I can't imagine not being friends with Annie. Even Mum admits that there is nothing malicious about her. She may have these wild and wacky ideas that get us into trouble, but she is warm, and funny, and generous, and is always making me laugh.

Last term she gave me this card. It was really beautiful, all decorated with little teensy pictures of flowers and animals that she'd done herself.

Inside it said:

TWELVE TODAY!

HIP HIP HOORAY!

HAPPY BIRTHDAY!

"What's this for?" I said.

Annie beamed and replied, "For your birthday."

But my birthday wasn't for another whole week! I couldn't believe that my very best friend in all the world had forgotten when my birthday was.

"It's not till the end of the month," I said. "Twenty-eighth of April!"

"I know," said Annie. "But I wanted you to have it now. I'll do you another one for your real birthday!"

"You're mad," I said. "Who gives people birthday cards when it's not their birthday?"

Annie giggled and said, "I do!" And then she said that maybe it was an *un*birthday card, and she started singing "Happy unbirthday to *you*, happy unbirthday to *you*, happy un*birth*day, dear Me-gan, happy unbirthday to *you*!"

I put my hands over my ears and begged her to stop. Annie has a voice like a screech owl. Really painful! Not that mine is much better.

Mum says it sounds like a gnat, buzzing to itself in a bottle. But it is not as loud as Annie's. And I wasn't the one singing happy unbirthday!

"I'm going to give you a really good birthday present," said Annie. "A *really* good one."

I said, "What?"

Annie said she hadn't yet decided, and even if she had she wouldn't tell me. "But it's going to be something you'll really, really like!"

"What I would really really like," I said, "is the latest Harriet Chance."

I'm sure I don't need to tell anyone who Harriet Chance is. She is just my all-time mega favourite author is all! Mine and about fifty million others. But I am her number-one fan! I have read almost every single book she's ever written. Which is *a lot of books*. Fifty-one, to be exact; I looked it up on one of the computers in our school library. Thirty-four of them are on the shelf in my bedroom. I call them my Harriet Chance Collection. I couldn't wait to get my hands on the latest one!

"It's called *Scarlet Feather*," I said. "Scarlet is this girl who goes to stay with her nan 'cos—"

Annie made an exaggerated groaning noise. She quite likes Harriet Chance, she is just not the huge fan that I am.

"Well, anyway," I said, "it's all right, I wouldn't expect you to get it for me. It's in hardback and costs simply loads." I heaved a sigh. Very dramatic. "I'll just have to wait till the paperback comes out."

"Why?" said Annie. "You can get it with your book tokens. You know you'll have lots."

It's true, I always ask for book tokens when it comes to my birthday or Christmas. Annie thinks it is just sooo boring.

"You get it with your book tokens," she said, "and I'll

think of something else... I'll think of something far more exciting!"

I said, "Nothing could be more exciting than a new Harriet Chance."

"Oh, no?" said Annie. "Wanna bet? I'll find something, don't you worry!"

"Not like last time," I begged.

For my last birthday she'd given me this long blonde wig and some spooky black eyelashes and plastic fingernails, "to make you look glamorous!" I did look glamorous. It was brilliant! Mum didn't approve, of course, but I sometimes think that my mum is just a tiny bit old-fashioned. Certainly compared to Annie's. But she didn't really mind, she let me dress up for my birthday party and paint the plastic fingernails purple. Unfortunately, I turned out to be allergic to the glue that stuck the eyelashes on, and next morning when I woke up my eyes were all swollen like footballs.

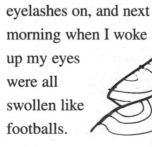

It wasn't Annie's fault, but I had to go to the doctor and get some special cream and couldn't leave the house for three whole days. Well, I could have done, but I was too embarrassed. This is the sort of thing that just always, somehow, seems to happen with Annie.

"I don't want more eyelashes!" I said.

"Not going to get more eyelashes."

"I don't want anything with *glue*."

"It won't be anything with glue! I'm going to think of something really special... hey!" Annie tiptoed over to the door (we were in her bedroom at the time) and peered out. "D'you want to go on the computer?"

I hesitated. "You mean... go to that site you told me about?"

Slowly, I shook my head. I would have liked to, I would *really* have liked to, but I'd promised Mum.

"When you're round at Annie's, I don't want you playing with that computer. I want you to give me your word!"

When Mum said "playing with the computer", what she really meant was chatrooms. She'd heard all these stories about middle-aged men pretending to be young boys, and girls going off to meet them, and they had scared her. They scared me a bit, too, though as I said to Mum, "I wouldn't ever go and *meet* anyone." Mum said she didn't care, she wanted me to promise her.

I do sometimes think Mum tends to fuss more than other people's mums. I suppose it is because I am all she has got, now that Nan is in a home. I don't remember what it was like when Dad was with us; I was too young. Perhaps it was after he left that Mum got nervous. Well, not nervous, exactly, but not wanting me to do things like go into chatrooms. Annie's mum and dad let her do pretty well whatever she wants. She even had her own computer in her bedroom. I didn't have a computer at all! Mum had always promised me one for when I was fourteen. She said we'd find the money somehow. I didn't really mind not having one. Not usually, I didn't. Not when I had all my Harriet Chances to read! Just now and again I thought that it would be fun and wished Mum didn't have to "count

every penny". But I knew it was a worry for her.

"Megs?" Annie was standing poised, with one finger on the mouse. She had this impish grin on her face. "Shall I?"

I muttered, "You know I'm not allowed into chatrooms."

"'Tisn't a chatroom!" said Annie. "It's a *book*room. Wouldn't go into a *chat*room." She looked at me reproachfully. "I know you're not allowed into *chat*rooms."

I was still doubtful. "So what's the difference?"

"This is for *bookworms*," said Annie. "You just talk about books, and say which ones you like, and write reviews and stuff. Honestly, you'd love it! It's your sort of thing."

It *was* my sort of thing; that was what made it so tempting. But I was quite surprised at Annie visiting a chatroom for bookworms. It's not her sort of thing at all! I mean, she does read, but only 'cos I do. I don't think, probably, that she'd bother with it if it weren't for me.

"What books do you talk about?" I said.

"Oh! Harriet Chance. Everyone talks about Harriet Chance. I'm only doing it," said Annie, "'cos of this project thing."

She meant our holiday task for English. We all had to review one of our favourite books and write a bit about the author. There are no prizes for guessing who I was going to do... Harriet Chance! I just hoped Annie didn't think she was going to do her, too.

I said this to her, and she said, "Well, I won't if you don't want me to, but who else could I do if I didn't do her?"

"Anyone!" I said. "J.K. Rowling."

"I can't do J.K. Rowling! *Harry Potter*'s too long."

"So do something short... do *Winnie the Pooh*."

"Oh. Yes." She brightened. "I could do that, couldn't I? I love *Winnie the Pooh*!" She then added that even if *she* didn't do Harriet Chance, half the rest of the class probably would. "There's more people that talk about her books than almost anyone else."

"That's because she's a totally brilliant writer," I said.

"Yes, and it's why you ought to visit the bookroom, so you can see for yourself," said Annie. "Look, it's ever so easy, all I have to do is just—"

"*Annie Watson, you fat little scumbag, I hope you're obeying the rules?*"

Annie dropped the mouse and spun round, guiltily.

It was her sister, Rachel, who'd crept up the stairs without our hearing. Rachel is four years older than Annie and me. She always house-sits when it's school holidays and her mum and dad are at work.

"I saw you!" she said. "You were going to use that computer!"

"I'm allowed!" shrieked Annie.

"You're not allowed to go on the Net. Not when Megan's here. You know that perfectly well."

"Wasn't going to go on the Net," said Annie.

"So what were you going to do?"

"I was going to... write something. For school."

"Like what?"

"Our project," said Annie. "F'r English."

*"Fringlish?"*

"Book reviews!" roared Annie.

Rachel narrowed her eyes. They are bright green, like a cat's, and very beautiful. Rachel herself is rather beautiful. While Annie is little and plump, Rachel is tall and slim. This is because of all the work-outs she does, and the games of hockey that she plays (instead of sitting in the stationery cupboard, trampling on the stationery).

They both have black hair, but Rachel's is thick and straight, like a shiny satin waterfall, while Annie's is all mad and messy, with some bits curling in one direction and some bits curling in another.

I have often thought that I should like to have a brother or sister, if my dad hadn't gone and left us before he and Mum could get round to it, but I'm not sure that I'd want a sister like Rachel. She is just *sooo* superior. Like she reckons anyone in Year Seven is simply beneath her notice. Like small crawling things in the grass; just too bad if they get trodden on. On the other hand she *was* supposed to be supervising us, so maybe it's not surprising if she came across a bit bossy.

"If you can't be trusted," she said, "you can go downstairs."

"We're not *doing* anything," said Annie.

"I still think it would be better if you went downstairs."

"We don't want to go downstairs! We're happy up here."

"Yes, well, I'm not happy with you up here! I'm the one that'll catch it if you do something you're not supposed to."

Annie flounced, and huffed, but I knew, really, that Rachel was right. Another minute and I might have given way to temptation. I had to admit that I didn't personally see anything so wrong in visiting a chatroom for bookworms; I mean you'd think it would be classed as educational, but I had given Mum my word. It was the only reason she let me go round to Annie's. I knew she wasn't terribly happy about it, because of Annie having her own computer and her mum and dad being a bit what Mum calls *lax*; but Mum couldn't always get time off in school holidays.

"I just have to trust you," she said.

It was probably all for the best that Rachel had stepped in. I don't *think* I would have been tempted, because in spite of what Mrs Gibson and Mum believe,

I do quite often stand up to Annie. Not if it's just something daft that she wants us to do, but if it's something I actually think is wrong. Like one time she showed me a packet of cigarettes she'd found and wanted us to try smoking one. I didn't do it because I think smoking cigarettes is just too gross. In the end Annie agreed with me and threw them away.

Then there was this other time when she thought it might be fun to write jokey comments in library books, such as "Ho ho!" or "Ha ha!" or "Yuck!" I told her off about that one. I said it was vandalism and that I really, truly *hated* people that wrote things in books. *Or* turned down the corners of the pages. That is another thing I hate. I don't so much mind them doing graffiti in the school toilets as the school toilets are quite dim and dismal places and graffiti can sometimes make them brighter and more interesting. But books are precious! Well, they are to me. I know they are not to Annie, but after I'd lectured her she got quite ashamed and said that if I felt that strongly, she wouldn't do it. She does listen to me! Sometimes.

But she hardly listens to Rachel at all. She grumbled all the way downstairs.

"We don't *want* to go downstairs! There isn't anything to *do* downstairs. We want to stay in my bedroom. It's not fair! It's my house as much as yours! What right have you got to tell me where I can go in my own house?"

"Every right!" snarled Rachel. "I'm the one who's been left in charge!"

"You're not supposed to push us about. You're only here to protect us in case anyone breaks in."

"I'm here to make sure you behave yourself!" shouted Rachel.

"I was behaving myself!"

"You were going to use that computer. You were going to do things you're not supposed to do! You get down there." Rachel gave Annie and me a little shove along the hall. "And you stay there!"

"But there isn't anything to *do* down here!" wailed Annie.

"Oh, don't be so useless!" Rachel herded us into the kitchen. "Go out in the garden and get some exercise!"

Rachel is a great one for exercise. She is an exercise *freak*. She is for ever charging fiercely up and down the hockey field, billowing clouds of steam, or dashing madly to and fro across the netball court. She also goes to the sports club twice a week and swims and jogs and does things with weights. This is why she is so lean and *toned*. In other words, super-fit. She thinks Annie and I ought to be super-fit, too. She is going to join the police when she is older. I just hope she goes and joins them up in Birmingham, or Manchester, or somewhere. Anywhere, so long as it is miles away from here! Here being Stone Heath, which is near Salisbury, and very quiet and peaceful, which it most certainly would not be if Rachel started bashing about with a truncheon. She'd whack people over the head just for *breathing*.

"Go on! Get out there," she said, flinging open the back door. "Go and get some fresh air, for a change. You're like a couple of couch potatoes!"

I said, "What's couch potatoes?"

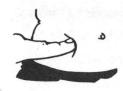"Human beings that sit around doing nothing all day, like vegetables. Look at you! Megan's like a stick of celery, and as for you" – she poked poor Annie in the stomach – "you're like a water melon!"

"Water melon's a fruit," I said.

"*Thank* you, Miss Know-it-All!"

"Don't you treat my friend like that," said Annie. "You've got no right to treat my friend like that, and just stop *shoving me*! Ow! Ouch! You're hurting!"

Rachel took absolutely no notice of Annie's howls; she is a really ruthless kind of person. She must have a heart like a block of cement. She drove me and Annie into the garden and for *over an hour* she made us throw balls at her so that she could whack them with a rounders bat. By the time she let us go back indoors we were completely exhausted.

"See what I mean?" she said. "You're so out of condition it's unbelievable! When I was your age I could run right round the playing field without even noticing it. You can't even run round the garden!"

She still wouldn't let us go back upstairs. She said *she* was going upstairs, and we were to stay in the sitting room until Mum came to collect me. Well! Quite honestly, we were so faint and wobbly from all the crashing about we'd done,

chasing after the balls she'd whacked, we just sank down side by side on the sofa – a big shiny water melon and a little trembly stick of celery – and watched videos all afternoon. One of them was *Candyfloss*, which was the very first Harriet Chance I ever read! I know the film practically off by heart, word for word. If ever we did it as a school production, I could play the part of Candy, no problem! I would already know all my lines. Except that Candy has bright blue eyes "the colour of periwinkles", and blonde hair which "froths and bubbles", whereas I have brown eyes, more the colour of mud, I would say, and mousy *flat* hair, not a bubble in sight; so probably no one would ever cast me as Candy, more is the pity. But it doesn't really bother me; I wouldn't want to be an actor. I am going to be a writer, like Harriet!

# RACHEL'S DIARY (THURSDAY)

I am just SO SICK of baby-sitting. Mum says, "For heaven's sake, Rachel! It's only a few weeks in the year." She also points out that I am being well paid for it, which is perfectly true. Mum and Dad pay me more than Jem gets paid for stacking shelves, AND I don't have to take fares out of it. Or food. But as I said to Mum, there is more to life than just money.

Mum pretended to be very surprised when I said this. Her eyebrows flew up and she went all sarcastic, saying, "Oh, really?" in this silly artificial voice. "Well, that's nice to know. You could certainly have fooled me!" A reference, I presume, to Christmas, when I was moaning — QUITE JUSTIFIABLY — about Gran giving me a box of bath salts. Bath salts, I ask you! LAVENDER bath salts. And a titchy little box, at that. Mum was quite cross. She reminded me that it was the thought that counted, to which I retorted that in Gran's case the thought obviously hadn't counted very much. Mum then told me not to be so grasping, but I don't see that it WAS grasping, considering Gran spends a small fortune going off on cruises every year, and that me and Annie are her only and dearly beloved grandchildren.

I mean, quite honestly, I wouldn't have minded so much if it had been something I wanted. But who in their right mind would pollute their bath water with stinky, flowery scents? Especially LAVENDER. Lavender's an old lady smell!

Anyway, that was then, and this is now. And right now I would rather be stacking shelves with Jem than stuck here in charge of a couple of horrible brats. Well, Annie is a horrible brat. She's plump, and she's spoilt! Her friend Megan isn't so bad, it's just that her mum is seriously weird, like some kind of pathetic old hen,

always fussing and bothering.
DON'T LET HER DO THIS,
DON'T LET HER DO THAT.
Plus she has this thing
about computers, like the
minute you log on someone's
going to leap out and grab
you. At least, thank goodness,
Mum and Dad have always been pretty relaxed about
trusting us to be sensible. I mean, how can you ever
LEARN to be sensible unless they let you just get on
with things? But Mum says if Mrs Hooper doesn't
want Megan going into chatrooms, then Annie has to
promise not to take her into chatrooms, and I have to
keep an eye on them both to make sure they're obeying
the rules. How am I supposed to do this? TIE THEM UP
AND HANDCUFF THEM??? Mum says don't be
ridiculous; just pop your head round the door every
now and then and check they're OK. But I don't see
why I should have to!

"Because it's what you're being paid for," says
Mum. "It's what I'd have to do, if I were here."

So why isn't she here? Because she wants to take
all of her holiday in one great lump and go off to

Spain for the summer. She seems to be under the impression that's what I want, too.

"Just think of those nice friends you made last year," she oozes.

Hm... I'm thinking of them. One in particular. The blond one. Kerry. He was gorgeous! But who's to say he'll be there again this year? In  any case, what  about Ty? He's gorgeous, too! And he's stacking shelves in the supermarket... I might drop by there tomorrow. Jem says she and him are on the same shift. She says that sometimes they even stand and stock the same shelves together... I'm just glad she doesn't fancy him!!! Well, she does, but she's got Kieron. Otherwise I'd be tearing my hair out! I think tomorrow I'll definitely go down there. Just to suss things out. The two dwarfs can manage on their own for an hour or so. I mean, they're nearly twelve years old, for heaven's sake! That's quite old enough to start taking responsibility for themselves.

They're downstairs at the moment, watching a video. Moaning and whining because I made them go into the garden and run about. Left to themselves, they'd never move anywhere at more than snail's pace. The little fat thing is all squashy, like an overripe plum. The other one is so skinny she looks like a puff of wind would blow her over. They don't get enough exercise! If I had my way I'd make them do two laps of the hockey field every morning, before school. I think I'll get them running round the garden again tomorrow, before I go and see Jem. That way, they'll be too EXHAUSTED to get up to mischief.

Even if they're not, who cares? I'm sick to death of them!

two

MUM CAME TO collect me at four o'clock. Annie and me were still collapsed on the sofa, watching videos.

"You look as if you've had a busy day," said Mum.

I couldn't decide if that was her idea of a joke, or if she was being serious. Rachel was there. She said, "I made them go into the garden and get some exercise."

"Good for you!" said Mum.

"She only did it because she wanted to practise *hitting* things," said Annie.

33

"Excuse me," said Rachel, "I did it because you need to lose weight."

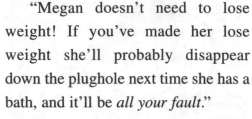

"Megan doesn't need to lose weight! If you've made her lose weight she'll probably disappear down the plughole next time she has a bath, and it'll be *all your fault*."

"I just hope they behaved themselves," said Mum. "It's very good of you, Rachel, to keep an eye on them."

"She's paid for it!" shrilled Annie.

"People are paid for emptying dustbins," said Mum, "but I wouldn't want to do it."

"It doesn't need any *skill*," said Annie. "You just have to be a big *bully*, is all."

Mum laughed. "Well! Sooner Rachel than me. I trust Megan hasn't been too much bother?"

"It's not Megan," said Rachel, looking hard at Annie. Annie stuck her tongue out. "It's *her*," said Rachel.

As Mum and me walked back through the Estate, Mum said that Annie was obviously "a bit of a handful".

Of course, I immediately leapt to the defence of my best friend.

"It's Rachel," I said. "She's so bossy!"

"It's difficult," said Mum, "when you're only sixteen. And after all, she has been left in charge."

I grumbled that it didn't give her the right to make us go and chase balls all round the garden.

"That's not what she's there for!"

"I'm sure she's doing her best," said Mum.

"*Bossy*," I muttered.

"Just keeping you out of trouble."

"We didn't need to be kept out of trouble! We weren't *in* trouble."

"Maybe she thought you were going to be."

"Well, we weren't!"

"You promise?"

"Promise!" I said. "We weren't *doing* anything."

"All right," said Mum. "I believe you."

Mum always does believe me, which is why I feel that I have to tell her the truth. It is quite hard at times!

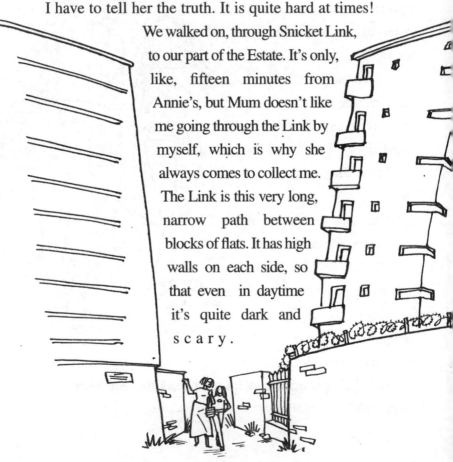

We walked on, through Snicket Link, to our part of the Estate. It's only, like, fifteen minutes from Annie's, but Mum doesn't like me going through the Link by myself, which is why she always comes to collect me. The Link is this very long, narrow path between blocks of flats. It has high walls on each side, so that even in daytime it's quite dark and s c a r y.

Annie's mum doesn't seem to mind Annie going through it when she comes to visit me, but Mum says it's too dangerous. She says anyone could be lurking there. If I go to Annie's by myself I always take the long way round, by the road.

Annie lives in a house, but Mum and me live in a maisonette, which I know from French lessons means a *little* house. What it is, it's two little houses, one on top of the other. We have the one on top. It is quite tiny, but it is a real *little house*; not a flat!

Mum asked me what I was going to do after tea, and I said I was going to write my book review for school.

"Harriet Chance, I suppose?" said Mum. Mum knows all about Harriet Chance! She can hardly help it, considering my room is full to bursting with Harriet Chance books. "Which one are you doing?"

I said I was going to do *Candyfloss*, because a) I'd just watched the video – for about the ninety-eighth time! – and b) it was one of my favourites. This is what I wrote:

# CANDYFLOSS

Candyfloss is eleven years old and lives with her mum. She has no brothers or sisters, but often wishes that she had. She has no dad, either. Her dad left home when Candy was only little, so that she can remember hardly anything about him. This makes her sad at times but mostly she is quite happy just to be with her mum.

I have just had a sudden thought: maybe this is why *Candyfloss* is one of my big favourites? Because Candy is like me! Lots of Harriet Chance characters are a bit like me, one way or another. For instance, there is Victoria Plum, who loves reading; and April Rose, who gets into trouble when her best friend leads her astray. But Candyfloss is the one who is *most* like me!

To continue.

Candy is quite a shy sort of person, who doesn't think very highly of herself. If anything happens, she always assumes she is in the wrong. Like if someone bumps into her in the street she will immediately say sorry, even if it was not her fault.

Like at school, just the other day, this big pushy girl called Madeleine Heffelump (that is what we  call her, her real name is Heffer) well, she came charging across the playground, straight towards me. I tried to get out of her way but I wasn't quick enough and she went crashing wham, bam, right into me, nearly knocking me over. And I was the one who said sorry. Just like Candy! Even though it was Madeleine Heffelump who was in the wrong, not me.

Crazy! Anyway. This is the rest of my review:

Candy is pretty, with bright blue eyes like periwinkles and bubbly blonde hair (as I already said, I don't look like her. Alas!) but she never thinks of herself as pretty, having this quite low opinion of herself most of the time. Then there is this girl at school, Tabitha Bigg, who bullies her and tells her she is useless and stupid, and Candy believes her, until one day a TV director comes to the school looking for someone to play a part in a TV show he is doing. Tabitha Bigg is sure he will choose her, because she is convinced she is the cat's whiskers and Utterly Irresistible. Candy is too shy to even show herself! She tries to hide in the lavatory, but she comes out too soon

and the director catches sight of her and immediately forgets all about Tabitha Bigg.

"THAT is the one I want!" he cries.

So Candy gets the part and it is yah boo and sucks to Tabitha Bigg, who is as sour as gooseberries and totally gutted. But everyone else is really glad that she didn't get chosen as they are all fed up with her.

When the show goes out on television, Candy's dad sees it (on the Net: he is in Australia) and he writes to Candy, and comes flying over to see her. It turns out that Candy's dad is a big name in Australian TV. He offers to take Candy back with him and make her a Big Star, but she chooses to stay with her mum.

Which is what I would do if ever my dad turned up! I wouldn't want to be a Big Star, and Candy doesn't, either. Another way that we are alike!

After I had written my review I read it out loud to Mum, who said that Candy sounded "a very sensible sort of girl".

I wondered if I was a sensible sort of girl, and whether sensible was an exciting thing to be. I decided that it wasn't, and that was why I needed Annie. I don't think anyone would call Annie sensible. But sometimes she is exciting. Like when she gets one of her mad ideas!

"When I go round there tomorrow," I said, "to Annie's, I mean, is it OK if I use her computer? Just to type out on?"

"What's wrong with your handwriting?" said Mum.

"It's horrible! No one can read it."

"Of course they can, if you just take care. Why don't you write it out again, nice and neatly? You can write beautifully when you try!"

I didn't want to try. I wanted to do it on Annie's computer! I wanted it to look like proper printing.

"Everyone else'll do it on the computer," I said.

"*Everyone?*" said Mum.

"Well... practically everyone."

"I don't believe you're the only person in your class who doesn't have their own PC."

"I said, *practically* everyone."

I think I must have looked a bit mutinous, a bit *rebellious*, 'cos Mum sighed and said, "Well, all right, if you really must. But I think it's a great shame if people are going to lose the ability to write by hand!"

"I don't mind for ordinary homework," I said, "but this is going to be made into a book. It's going to go on display. Miss Morton's going to put it in the library! So it needs to look *nice*, Mum. It—"

"Yes, yes, yes!" Mum held up her hands. "Enough! You've made your point."

"I wouldn't go into a chatroom," I said. "Honest! All I'm going to do is just type out the review. I wouldn't *ever* go into a chatroom," I said. "'cos we've talked about it. And I've given you my word. And I wouldn't ever break my word, Mum, I promise!"

"Oh, Megan." Mum reached out and patted my hand. "I know you think I'm a terrible old fusspot—"

"I don't, Mum," I said. "Truly!" I mean, I did, a bit; but I wanted her to know that I understood and that it didn't bother me.

"It's just that Annie is such a strong character—"

Did Mum mean that I was a weak one???

"—and you do tend to follow wherever she leads."

"Not always!" I said.

"Most of the time," said Mum.

"Only when it's something funny! I wouldn't do anything *bad*."

"I'm sure you wouldn't mean to. But it does worry me that Annie's parents are so lax."

I crinkled my forehead. "What does it mean? *Lax?*"

"They're not very strict with her. They let her do things that other parents wouldn't. Like going into chatrooms without supervision, or—"

"She knows not to give her address!" I said.

"Even so," said Mum. "She's only eleven years old. You can do very silly things when you're that age."

"Did you ever do silly things?" I said.

"Of course I did!" said Mum. "Everybody does. You don't have the experience to know any better."

"What were some of the silly things that you did?" I said.

"Oh, come on, Megs! You really don't want to hear about them."

"I do," I said. "I do!"

So then we got sidetracked, with Mum telling me how she'd once tried to turn herself blonde by using a bottle of household bleach – "I had to have all my hair cut off!" – and how another time she'd plucked her eyebrows almost raw, trying to look like some movie star I'd never heard of.

"Mum! To think you were so vain," I said.

"You'd be hard put to believe it now, wouldn't you?" said Mum, tweaking at the side of her hair where it is just starting to turn grey. "At least it's one thing I wouldn't accuse you of."

 It is true that on the whole I am not a vain sort of person, which is mainly because I don't really have anything to be vain about. Maybe if I was in a competition to find the human being that looks most like a stick of celery I might get a bit high and mighty, since I would almost certainly win first prize; or even, perhaps, a competition for the person with the most knobbly knees. My knees are *really* knobbly! A boy at school was once rude enough to say that my knees looked like big ball-bearings with twigs sticking out of them. Some cheek! But I have to admit he was right. So this is why I am not vain, as it would be rather pathetic if I was.

I told Mum about the celery competition and the ball-bearing knees, and Mum said, "Oh, sweetheart, don't worry! You'll fill out," as if she thought I needed comforting. But I don't! I don't mind looking like a stick of celery. I don't even mind knobbly knees! If ever I start to get a bit depressed or self-conscious, I just go and read one of my Harriet Chances. Every single one of Harriet's characters has secret worries about the way she looks. April Rose, for instance, has *no waist*. Me, neither! Victoria Plum has "hair like a limp dishcloth". Just like me! Then there is poor little Sugar Mouse, who agonises about

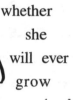

whether she will ever grow

any boobs, and Fudge Cassidy, who can't stop eating chocolates and putting on weight.

I don't personally care overmuch about growing boobs, in fact I sometimes think I'd just as soon not bother with them. And as for putting on weight, Mum says I hardly eat enough to keep a flea alive (not true!) but there are lots of people who *do* agonise over these things. Harriet Chance knows everything there is to know about teenage anxieties. She can get right into your mind!

\*

When Mum dropped me off at Annie's the next day, I said that I was allowed to use her computer just to type out my book review.

"We'd better tell *her*," said Annie. "Old Bossyboots."

"Oh, do what you like!" said Rachel, when Annie told her. "I've washed my hands of you."

"That's good," said Annie, as we scampered back to her bedroom. "P'raps now she'll leave us alone."

But she didn't. I'd just finished typing out my review when she came banging and hammering at the door, shouting to us "Get yourselves downstairs! Time for exercise!"

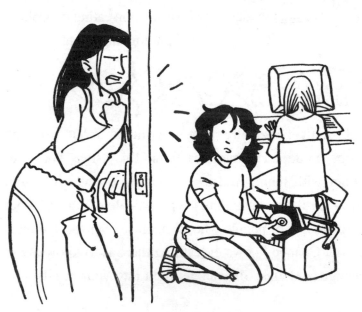

"We exercised yesterday," wailed Annie.

"So you can exercise again today!"

There wasn't any arguing with her.

"You get out there," she said. "It's good for you! You heard what your mother said, Megan."

She kept us at it until midday, by which time we had gone all quivering and jellified again.

"OK," she said. "That's enough! You can go back indoors now. I'm going out for a couple of hours. I want you to behave yourselves. *Otherwise*—" she twisted Annie's ear. Annie squawked.

"Otherwise, there'll be trouble. Geddit?"

"Goddit," said Annie. And, "Geddoff!" she bawled. "You're breaking my ear!"

"I'll do more than just break your ear," said Rachel, "if I get back and find you've been up to nonsense."

"She's not supposed to leave us on our own," said Annie, when Rachel had gone. "I'll tell Mum if she's not careful!" And then this big sly beam slid across her face, and she said, "This means we can do *whatever we want*, 'cos a) she won't find out and b) even if she does, there's nothing she can do about it! 'Cos if I tell Mum, Mum'll be furious with her. She promised your mum that Rachel would be here with us *all the time*."

"So what shall we do?" I said. "Watch more videos?"

"No! Let's get some lunch and take it upstairs."

"And then what?"

"Then we'll think," said Annie.

So we grabbed some food and went back to Annie's bedroom to eat it.

"Sure you don't want to visit the bookroom?" said Annie.

I said, "No! Don't keep pushing me."

"You don't know what you're missing," said Annie. "You'll never guess who I talked to!"

"Who?" I said.

"Harriet Chance's daughter!"

"*Lori?*"

"Mm!"

"You spoke to *Lori*?"

"Yes!"

I swallowed. "What did you talk about?"

Annie giggled and said, "You!"

"M-me?"

"I told her that you were Harriet's number-one fan. I told her you'd got every single book she'd ever written—"

"I haven't!" I cried. There are three of her early ones that I've only been able to find in the library, and one, called *Patsy Puffball*, that I have never even seen. (Though I did read somewhere that Harriet Chance was ashamed of it and wished she'd never written it.)

"I've got *most* of them," I said, "but I haven't got *all*."

"So what?" said Annie. "You're still her number-one fan! I thought you'd be *pleased* I'd talked about you!"

I suppose I should have been, but mainly what I was feeling at that moment was jealousy. Huge, raging, bright-green JEALOUSY. *I* was the bookworm! Not Annie. *I* was the one that ought to be talking to Harriet's daughter!

"We could visit right now," said Annie, "and see if she's there."

I pursed my lips and shook my head. Inside, I was seething and heaving like a volcano about to erupt.

"Megs, it's *harmless*!"

If I did erupt, I would spew bright-green vomit all over Annie. Great gobbets of it, splatting in her face and dripping through her hair.

"It's just *books*. Just people talking about *books*."

Annie didn't even like books. She only read them because of me.

"There's no grown ups. Nothing bad. No one talks about sex, or anything like that. It's just kids! Nobody over fourteen."

I came back to life. "If it's nobody over fourteen," I said, "what's Lori doing there?"

"Why?" Annie blinked, owlishly. "Is she over fourteen?"

"Yes, she is!" I knew all about Harriet Chance's daughter. I knew *everything there was to know* about Harriet Chance. Well, everything that had ever been written.

"So how old is she?"

"She's *fif*teen," I said. "She was fifteen in January."

"Oh! Wow! Fifteen!" Annie went into a mock fainting fit on the bed.

"You said nobody over *four*teen," I reminded her. "Anyone could just *say* they were fourteen!"

"Why would they want to? Just to talk about books!"

I hunched a shoulder. Annie had made me feel all cross and hot.

"OK, if you don't want to," she said. "I'll probably visit later and have a chat. I'll tell her you're too shy."

"Don't you dare!" I said.

"So what shall I tell her?"

"Tell her... tell her that I've chosen Harriet Chance as my favourite author and I'm writing a review of *Candyfloss* for the school library!"

"All right," said Annie. "I don't mind doing that."

Annie is a very generous and good-natured person. More good-natured than me, probably. She knew I was cross, but she didn't want to quarrel. Annie never quarrels. Rachel is the only person she ever gets ratty with; but then Rachel is enough to make a saint ratty, I would think.

"Hey!" Annie suddenly went bouncing off the bed. "Look what I've got!" She snatched up a box and rattled it at me.

"What is it?"

"Make-up! All Mum's old stuff that she doesn't want any more." Annie tipped the contents of the box on to her dressing table. Little tubs and pots rolled everywhere. "Loads of it!" she said. "Let's practise making ourselves up!"

So that was what we did. I still felt sore at the thought of Annie talking to Harriet Chance's daughter, but I was determined not to be tempted and I really didn't want to go on being cross, and messing about with the make-up was quite fun. After we'd made ourselves up to look beautiful – we thought! – we went a bit mad and started on Dracula make-up, and Cruella de Vil make-up. Alien-from-Outer-Space make-up. Monster-with-Red-Eyes make-up. Anything we could think of! We forgot all about Rachel. We were taken by surprise when she put her head round the door. She was taken by surprise, too.

"What on earth do you think you're doing?" she screeched.

Me and Annie flashed toothy lipsticky smiles at her. Annie had drawn black spider legs all round her eyes and daubed big red splotches on her cheeks. I had painted my mouth green and my eyes purple. In addition, we had both tied scarves round our chests, beneath our T-shirts, and stuffed them with knickers to give ourselves boobs. We could hardly look at each other without collapsing into giggles. It was really funny! Needless to say, Rachel didn't think so. She has *no* sense of humour. (She exercises too much. Well, that is my theory.)

"Honestly, you look a total sight," she said. "You'd better just scrub all that muck off yourself, Megan Hooper, before your mum comes for you!"

# RACHEL'S DIARY (SATURDAY)

That tubby little scumbag has been whining to Mum about me making her exercise.

"M-u-u-u-um," she goes, "it's not fair! She hasn't any right!"

The really irritating thing is that Mum agrees with her. That is what is NOT FAIR. Mum always takes her side! She is so spoilt it is just not true. I was never spoilt like that.

Old Tubbo goes on wailing and moaning. "She made us run round the garden, Mum! She kept us out there for HOURS."

So Mum then tells me to "just let them be. Let them do their own thing."

I snap, "I thought I was supposed to be keeping an eye on them! How can I keep an eye on them if they're locked away upstairs?"

Mum says, "You wouldn't do anything naughty, would you, Annie? You know Megan's mum doesn't want her going into chatrooms?"

  To which Tub, all big-eyed and positively OOZING virtue, goes, "Mum, I KNOW. And I wouldn't, EVER. I wouldn't, Mum! HONESTLY."

And Mum believes her! Quite extraordinary. She never believed ME. She still doesn't. It always, like, the third degree when I've been anywhere.

"Are you SURE you didn't? Are you SURE you haven't? Are you telling me the truth?"

But with old Tub, it's like butter wouldn't melt in her mouth. She's such a sly boots! I wouldn't trust her further than I can spit.

"SEE?" She's all gloating and full of evil triumph. She doesn't actually say it out loud; she just mouths it at me. I mouth back at her. Something really rude, behind Mum's back. Fatso sticks her 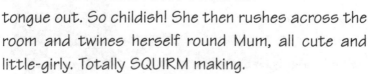 tongue out. So childish! She then rushes across the room and twines herself round Mum, all cute and little-girly. Totally SQUIRM making.

"Tell her, Mum! Tell her she's not to boss us!"

"I'm sure she won't," says Mum, "so long as you behave yourselves."

"Mum, we do!"

Huh! is all I say to that. Huh huh HUH. But Mum accepts it. She says all right, that's all she wanted to hear. Later she gets me on my own and tells me to cool it.

"Give them a bit of leeway. They're not bad kids. You get on and do your thing, and let them do theirs." She then adds that, "You're not in the police force yet, you know!"

I tell her that it's the police SERVICE, not the police FORCE, which in fact I have already told her about two dozen times before, but Mum just waves a hand, like it's not important, and says, "Whatever! Go easy on them."

It's absolutely no use looking to Dad for support; he keeps well out of it. Bringing up girls is a woman's job. It's always "Ask your mum. See what your mum says." What a cop out! But then Dad is a bit of a throwback. Not a modern man at all.

Anyway, that has done it, as far as I am concerned. I wash my hands! They can stay upstairs and moulder all day long. What do I care if Little Goody Two-Shoes is led astray?

Besides, I have other things to think about. Well, one other thing, basically. TYRONE! Tyrone Patrick O'Malley. He's far more gorgeous than anyone I met on holiday. Mum can keep her Spanish boys! Jem says if it weren't for having Kieron, she would quite fancy him herself. But she has promised me faithfully not to do any ogling! I am still consumed with jealousy as they are still stacking shelves together.

Oh, I can't bear it! The thought of Jem actually standing next to him – maybe even TOUCHING him!!! It is agony. She says they're both on early shift next week, which means they finish at one, so if I go down there I can join them in the canteen for lunch. THEY get to eat free, but Jem says loads of people just drop in for a quick bowl of soup and a roll and butter. I can afford that! I could afford a whole three-course meal if it meant being with Ty!!!

The dear little girls will just have to get on by themselves. After all, it's only a couple of hours.

# three

ON SUNDAYS ME and Mum always go off to visit my gran. It's a really long journey, as we have to catch a bus into town, then another bus out of town. It takes over two hours and is quite boring. Unfortunately, it is equally boring when we get there, as Gran's home where she lives is full of old ladies (and a few old men, though not very many) and there is absolutely nothing whatever to do. We can't even talk to Gran any more, as her mind has wandered and she doesn't know who we are. Sometimes she calls Mum "Molly", which we think was a friend of hers when she was young. Other times she calls her "Kathryn". We don't know who Kathryn was. She doesn't call me anything at all, which is sad, 'cos me and Gran were the hugest of friends when she lived with us.

In those days I didn't have to go round to Annie's in holiday time, as Gran was always there to look after me. We used to have such fun! We used to play board games, and word games, and read things to each other. Sometimes Annie would come and spend the day, and then we'd have even more fun! Gran used to laugh at Annie and the things she got up to. That was when she called her doolally.

"That girl is completely *doo*lally!"

I can't remember when Gran stopped laughing; when I was about ten, I think. Now she just sits there, staring. I don't really enjoy going to visit her. I don't mind so much about being bored, as I can always take a book to read, but it makes me unhappy to see Gran just sitting staring. And I *hate* that she doesn't know who I am! Mum says maybe she does know, somewhere deep inside. She says that is why we have to keep visiting.

"Imagine how hurt she'd be if there's a little part of her which can still recognise us, and we didn't come any more."

I couldn't bear for Gran to be hurt! Once or twice, when I've been really upset, Mum has said that perhaps she ought to leave me behind. Except that who could she leave me with?

"I can't keep parking you at Annie's."

Annie wouldn't mind; but when I think about what Mum said, that maybe there is a little part of Gran, somewhere deep down, that still recognises us, I know that I can't let Mum go by herself. I have to go with her; just in case.

To make myself a bit braver I always remember Clover in *Daisy and Clover*. Clover has to go and visit *her* gran in a home, and she feels just the same as I do. When Clover's gran doesn't know who she is, Clover says, "I wanted to burst into tears and cry, 'Gran, it's me! Don't you remember? All the things we used to do together?' But I didn't, because I knew it wouldn't be any use. Gran had gone, and there was no way of reaching her."

It is truly amazing how Harriet Chance describes every single thing I have ever felt or thought. Surely she must have been through it all herself? Or maybe she just has this incredible understanding of how it is to be a young person.

Some of the old ladies in Gran's home are what Mum calls "real characters". (What Gran would probably have called *doo*lally.) There is one who is a particular friend of mine. Her name is Mrs Laski, but I call her Birdy as she is very tiny and fragile, and she speaks in this high twittery voice, like a bird. Me and Birdy have these long, interesting conversations together. Like Birdy might say, "It's very whizzbang out there today." That is one of her expressions: *whizzbang*. I don't quite know what it means, but lots of things are whizzbang.

"Whizzbangs all over the place! They're arriving in hordes! Did you find any?"

And I will cry, "Yes! I found loads!"

She likes it when I play the game the way she wants it played. She does *not* like it if I am stupid enough to say something such as, "Found any what?" That makes her cross. But so long as I answer *intelligently*, we can go on for ages! Birdy will ask me what colour they were, these things that I had found loads of. I will say, "Red! Bright red!" Then Birdy will say, "Not green?" – I mean, this is just an example – and I will say, "Well, maybe some of them were," and she will nod and say, "I thought so! It's the time the of year. Very whizzbang! They're all on their way. Swarms of them!" And before I know it we will be in outer

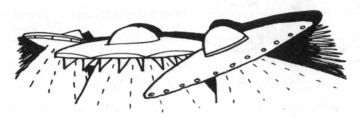

space, surrounded by aliens, all whizzbanging about in their flying saucers, on their way to earth to suck out our brains. Everything always comes back to the aliens sucking out our brains.

Harriet Chance has never written about anyone like Birdy. Maybe I should write and suggest it to her! Except that I once read she almost never uses ideas that come from other people. She says she has "a resistance" to them.

There is another old lady in Gran's home whose name I don't know so I call her Mrs Yo-Yo, because her favourite toy is a yo-yo. She yo-yo's away like crazy! I know it is very sad, when maybe she has been something important in life, and had a job and brought up children,

and now she does nothing but play with a yo-yo all day, but at least she is happy. She beams, and laughs, and skips. I would rather Gran played with a yo-yo than just sat in a chair doing nothing.

Mrs Yo-Yo wasn't there that Sunday, but Birdy was. We had a bit of a chat about whizzbang dustbins full of aliens come to suck our brains out, then a woman that I think is her daughter came and took her away. She said, "She's not on about aliens again, is she?"

I said, "Yes, they're hiding in the dustbins," and the woman looked embarrassed and said she was so sorry and that I wasn't to take any notice. I don't know what she said she was sorry for! I enjoy my conversations with Birdy. She has a really good imagination.

After she had gone, and Mum was sitting with Gran, telling her all the things that had been going on in our lives during the week (which was not a lot. Nothing as interesting as aliens hiding in dustbins) I settled down to finish my project for school. I'd done the review; now I had to do the biography. Biography of Harriet!

I'd looked her up on the Internet at school, and I'd also read about her in a book called *Children's Writers*. Plus, of course, the little bits that publishers put at the front of books, like telling you where the author lives and how many children they've got. Plus an interview that she had done for a magazine which is in the school library. I knew everything there was to know! I could have written a whole book about Harriet. But our teacher had said not more than three hundred words, so I thought it would give me good practice in picking out the things which were most important. Otherwise I would just go on for ever! Annie had asked what was the *least* number of words, as she didn't think she'd be able to manage more than about twenty. Other people were just going to copy out stuff they'd read. I don't think there is any fun in that.

I settled myself at a little table in the corner and turned back the cover of my nice new writing block.

# BIOGRAPHY OF HARRIET CHANCE

Harriet Chance was born in Epsom, Surrey, on 12th March 1962. She went to school at the Convent of the Sacred Heart. She was very good at English, French and German, and very bad at maths and geography. She hated playing hockey. (Just like me!)

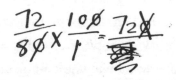

When she left school she went to university in London and did English. After that she went to teach at a school in Birmingham, where she met her husband and got married. She now lives in London with her husband and her daughter Lori, who is fifteen.

Harriet Chance started writing books while she was at school. When she was twelve she wrote a book called PAPER DOLLS, but she never tried to get it published. When she was at university she wrote some poetry which was not very good. While she was a teacher she wrote a book for grown-ups, but that was not very good either so for a while she gave up writing.

Then she got married and had a baby and didn't work any more but she got bored just being at home all the time and so she started writing again.

Her very first book that was published was called PATSY PUFFBALL, but now she wishes she had never written it. She would like all the copies to be put into a shredding machine. She really hates that book!

Other books she has written include: CANDYFLOSS, VICTORIA PLUM, APRIL ROSE, SUGAR MOUSE and FUDGE CASSIDY. In all she has written fifty-four. Her latest one is called SCARLET FEATHER. It is about this girl called Scarlet whose mum and dad split up and Scarlet has to decide which one she will live with. I cannot say which one she chooses as the book is not yet published. But I can say that Harriet Chance is my ACE FAVOURITE AUTHOR!

~~~~~

I had just written the last words and put a little squiggly bit underneath to show that that was The End, when an old lady I had never seen before suddenly spoke to me.

"And what are *you* writing?" she said. "Love letters?"

My cheeks immediately went bright pink. (I don't know why, but I am very easily embarrassed.) I said, "No, I'm doing a project for school."

"What is it about? Is it about love?"

I shook my head, turning even pinker.

"Is it about *boys*?"

"N-no," I said. "It's about my f-favourite author."

"Does she write about *love*?"

I shook my head again; more vehemently, this time.

"So what does she write about?"

"J-just... ordinary p-people," I said. "And their p-problems."

"Ah. An agony aunt! I used to read Enid Blyton. Do you read Enid Blyton?"

I said, "S-sometimes."

"I used to read her *all* the time. Which ones have you read?"

"Um... *F-Five on a T-Treasure Island*?"

"Ah, yes! The Famous Five. What else?"

"N-Noddy?"

"Noddy? I should have thought you were rather too old for Noddy."

"When I was l-little," I said.

"Oh, my dear," said this strange old woman, "you are still little! But too old for Noddy. Try *The Secret Island*. That was one of my favourites!"

With this she wandered off, and I was quite relieved. I didn't mind talking to Birdy about aliens, but I don't like the sort of conversations that make my cheeks go pink. It may be *silly* that they turn pink, but there is nothing that I can do about it. It is just something that happens.

I watched the old lady shuffle across the room. I wondered how old she was. I thought probably about eighty. I mean, she was *really* old. Older than Gran, even though Gran sat staring and this old lady could still walk and talk. To think that she was reading Enid Blyton over sixty years ago! Over *seventy* years ago. I tried to imagine how it might be when I was her age, tottering about in an old people's home, asking young girls who had come to visit their grans if they had ever read Harriet Chance. I couldn't! I just couldn't  *imagine* being eighty years old. But I could imagine people still reading Harriet Chance. I bet they'll still be reading her in a hundred years' time!

"What was that all about?" said Mum, as we walked up the road to catch our bus back to town.

"She wanted to know what I was writing," I said.

"And what were you writing?"

"My biography of Harriet!"

"Oh, yes... didn't you say something about a new book being published?"

"*Scarlet Feather*," I said; and I sighed.

"What's the sigh for?" said Mum.

"It's in hardback... it won't be out in paperback for *ages*."

"Well, who knows?" said Mum. She patted her bag. "Gran's just given me your birthday present... so maybe you'll be able to buy it?"

Gran doesn't really give me birthday presents any more. It's Mum who buys the book tokens and then guides Gran's hand as she signs the birthday card. But we both pretend. I always give Gran a big kiss and say thank you. Maybe somewhere deep inside she knows what it's for.

The phone was ringing as we got back home. It was Annie, all bright and bubbling. She is always bright and bubbling.

"Hey! Guess what?" she went. "I think I know what your birthday prezzie's going to be!"

I said, "What? What?"

"Can't tell you! I'm still arranging it. But it's something you're absolutely going to *love*."

I went, "Hm!" thinking that if it was anything gluey I wouldn't use it. I didn't care how much it hurt Annie's feelings. I didn't want my eyes swelling up again! I looked like a football that'd been kicked by David Beckham.

"I've been speaking to you-know-who," said Annie.

I squeaked, "*Lori?* You've been speaking to Lori again?"

"For ages!"

Now I'd gone all green and jealous.

"What did you speak about?"

"'Bout you."

"About *me*? What did you say?"

"Tell you tomorrow! It's so exciting!"

"What? What is?"

"What we've been speaking about!"

"*Annieeeee!* Tell me!"

But she wouldn't. She just giggled, and bounced the phone back down. I went into the kitchen and said, "Mum, I'm so envious! I can't help it."

"Envious of what?" said Mum.

"Envious of Annie! She's been talking—" I took a breath "—to *Harriet Chance's daughter!*"

"Oh, my goodness," said Mum. "Where did she meet her?"

"In a bookroom. On the Internet." I could already see the frown lines gathering on Mum's forehead.

Hastily, I gabbled on. "It's this special site, just for bookworms. That's what it's called... *Bookworms*."

"I see." Mum smiled. The frown lines had disappeared. Hooray! "Now, I suppose, you're just dying to get on there and talk to her yourself?"

"Couldn't I, Mum? Just this once? It's not a chatroom! It's *educational*. All about books. It would be just *sooo* useful, for my project!"

"I'll tell you what," said Mum. "I'll make you a promise... birthday treat! Next weekend we'll ask Annie's mum if we can both call round and you can use Annie's computer and go and have a little chat. On your birthday! How about that?"

Of course I said that it would be lovely; I didn't want to sound ungrateful. But somehow I just couldn't manage to feel enthusiastic. It was something to do with the fact that Mum would be there, and that it was all being planned in advance. Annie didn't have to plan in advance! She just logged on, and started chatting. She didn't have her mum looking over her shoulder to check what she was talking about. If I talked to Harriet's daughter, I wanted it to be strictly confidential! Just the two of us. Otherwise I'd get embarrassed. There'd be things I couldn't say, if I thought Mum was watching.

"Tell Annie, tomorrow," said Mum. "I'll have a word with her mum. I'm sure it'll be all right... Bookworms in the morning, party in the afternoon. Never say I don't indulge you!"

# RACHEL'S DIARY (SUNDAY)

That Annie! She's up to something, I know she is. The
phone rang this evening and I
went to answer it and it was
Mrs Hooper, wanting to speak
Mum. I thought she was
ringing to complain about me
making them take a bit of exercise.
Either that, or she'd discovered that old
Tubby Scumbag had gone and got her dear little
angel to visit a site with her, which would never
surprise me. She is certainly up to SOMETHING.

So, anyway, I braced myself for trouble, thinking
either way I'd be the one to get the blame, I mean I
always am. Leastways, that's how it seems to me.
Of course I may just have a persecution complex, but
I doubt it. I don't IMAGINE these things. Well, but
hooray! This time it wasn't anything to do with me.

Wonders will never cease. For once in my life, I haven't done anything wrong.

All it was, was the little angel's mum wanting to know if the little angel could come round on Saturday and play with the computer. UNDER SUPERVISION. Natch! Mum said, "I told her that would be all right. It seems there's some special chatroom she wants to visit... something to do with books?"

"Bookworms," said the Scumbag.

"Well, that sounds harmless enough. But her mum wants to be there with her."

"Really?" said Dad.

"She's read all these scare stories... people pretending to be what they're not."

The Scumbag said that didn't happen in the bookroom. "Everyone just talks about books. Children's books. Grown-ups don't read children's books."

I said, "So what?"

"So they wouldn't be able to talk about them," said my little clever clogs sister. I pointed out that they might be able to talk about Harry Potter, everyone can talk about Harry Potter, but she said Megan wouldn't want to.

"She's not into Harry Potter. She'd want to talk about H.C."

Mum said, "Who's H.C.?" but at this the Scumbag went all silly and dissolved into giggles.

"I can understand her worries," said Mum (referring, I suppose, to Mrs Hooper). "Megan's her only child, and it can't be easy, bringing a child up on your own... but I do think she keeps her a bit too wrapped up in cotton wool."

"Or maybe we're being a bit complacent?" suggested Dad.

"But they've got to learn," said Mum. "How are they going to learn if they're never allowed to take any responsibility? We've already been through this, haven't we, Annie?"

"Yes," said the Scumbag, with a big saintly beam.

"You never give your address to anyone, do you?"

"No way!" said the Scumbag, beaming brighter than ever.

"Or your telephone number?"

"Mum, I wouldn't!"

"You see? Annie KNOWS," said Mum. "Poor little Megan's still a total innocent. She could never be left on her own, she'd get into all sorts of trouble. Anyway, they're coming round Saturday morning, then you're off to her party in the afternoon. Have you got her a present yet?"

"Working on it," said the Scumbag.

"Well, don't leave it too late. What are you going to buy?"

The Scumbag said she wasn't going to BUY anything.

"You mean you're making something?" said Mum. "That's nice!"

So then the Scumbag giggled again, for absolutely no reason whatever as far as I could see. That is what makes me suspicious. She is being all secretive and over-excited about something. I notice these things! With Mum and Dad, it's like they're wearing blindfolds.

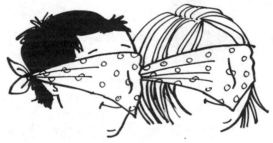

Another thing that makes me suspicious. A few minutes ago I angrily hammered on her bedroom door demanding to know what she'd done with my heated rollers that she keeps snitching. She actually APOLOGISED. Which come to think of it is quite suspicious in itself. The Scumbag saying sorry!!!

"I forgot," she said. "I put them in my cupboard."

While she was getting them out of the cupboard (but what cheek to put them in there in the first place!) I happened to glance down at some drawing she was doing.

"What's this?" I said. "Is this Megan's birthday present?"

"It's her birthday card."

"Weird kind of card," I said. She'd drawn this picture of a sticklike child on her knees, and a woman wearing a halo round her head, with a speech bubble coming out of her mouth saying, HAPPY BIRTHDAY! "What's it meant to be?"

By way of reply, the Scumbag picked up a felt tip pen and wrote H.C. in big bold letters with an arrow pointing to the woman.

"Who is H.C.?"

She wouldn't tell me. All she did was giggle again. Definitely something going on! But I have washed my hands. It's the parents' job to know what their children are up to.

# four

I COULD HARDLY wait to get round to Annie's the next day! I was, like, jigging up and down with impatience all the time Mum was getting ready. Usually in the mornings she just grabs her bag and that's that, we're off! Today, wouldn't you know it, she suddenly decides her shoes are killing her and she's got to change into different ones. Then while she's changing her shoes she notices this *teeny little hole* in her tights, and instead of sticking it up with nail varnish, which is what she'd normally do, she has to take the tights off and find herself a new pair.

I felt like screaming, "Mum! Who's going to see them?" I mean, she works in an office, sitting at a desk. No one's going to notice holes in her tights! Specially not ones you'd need a *magnifying glass* to find. But Mum likes to keep herself looking nice. She's always very neat. Unlike Annie's mum, who looks like a haystack! A very soft, comfortable sort of haystack; but still a haystack.

"What's the matter?" said Mum, as I stood in her bedroom doorway, wrapping one leg round the other. "Do you want to go to the toilet?"

I said, "*Muuum!*"

"Well, what are you jigging about for?"

"It's late," I said. "You'll be late for work!"

Mum's never late for work; she's a very punctual sort of person. "It's nearly half-past nine," I said.

"That's all right," said Mum. "I don't have to be in till ten... stocktaking on Thursday, right? Late night. So I get a ten o'clock start the rest of the week! What's your rush, anyway?"

"Got things to do," I said.

"Oh! I suppose you want to talk to Annie about Saturday?" Mum laughed. "Come on, then! Let's get you over there."

I did feel a bit mean, not being more enthusiastic about Mum's idea of letting me visit the bookroom. I knew it was a big thing for her. She is not scared of technology as she uses a computer for work; but she definitely gets twitchy when I want to do some of the things that anyone else's mum would let them do without even winking an eyelash. Or is it batting an eyelid? (But how could you *bat* an eyelid? It would hurt!) I knew she'd spoken to Annie's mum and Annie's mum had said it would be OK, and I was quite looking forward to it;

but mostly I wanted to hear what Annie had been saying to Lori. What had she been telling her about me???

When we arrived at Sylvan Close, which is the road where Annie lives, Annie's mum and dad had already left for work and Annie was in the middle of a big shouting match with Rachel. You could hear them going at it as you went up the path.

"This sounds serious," said Mum. "Is it safe to go off and leave them?"

"It's OK," I said, "they're always having rows. They don't *do* anything. They just yell."

SYLVAN WAY

It was all about heated rollers, which Rachel said Annie had taken, and Annie swore she'd given back.

"I gave them back *last night*!"

"So where are they, then?"

"How should I know? You took them!"

"I beg your pardon, *you* were the one that took them!"

Rachel then shouted that she was sick of Annie just helping herself to things that didn't belong to her and if there was any more of it she was going to put a padlock on her bedroom door. "Because you're a thieving little toerag!"

*Phew*. I am sometimes quite glad that I am an only child.

"Can we go upstairs now?" I said.

"You can do whatever you like!" snapped Rachel. "I've washed my hands of you!"

With that she stalked off in a huff and Annie and me went up to Annie's bedroom.

"Good riddance!" yelled Annie, as somewhere downstairs a door slammed shut. "I gave her back her stupid rollers! How should I know what she's gone and done with them? W—"

"Oh, look, just shut up!" I begged. "I want to hear what you talked to Lori about!"

"Yes. Well!" Annie hurled herself down on to her bed. "I was telling her all about you, right? About you being a big fan, and everything. How you were doing this project for school. How you had all these books, and—"

"Yes, yes, you told her that before!" I said.

"So, OK, I told her again. I wanted her to know that you were this huge great admirer, and I said how it was your birthday on Saturday and how you really, really wanted this new book, this Feather thing—"

"*Scarlet Feather!*"

"*Scarlet Feather*, and—"

"You weren't trying to get her to send me one?" I said, horrified.

"Why not? I thought you wanted one!"

"I do, but not like that! That's like *begging*."

"Well, it's all right," said Annie, "'cos she didn't offer anyway. I thought she might have, 'cos I bet when books are published the authors get given loads of free copies,

I mean like stacks and stacks, so it wouldn't have hurt, but—"

"It would've hurt me!" I said.

Annie looked at me and shook her head. "You're weird," she said. "You know that? You're really weird!"

"Now she probably won't ever want to talk to me!" I wailed. "She'll think you were just trying to get a book out of her!"

"No, she won't," said Annie. "I've got it all arranged."

"Got what all arranged?"

Annie bounced upright, on the bed. She hugged her knees to her chest and grinned this big triumphant grin, almost splitting her face in two. "Your birthday present. I'm arranging it. *Lori's* arranging it. With her mum."

"With Harriet?"

Annie nodded, happily. "She's really nice! Really friendly. Not a bit stuck up. She asked me if you'd ever met her mum, and I said no, but you would absolutely love to. I said if you could meet her it would be the most exciting thing that had ever happened to you – 'cos it would, wouldn't it?" said Annie.

I gulped. "Yes, it would!"

"So Lori said, being as you're such a huge great fan and you're doing this project and everything, she'd ask her mum if it could be arranged. She's almost sure her mum'll say yes. So there you are!"

Annie flung her legs in the air and exultantly rolled backwards on the bed. "You're going to meet Harriet Chance!"

"B-but... h-how?" I said.

"What d'you mean, how?"

"Well, I mean... she's in London!"

"No, she's not."

"She used to be."

"So people move! We can get to her easy as anything on the bus. I didn't give her your *address*," said Annie, "'cos I know you're not supposed to—"

"She's got it anyway," I said. "I mean, Harriet has." When I was ten I wrote her this creepy crawly fan letter, all decorated with hearts and flowers, and she wrote back, saying *Love from Harriet, XXX,* and I was so thrilled! I put the letter in a special frame and hung it on the wall. It's still there, even now.

"Yes, well, this is it," said Annie. "I probably *would* have given it to her if she'd offered to send you a book, but all she did was just ask what part of the country we lived, and when I said Wiltshire she said was it anywhere near Salisbury, so I said yes, and she said in that case there was no problem. She's going to ask her mum and see when to do it. It will be your birthday treat," said Annie, all self-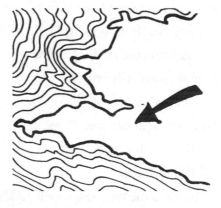important. "A special present from me to you! You might try to look a bit *happy* about it."

I said, "I am happy! It would be the most brilliant birthday present I've ever had!"

"So why are you looking worried?"

"I'm just scared in case it doesn't happen!"

"It will happen. Lori's promised."

"But why should someone important like Harriet want to see *me*?"

"Because you're her number-one fan! Because you're doing this thing about her! Because it's your *birthday*. I told you I was going to give you a really good present! You didn't believe me, did you? You thought I was going to give you something stupid, like last year."

I bleated a protest. "I didn't!" The reason I bleated was that I was in such a tremor my voice had gone. I'd swallowed my voice! "I didn't," I said, "honestly!"

"Bet you did," said Annie.

"I did *not*. You always give me good presents!"

"Not as good as this. I'm your fairy godmother!" Annie sprang off the bed and did a little twirl. "I'm the one that makes your dreams come true!"

I thought that meeting Harriet really would be a dream come true. I'd read once where she'd visited a school to talk about her books, and I had just been *so jealous* of the people at that school. Annie couldn't understand, as her dream would be to meet someone from her favourite band, which at that moment was Dead Freaks.

I thought Dead Freaks were really creepy! But Annie had all their albums, just like I have all of Harriet's books, so sometimes I would listen to Dead Freaks and sometimes Annie would read Harriet Chance. That is what friendship is all about, sharing each other's interests even if you don't really understand them.

"When do you think we'll know?" I said.

"Soon as Lori's spoken to Harriet. Tomorrow, maybe? I said it would be best if it was in the afternoon, 'cos then we could go while old Bossyboots is out, so she wouldn't be able to stop us."

"How d'you know she'll be out?"

"'Cos she's got this thing about one of the boys in Savemore. Ty*rone*." Annie pulled a face. "He's really gross!

96

But she's got the hots for him. So she has to keep going there every day to check her friend Jem hasn't pinched him. See, they're stacking shelves and she's stuck here babysitting, which is why she's in such a tetch. But it means we can go and meet Harriet and she won't know anything about it! Well, not until we get back, and she won't be able to say anything 'cos she's not meant to leave us on our own. And I don't think, probably, that we ought to say anything, either. Not even to your mum, 'cos I know what you're like."

I said, "What am I like?"

"You tell her everything," said Annie.

"I don't tell her *everything*." I'd never told her about hiding in the stationery cupboard. I'd never told her about the birds' nests.

"Well, you'd better not tell her about this," said Annie. "Not unless you want her coming with us! She's already going to listen in on Saturday. You don't want her sitting there while you talk to Harriet, do you?"

I had to admit, I didn't. I definitely didn't! If I was going to meet Harriet I wanted it to be *private*. Just the two of us. Well, and Annie, of course. But I didn't mind Annie. She's my best friend and we don't have any secrets. But it would be really offputting if Mum was there!

"Let's listen to music," said Annie; and she snatched up this one CD that is my least, *least* favourite of Dead Freaks as it is quite scary, well I think it is, but Annie just loves it. She doesn't usually play it when I am around, but this time she said that I "owed her", and I couldn't deny it, so we were sitting there listening when the door crashed open and it was Rachel, shouting at us to "Turn that music down! They'll complain next door, and I'll be the one that gets into trouble!" She then added that she was going out and would be back in a couple of hours and we were to just behave ourselves *or else*.

"Else what?" said Annie.

"Else you'll be in deep ****!"

The reason I have put **** is so as not to write what she actually said, as what she actually said was quite rude and I don't think really she ought to have said it; but as she was in this strop on account of having to baby-sit for me and Annie instead of stacking shelves with Ty*rone*, I forgave her. The minute she'd gone, Annie turned the music up again.

"Now we can have *fun!*" she said.

I was in a state of jitters again next morning, desperate to get round to Annie's and discover if she'd managed to speak to Lori again, but I did my best to contain myself as I didn't want Mum growing suspicious, thinking I was up to something. The minute she dropped me off, we raced upstairs to Annie's bedroom. I could see that Annie was bursting with news.

I said, "Well? Did you speak to her?"

Annie's face broke into a big beam. "Yes! It's all arranged. We're going to have tea with her!"

I said, "*Tea*..." I could hear my voice, all hushed and breathy, like it was going to be tea with the Queen.

Only this was far more exciting! I wouldn't have anything very much to say to the Queen. I'd got simply loads to say to Harriet!

"We're going on Thursday," said Annie. "I thought Friday would have been better, 'cos of being nearer to your birthday, but Lori said her mum couldn't manage Friday. And I said we couldn't manage Saturday 'cos of your birthday party, so she said what about Thursday, and I said Thursday would be OK, so—"

"Thursday is good!" I said. "Mum has to work late on Thursday!"

"Anyway, we'll be back ages before then," said Annie. "It's only *tea*. What we've got to do, she said, is get a bus to Brafferton Bridge—"

"We go through there on the way to visit Gran!" I knew exactly which bus, and where to catch it: a number six, at the back of Market Square. "Is Brafferton Bridge where she lives?" I said, thinking that I would have to change the first bit of my biography.

"Near Brafferton Bridge. She said her mum will meet us and take us back. Lori won't be able to come 'cos she's already doing something else, but—"

"That's all right."

I didn't care about Lori; Harriet was the one I cared

about. In fact I thought I might be a bit shy if Lori were there, so I was quite glad she wasn't going to be.

"She said maybe we could meet another time," said Annie. "She sounds really nice! Oh, and it's got to be kept a secret. She said her mum doesn't usually meet her fans 'cos if she met all the people that read her books she'd never have time for writing."

"Yes." I nodded. I'd read that somewhere, in one of the interviews that Harriet had given. She had said that she was a very private person. She loved to hear from her readers, and she always, *always* wrote back; but she didn't very often make public appearances. I could understand that! That is probably how I would be, if I were a famous writer.

"So we've not got to tell *anybody*," said Annie. "In case it gets back to people and they all want to come."

"Absolutely!" I said. This was *my* treat. I could think of several girls in our class who would be really envious... but I certainly didn't want them intruding on my birthday present!

"I said what we'd do," said Annie, "we'd look up the times of buses so I could tell Lori which one we were getting so Harriet doesn't have to be kept waiting."

I was ever so impressed! Annie isn't normally what I would call an efficient sort of person. Mrs Glover at school once told her she was "slapdash". But because this was my birthday present, and she did so much want me to enjoy it, she was making this huge great effort. She even knew how to look up bus timetables on the Internet!

"See, look? There's one that gets to Brafferton Bridge at ten past two. I'll tell her that one. Then you talk as much as you like, all about books, you could even do an interview, then we can have tea and come back home and nobody will ever know! Now you're looking worried again. What's the matter *now*?"

"How are we going to recognise her?" I said.

"Who, Harriet?"

"There aren't any photos!"

I'd searched and searched, but being such a private person she obviously didn't like having her photograph taken. (I agree! I don't, either.) All these other old ugly authors had their pictures all over the place – well, they weren't all old and ugly, but they weren't very beautiful, either, which I suppose oughtn't to matter as it is their books you are interested in, and not their faces, and even if Harriet turned out to be old and ugly I would still be her number one fan! But the only photographs I had been able to find were taken when she was young. I knew it was when she was young as she was holding Lori, and Lori was just a baby. Harriet had looked really pretty, then, with a nice little round squashy face and dark hair, with a fringe. I did hope she still looked like that! But I knew it was a long time ago, almost fifteen years. People could change a whole lot in fifteen years. I mean, anyone who had last seen me when I was, say, *two*, certainly wouldn't recognise me as I am now. So I thought probably she was bound to look a little bit different.

"We don't want to get in a car with the wrong person!" I said.

Annie rolled her eyes. "You are such a worrygut! Maybe she could hold a copy of one of her books? Or d'you think there might be hundreds of people waiting at Brafferton Bridge holding copies of books?"

I giggled at that.

"I'll ask Lori," said Annie. "Just leave it to me. And *stop FUSSING!*"

# RACHEL'S DIARY (THURSDAY)

My sister is a brat. An obnoxious, odious, beastly little BRAT. She was playing music really loud this morning. So loud the floors were practically shaking. I told her to turn it down, but the minute I left the house she went and turned it back up again. I could hear it thumping and banging all the way down the road. Next Door's going to create, I just know they are. Then Mum'll say, "Rachel, how could you let her annoy the neighbours like that? You KNOW what Mrs Hawthorn's like about noise!" And it will stand there looking all simpering and saintly, and pulling faces at me behind Mum's back. It knows I can't say anything. If I complain about it not doing what it's told, it'll go and tell Mum about me going off to meet Ty instead of staying here and playing nursemaid. It's blackmail!

Well, and what do I care? Seeing Ty is the only thing I care about. He's asked me to go to a party with him on Saturday!!! I bet he never would have if it weren't for me going in every day and sitting there right under his nose. He probably wouldn't ever have noticed me! You have to work at these things, they don't happen by themselves. Well, sometimes they do, if you're lucky, but mostly I think you have to make a bit of an effort, specially if it's someone like Ty that could have the pick of the bunch. He's so gorgeous! He used to go out with Marsha Williams, but he doesn't any more so it's not like I'm stealing him. He was up for grabs! I wouldn't have made a play for him if he'd still been going with Marsha. At least, I don't think I would. But then again, I might have! All's fair in love and war, and Marsha is a total dimbo anyway. She may have the boobs but she certainly hasn't got the brains. She doesn't deserve a boy like Ty.

The brat and its friend are downstairs now, hatching plots. I know they're hatching plots because whenever I come into the room they immediately stop talking and look guilty. MEGAN looks guilty. Annie looks furtive. When I ask what's going on, Megan turns bright pink and Annie says, "Nothing. Why?" I say, "Because your eyes have suddenly bunched up and gone all shifty." So then she crosses her eyes and sticks out her tongue, and I tell her she ought to have a bit more respect for those in authority — i.e. me — to which she retorts that I am not in the police force YET. I snap, "Service!" and flounce from the room; whereupon they both start giggling.

They just don't seem to teach kids any manners these days. I'm sure when I was that age I wouldn't have cheeked my older sister like Annie cheeks me. If I'd had an older sister. If I had, I'd have paid attention and done what she told me. I would have taken the opportunity to LEARN. This one just doesn't care. Well, and neither do I! Let them get on with it.

# five

THURSDAY CAME – THE day of my birthday treat! I was so excited, but a bit nervous, as well. I had been Harriet's number-one fan for so long! Ever since I was eight years old, and read *Candyfloss*. I just loved that book! I read it so many times that in the end it fell to pieces and Mum had to buy me another one. Now I was actually going to meet the person who had written it!

I couldn't make up my mind what to wear. I don't have all that many clothes in my wardrobe, and I am not one of those hugely fashion-conscious people, like this girl at school, Rozalie Dunkin, who is trendy as can be and always dressed in the latest gear, which Mum won't let me have. Or at least, not very often. She either says it's cheap and tacky, or she says it's not suitable. Meaning that she doesn't approve of eleven-year-olds dressing up like they're eighteen. She really is very old-fashioned, my mum. It doesn't usually bother me as I don't specially want to go round pretending to be eighteen, and am probably a little bit old-fashioned myself. Annie sometimes says I am. But I did want to look nice for Harriet!

I dithered for ages, trying to decide. Most of the stuff in my wardrobe is stuff that Rozalie Dunkin wouldn't be seen dead in. But I had to wear something! Mum was calling to me from the kitchen: "Megan, your breakfast is ready! What are you doing?"

I stuck my head out of the door and yelled, "Getting dressed!"

"Well, just be quick! I haven't got all day."

Now it was Mum agitating to go, and me holding things up. I stopped dithering, grabbed a top which was not new but which I just happen to love – it is blue, with little bunched sleeves, and ties round the middle – and my best pair of jeans, which *were* new. So new I hadn't yet worn them! They had beautiful embroidered bits round the bottom, bright reds and greens, all curling and swirling. I thought maybe they were the one thing I owned that Rozalie Dunkin might not mind being seen dead in. I didn't have any trendy sort of shoes, so I just put on my trainers, which she definitely would *not* have been seen dead in! They were quite old and tatty, but I hoped that Harriet wouldn't notice.

Mum did! Well, she noticed the jeans.

"You're wearing your new trousers!" she said. "I thought you were keeping those for the party?"

"I'll probably wear a dress for the party," I said. "I might get a bit hot in these."

"You'll get a bit hot in them today! It's going to be well over 20 degrees. If I were you, I'd go and put some shorts on."

I couldn't go to tea with Harriet wearing *shorts*. I had this sudden great urge to tell Mum what I was doing, but I knew that I couldn't. Mum is such a worrier! She might even tell me that I wasn't to go. In any case, I had promised Annie not to say anything, and I couldn't break my promise. Not when it was her birthday present to me, and she had worked so hard at it.

"Well, it's up to you," said Mum. "Wear what you like, I don't have time to argue! Now, I'll be picking you up at 6.30 tonight, OK? So you'll be having tea with Annie."

With Harriet, I thought; and I couldn't help a little giggle bursting out of me. Oops! I promptly clapped a hand to my mouth.

"You're in a very odd mood," said Mum. "What's brought all this on?"

"I'll tell you about it later," I said.

"Why can't you tell me now?"

"'Cos I can't! It's a secret."

"I suppose Annie's in on it?"

I said, "Yes, but we're sworn to utter silence."

"Oh! Well... in that case," said Mum.

She didn't try to get it out of me. I am allowed to have secrets! She just told me to eat up my breakfast or I'd make her late for work.

Needless to say I
spent the morning
jittering, in case for once Rachel
didn't go off to gaze at Tyrone and
make sure her best friend wasn't pinching him.

"What'd we do? If she doesn't go? How'd we get out?"

"We could always climb through the window," said Annie.

I ran across to look. It's true there is an apple tree
outside Annie's window, but I knew I'd never be able to
reach it. Heights make me go dizzy. And Annie has *never*
been able to get more than a quarter of the way up the
ropes when we do gym.

"We'd break our necks," I wailed.

"I wasn't serious," said Annie. "I only said it 'cos of
all the dithering you do."

"But Rachel," I moaned.

"You don't have to worry about Rachel. She couldn't stay away from Ty*rone* if you offered her a million dollars. I heard her on the phone last night. She's got it so bad she couldn't even say his name without stuttering... T-T-Ty*rone*!"

"I hope you're right," I said.

"I'm always right," said Annie. "I'm your fairy godmother. When I wave my magic wand—" she snatched up a ruler from her desk and wafted it about "—all your wishes come true!"

She was right about Rachel. She isn't always right; she is sometimes spectacularly *wrong*. But in this case she was right! Rachel came upstairs a bit later, when we were sitting good as gold, quiet as mice, with the CD player turned low as low could be, to tell us that she was going out for a couple of hours.

"You two just behave yourselves—"

"Or else," said Annie.

"Yes! *Or else*. And keep that music down!"

What cheek! We couldn't have turned it any lower if we'd tried.

"Some people are just never satisfied," grumbled Annie.

A few seconds later the front door slammed shut.

"Now we can listen properly," said Annie; and she turned the CD player up to practically full blast. "Let's go and spy on her!"

We raced along the landing, into Annie's mum and dad's bedroom, which is at the front of the house.

"Hide behind the curtain! We don't want her to see us."

Giggling, I wrapped myself up in the curtain and watched as Rachel set off down the road.

"We'll just give her time to get her bus," said Annie. "We don't want to go and bump into her at the bus stop."

Help! I hadn't thought of that! Suppose the bus was cancelled? Suppose we got there and she was still waiting?

"Oh, shut up!" said Annie, when I said this to her. "You're behaving like your mum."

Well! The last thing anyone wants to do is behave like their mum, so I obediently kept quiet and just worried silently inside my head, instead of out loud.

"You're still doing it," said Annie.

"Doing what?" I said.

"*Flapping*. I can tell from just looking at you."

"Well, but you don't think—"

"No, I don't," said Annie, without even waiting to hear what it was that I was going to say. "I've got it all *planned*.

Just leave it to me." She looked at her watch. "Every quarter of an hour. That's when the buses run. We'll go in *quarter of an hour*."

Unlike me, Annie hadn't bothered to get dressed up. She was wearing the same pink joggers she'd been wearing all week, though she had put on a clean top and a big old swanky cap (all pink and puffy) that she's had for ages. But that was all right! It wasn't Annie's birthday treat. She wasn't Harriet's number one fan.

"I'll just do a note for old Bossyboots," she said.

She showed me what she'd written: WE HAVE GONE TO HAVE TEA WITH HARRIET CHANCE. WE WILL BE BACK SOON.

"*Annieeee!*" I stared at her, reproachfully. "I thought we weren't supposed to tell anyone?"

"I've got to leave her a note," said Annie. "We don't want her getting in a panic and phoning the police."

"But you promised!"

Annie stuck out her lower lip. What I call her stubborn look.

"Annie, you *promised*," I said.

"OK! I'll write another one."

WE HAVE GONE TO TEA WITH HARRIET. WE WILL BE BACK SOON.

115

"How's that? If I just say *Harriet*?"

I told her that that was much better. "It'll keep her from worrying, but she won't actually know where we've gone."

"Right. So now will you please just stop *flapping*?"

I was still a bit scared what we might find when we got to the bus stop. If Rachel was there, we would have to hide in a shop doorway until after she'd gone. Then we'd miss our bus! Harriet would be kept waiting. She would be so cross – it would be so rude! I couldn't bear it!

But then we got there, and I breathed this huge sigh of relief. Rachel was nowhere to be seen!

"Told you so," said Annie. "All that flapping and fussing!"

"I can't help it," I said. "It's my anatomy."

"Your *what*?"

I hesitated. Perhaps I'd got the wrong word. "It's the way I'm made. You can't help the way you're made."

"You don't have to give in to it," said Annie. "When you feel a worry fit coming on, just think, *everything will be all right... Annie says so!*"

I muttered that it hadn't been all right when we'd fallen out of the stationery cupboard, but at that moment our bus came and Annie didn't hear me. Which probably just as well.

All the way into town my heart was hammering, but now it was with excitement, not worry! I had a tiny touch of anxiety when we reached Market Square, for really no reason at all, but as soon as we were safely on the number six bus, headed for Brafferton Bridge, it disappeared. I suppose I could have started worrying about pile-ups, or being hijacked, but even I am not that sad.

*However...* when the bus stopped at Brafferton Bridge, and we got out, and there wasn't anyone there to meet us, my heart stopped hammering and went *flomp*! like a dead fish inside my rib  cage. I could see that even Annie was a bit concerned.

"Don't worry, don't worry," she said. "She'll be here!"

The bus went on its way, leaving us all by ourselves. Stranded! In the middle of absolutely nowhere.

There aren't any houses at Brafferton Bridge. No one actually lives there. It is just this old ancient bridge over a stream, with fields stretching out on either side as far as the eye can see.

"She'll *be* here," said Annie.

Even as Annie spoke, a red car drew up beside us and a woman got out. It had to be Harriet! She was holding a copy of *Victoria Plum*. A very old, battered copy, like my one of *Candyfloss* before Mum had replaced it. She came over to us, smiling.

"Oh!" she said. "There are two of you! I hadn't realised you were both coming."

I glanced anxiously at Annie. It takes a LOT to make Annie feel uncomfortable, but I could see she was a bit thrown. After all, she was the one who'd set everything up. In any case, I wouldn't have been brave enough to come by myself.

"I th-thought it was w-what we'd arranged," mumbled Annie.

"Of course! That's all right. Two of you is lovely! So which one is the birthday girl?"

Annie beamed and shoved me forward. "Megan! She's your number-one fan."

Harriet held out a hand. "Happy birthday, Megan! Sorry I'm late. I hope you haven't been waiting long?"

I shook my head. I wanted to say, "No, we only just got here," but I couldn't. I was suddenly struck dumb! I could feel my cheeks turning hot tomato. It was Annie who assured her that we had only that minute got off the bus.

"Thank heavens for that! I had visions of you giving up and going back home."

"Wild horses wouldn't get Megan back home," said Annie. "She's been, like, *oh-my-goodness help-help I-can't-believe-it* ever since we set out!"

By now, my cheeks were starting to sizzle. It was just too embarrassing!

"Well, let's get you into the car," said Harriet, "and we'll all go back and have some tea. Who wants to come in front? Megan?"

Annie gave me another shove. "Go on! It's your treat." She then added, beaming, that "Megan always gets sick if she sits in the back."

I don't know why she found it necessary to say that. Getting car sick is such a childish thing to do! But Harriet was really sympathetic. She said, "Oh, join the club! I always had to take pills if I was going a long journey."

"Megs has to stick her head out of the window," said Annie. "Even then it doesn't always stop her throwing up. One time she did it and it all went *splat* down the door. D'you remember?" She leaned forward, chummily, from the back seat. "That time we went to Alton Towers with Mum and Dad?"

I did remember, but I didn't particularly want to be reminded of it. Not in front of Harriet!

"We'd been eating *sardine sandwiches*," said Annie.

"Oh, horrible! Sardine sandwiches aren't at all the right thing to eat if you suffer from car sickness. But don't worry, Megan! There are some peppermints in the glove compartment. They'll help."

"She doesn't usually get sick in front," carolled Annie. "The worst things are those things at fairgrounds that go round and round."

Harriet looked puzzled. "Roundabouts?"

"No, those things where you stick to the side."

"Oh! You mean, like a centrifuge."

"Yes. She gets *really* sick in those!"

"Poor Megan!" Harriet smiled at me as she started the car. "You're obviously like me, you have a delicate stomach."

"You could write a story about someone like that." Annie draped herself, eagerly, over the back of Harriet's seat. "Someone who throws up everywhere she goes... you could call it *Sickly Susan*!"

"Well, it's an idea," said Harriet. "I'll certainly bear it in mind."

She was only being polite; she never used other people's ideas. I knew that, from my reading. She'd said she had "a resistance" to them. I felt like telling Annie to just be quiet. She'd done nothing but burble ever since Harriet had met us! But something had happened to my tongue; it was like a great wodge of foam rubber in my mouth. I couldn't talk! It was really annoying. Although I am not as bubbly and up-front as Annie, I am not usually shy; but when you are in the presence of greatness it is all too easy to just shrivel. Yet I had so many things I wanted to say! So many questions I wanted to ask! Anyone would have thought it was Annie who was the number-one fan rather than me.

"So how long have you been reading my books?" said Harriet.

I whispered, "Since I was about... s-seven."

"She's read them all!" crowed Annie.

"I haven't read them *all*," I said.

"Most of them!"

"Have you read this one?" said Harriet. She pointed at her old battered copy of *Victoria Plum*.

"Yes!" I found it a bit easier, now that we were talking about books. "It's one of my favourites, 'cos Victoria's always having bad hair days. I like the bit where she tries to make it curly and she goes to bed in rollers and says it's like sleeping on a hedgehog!"

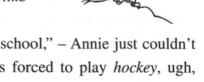

"And then she goes to school," – Annie just couldn't resist joining in – "and is forced to play *hockey*, ugh, yuck! And it rains, and all the curls come out!"

"And she says how for a little while she'd looked like a bubble bath but now she's gone back to being a limp dish mop, and she's just so ashamed she runs away and hides in the loo!"

"We used to think that maybe you had hair like a limp dish mop," said Annie. "But you haven't! You've got *nice* hair."

Harriet's hair was beautifully thick and curly – but it was going grey. Harriet was going grey! I felt sad about that, though I knew, of course, she couldn't still look the same as she had fifteen years ago. She was wearing glasses, too. Just for a moment I wished that I could have met her when she was young; but then I thought that that was a very ageist thing to think, and very ungrateful. After all, she was still Harriet. She was still writing wonderful, marvellous books! And she did look warm and friendly; just a bit... mumsy. But that was quite comforting, in a way. If she had been young and glamorous I would probably have been struck dumb for all eternity.

Rather timidly, I said, "How did you manage to know what it's like, having limp hair?"

"Megan's got limp hair," said Annie. "She's always going on about it."

"Like Victoria," I said. "I really love the way you understand how people *feel*. Like having bad hair, or spots, or being plump, or not having any boobs. Like Sugar Mouse. I don't know how you do it!"

"Well... there is such a thing as imagination," said Harriet. "Very important, if you want to be a writer!"

"Megan wants to be a writer," said Annie.

"In that case," said Harriet, "I very much hope that you will be. Do you have a copy of this one, by the way?"

"She's got all of them," said Annie.

"I haven't got *all* of them." Annie did exaggerate so!

"You've got a whole shelf full."

"I've got thirty-four," I said.

"Good heavens!" Harriet laughed. "You *are* a fan, aren't you?"

I nodded, bashfully. "*Victoria Plum* was one of the first ones I had."

"And I bet it's in better condition than this! I'm afraid this one's been read to bits."

I have read my copy over and over, but I do try to look after my books and keep them nice. I was only young when I ruined *Candyfloss*. Now that I'm older I wouldn't ever turn down the corners of pages or stand mugs of hot chocolate on them or leave them out in the rain. Poor *Victoria Plum* looked as if all those things had happened to her. I picked her up, and opened her at the title page. Across the top someone had written, "For Jan, with all my love, Mummy". I wondered who Jan was, and why she didn't take better care of her books. Maybe she was Harriet's niece and knew that she could always ask for new ones. It made me feel quite jealous. Imagine having a famous writer as your aunt!

"Hey, look, Megs." Annie lunged forward and poked a finger at me. "Isn't that where we went when we visited your gran?"

Annie had come with me a couple of times, to visit Gran. Mum had thought she would be company for me, but then she had said we couldn't behave ourselves properly, and made too much noise, and upset the old people, so now I had to go on my own.

"Megan's gran is in a home," said Annie. "She has Oldheimer's."

"Alzheimer's," I said.

"Oh, dear! That must be very upsetting," said Harriet.

I said, "Yes, it is, 'cos me and Gran used to be best friends. Now she doesn't even know me... like Clover's gran, in *Daisy & Clover*. I cried when I read the bit where Clover wants to burst into tears. That's just how I feel, when I see Gran... you always seem to be writing about how I feel! Like when Clover says about remembering all the things that she and her gran used to do together—"

"That was me," said Harriet, "remembering *my* gran! She had Alzheimer's, too. That's what made me want to write about it."

"Except that... Clover's gran doesn't actually have *Alzheimer's*," I said.

"She has a stroke," said Annie.

"Oh! Well, yes. I changed it to a stroke for the purposes of the book. It would have been too painful," said Harriet, "actually writing about Alzheimer's. It would have brought back too many memories. So you know this area quite well, do you, Megan?"

"Only from coming to see Gran," I said. "Over there's where we get off the bus."

"Darnley Manor. A very pleasant spot! We're just a few miles further on. Are you feeling all right? Not getting sick?"

"She doesn't give you any warning," said Annie. "She just opens her mouth and does it... *blurgh*! All over the door."

Annie doesn't say these things on purpose to embarrass me. She just opens *her* mouth and words come tumbling out. Mostly I try not to mind.

"Well, just yell," said Harriet, "if you want to stop. We've got a few twisty turny bits coming up. They're always the worst, if you have a funny tum."

I thought that Harriet was so nice! Every bit as understanding as she seemed from her books. A girl at school had once met this other author she was keen on and said she had turned out to be really cold and snooty. A huge disappointment! Harriet wasn't in the least bit snooty. Or cold. She was just like one of us.

"I'll tell you what," she said, "I must just quickly ring home and... bother!" She was rummaging with one hand in her bag. "Would you believe it, I've gone and forgotten my mobile! Honestly, I'd leave my head behind if it weren't attached to my shoulders! I don't suppose either of you has one I could borrow?"

I said, "I do!" I felt
quite honoured,
offering my
phone to Harriet!
"You can use
mine."

"Bless you!" Harriet slammed the glove compartment shut and blew me a kiss. "You've saved my bacon. I should have rung half an hour ago! I'll just pull up in this lay-by... mustn't use a mobile while you're driving. Very dangerous!"

I thought that Mum would approve of that. When we had gone to Alton Towers – the time I got sick and it sprayed over the door. On the *outside*, I should add – Annie's dad had done lots of talking on his mobile. Mum had said afterwards that she hadn't liked to say anything, as it wasn't her car, but she had been on tenterhooks the whole time. So that was ten out of ten for Harriet. Hooray!

I felt very privileged and important, sitting next to a famous author as she rang home. I wondered who she was going to talk to. Could it be Lori? I knew it wouldn't be her husband 'cos I'd read somewhere that she was divorced.

Harriet pulled a face. "Answerphone... I hate when it's the answerphone!"

Me, too. I knew how she felt. Sometimes if I get an answerphone I just hang up, though I know it's a bit rude and you ought really to say who you are and leave a message, which was what Harriet was doing.

"Darling, where are you? This is Mummy here! Where have you gone?" She sounded a bit upset. I guessed that Lori had gone off without telling her. "Can you hear me? Are you listening? Please speak to me! If you're there... please! Pick up!"

Just for a moment it was like really tense. Even Annie must have felt it. She leaned forward intently across the back of the seat as we waited for Lori to pick up the phone. But she didn't.

"Call me," whispered Harriet. "Please, darling, call me!"

After that there was this long silence, and then she gave a little laugh, sort of half ashamed, like pulling herself together, and said, "Oh, dear! Mothers do worry so. Does your mother worry, Megan?"

I said that she did.

"Megan's mum gets into total flaps," said Annie.

"I'm afraid I do, too. You just never know... what might have happened... " Harriet's voice faded out.

Trying to be helpful, I said, "Couldn't you try her mobile?"

"Her mobile? No, she doesn't have a mobile. If only she had had a mobile. She's not answering... she doesn't answer... I hope you have your mobile with you, Annie?"

Annie confessed that she hadn't. "We came out in such a rush. I think it's on the kitchen table."

"That's naughty! What would you do if Megan's ran out?"

"Find a call box," said Annie.

"Not good enough! You should always take your phone with you. If only—" Harriet stopped. "Well, anyway!" she said. "Let's get on. I'm so sorry if I'm sounding a bit vague, but I'm in the middle of writing a new book and it's going round and round in my head."

"What's it called?" said Annie. "Has it got a title?"
"Um... yes. How about... *Jampot Jane*?"

I giggled. Annie, in her bold way, said, "That's a funny title! What's it about?"

"I'm afraid I can't tell you that," said Harriet. "I never discuss my books before they're published!"

I hoped that Annie felt properly put in her place. Such nosiness! It was one thing to be a fan, and to show interest; but to poke and pry was just bad manners.

"I'll keep the phone by me, Megan, if I may," said Harriet, "just in case. And I'll try to stop thinking about work and concentrate on you, instead. This is your birthday treat, and I want you to enjoy it."

# RACHEL'S DIARY (THURSDAY)

I am just so absolutely ANNOYED. That little fat freak and her skinny little friend have gone and done a runner. They have had the NERVE to leave me a note. Gone to tea with Harriet, whoever Harriet is. How dare they??? They know perfectly well they're not supposed to go off without telling me. They'd better just get back before Mum comes home or we shall all be in trouble. AND it hasn't taken its phone with it. What's the point of having a mobile if it's just going to leave it lying around on the kitchen table when it goes out? It shouldn't be out! It's just taking a mean advantage. It thinks it can get away with it because I daren't tell Mum. It's a rotten thing to do! It knows how I feel about Ty.

Oh, and I was so happy! It's Jem's day off so me and Ty had lunch together, all by ourselves. He's going to call round at seven on Saturday, to take me to the party. Jem is going as well, with Kieron, so it should be lots of fun. I wasn't a bit tongue-tied today, on my own with Ty. We just have so many things in

common. So many things to talk about! We are both into sport in a big way, are both huge fans of Man U, and our ace fave band is Hot Brits. So no embarrassing pauses while I rack my brain trying to think what to say! We could just go on for ever. I think it's truly important that when you are attracted to someone it should be more than merely physical. Ty is gorgeous — but we can TALK. For instance we had this really in-depth discussion about our aims and ambitions. Not just to stack shelves from now till the end of time! Ty is thinking of going into the army, but I am trying to persuade him to join the police. He is definitely interested!

In the meantime, I WAS going to go and try things on ready for Saturday. I have to look my best!!! But now I'm too cross and angry, because of the

Scumbag taking advantage. She might at least have given me a telephone number. I bet she didn't on purpose. I bet that's why she left her phone, as well, so I couldn't get hold of her. Then she'll pretend she just forgot. It's such a scummy thing to do! I'm surprised at the Stick Insect; I should have thought she'd know better. She always comes across like butter wouldn't melt in her mouth, and for an eleven-year-old she is quite sensible, on the whole. Unlike my dear little sister, who is just one great big PAIN.

To think that out of the goodness of my heart, because I was feeling so happy, I actually brought back some cakes for tea! Squidgy ones full of cream, as a special treat, to make up for yelling at her about the music. I think I'll try ringing Jem and see if she feels like coming over and helping me eat them. Then we can go through my wardrobe together and decide what I'm going to wear. I am NOT going to worry myself about little Tubby Scumbag. She is old enough to know better, and I don't see why I should.

# six

WE DROVE ON through the countryside, down lots of twisty turny lanes, just like Harriet had said. I opened the window and ate peppermints and didn't get sick, but it did seem a long way to drive. Well, to me it did. I thought probably it was because I wasn't used to car journeys. Mum can't afford a car, so we don't really travel very much. It obviously didn't bother Annie. She was bouncing all over the place like a rubber ball. She kept suddenly appearing over the back of my seat and poking at me.

"Hey, look! There's a rabbit!" "Oh, look! Donkeys!" "Look, look! Lambs!"

"Yes, we're way out in the country now," said Harriet.

Rather shyly, not wanting it to seem like I was prying, I said, "I thought you lived in London?"

"Oh! Yes. London's where I *live*. But in the country is where I write my books. Not many people know where I do my writing! I like to keep it a secret."

She explained how nothing was worse, when you were concentrating really hard, and trying to think what to write next, than to have people come knocking at the door expecting to be invited in for a cup of tea, or ringing you up "just for a chat".

I knew how she felt. It was what I sometimes feel when I'm writing an essay for school and Mum says, "Megan, put that away now, it's time for tea." I always wail, "Mum, I can't stop in the middle of something!" But Mum never understands, because Mum isn't a writer. By the time I've had tea and gone back to my essay, I have totally forgotten what I was going to write. I said this to Harriet, and she said, "Oh, you understand! We are obviously on the same wavelength."

I just, like, *glowed*. I felt so proud at being taken into Harriet's confidence! If I hadn't been in the car I would

 have written things down in my reporter's book that I had brought with me; but I can't write – or read – in cars, because of car sickness. However, I knew that I wouldn't forget it. It was something that Harriet and I had in common. We were both writers! And we didn't like to be disturbed.

"This was another reason," said Harriet, "why I didn't want you telling anyone about our secret meeting... if readers discovered my hideaway, it would be the end! I'd never have a moment's peace. I would have to move."

Earnestly, I assured her that we hadn't told a soul. "And we won't. I promise!" I then turned round and pulled a face at Annie, 'cos Annie very nearly *had* told.

"Wouldn't have made any difference," said Annie.

"What's that?" said Harriet. "What wouldn't have made any difference?"

"If I'd told my sister we were coming to meet you."

"But she didn't!" I said, quickly. "I stopped her."

"Good girl," said Harriet.

"She still wouldn't have known where you lived," said Annie.

"She might have found out," I said.

"Well, she probably wouldn't have been able to," said Harriet, "because not even my publishers have my country address. I don't give my country address to anyone! It's my very secret hideaway where I can be private."

"Even from Lori?" I said.

"Lori? Oh, no not from Lori. of course not. But from the rest of the world... You have no idea what it's like to be constantly bombarded by total strangers turning up on the doorstep wanting autographs, or wanting books signed, or just to come in for a chat."

"It must be horrible!" I said. I really meant it. I wouldn't want to be a celeb! Annie, however, said she thought it would be quite fun.

"It might seem so, just at first," said Harriet, "but in the end it wears you down."

"That's right," I said. "You want to write books, not keep on being bothered all the time."

"Oh, Megan! You and I are kindred spirits," said Harriet. Which made me glow all over again!

We finally reached what Harriet called her secret hideaway.

"Wasn't there some writer," she said, "who had a shed in the garden?"

"Roald Dahl," I said.

"Roald Dahl! I knew it was someone famous. He had his shed, I have my cottage."

The cottage was at the bottom of a narrow lane. The lane ended up in a woody area, with a field on one side. It was rutted and bumpy, and hardly wide enough for a car.

"Sorry for the rough ride," said Harriet, as we jolted and bounced. "Not many people come down here – which is why I love it so! Complete peace and quiet."

"Don't you get lonely?" said Annie.

"Lonely? Not at all! How could I get lonely when I have all my characters for company?"

"I would," said Annie.

"You're not a writer," I said.

Harriet's hideaway was like a little dolls' house. Really cute! Harriet apologised for the fact that it was a bit tumbledown. She said, "It needs a lot of work done on it, but it's such an upheaval!"

"It's like the one in Hansel and Gretel," said Annie.

"The witch's cottage? Was that tumbledown?"

"No, but it was kind of... spooky."

"Annieee!" I was horrified. How could she be so rude? "It's not spooky, it's lovely!"

I thought that if I were writing a description of it for English, I would say that it was *picturesque*. Just right for an author!

"I always have to watch my head," said Harriet, ducking as she opened the door.

The door gave straight on to the sitting room, which was quite bare. Just a chair and table, and an old saggy sofa. No books! That surprised me, but Harriet explained that if she had books there she would keep breaking off to read them.

"I am so easily distracted! I have a mind like a flea."

I was a bit puzzled by this as I had once read how Harriet Chance liked to sit at her kitchen table and write her first draft by hand, surrounded by her four cats. Surely cats would distract her? The lady who lives downstairs from us has a cat called Biddy, and when she comes to visit us, Biddy I mean, she always spreads herself out across my homework, if I'm doing homework, and starts grooming herself or purring. I find that very distracting!

I told this to Harriet. "Sometimes," I said, "she even tries to chew the paper!"

"Oh, I couldn't be doing with that," said Harriet. "I couldn't write with cats around! And I couldn't write on paper... far too slow!"

Falteringly, I said, "I read this interview where you said how you always did your first draft by hand... you said you couldn't write straight on to a computer."

"Did I?" She laughed. "Well, I've been dragged kicking and screaming into the twenty-first century! One has to move with the times."

"I still write by hand," I said.

"That's only 'cos you don't have a computer," said Annie.

"They are one of the blessings of modern technology," said Harriet. "Imagine! If I didn't have a computer, we would never have met. Now, then! How about some tea? Annie, clear a space on the table while I go and get it."

I needed to go to the loo – I always do after a car journey. Harriet told me the bathroom was "directly ahead, up the stairs... but be warned, it's a bit primitive!"

It was such a funny little place, the bathroom. Like a little cell. All it had was a washbasin and a toilet, with a cracked bit of mirror on the wall. Both the washbasin and the toilet were very old-fashioned. The washbasin was propped up on a sort of iron stand, and the toilet had a broken

142

seat and a long chain with a handle that you had to pull when you'd finished, except that it didn't seem to work, which was rather embarrassing. Red-faced, I told Harriet about it, and she said, "Oh, dear! Never mind. At least it's better than having to go outside… imagine that on a dark night!"

"You could write a book about someone living in a place like this," said Annie. "You could call it *Spooky Cottage*."

I cringed, but Harriet said, "Do you know, that's a really good idea? I might well do that! And then I could dedicate it to you both. *To Annie and Megan, who came to tea.* Speaking of which—" she whisked away a cloth which was covering the table. "How about that?"

I gasped. I couldn't believe it! It was like a fairy tale... all my favourite food was there! A bowl full of tiny weeny Easter eggs – another bowl full of Cadbury's Creme ones – a *big* bowl of crisps – a plate of ham sandwiches and a baby birthday cake, with twelve candles crowded on the top.

"This was *our* secret," gloated Annie. "I told Harriet all the stuff you loved to eat!"

"I hope we got it right," said Harriet.

"We did!" said Annie. "She adores all this stuff!"

I'm afraid it is true. It is exactly the sort of food that I would like to have on a desert island. The sort of food that Mum only lets me eat in what Gran would have called "dribs and drabs". Certainly not all in one go!

"Fortunately," said Harriet, "I bought enough to feed an army, so get stuck in, the pair of you."

Annie and I sat munching side by side on the saggy sofa. Harriet sat at the table. I was quite surprised to see that she was eating ham sandwiches as I had once read that she was a vegetarian; but I thought perhaps she was only doing it to be polite, what with me being a guest, and so I didn't say anything. It would have seemed ungracious.

After we'd eaten as much as we could, and I'd blown out the candles on the cake and made a birthday wish – even though it wasn't yet properly my birthday – I settled down with my reporter's notebook to interview Harriet. Annie kept nagging to know what I'd wished for, but Harriet told her that birthday wishes had to be secret, "Otherwise they won't come true."

Annie said, "Will you tell me if it *does* come true?"

I said, "Yes, but it won't be for ages yet!" Not unless you could have books published and get famous while you were still at school... Was that possible? I opened my notepad and wrote it down, as a question to ask Harriet. I had a long list of questions! I had carefully worked them all out in advance. I had decided there wasn't any point asking her things I already had the answers to, so I'd tried to think of questions she maybe hadn't been asked before. This was my list:

## Questions for Harriet Chance

What was Paper Dolls about?

What was your grown-up book about and what was it called?

In Scarlet Feather, does Scarlet choose to go with her mum or her dad?

Were you ever like any of your characters when you were young? If so, which ones?

Have you ever written a book using an idea that was given to you by someone else?

What made you decide to become a vegetarian?

Do you think a person could have a book published while they were still at school?

"Right! You come and sit at the table," said Harriet, "I'll sit on the sofa with Annie. Now! Fire away."

I cleared my throat. "Can you tell me what your book *Paper Dolls* was about?"

"*Paper Dolls?* Oh! Well... it was about paper dolls. Is that one you haven't read?"

"It was the one you wrote when you were at s-school," I said. "It... it wasn't ever published."

"Oh, good heavens, you're right!" Harriet banged a clenched fist to her forehead. "Silly of me! Memory like a sieve. But it was definitely about paper dolls. I used to play with them, when I was a child."

Dutifully, I wrote it down. I wasn't quite sure what a paper doll was, but I didn't want to bore Harriet by asking too many questions, especially silly ones.

"Sorry about that," said Harriet. "But I was at school a very long time ago!"

"That's all right," I said. "What about your grown-up book that you wrote?"

"Ah, yes," said Harriet. "My grown-up book."

"What was that about?"

"Um... well! It was... you know!" She waved a hand. "Best not talked about."

I thought perhaps she meant that it was rude.

All about sex, or maybe drugs.

"Not the sort of thing you'd want to read," she said. "Next question!"

"In *Scarlet Feather*, when Scarlet's mum and dad split up, which of them does Scarlet choose to go and live with?"

Harriet hesitated. "That's not fair!" shrilled Annie. "You shouldn't ask the ending of a book before you've read it!"

"No, you certainly should not," said Harriet.

"It's cheating! Don't tell her!"

"I don't intend to," said Harriet. "But it was a good try!"

"I just wanted to get a scoop," I said. "Like in the newspapers."

"But if you give all my plots away, no one will bother to buy the books!"

I hadn't thought of that.

"Next question!"

I consulted my list. "Were you ever like any of your characters when you were young, and if so, which ones?"

"Oh, dear! That's asking."

"You don't have to tell me if you don't want," I said. "It's just that you always seem to know how people feel. Like Victoria Plum and her hair. And Sugar Mouse and—"

"Sugar Mouse! That was me. That was my nickname, when I was at school... Mouse. Because I was so mouse-like! Wouldn't say boo to a goose. You probably wouldn't think it now," said Harriet, "but I was just so shy! Always scuttling off into the corner." She made little scuttling motions with her hands. "So, yes, you're right! I know all about being mouse-like."

There was a bit of a silence.

"Well, aren't you going to write it down?" said Annie.

I swallowed, and started writing. Perhaps *Sugar Mouse* was one that Annie hadn't read. Or perhaps she'd forgotten it. It seemed like Harriet had forgotten it, too. Sugar Mouse doesn't get her nickname because she's mouse-like, she gets it because she dances the *part* of a sugar mouse in the end-of-term show at her ballet school. She's chosen because she's very tiny and dainty. But she's also very perky and up-front! She has people in stitches doing really wicked imitations of her ballet teacher. She's not mouse-like at all.

It was worrying how Harriet didn't seem able to remember things. It reminded me of Gran, and her Alzheimer's. But Harriet was too young to have Alzheimer's! And she didn't behave like Gran used to behave. She didn't suddenly stop speaking, and look lost, or go out of the room to fetch one thing and come back with another. She seemed absolutely totally normal, except for not being able to remember the characters in her own books.

Maybe that was what happened when you wrote a lot of books? Maybe you forgot what you'd written in them? It was a bit disappointing, as I'd been looking forward to asking lots of questions about my favourite characters; but I reminded myself that I was really lucky to be here at all.

"So how are we doing?" said Harriet. "Got any more?"

"J-just t-two," I said. I decided I wouldn't bother asking her the one I'd added, about getting books published while you were at school. I didn't want to wear her out.

"Right, then! Let's be having them."

I seemed to have a ping-pong ball in my throat. I swallowed, and forced it back down.

"Have you ever written a book using an idea that's been given to you by someone else?"

I expected her to say a very firm no, because of what I'd read. If she'd have said no, I was going to ask her *why* she had resistance. But she didn't say no. She said yes! She said, "Yes, yes, absolutely! People are always giving me ideas. It's very important to listen when people tell you things. They have such extraordinary stories! Things you couldn't possibly make up. They give you all sorts of wonderful ideas!"

"Like *Spooky Cottage*," said Annie.

"Exactly! Yes!"

Maybe, I thought, the person who had interviewed her before had got it wrong. It was the only explanation.

"So which books," I said, "have come from ideas that other people have given you?"

"Oh... loads of them! That one." She pointed at the battered copy of *Victoria Plum*. "I had a friend with limp hair. She was always having bad hair days. So I put her in a book!"

I was sure I'd read that it was Harriet herself who had bad hair days and limp hair, and *that* was why she wrote the book. But she didn't have limp hair, she had lovely thick curly hair, even though it was going grey. It was really difficult, knowing what to think. Maybe she had just pretended it was based on herself. Authors probably did that sort of thing.

Now I had only one question left.

"What made you decide to become a vegetarian?"

I had blurted it out before I could stop myself. I went red as soon as I'd said it. Harriet went a bit red, too.

"Oh, dear!" she said. "You've properly caught me out, haven't you?"

I hadn't meant to. I didn't want to embarrass her! "It's just that I r-read somewhere that you were a v-vegetarian—"

"And now I've been caught red-handed, eating ham sandwiches! Well, that's my credibility gone. You'll never trust me again, will you?"

"Sometimes people who are vegetarians eat meat," said Annie.

"Only if they give way to a moment of weakness," said Harriet. "I'm sorry, Megan! Ham sandwiches are my weakness."

I didn't point out that she had said in the interview it was something she felt quite passionately about. It seemed that you couldn't rely on interviews. Either the people that did the interviewing made things up, or... or the people that were being interviewed didn't always tell the truth. I just didn't know what to believe!

"Is that the lot?" said Harriet. "Have you finished grilling me? Good! In that case—" she reached out for her bag, which was on the floor beside her. "I have a birthday present for you. Here!"

She handed me a book-shaped package. Just for a moment my heart leapt, as I thought perhaps it might be a copy of *Scarlet Feather*; but I knew at once it wasn't heavy enough for a hardback. I tore off the wrapping, and there inside was an old dog-eared copy of... *Patsy Puffball*! Harriet Chance's very first book. The one she was ashamed of, and would like all copies of it destroyed. In

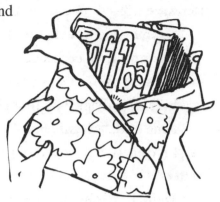

spite of that, I was quite pleased to have it, because it was one I'd never been able to find.

"I'm afraid it's only second-hand," said Harriet. "I wish I could have found a good copy for you, but after all this time I don't have any left. If you look at the publication date, you'll see that it's very old."

Obediently, I looked. Inside were the words, "For Jan on her birthday, with love from Mummy xxx." And then, inside the front cover: "Janis Patmore: her book."

"You don't already have it, do you?"

"N-no." I shook my head "No, I don't. Thank you very much!"

"You're welcome. It may be an early work," said Harriet, "but it's one I'm still proud of! That's why I just couldn't resist, when I saw it going second-hand. I had to rescue it!"

"So you – you wouldn't want it to be destroyed?" I said.

"Destroyed? Good heavens, no! Why should I want it to be destroyed?"

"Like if, perhaps, you thought it wasn't very good?"

Annie said, "Meg*annnnn*!"

"Like maybe if you thought your later books were better?"

"Well, I'm sure they are," said Harriet. "In fact, I should hope they are! This must be one of the very first books I ever wrote."

"It was," I said; and I could hear my voice, all small and tight. "It was the *very* first."

There was a pause.

"The first to be published," I said.

"Oh, goodness! Was it really?" said Harriet. "My memory!" She banged her fist against her forehead. "It's getting to be like a leaking bucket! What must you think of me?"

Gravely I said, "That's all right."

"It's not all right! You know more about me than I do!"

Harriet laughed, and so did Annie, but I felt this strange little shiver go prickling down my spine.

"I'll read the book," said Annie, snatching it from me, "if she thinks it's beneath her."

"I didn't *say* that," I said. "I just... I thought... it was a book you didn't like any more!"

"Whatever gave you that idea?" wondered Harriet.

"It was... s-something I read."

"Oh! You don't want to take any notice of things you read. You've probably read all sorts of things. Haven't you?"

"Y-yes." I swallowed, rather desperately. "Actually," I said, "thank you very much for the tea but I think perhaps we ought to go now."

"Go?" Annie glared at me. "What for? We're not in a rush!"

"No, and surely you'd like your photos taken?" said Harriet. "For your project?"

"Yessss!" Annie punched the air, exultantly. She just loves having her photo taken.

"Let me have your address," said Harriet, "and I'll send them on to you."

Annie opened her mouth to blurt out where she lived. I got in, just in time.

"Really," I said, "it doesn't matter." I knew enough to know that you never give your address to strangers. And Harriet *was* a stranger, even if I did love her books.

If they were her books. I was beginning to have the most horrible doubts.

"We do honestly have to go," I said.

"No, we don't!" said Annie. "We can stay till—" she looked at her watch – "at least five o'clock."

"Oh, that will give us plenty of time for photographs! You must have your photographs. After all, it's probably the only opportunity you'll ever get."

By now I was in a bit of a panic. I just knew that something wasn't right.

"Please could I ring my mum?" I said.

"Of course you can ring your mum!" said Harriet. "Where's your phone? Did I leave it in the car? I must have left it in the car!"

"I'll go and get it," I said.

I made a run for the door, but Harriet got there first.

"No, no! You wait here." She smiled. "I'll go!"

There wasn't anything I could do.

# RACHEL'S DIARY (THURSDAY)

I am getting worried. I don't know what to do! I think I'm going to have to ring Mum.

It's just gone four o'clock and Jem has left. There isn't any sign of Annie or Megan. While Jem was here I looked on the computer and found the email addresses of people that I think are in their class at school. People I've heard them talk about. I was hoping there'd be someone called Harriet, but there wasn't. Jem said, "Well, she must be a friend or they wouldn't have gone to tea with her. Haven't they ever mentioned anyone called Harriet?"

I thought about it, and I said maybe they had. It did sound sort of familiar.

"In that case, it's obviously a friend that doesn't have email," said Jem. She suggested I try ringing up some of the other people and seeing if they knew who she was, which I thought was a good idea. I took a couple of people off the computer, ones with unusual surnames, Ravjani and Caldecott, that I thought there couldn't be too many of, and looked them up in the local directory. I got through to both of them. They were both in Annie's class but they said they didn't know anyone called Harriet. There wasn't any Harriet in Year Seven.

There aren't any in our year, either. There aren't any in the netball teams, or the hockey teams, or the gym squad. There aren't any prefects called Harriet. There isn't ANYONE called Harriet, that I can think of.

Jem could see that I was starting to grow a bit agitated. She knows I'll be in trouble if Mum finds out about me going off and leaving them every day.

"Clues," said Jem. "She might have had a letter, or something."

"She doesn't get letters," I said.

Jem said well, it wouldn't hurt to look, so between us we ransacked Annie's bedroom. I know bedrooms are private, but it's her own stupid fault! It was Jem who went through the waste paper basket and found the note: HAVE GONE TO HAVE TEA WITH HARRIET CHANCE. Exactly the same as the one she left for me to read, except that my one just says "Harriet". I immediately rushed back downstairs to look up Harriet Chance in the directory. She wasn't there!

"She must be local," I wailed, "if they've gone to have tea with her!"

I'm the one who wants to go into the CID, but it was Jem – AGAIN – who came up with a clue. Well, it seemed like a clue. She suddenly remembered who Harriet Chance was.

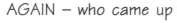

"She's a writer!"

Of course, as soon as she said it I realised why the name sounded familiar. I think I read one of her books once. And Megan is like, this really big bookworm. It was all starting to come together! They'd gone to have tea with one of their favourite writers. Now all we had to do was find out where.

"Ring the publisher," said Jem. "Ask where she lives!"

I'd have thought of it myself if I hadn't been in such a frazzle. If I was in the CID they wouldn't let me work on a case that I was personally involved in.

We raced back upstairs and into Annie's bedroom. Please, PLEASE, I was thinking, let her have one of the woman's books! She's got this one called Candytuft – Candyfloss. Something like that. Inside it says the name of the publisher, so I at once got the number from Directory Enquiries and rang and asked to speak to "someone who knows about Harriet Chance". I was actually, almost, beginning to feel a bit pleased with myself. I mean I was being really efficient. Really probing. CID, here I come!

All I wanted was an address and telephone number, but they wouldn't give them to me. Not even when I told them how my little sister had gone off to have tea.

"I need to talk to her! It's urgent!"

In the end they put me through to this person called Caroline Something who said she was Harriet Chance's editor. She said she was very sorry, but they didn't give out the addresses of their authors. Or their telephone numbers. Or their email addresses. But I think I rattled her a bit, because after I'd told the story all over again, about Annie going off to have tea, she said that she would get in touch with Harriet Chance herself and ring me back.

I'm still waiting! It's been nearly half an hour. Jem has had to go, and I'm all by myself. I don't know what to do! I ought to ring Mum, but I really don't want to. It's still only four o'clock. They could come back any minute. And when they do, I won't half give them what for! Going off like that, w—

I stopped there, because the telephone rang. I grabbed at it, hoping it would be Annie, but it wasn't. It was the Caroline person. She says she's spoken to Harriet Chance, and Harriet Chance is at home in London doing her writing and doesn't know anything about having tea with my sister. She made me go right through the story for the third time. She kept asking me these questions, like was I sure it was THE Harriet Chance, and had Annie ever had a letter from Harriet Chance, and did she read Harriet Chance's books, and did she ever go into chatrooms. It was only when I said yes about the chatrooms that she kind of went into overdrive and said she thought she'd better get in touch with the police.

Now I wish I'd never rung her! Dad will have a fit if the police suddenly turn up. And anyway, what's the point? They're not MISSING. The little tubby beast has just gone off somewhere on purpose to annoy me and get me into trouble and pay me back for telling her to turn her music down. I know her!

I bet she's gone up to London. I bet she was going to go and have tea with Harriet Chance, and then at the last minute changed her mind. I bet that's what happened.

But why would Harriet Chance say she didn't know anything about it?

Because maybe she didn't know anything about it! Maybe somehow Annie got hold of her address and talked Megan into going with her, and it was going to be a surprise visit. Turn up on the doorstep and get themselves invited in for tea. That would be JUST like Annie. Just the stupid, thoughtless, inconsiderate sort of thing she'd do. And then she'd suddenly have got cold feet, or most likely Megan would. She's more timid than Annie, and she's got a bit more sense. They're probably on their way back right now.

I just hope they turn up before Mum comes home!

# seven

THE MINUTE THE door closed, Annie turned on me.

"What's the matter with you? This is meant to be a birthday treat, and you're going and ruining it! Why are you being so horrid, when Harriet's being so nice?"

I said, "Because—"

"Because *what*?"

"Because I don't think it *is* Harriet!"

Annie stared at me like I'd suddenly gone mad. "What d'you mean? Of course it's Harriet! Who else would it be?"

I said, "I d-don't know, but—"

Annie put her hands on her hips and stood there, waiting. "*But?*"

"Something's not right!"

"Like what?"

"Like – she doesn't know things! Things she ought to know. Things she's said—"

"She's just forgotten!"

"She can't have forgotten *everything*. She can't have forgotten her own books!"

Annie frowned.

"She didn't even know that Clover's gran had a stroke," I said. "She thought it was Alzheimer's. And *Sugar Mouse*, she thought she was called that because she was mouse-like! And how could she have forgotten that *Patsy Puffball* was her very first book?"

"Well, I – I don't know! I—"

"She couldn't!" I said. "Nobody could forget their very first book! And that copy of *Victoria Plum* that she bought? She got it second-hand. It's got the same name in it that's in *Patsy Puffball*."

"I don't see that's anything to go by," muttered Annie; but I could see that she was beginning to have doubts by the way her mouth was puckering.

"There's another thing," I said. "Why did she keep my mobile? And why wouldn't she let me go and get it?"

"She didn't actually *stop* you going and getting it. And she did ring Lori!"

"If it really was Lori."

"Well, who else could it have been?"

"Anyone! *No* one. She said it was an answerphone."

"But she left a message! She said, 'This is Mummy'."

"She could just have been pretending."

Annie's voice quivered. "W-what would she do that for?"

"To make us believe that she was Harriet! Don't you see?"

Annie gazed at me, doubtfully.

"She wanted to get hold of my phone." I was remembering how just afterwards she'd ask Annie whether she had her mobile with her and Annie had said no. What would have happened if Annie had said yes? Would she have found some way of getting it off her? Like saying she had to make another call and mine had run out of money, or—

"Megan!" Annie was tugging urgently at my sleeve. "Stop it!"

"I don't think we ought to be here," I said. "I don't think we ought to have come!"

"But... *I* talked to Lori. We had this long conversation! In the bookroom!"

"How do you know that it was really her?"

"Well... b-because— " Annie faltered, and came to a stop.

"You don't!" I said. Anyone could pretend to be anyone, in a chatroom.

And anyone could look up Harriet Chance and see what had been written about her, like I had. Except that I had remembered it all; this woman hadn't.

We heard the sound of a key turning in the lock. She was coming back.

"Ask her when Lori's birthday is," I hissed.

"W-why? When is it?"

"New Year's Day. See if she knows."

I knew, because there wasn't anything that had been published about Harriet Chance that I didn't know.

The door creaked open, and Harriet – if it was Harriet – ducked her head and came in. Annie mouthed at me: "Ring your mum!"

"Megan, I'm so sorry," said the woman. She wasn't Harriet! I knew she wasn't. How could I ever have thought she was?

She didn't have Harriet's hair. She didn't know the characters in her own books. She didn't know that she never used other people's ideas. This person wasn't Harriet Chance!

"I'm really sorry," she said. "But your phone has gone dead. You must have forgotten to recharge the battery. You are a naughty girl!"

I felt my cheeks turn crimson. I was sure I hadn't forgotten; Mum was always reminding me.

"C-could I have a look at it?" I said.

"Well, I've left it in the car. It isn't any use, it's completely dead."

"But I need to ring my mum!" I said.

"Oh, dear! What shall we do? Your phone's dead, and Annie and I have left ours behind. How stupid of us. Now your Mum will never know where you are."

That was the moment when I knew for certain sure. Annie and I had made a terrible mistake. I didn't need Annie to suddenly blurt out, "When is your daughter's birthday?" Even if the woman had said "New Year's Day" I still wouldn't have believed she was the real Harriet. But she didn't.

She stared at Annie with these strange glassy eyes and said, "My daughter's birthday? I don't have a daughter…

my daughter is dead. My little girl is dead! That's why she doesn't answer when I ring her… she's not here any more! She's left me!"

Cold, wet goose feet went plapping down my spine. I could feel Annie trembling beside me and I knew that she was just as terrified as I was.

"You're not my little girl, are you?" The woman turned, slowly, to look at me. "You're just pretending to be her."

"No!" My voice came out in a horrified squawk. "I'm n-not! I'm not pretending!"

"You are. You're trying to make me believe that she's come back to me!"

I tried to swallow, but I couldn't, my throat had gone dry. Next to me, Annie was trembling like a leaf. I knew that we were in the most horrible situation, but I couldn't think how to get out of it. If we ran for the door, the woman would get there before us, and also it might make her angry.

The one thing I knew I mustn't do was panic. I looked at my watch and in this very calm, controlled voice I said, "I really do think we ought to be going now, if you don't mind."

"Going?" said the woman. "Going where?"

"G-going h-home," I said; and I edged desperately towards the door, tugging Annie with me. The woman at once moved across, to block our path.

"What do you mean, you're going home? This is your home!"

"No," I shouted, "it's not! It's not our home, and we don't belong here! We're nothing to do with you?"

"What?" The woman stopped, like someone had plunged a knife into her. She looked totally bewildered then suddenly wrenched open the door and cried, "Go! The pair of you! Go, now! Quickly!"

I didn't wait. I grabbed Annie by the arm and dragged her out of the cottage. I didn't dare use the road, she might follow in the car, so I dragged Annie into the surrounding woods, and together we ran. We ran and we ran, tripping over roots, falling into brambles.

Horrid scratchy things tore at us, overhanging branches nearly poked our eyes out, and still we went on running. I wouldn't let Annie stop. She was sobbing and gasping, with tears rolling down her cheeks and blood streaking her forehead, but I forced her to go on.

It is usually Annie who takes the lead; she is the one who makes the decisions and says what we're going to do. That day, it was me. I ran like I have never run before, with Annie stumbling after me.

I just knew that we had to get as far away from that cottage as we possibly could.

# RACHEL'S DIARY (THURSDAY)

Jem has just rung to ask if they are back yet. When I said no, she said why didn't I see if I could find the number for Megan's mobile and try ringing her at it.

I felt so ashamed, because why didn't I think of that? Not that it has done any good. If anything, it has just made matters worse, because I am more worried now than I was before.

I found the number on Mum's telephone pad, but when I rang it there was no reply. It just rang and rang until a recorded voice came on saying that the person I'd called was not available.

I don't know whether this means that Megan has also gone off without her phone, or whether it means she's just not answering. But Megan wouldn't go off without her phone!

Megan
6782 7721
6800

And she wouldn't not answer. Not if she heard it ringing. She is such an ORDERED little thing.

This is like a nightmare. The Caroline person rang to say that the police were on their way, so now I'm going to have to ring Mum. I don't care any more if she gets mad at me. I just want them to come back safe!

# eight

WELL! SO THAT was my birthday treat. Some treat! Not
that I am blaming Annie, it was every bit as much my
fault as hers. We should both of us have known better. As
Mum says, "You'd been told often enough!" I still don't
know how we could have been so stupid. Stupid, stupid,
STUPID. Even now, after all these months, I really don't
like to think about it. It was just so so frightening. So
really scary. The most scary thing that has ever happened
to me. Annie and I both had nightmares for ages

175

afterwards. I still do, sometimes, and I think Annie does too, though she wouldn't admit it.

When we came to the edge of the woods that day, all scraped and scratched and doubled over with stitches, we found ourselves in the middle of a housing estate. I don't think either of us could have run any further. Annie had ricked her ankle and was hobbling badly, and now that we had stopped I could feel my cuts throbbing, making me feel sick.

We managed to stagger to the nearest house and ring the bell. It was an old lady who answered the door. I was just so relieved that she was old! She looked a bit like my gran. She was horrified when she saw the state we were in. We tried to tell her what had happened, but Annie was sobbing too much and I was shaking so violently I could hardly speak.

In the end I just begged to be allowed to ring my mum; but even then, when I heard Mum's voice, all I could do was weep. The old lady had to take the phone from me and tell Mum where we were. Then Annie rang home and Rachel was there, and I heard her screaming down the phone.

"Where are you? Where have you been? I've been going crazy! We've called the police!"

After that, it is all a bit of a blur. Mum arrived in a cab, and Rachel's mum in her car, and Rachel in the police car, and we had to tell the police the whole story. We had to do it in front of our mums. That was almost the worst part. The old lady said she knew the cottage where we had been; she said it had stood empty for months. It was empty when the police went round to investigate. The woman who had pretended to be Harriet had disappeared. But she had left a note which said, I AM SO SORRY. My bag was still there, though not my mobile.

The police told us that they'd put a trace on the phone, but she must have dumped it somewhere 'cos it's never turned up. Ages afterwards, Annie came across the number written on a scrap of paper in her purse. "Megan's mobile". She wanted me to try ringing it, just to see, but I wouldn't; I would have been too scared, in case anyone answered. I told Annie that she ought to throw it away.

"We don't want to keep being reminded!"

It was like with my bag. It still had all my stuff in it, but I just couldn't even bear to touch it, it was like it had been contaminated, like diseased fingers had pawed and palped at it, so Mum emptied everything out and put the bag in the dustbin. I said to Annie that she should do the same with my mobile phone number.

There was a time when Annie would have argued, or even rung the number herself, but sometimes, these days, she actually listens to what I say. Sometimes she even does what I tell her! Which is what she did on this occasion.

"I 'spect you're probably right," she said. And lo and behold, she screwed up the paper and tossed it into the bin. I felt a whole lot better once she'd done that. Even if the phone did turn up one day, I couldn't ever bring myself to use it again.

Another thing the police did was take Annie's computer away. I don't know exactly what they do when they take computers away, but I think they were hoping to find out who it was that Annie was talking to in the chatroom. I mean, it was obviously the same person that was pretending to be Harriet Chance pretending to be Harriet's daughter Lori, but what they wanted to know was: *who was this person*?

Me and Annie both had to go to the police station, with our mums, and look through all these photographs in the hope that one of them would turn out to be her. The woman. We looked and looked as hard as we could, until our eyes started aching with the strain of it, but there wasn't any photograph that was even the least little bit like. I felt quite guilty that we couldn't be more helpful. There was this nice policewoman who told us to take our time and not to worry if we couldn't identify anybody, but I felt that we had behaved so stupidly, and put everyone to so much trouble, not to mention upsetting our mums, and Annie's dad, and Rachel, that I really would have liked to be able to point my finger and say "That one!" But in the end I couldn't, and neither could Annie.

We couldn't even be helpful about the car. All we could remember for sure was that it was red. So then we had to look at pictures of cars, and Annie thought it was a VW and I thought it was a Ford, and neither of us had noticed the number at all. Not even just one digit. Not even a letter! But I remembered the name "Jan" in the books, and "Love from Mummy," and then a bit later I remembered how one of the books had had the words "Janis Patmore: her book" written in it. I told Mum, and Mum said we must tell the police immediately. It turned out to be the clue that they needed, 'cos they actually managed to trace the woman. She hadn't really bothered to cover her tracks, so once they'd got the name it was quite easy. Maybe – this was what Mum said – she secretly wanted to be caught. "To stop her doing to anyone else what she did to you."

She obviously felt bad about it, or she wouldn't have left the note saying sorry. And what the police discovered was really sad. Janis Patmore had been the woman's daughter, her only daughter, and just a few months ago she had been killed in a terrible motor accident. She had only been twelve years old, and Harriet Chance had been her favourite author, just like she is mine.

The police said they thought the woman's brain had got muddled by grief, and that she had gone into the chatroom hoping to find her lost daughter – and instead, through Annie, she had found me. With one part of her brain, the muddled part, she might actually have thought that I *was* her daughter. But with the other part she would have known that I wasn't; which was why, at the end, she had come to her senses and shouted at us to go. It was like she had suddenly woken up to the truth and realised what she was doing.

When Mum heard this she said, "That is so tragic! The woman needs help, not punishment." The police assured us that she was getting help, and Mum said "Thank goodness. I know that what she did was terribly wrong, but she was obviously beside herself." And then she said, "That poor woman!"

I was somewhat indignant, at first. I mean, that poor woman had given me and Annie the worst fright either of us had ever had; and as I said to Mum, "Suppose she hadn't let us go?"

Mum said, "Then I would probably have ended up every bit as distraught and disturbed as that poor soul." She said that losing a child was just about the worst thing that could happen to a parent, and I knew that I should feel sorry for the woman, and I do try to, thought it is not easy. Mum says that when I'm older I will be more understanding. At the moment, it is still too close and I still get too scared. But sometimes I find myself remembering how the woman spoke on the answerphone, saying "Darling, where are you?" and "Please speak to me" and then I do, genuinely, feel sorry for her and think that maybe one day I shall be able to forgive her.

In the meantime, our story has been all over the papers, and on the radio and TV. It has been so embarrassing and horrible! I have felt all the time that everyone is looking at me and going, "That is the girl who was so stupid and has caused so much trouble." For ages I didn't want to go out for fear of being stared at. Annie felt the same. She always used to say that when she grew up she wanted to be a celeb, but I think she has changed her mind. She says that being famous is no fun and she would just like to be plain Annabel Watson that no one has ever heard of.

Our mums, I must say, were not very sympathetic. They were right at the beginning, but once they had got over the first shock, and the relief at having us back, they became a bit stern and told us that we had brought it all on ourselves. Mum did say that at least if other children could learn from our mistakes it would be one good thing to come out of "the whole sorry episode". She said, "You have both got off very lightly, and if a little bit of embarrassment is the price you have to pay, so be it."

I couldn't really argue with her. Even now when I think what *could* have happened, I get so tied up inside that I have to immediately start doing multiplication tables very quickly in my head, or gabbling nonsense like Mary-had-a-little-lamb, its-fleece-was-white-as-snow-as-snow-as-snow, until the knots have untied and the panic has stopped.

Before that terrible day, I don't think, probably, that many people at school knew who we were. We were just nonentities. Now – unfortunately – we are known throughout the school. We've had visits from the police, we've had lectures from teachers, we've even had a talk from Mrs Gibson in morning assembly, everybody from Year Seven to the Sixth Form, warning us about the dangers of meeting strangers from chatrooms. Mrs Gibson didn't actually mention me and Annie by name, but by then we'd been in the papers, so she didn't have to. Everybody knew. Heads turned, all over the hall. People around us started whispering. In the playground at break we could feel that we were being pointed at and talked about.

Most of the people in our class were really nice and said that what had happened could just as easily have happened to any of them – "We can all make mistakes!" But one or two said how dumb could you get, and one girl, Rozalie Dunkin, even blamed us for the fact that her parents had now taken her computer away and would only let her use it under supervision. She said it was so unfair.

"I'd never do anything that stupid!"

Me and Annie hung our heads, not knowing what to say, but another girl came to our rescue. Katie Purvis. (Who we are now really good friends with.) Katie pointed out that *at the time* you don't always realise you're being stupid.

"If you realised, you wouldn't do it."

Rozalie just tossed her head and said, "*I'd* realise. I'm not an idiot! Now we've got to put up with all these boring lectures."

Fortunately, not everyone thought they were boring, but Annie and me did feel quite bad about it.

We've both had to go for counselling (though not together). We've had to talk about what happened, and say how we feel. I didn't want to, at first. I didn't even want to think about it, but you can't always choose what you're going to think about. Thoughts pop into your brain when you are least expecting them. So in the end I started talking, telling it all over again, though I'd already been through it with Mum, and the police. And after a while it started to get easier, so that I now feel a bit better than I did. But I know that it will always be with me, and that I will never again do anything so foolish, not if I live to be a hundred.

Annie and I never really talk about that day. I think we are both too ashamed, and also it was just too scary. It scared me so much that I stopped nagging Mum to let me go into chatrooms. I even stopped nagging at her to let me have a computer. I thought Mum would be pleased. I thought she would say, "Well, at least you have learnt your lesson!" I couldn't really blame her if that's what she'd said. I'm all Mum's got in the world, and she might have lost me. She'd already told me that it made her blood run cold to think what might have happened.

"You're so precious to me, Megan!"

I said, "You're precious to me, Mum! That's why I don't care any more if we don't have a computer. I don't want one!"

You'll never guess what Mum said? In this very brisk tone of voice she said, "Well, that's where I beg to differ. *I* think we need to get you one as soon as possible, so that you can learn to use it properly and responsibly, without putting yourself at risk."

Anxiously I said, "But I don't ever want to go into a chatroom!" To which Mum said, "Nonsense! Of course you'll go into chatrooms. But you'll do it with me, and you'll stick to the rules. I don't want you growing up not knowing how to take care of yourself!"

*Well.* There are times when Mum can really surprise me. I thought she'd be so angry she'd never trust me ever again. But she said that in some ways she blamed herself.

"I've kept you too wrapped up in cotton wool."

At the time when she said it, when I was still feeling all shaky and terribly, horribly scared, I thought to myself that I liked being wrapped up in cotton wool. I didn't ever want to be unwrapped! But Mum says you can't live in a cocoon for ever, and I expect she is right. I am beginning to come out of it a bit now.

Annie has almost gone back to being her old bouncy self, which for a long while she wasn't. I hated seeing Annie all meek and subdued. I was quite relieved when she said to me one day that it might be fun to visit the joke shop in the shopping centre and buy some pretend scabs to stick on ourselves.

"Really gruesome ones... and grollies! You can buy grollies, all green and yucky!"

I knew then that she was still the same old Annie. We did go to the joke shop and buy scabs – and grollies, and some boils-on-the-point-of-bursting – but I said I didn't think we ought to wear them to school. I mean, we were in enough trouble as it was. For once, Annie agreed with me. Wonders will never cease! But like I said, Annie does now actually listen to me occasionally. Sometimes. Just now and again. If she always did *everything* I told her, I would know there was something seriously wrong.

Annie's mum was really across with her that day. Once she'd stopped hugging her, and crying, that is. Both our mums hugged and cried. Even Rachel did. But afterwards, Annie's mum told her that she should have known better. She had been warned over and over about going to meet people from chatrooms. Annie sobbed and said that she had thought it would be all right, because it was a woman, but her mum said that didn't make any difference.

"Besides, how did you know that it was a woman? It could have been a man. It could have been anyone!"

Rachel said, "It *was* anyone."

It certainly wasn't Harriet Chance. One of the horridest things is that for a while I thought I wouldn't ever want to read a Harriet Chance book again. I couldn't bear to see them all, in my bedroom! It was like I was muddling the real Harriet with the pretend one. It gave me a sick feeling in my stomach. But then something wonderful occurred. Caroline, Harriet's editor, rang up and said that Harriet was very upset about somebody impersonating her, and the terrible time that we'd had, and she wanted to do something to make up for it. She'd suggested that perhaps she might visit our school and talk to all of Year Seven about her books, and how she wrote them. And Mrs Gibson agreed! She said, "You've had all the lectures. Now it's time to move on."

Harriet came last week. I was really on tenterhooks, wondering what she would be like, and how I would feel. I kept thinking, what would I do if she walked into the library and it was *her*? The one that had pretended. What if she hadn't pretended? What if it had been the real Harriet all along?

Well, but it wasn't. That was just my fevered brain. The woman who came into the library was as different as could be from that other one. She was just as I had always imagined her. Small, and slim, and friendly, with mousey hair – a bit limp, but not grey – and rather quiet and shy. But really, really nice!

Afterwards, she talked to me and Annie on our own. She said that although she didn't usually use other people's ideas – "I just have this resistance! I don't know why" – she wanted to make an exception in our case. She wanted to write our story so that everyone who read it would know not to behave as foolishly as we had. (*She* didn't say foolishly. I'm the one that said that.)

"Is that all right?" she asked. "Would you mind?"

Annie and I just blushed and beamed and said we thought that would be really neat.

"And naturally," she said, "I'll dedicate it to you both."

So we really will have a book with our names inside! Mum says it is more than we deserve. Annie's mum says that what Harriet ought to put is "To Megan, who was led astray by her very stupid friend".

Poor Annie! It is so unfair. She feels extra bad about it, since she was the one who arranged it all.

"It was supposed to be your birthday treat!"

But I don't blame Annie. I was just as much in the wrong as she was. I have told her this.

"I know you *suggested* it, but I didn't have to agree."

She thought that I would hate her, but of course I don't. How could I hate Annie? Especially after all we have been through together. She's my best friend! My very *very* best friend.

She always will be.

# Is Anybody There?

# JEAN URE

Illustrated by Karen Donnelly

For Emily Crye

# one

LAST CHRISTMAS WHEN I was in Year 8, I did this really dumb thing. The dumbest thing I have ever done in all my life. *I got into a car with someone I didn't know.*

OK, so I was only just turned thirteen, which in my experience is an age when you tend to act a bit stupid, thinking to yourself that you are now practically grown up and don't need to obey your mum's silly little niggly rules any more. Also, I have to say, it wasn't like I'd never met the guy. I mean, I knew his name, I knew who he was. I even knew where he lived. But I'd only met him just the one time, just to say hello to, and even that was enough to tell me that he was a bit – well, different. Definitely not the same as other people. In any case, thirteen is *way* old enough to know better. We're all taught back in Reception that you don't go off with strangers.

"And that," as Mum was always drumming into me, "means the man next door, the man over the road, the butcher, the baker, the candlestick maker... you don't go with *anyone*. Got it?" And out loud I would say, "Yes, Mum!" while inside I would be thinking, "This is just *so* too much."

Mind you, Dad is every bit as bad, in fact I'm not sure he's not even worse. Whenever I go up to Birmingham, to stay with him and his new wife Irene, it's, "Where do you want to go? We'll take you! You can't go on your own. Not in Birmingham." Like Birmingham is one big bad place full of child molesters. Dad says it's not that, it's just that Birmingham is a city, and I am not used to being in a city.

"I'm sure at home your mother lets you go wherever you want."

I wish! Though actually, to be honest, after last Christmas, I didn't want to go anywhere on my own. It took me ages to get my confidence back.

\*

How it all started, really, was one wet Saturday afternoon towards the end of term; the Christmas term. Chloe and Dee had come round, and we were up in my bedroom. We were huge best mates in those days, the three of us. We'd all gone to St Mary Day from different schools, but we'd palled up immediately. We spent most Saturdays either round at my house, or Dee's; just occasionally we'd go to Chloe's, but Chloe had to share a bedroom with her little sister, who was one big pain and totally hyperactive, if you ask me. So we didn't go there often as it led to *scenes*, with Jade and Chloe threatening to punch each other's teeth down their

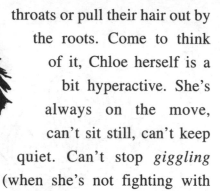

throats or pull their hair out by the roots. Come to think of it, Chloe herself is a bit hyperactive. She's always on the move, can't sit still, can't keep quiet. Can't stop *giggling* (when she's not fighting with her sister). It gets her into terrible trouble at school.

Dee, on the other hand, is quite cool and laid back. She is a very serious sort of person. I suppose I would have to say that I am midway between the two. Sometimes I have fits of the giggles, other times I contemplate life and what it all means,

and try to think deeply about God and religion and stuff. But I can see, now, looking back on it, that we were a fairly odd sort of threesome. However, we did have a lot of fun, before I went and ruined it all.

That particular Saturday afternoon, that Saturday at the end of term, it was pouring with rain drip drip dripping off the trees, plink plonk into the water butt. We were upstairs in my room, all cosily huddled under my duvet with Dee and Chloe doing their best to push me into playing The Game – which makes me think that really, I suppose, before going any further, I should stop and explain what the Game is all about.

OK. Basically it's about me being a bit psychic. Well, more than a bit, actually. According to Mum, I have "the gift". Mum is also psychic; I get it from her. Only she says that with me it is even stronger than it is with her, or will be, when I am grown up. Mum makes her living as a professional clairvoyant. People come to visit her, and she does

*Not my mum!*

readings for them. It is all quite honest and above board. Mum is *not* a charlatan! She explained to me, once, how clairvoyant simply means "seeing clearly". She doesn't pretend to be able to tell what is going to happen in the future. She can tell what *might* happen, if people keep on

doing the things that they are doing, but it is up to them whether they act on what she says. She is not here to change people's lives for them; only they can do that. She doesn't use tarot cards or a ouija board, she doesn't use a crystal ball, or call up spirits from the other side.

What Mum does, she asks people to give her some object that they have handled, like it might be a watch, or a bracelet, just something small and personal, and by holding it, and concentrating, she can, like, see inside a person's mind. She can tell them things about themselves that they hadn't realised they knew; things that are hidden deep within them. Things, sometimes, that they have deliberately suppressed.

Or maybe she'll dredge up something from their past that they'd forgotten, and suddenly everything will fall into place and make sense and they'll say, "Ah! Yes. *Now* I understand."

Some people just come to her out of curiosity; others come because they are unhappy or in trouble. It is very satisfying, Mum says, when you can help someone, but it is also very draining. It takes ever such a lot out of her, which is why she tries not to do more than three sessions in a day. Unfortunately, these sessions quite often take place in the evening or at weekends, which is a bit of a drag, but I have grown used to it. I don't think Dad ever did, only with him it wasn't just people coming round and spoiling his evenings, it was the whole thing about Mum being psychic. He just couldn't handle it, is what Mum says.

"He found it a bit creepy; it really used to upset him, poor man! But if you've got it, you've got it. It's not something you can just ignore."

It was quite by chance that we discovered I had it. I mean, Mum didn't give me tests, or anything like that. It happened unexpectedly, without any warning, when I was nine years old. My nan had just died, and Mum was very sad about it, and so was I, although Nan had been ill for a long time and I had never really known her any other way. I'd gone over to the nursing home with Mum, to collect Nan's stuff, and when we brought it back Mum said that I could have Nan's gold propelling pencil to keep, in memory of her.

"Nan loved that pencil! Grandad gave it to her, when they were first married. She'd have liked you to have it."

I don't think I'd ever handled a propelling pencil before. While Mum was in the kitchen making tea, I sat playing with it, twiddling the top and making the lead go up and down, and all of a sudden this great surge of joy came over me; I laughed and jumped up, and started dancing all around the room. Mum came in in the middle of it.

"Well, I'm glad to see one of us is happy," she said. There was just this tiny note of reproach in her voice, and it made me feel guilty because how could I be laughing and dancing when Nan had just died? I said to Mum, "I don't really feel happy. It was Nan! She's the one that was happy."

"How do you mean?" said Mum.

"She was with someone – a man – and they were laughing. And then she kissed him, and they started dancing. And she was just so happy!"

"Jo," said Mum, "what are you talking about?"

"Nan!" I held out the pencil. "I saw her! When she was young." And then I stopped, because obviously I hadn't even been born when Nan was young, so how could I possibly have known that it was her? But I had!

Mum questioned me closely. She made me look at pictures, and I found the man that Nan had been dancing with. It was my grandad, who I'd never met. Doubtfully, Mum said, "Of course, you've seen photographs of him. But all the same..."

Mum was really upset, and I couldn't understand it. "Mum, she was happy!" I cried. "Nan was happy!"

I thought it would make Mum happy, knowing that, but it didn't seem to. She said, "Oh, this cursed legacy!" I said, "Who's Kirsty Leggaty?" Well, I mean, I was only nine; what did I know? Mum then told me that I had the gift. She said she'd been hoping and praying that I wouldn't have, because although it could be a power for good it didn't make for an easy life.

I said, "But it was nice, seeing Nan!"

I think my face must have crumpled, because Mum hugged me and said, "Oh, darling, I'm sure it was. May all your visions be as happy!"

We didn't talk any more about it for a while after that. I didn't have any more visions, either; not that I can remember. Just one or two when I was in Year 6, but nothing to worry about. Nothing upsetting. It got a bit annoying when I changed schools and it started happening more regularly, but I very soon learnt how to recognise the signs and take avoiding action. Nowadays, I can almost always blot it out. You have to blot things out, or life would become intolerable. Mum is lucky that way, she doesn't have to. This is why she says my gift is more powerful than hers. Mum actually needs someone to be there, in person, before anything can get through. On the other hand she has to concentrate far harder than I do, which is why it tends to wear her out.

On my eleventh birthday, Mum told me that I was old enough, now, to take responsibility for the gift I had been given.

"I nearly said, 'saddled with', but that wouldn't be fair. You can do so much good with it, Jo! But you must treat it with respect. It's not something to just play around with. It's not a toy."

She told me that just as I could do good with it, I could also do harm.

"Do you understand me? I hope you do, because this is serious."

I *said* that I understood, but I don't really think I did. It was hard to see what harm it could do, just amusing my friends now and again. Anyway I didn't ever boast about being clairvoyant, but when Chloe and Dee asked me one day what my mum did, and I told them, and they wanted to know whether I could do it, too – well, naturally, I said yes. So then they wanted me to show them, which I knew Mum would have said I shouldn't; I knew she would have said it was treating my gift like a toy. But I just didn't see what was so wrong about it!

"It's only a bit of *fun*."

That was Chloe. Everything is a bit of fun with Chloe. If things aren't fun, she can't see any point in doing them. An attitude which does not go down too well with some of our teachers! Dee, being more serious, said that she could "sort of understand" why Mum was concerned.

"After all, being clairvoyant isn't exactly the same as being musical, or being able to dance, or... do gymnastics, or something."

"Whoever said it was?" wondered Chloe.

"What I *mean*," said Dee, "is you're not going to hurt anyone, just playing the piano. But you might hurt

someone getting into their mind. Specially if they didn't want you to, or you discovered something scary."

"Like what?" said Chloe.

"Like if someone was going to die." said Dee. At which Chloe gave a delighted screech and clutched herself round the middle. Honestly! She is just *so* ghoulish. She is totally mad about horror films, or anything with blood. Not me! *Urgh*.

"That would be so gross!" squealed Chloe.

I said, "Yes, it would. How would you like it if I saw that *you* were going to die?"

That shut her up. Well, for a little bit. But there and then, we laid down rules. *If* we were going to play the Game, we were only going to do it using objects that belonged to people who'd given their permission.

"Otherwise," I said, "it'd be like...well, like prying into someone's private affairs."

Dee agreed immediately, and after a bit so did Chloe. She said she thought it was a pity, as she would have liked me to do some of the teachers, she thought that would be fun, but Dee and I made her promise – "On your honour!" – that she wouldn't ever cheat. That way, we thought it would be safe.

Even so, we didn't play The Game too often. For one thing, I had to be in the mood, and for another I always had this slight guilt feeling, like maybe I was doing what Mum had warned me not to: using my gift "irresponsibly". It did niggle at me every now and again, but I told myself that it was just Mum, fussing. Mums do fuss! All the time, over just about everything. You have to decide for yourself whether it's a justified fuss, or just a Mum fuss. If it's just a Mum fuss, then it's OK to ignore it. Well, anyway, that's what I told myself.

That particular Saturday, what with it being nearly the end of term and Christmas only a couple of weeks away,

I guess it was a bit like, "So what? Just a M u m fuss!" We m e s s e d about for a while, and I did Chloe's cousin Dulcie, and had Chloe in fits of the giggles when I saw "Seven little people... I am definitely seeing seven little people! I can't work out what it means."

Dee said, "Maybe she's going to get married and have seven babies." and Chloe squealed and rolled herself up in the duvet.

"Is she happy about it?" said Dee.

"Mm... yes. I think so. But she's kind of a bit... anxious."

"You would be," said Dee, "if you were going to have seven babies!"

Chloe squealed again and shot out of the duvet. "She's not going to have seven babies! She's playing Snow White in her end-of-term play... *Snow White and the Seven Dwarfs*!"

"That is *so* politically incorrect," said Dee.

"It's better than having seven babies," said Chloe. "Let's do another one! Do my Auntie Podge. Look! This is her hanky. I did ask her."

But I didn't want to do Chloe's Auntie Podge. "I'm tired," I said. "I've had enough."

"But I promised!" wailed Chloe. "I said you'd do her!"

"I'll do her another day."

For a minute it looked like Chloe was going to go off into one of her sulks, but then she suddenly snatched my nightie from under the pillow and cried, "OK, I'll do you! I'll tell you what *you're* thinking..." She scrunched the nightie into a ball and made this big production of screwing her eyes tight shut and swaying to and fro (which I do *not* do, though I do close my eyes). After almost swaying herself dizzy, she began to chant in this silly, spooky voice.

"Is anybody the-e-e-re? Is anybody the-e-e-re? I see something! I see... a shape! I see... a boy! I see... *DANNY HARVEY*!"

I immediately turned bright pillar-box red.

"Told you so, told you so!" Triumphantly, Chloe hurled my scrunched up nightie at Dee. "Told you she was mad about him!"

"I am not," I snapped; but by now my face was practically in flames, so fat chance of anyone believing me. The truth was, I'd had a thing about Danny Harvey ever since half term, when he'd come to our Fête Day with his mum and dad. (His sister Claire's in Year 7.)

He'd visited the cuddly toy stall that I was helping look after. He'd bought a pink bunny rabbit! From *me*. I thought it was so cool, a Year 10 boy buying a bunny rabbit. I may not know as much as I

would like to
about boys, but even I know that
they would mostly be too embarrassed to buy a cuddly toy!

Mary Day, unfortunately, is an all-girls' school, so we don't get much of a chance to mix with boys; and if, like me, you are an only child, and specially if your mum and dad have split up, you practically live the life of a nun. Like, the opposite sex is utterly mysterious and you might just as well hope to meet aliens from outer space as an actual *boy*. But I knew where Danny went to school, it was Cromwell House, just down the road from Mary's, so by

using a different bus stop, and doing a bit of carefully timed lingering and lurking, I did occasionally manage to catch a glimpse of him. For weeks and weeks a glimpse was all, but just a few days ago, joy and bliss! He'd smiled at me and said "Hi". He'd remembered! He'd recognised me! He knew I was the one that had sold him the bunny! Which, needless to say, had set me off all over again. Just as I thought I might be getting over it...

"Poor you," said Dee; and I sighed, and she hugged me. And although she didn't say it, I knew what she was thinking: *Poor old Jo! She doesn't stand a chance.*

213

It was then that Chloe had her bright idea. We knew that Danny worked weekends and Thursday evenings at the Pizza Palace in the High Street (I had my spies!), so why didn't we organise an end-of-term celebration for the day we broke up, which just happened to be a Thursday?

"We could say it's for everyone in our class, 'cos they won't all come, but if it's just the three of us it might look kind of obvious, or *parents* might even want to be there..."

Dee and I groaned.

"Whereas if it's for the whole class," said Chloe, "they're more likely to let us go by ourselves. And *then*" – she beamed at me – "you can get all dressed up and flirt as much as you like!"

Naturally I denied that I would do any such thing; but already I was mentally whizzing through my wardrobe wondering what to wear...

# two

FIFTEEN OF US signed up for our end-of-term celebration. We arranged to meet at the Pizza Place at six o'clock so that we could be home by nine, which was what most people's parents laid down as the deadline, it being December, and dark, and the High Street being full of pubs and clubs and wine bars, not to mention Unsavoury Types that hung about in shop doorways. It was Mum who said they were unsavoury.

"Why do you have to go into town? Why can't you find somewhere local?"

I said, "Because not everybody lives somewhere local." Plus anywhere local is totally naff. "Anyway," I said, "you don't have to worry... Dee's dad will come and pick us up."

"So long as he does," said Mum.

I said, "Mum, he *will*."

Dee lives just a bit further out from Tanfield, which is the boring suburb where I am doomed to dwell; her dad always gives me a lift. So Mum said all right, in that case she would let me go, and I rushed off to ransack my wardrobe and see what I had that was even remotely wearable, and to ring Dee and tell her that she could go ahead and book a table, or get her mum to.

Of the three of us, it was always Dee who did the organising. Chloe was too scatty, she would be bound to get the wrong day, or the wrong time; even wrong *year*. Mum used to say she was "mercurial". Dee and I just said she was useless. I am not useless, but Dee is one of those people who always has everything under control. She's the same at school. She always knows what's been set for homework, she's always *done* her homework. She's the one who's always filled in her timetable correctly, the one who tells the rest of us where we're meant to be, and when. I bet you anything you like she'll end up as head girl, keeping us all in order.

But, oh dear, it was so sad! So *unfair*. The day before our celebration poor old Dee was carted off to hospital with an asthma attack. She has asthma really badly; her mum said she would never be fit enough by Thursday evening.

I was really upset for her, especially after all the hard work she'd put in, but also it meant I had to tell Mum that Mr Franklin wouldn't be picking me up any more.

He probably would have done, if I'd asked him, but Mum wouldn't hear of it. She said, "We can't impose on people like that!" But Mum herself couldn't come and fetch me, she had two sessions booked for that evening, and she said she certainly wasn't letting me make my own way back.

"Not at that time of night. Not in this town. No way!"

She told me I was to ring Albert and get myself a cab. Albert is one of her regulars, he's been coming to her for years. He also happens to run a minicab service, which comes in useful as Mum says he can be relied upon. She wouldn't normally let me go anywhere near a minicab, but Albert is like a mother hen. When I was little he quite often used to pick me up after school, and always got most tremendously fussed if I wasn't waiting exactly where I had been told to wait.

"A lot of bad people around! You can't be too careful."

I couldn't help feeling that a cab all the way from the High Street out to Tanfield was a bit of an extravagance when there was a perfectly good bus that would take me practically door to door, but I didn't say anything as I knew Mum would freak if I even so much as hinted at jumping on a bus. Instead, I concentrated all my energies on what I was going to wear.

It is so important, deciding what you are going to wear! There are different clothes for different occasions, and if you don't get it right you can find that you have turned up in jeans and trainers while everyone else is dressed to kill. Or even worse, *you* are dressed to kill and everyone else is in jeans and trainers. That is truly squirm-making!

Actually, however, since the contents of my wardrobe would probably fit quite comfortably into a couple of carrier bags, I didn't really have much choice. I only seem to have clothes for two occasions, one of them being school and the other being – everything else!

Which is OK as I am not really a dressing-up sort of person, being tallish and skinnyish without actually having any figure; not to speak of. No bum, no boobs. Just straight up and down. What can you do?

I used to envy the others so much! They might not be drop dead gorgeous, but even Dee, who is so slim and bendy, has some shape. She also has silvery blonde hair, cut very smooth and shiny, and always looks just so so neat. Chloe is just the opposite. She is very small and chunky and has no dress sense whatsoever, but because of being vivacious manages to look really bright and perky, like a little animated pixie. I probably look more like a sort of... stick arrangement. Mum says that I will "grow into myself". Meaning, I think, that I will be OK when I finally manage to achieve something resembling a figure.

Meanwhile, as I await that glorious day, I tend to wear... you've got it! Jeans and trainers. Which is what I put on for the celebration. Dee once told me that I looked good in jeans as I have these very long legs, like I'm walking on stilts. They are, however, not particularly inspiring – the jeans, that is. So to go with them I found a sparkly top, pale pink, that I'd hardly ever worn. I did my hair into a plait, one of those that's tight into your head rather than a pigtail. I think pigtails are a bit childish, all thumping about, but Dee said that having my hair pulled back made me look sophisticated. To top it off, I wore this very chic hat that I found in a charity shop. It's like a man's hat, I think it's called a fedora. It's got a high crown and a small brim, and is made from soft felt. It looks really great with jeans!

I was quite pleased when I studied myself in the mirror. The only thing wrong was the trainers. What I would really like to have had, what I had been positively lusting after ever since I'd seen them in a shoe shop  in town, was a pair of glitter boots. You could get them in either silver with red tassels, or gold with green. It was the silver ones I was lusting after! I'd shown them to Mum, who *predictably* had said they were totally impractical and wouldn't last five minutes. But five minutes was all I needed! I was busy saving up, and was praying they would still be there when I'd reached my goal. Saving money, though, is *so* difficult. I kept finding other things that I just desperately had to have! Entire continents could come and go by the time I managed to get fifty pounds in my account.

So I wore my tatty old trainers and my tatty old denim jacket, and Mum got the car out and drove me into town. As she dropped me off outside the Pizza Palace she said, "Shall I ring Albert and book a cab for you?" I was horrified. I said, "Mum, no! I can do it." The last thing I wanted was Albert turning up, all mother hennish, and dragging me off before we'd properly finished. It's horrid if you're the first one to leave. You imagine all the others staying on to have fun after you've gone.

Mum said, "Well, all right, have it your way – but I want you back no later than nine o'clock. You'd better ring for a cab at 8.30, just to be on the safe side. And don't you pull that face at me, my girl! You may think you're some kind of big shot, being in Year 8, but you're still only th—"

"Yeah, yeah!" I hopped out of the car and slammed the door shut behind me. I'd just seen Mel Sanders go mincing into the restaurant, all got up like a Christmas tree.

What was more, *she was wearing my boots*. I could see the little tassels swinging as she walked. Fortunately she'd gone for the gold ones, not the silver; all the same, it was a bad moment.

"Joanne?" Mum was banging on the window at me, pointing at her watch. I flapped a hand.

"It's all right, I heard you. *Don't fuss!*"

Of the fifteen of us, only ten actually turned up, but ten was probably about right, given the amount of noise we made! To be honest, I didn't actually realise we were making any until a woman at a table nearby came over and asked if we could "be a little bit quieter... I can hardly hear myself think!"

So then I stopped to listen, and I had to admit, she had a point. I have noticed that adults are very sensitive to decibel levels, and ours was certainly well up. Chloe, sitting next to me, was screeching at the top of her voice, which is quite loud enough even when she isn't screeching. Louise Patterson, at the far end of the table, was doing her best to stuff half her pizza into someone's mouth, Carrie Newman was having hysterics (well, that's what it sounded like), Lee Williams seemed to have got drunk on Coca Cola and Marsha Tate was tipping backwards on her chair, and honking like a car horn.

Our mums would *not* have been pleased. Nor would our class teacher, Mrs Monahan. She was always on about "gracious behaviour in public". We weren't behaving very graciously! But most of us hadn't ever been out for a meal on our own before, i.e. without grown-ups to keep us in their vice-like grip. I know I hadn't. I suppose it rather went to our heads, but it was the best fun.

I have to say, however, that it would have been even huger fun if Mel Sanders hadn't been there. That girl is so... obnoxious! She is so *obvious*. Where members of the opposite sex are concerned, I mean. She is one of those people, she only has to catch the merest glimpse of a boy in the far dim distance and she goes completely hyper. If there is one actually sharing her breathing space, well, wow! That is *it*. Fizz, bang, wallop, firing on all cylinders. Eyes flashing, teeth gleaming, boobs thrust out as far as they will go. (Which isn't very far, as a matter of fact, but she makes it look as if it is.) I guess it's something to do with her hormones, she probably has too many of them, and she just can't help herself. For all I know, it could even be some kind of disease. All I can say is that the effect is extremely irritating since boys, poor things, seem incapable of taking their eyes off her. It's like she has some kind of mesmeric power.

In this case it was specially irritating as clever Chloe 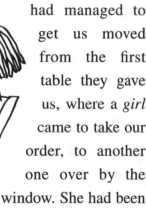 had managed to get us moved from the first table they gave us, where a *girl* came to take our order, to another one over by the window. She had been watching, with her beady eyes, and had seen that over by the window was where Dreamboy Danny operated. I hasten to add that *I* didn't call him Dreamboy. I have better taste than that! Dreamboy was Chloe's nickname for him.

"He's over there," she whispered. "Let's move!"

She claimed she was too near the smoking area ("I get this *really* bad asthma") so we all trooped over to the windows and there was Danny, with his order pad – and there was Mel, with her eyes going into overdrive, and I might just as well not have been there. If it *is* a disease that she's got, I wouldn't mind having a bit of it myself. Not enough to make me ill, or anything; but it would be nice to be able to mesmerise boys. As it was, I don't think Danny even noticed me; or if he did, he didn't show any signs of actual recognition. I guess maybe I look different when I'm not in school uniform. All the same... big sigh! He'd recognise Mel if she turned up in a bin bag.

Round about half past eight, people's parents started arriving and I dutifully rang Albert on my mobile, only I couldn't get through as the number was engaged, and while I was waiting for it to become unengaged I started thinking things to myself. It was totally stupid spending all that money on a cab when I could just as easily walk a few hundred yards up the road and catch a bus. I'd still be home by nine – well, nine*ish* – and I wouldn't need to tell Mum how I'd got there. Which meant I could put the money I'd saved towards the glitter boots! I wanted those boots more than ever after seeing Mel in a pair. I think I felt that if I had the boots I might also have the hypnosis thing and be able to get boys to take notice of me. Maybe. I know it was bad, when I'd given Mum my word, but I was, like, desperate. I'd just spent the whole evening being totally overlooked by the boy I loved! Well, OK, perhaps love is a bit strong, but I truly did fancy him like crazy. Believe me, if you have never experienced it, I am here to tell you that fancying a boy who has eyes Only for Another can make you behave in ways you normally wouldn't dream of. At any rate, that is my excuse because it is the only one I can think of.

I snatched up my jacket and rushed out into the night. I wasn't bothered about being one of the first to leave; I just wanted to add Mum's cab money to my boot fund! Unfortunately, owing to the stupid one-way system, you can't actually catch a bus to Tanfield directly outside the Pizza Palace but have to go trailing round the side roads, which at that time of night are more or less deserted.

I am not at all a nervous kind of person. I really don't mind being out on my own in the dark – not that I am ever allowed to be – but I must admit, it was a bit scary, waiting for the bus at an empty bus stop in this great concrete canyon, nothing but slab-sided office blocks rising up on either side, and gaping dark holes leading into the bowels of underground car parks. Plus this really spooky orange lighting, and not a single human being to be seen.

I was just beginning to think that maybe I had better go back to the restaurant and ring Albert after all, when a little blue Ka pulled up and the driver wound down the window and called out to me.

"Joanne? It is Joanne, isn't it?"

I'd been all prepared to turn and run. You'd better believe it! But when he called my name, I hesitated.

"Joanne? It's Paul – Dee's brother. Can I give you a lift?"

Well! I relaxed when he said he was Dee's brother. I'd only met him once, a few weeks back, when mostly all we'd said was "Hi"; but obviously, being Dee's brother, he had to be all right. So I said that I would love a lift, and I hopped into the car as quick as could be, feeling mightily pleased with myself. I'd be home well before nine, and could keep *all* of the cab money!

Cosily, as we drove, I prattled on about my boot fund, and our end-of-term celebration, and how Dee had done all the organising and how rotten it was that she hadn't been able to come. I asked Paul how she was, and he said

that she was much
better and was out
of hospital, and
then for a while we
talked about Dee
and her asthma,
and how it stopped
her doing some of
the things she
would really have
liked to do, such as horse riding (because of being
allergic to horses) and playing hockey (to which I went
"Yuck!" as I am forced to play hockey and would far
rather not), but I have to say it was quite hard work as I
was the one that had to do most of the talking.
Fortunately I am not at all shy, but on the other hand I am
not a natural chatterer like Chloe, and after a bit I began
to run out of things to talk about.

Paul didn't seem bothered, he just smiled and nodded.
He did a lot of smiling, but practically no talking at all. I
think it is so weird, when people don't communicate.
Even if I asked him a question, he mostly only grunted.
Or smiled. *Not* very helpful. You do expect some kind of
feedback when you're making all that effort. If it hadn't

been for me we would have sat there in total silence. But it shouldn't have been up to me! He was the adult. I couldn't remember how old Dee had said he was, or even *if* she had said, but I knew he was her half brother and was loads older than we were. He must have been at least in his twenties. Mid-twenties, at that. I was only just a teenager, for goodness' sake! Why should I have to carry the burden? It wasn't fair, leaving it all to me.

I looked out of the window in a kind of desperation, wondering where we were, and if we were nearly home, and discovered, to my horror, that we

were nowhere near home. Spiders' legs of fright went whispering down my spine. We were on totally the wrong road! Instead of taking the  left fork out of town, through Crossley and Benbridge, he'd gone and swung off to the right, down Gravelpit Hill. I'd been too preoccupied racking my brain for things to say to notice.

"Why—" my voice came out in a strangulated squawk. I had to swallow, and start again. "Why are we driving down G-Gravelpit Hill?"

He turned, to look at me. "Didn't Dee say you lived in Tanfield?"

"Y-yes." I swallowed again. "But th-this isn't the way to get there!"

"It does get there," he said. "I promise you! I know where I'm going." He had this very quiet, husky voice, without much expression. It was more frightening than if he'd shouted. "I realise it adds a bit to the journey, but—"

It didn't just add a *bit*, it took us miles out of our way. It took us through open countryside. Fields, and woods, and isolation. And, in the end, it took us to the gravel pits...

"I always come by this route," he said. "I prefer it to the other."

"But it's such a w-waste of p-petrol!" I said.

"Well – yes." He smiled. "I suppose it is; I never thought of it like that. But it's so much nicer than the main road. Don't you think?"

I couldn't answer him; my mouth had gone dry. I suddenly sensed that I was in terrible danger. I had made the most stupid mistake... I should never have got into the car! And oh, it is true, it is absolutely true, what they say, that at moments like that your blood just seems to turn to water, the bottom of your stomach feels like it has dropped out, and you get cold and shaky and a kind of dread comes over you. The one thing I knew, I had to keep calm. I mustn't panic! If he sussed that I was frightened, it would give him power over me. So long as I just kept my head, I might be able to find a way out.

Doing my best to keep my voice from quavering, I told him that if I didn't get back by nine, Mum would start to worry. "She'll be going frantic!"

In this soft voice, with just a

touch of reproach, he said, "Joanne, I really don't think you'd have got home by nine if you'd waited for the bus."

No, but at least I *would* have got home.

"I promised her," I said, "I gave her my word! She'll be worried sick! I think I'd better ring her, and—"

"Yes," he said, "do that."

I scrabbled frantically in my bag, for my mobile. Where was it? *Where was my mobile?* It wasn't there! My mobile wasn't there! I must have left it in the restaurant. In my rush to get away, and catch a bus, and save a few measly pounds, I'd gone and left my mobile in the Pizza Palace. I'd put my entire life in jeopardy for a pair of stupid boots!

Paul said, "What's the matter?"

"My phone," I said. "I've left it behind. I've got to ring Mum, I'll have to go back!"

"There might be one in the glove compartment," he said. He leaned across me to open it and, oh God, I thought my last hour had come! There was a screwdriver in there... one of those really long ones.

I saw his hand close over it, and I immediately lunged sideways in my seat, which threw him off balance so that he jerked at the wheel and the car did this great kangaroo leap. I screamed, and he said, "Sorry! Sorry!" and pulled us back again. "Phew! That was a close shave. Sorry about that. You OK?" He glanced at me as he shut the glove compartment. "It doesn't look as if I've got my phone with me, I'm afraid. But don't worry!" He smiled. "We'll be back in no time. At least coming this way the roads are clear."

I didn't want them to be clear! I wanted them full of traffic, and hold-ups. *I had to get out of that car.*

"You must admit," he said, "it's one of the advantages. And just look at the countryside!" He gestured out of the window, at the dark shapes of pine trees, and the woods looming behind. "I love it out here. You can drive for hours without seeing anyone. It's hard to believe the town's just a couple of miles away."

I knew why he was starting to talk: it was to make me think that everything was normal. But everything wasn't normal!

In a small, tight voice, I said, "I really do need to ring my mum. If I don't ring her she'll wonder where I am. She'll get really worried if she doesn't hear from me. She'll do something stupid, like call the police. I really do think I ought to go back and get my phone!"

"And I really think," he said, firmly, "that it would be better to get you home first and set your mum's mind at rest. We'll be there in a few minutes."

"But I want my phone!" I could hear my voice coming out in this panic-stricken wail. "I need it!"

"You can always call the restaurant when you get in. I'm sure they'll keep it for you. I'll even drive back into town and pick it up for you, if you like. But let's just get you home first. We don't want your mum being worried."

"Please!" I said. I was begging him, now. "I need to go back! I want my phone!"

"Joanne," he said, "mobile phones are not that important. Your mum's peace of mind is at stake here. But OK. OK! If that's what you want, I'll take you back."

I wanted to believe him. I did so want to believe him! But I knew he was only saying it to keep me quiet. If he

had really been going to take me back, he would have
slowed the car and turned round. Instead, he continued
straight on, barrelling down the hill towards the gravel
pits. It was the most terrifying moment of my whole life.
You just can't believe, until you find yourself in it, that
you could ever get yourself in such a situation. This was
something that happened to other people! It couldn't be
happening to me!

The thing that saved me was the traffic lights. The
lights at the intersection with the main Benbridge Road.
They were on red, and he was forced to stop. I was out
of that car so fast I almost fell over. Coming towards us,

up the hill, heading back into town, was a bus. I regained my balance and hared across the road towards it. I got to the stop just in time... another second and I would have been too late.

I heard him calling after me, "Joanne! I'd have taken you! I was going to go round the roundabout!"

But the roundabout was at the bottom of the hill, where the gravelpits were. I somehow didn't think, if we'd gone that far, that I would ever have come back...

# three

IT WAS TWENTY past nine when I finally arrived home. I rang Mum from the cab to tell her that I was on my way; I said I'd had trouble getting through to Albert, and that when I had finally got through, he didn't have a spare cab (keeping fingers firmly crossed that he and Mum would never talk together about it). Mum said rather sharply that that was no excuse, I obviously hadn't rung him early enough.

"I knew you couldn't be trusted! I knew I should have booked in advance."

Then she added that she didn't have time to tell me off right now.

"Miss Allardyce has just called round, she's in one of her states. I've got to go, I shall speak to you later."

By which time, with any luck, she would be too tired to make the effort.
Three cheers for Miss
Allardyce! Though I have
to say that I have never
understood how Mum puts
up with her. When I was little I
used to call her the Handkerchief
Lady, because she was always
turning up on the doorstep
in floods of tears with a
handkerchief pressed to her
face. In my view she is a total
pain, and personally I couldn't be
bothered with her, but Mum seems to have masses
of patience. She says that she is "a fragile personality", and this, apparently, excuses everything.

Anyway, for once I blessed her – the Handkerchief Lady, that is. I hadn't been looking forward to getting home and having Mum lay into me. I was still feeling quite shaky after my narrow escape. When I'd got back to the Pizza Palace all the others had left but luckily someone had actually picked up my mobile and handed it in, which was not only a major relief ('cos I'd already lost two of them) but also somewhat amazing, since all you ever hear about is mobile phones being stolen. But then I rang Albert, and my hand was so trembly and quaking that I had to have three goes at putting the number in. Even when at last I managed to get through I was terrified that my voice would give me away, because

that was all trembly and quaking, as well. The last thing I wanted was for Albert to start doing his mother hen act.

"What's wrong, poppet? Tell your Uncle Albert! 'fess up... something's happened."

Albert is a darling man and I love him to bits, and so does Mum, but I desperately, desperately didn't want Mum finding out what I'd done. Partly this was because I felt so stupid, and embarrassed, and ashamed;

and partly, of course, because I felt guilty. Not to mention the fact that Mum would never let me out of her sight again.

When I got in, the door of her consulting room was closed, so I guessed that she was with the Handkerchief Lady. Dear, sweet, Handkerchief Lady! If Mum gave her a full hour, it meant I could be safely tucked up in bed before she was through.

While I was getting undressed, my mobile rang. It was Chloe, eager to chat about the night.

"What did you think? Did you enjoy it? I thought it was great! I think we ought to do it again. Only in future," said Chloe, "we'll just ask a *few* people."

I said, "Yes, and Mel Sanders won't be one of them."

Chloe agreed that Mel Sanders would definitely not be one of them. "That girl is just *so* disgusting. She was even making eyes at the old guy behind the bar!"

"He was encouraging her," I said. "They always encourage her. All of them! It's like she has this spell that she casts."

"There isn't anything *magic* about it," said Chloe. "Anyone could do it if they wanted. It's just that some of us happen to have a bit better taste."

"Oh," I said. "Is that what it is?"

"Well, what did you think it was?" said Chloe.

Glumly I said, "Lack of sex appeal?"

Chloe snorted. "Doesn't strike me as very *sex appealing*, going round like a bunch of animated candyfloss."

What on earth was she talking about?

"That hair," said Chloe. "All puffed up. And that ridiculous top! I couldn't decide whether it was meant to be on the shoulder or off."

 Mostly it had been off. Quite a long way off. I had watched Danny's eyes, going round like Catherine wheels.

"And *did* you see those boots?"

Boots? I froze. What boots? My boots?

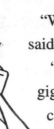

"What was wrong with them?" I said.

"Tart boots," said Chloe. She giggled. "That's what my mum called them!"

Chloe's mum was obviously an idiot. What did she know? I huffed, grumpily, into the phone.

"What's going on?" said Chloe. "You sound all humpish."

I said, "I'm tired."

"*Tired?* Really? I'm so wide awake I could stay up all night! Listen, I was thinking, if Dee's out of hospital—"

"She is," I said.

"Oh." Chloe sounded surprised. "How do you know? Did you ring?"

"No, I mean... she's *probably* out of hospital. I mean, she usually is. When she goes in. She usually comes out next day. I mean, like – well! She's never in for more than one night. You know?" I was growing more flustered by the second. I didn't want even Chloe to know how stupid I'd been. If Chloe knew, she would tell Dee for sure, because Chloe is quite incapable of keeping a secret, and I certainly didn't want Dee knowing. It would only upset her.

"Well! I'll ring and find out," said Chloe. "If she's home, shall we go and see her?"

I mumbled, "Could, I s'ppose."

"We ought," said Chloe. "She'll be dying to know how it went!"

"You could both come round here," I said.

"It'd be better if we went to her place."

I sighed. "All right."

"You're sounding all humpish again," said Chloe. "It's not Mel, is it? You're not letting her get to you? She is just so *nothing*. She's rubbish! Don't worry about her."

I wasn't worried about Mel, I was worried about going round to visit Dee and bumping into her brother. What would I say? What would I do? I didn't ever want to set eyes on him again!

"Let's go tomorrow morning," said Chloe. "I'll text you."

I said OK, but my brain was whirring furiously,

thinking of what excuses I could make. I would have to be ill! Or going somewhere with Mum. Or the dentist, or the doctor, or just anywhere. I couldn't face the thought of seeing Dee! Except... I would have to see her some time. We were always going round to each other's places. I couldn't just suddenly stop. She would think I didn't want to be friends with her any more. I didn't know what to do!

Seconds after Chloe rang off, the phone started up again. It was Dee...

"Oh!" she said. "You're back!"

Trying hard to sound bright and cheery, I said, "Nine o'clock curfew."

"Yes, but what happened? Paul was worried about you! He said he was giving you a lift and you jumped out of the car. What d'you go and do that for?"

She sounded reproachful. More than reproachful: she sounded quite cross. She had some nerve! She'd only got his side of the story; what about mine?

"Jo? What d'you go and jump out of the car for?"

I swallowed. "I s-suddenly realised... I'd left my phone in the restaurant."

"I know, Paul said. But he was going to take you back there! You might have given him a chance. He said you frightened the life out of him, tearing across the road like that."

How could I tell her that he had frightened the life out of me? He was her brother, and she probably loved him. When she'd introduced him to us, me and Chloe, that one time, she'd seemed, like, really proud. Like he was something special. Even if I told her why I'd jumped out of the car, she probably wouldn't believe me. She

249

wouldn't believe that her beloved brother could kidnap someone. Because that *was* what he'd done. Dee would say I was imagining it. But I wasn't! He'd deliberately driven the wrong way. How would she explain that? And the screwdriver in the glove compartment? And pretending not to have a mobile phone! Everyone had a mobile phone. If I hadn't left mine in the restaurant, if I'd had it with me and I'd tried to use it, he would never have let me. He would never have let me ring home! If it hadn't been for the traffic lights being on red, I would never have got home. Mum would have waited and waited for me, getting more and more distraught, until in the end she would have had to call the police. And then it would have been on television, and in the papers. *Has anyone seen this girl?* And poor Mum, weeping, as she begged whoever had taken me to let me go. Only by then it would be too late. And one day somebody walking a dog round the gravelpits would come across a body, and it would Mum's worst nightmare come true. But how could I explain any of this to Dee?

"*Jo?*" The way she said it, it was like... accusing. Like I was the one who'd done something wrong, upsetting her brother. I was quite surprised that he had mentioned it to her. I would have thought he'd have wanted to keep quiet about it, but no doubt he'd decided it was best to get in first and make like he was the injured party, in case I reported him, or anything. Not that I would. I still desperately didn't want Mum finding out.

"Jo, are you there?" She was getting impatient, now. "Say something! Don't just go all quiet on me!"

"Look, I'm really tired," I said. "I want to go to bed."

"Just tell me why you ran off like that!"

"I don't know! I wasn't thinking. I just saw this bus and... I had to get my phone! I've already lost two, Mum would have gone spare."

"But Paul would have *taken* you."

"I didn't want to put him to any trouble," I said. "Anyway, it's OK, 'cos I got the phone back. I've just been speaking to Chloe, and she said she's going to ring you and see if you're home. Which you obviously are," I said, brightly, though I wasn't actually feeling bright, I was feeling quite limp and weak; with shock, I suppose. Thinking of Mum sitting at home waiting for me had brought back all the horror of being in that car and knowing that I had made this terrible mistake. "You are home," I said, "aren't you?"

"Yes, of course I am!" snapped Dee. "Paul told you I was."

"Oh. Yes! So he did. Well!"

"Well what?" said Dee.

"I hope you're feeling better," I said. But Dee just made an exasperated sound and rang off.

I really hated falling out with Dee, but I just didn't know what to say to her. Also, to be honest, I couldn't understand what her problem was. So I'd jumped out of the car and leapt on to a bus. So what? It hardly seemed any good reason for her to be mad at me. What could he have said to make her so mad? Maybe he'd told her how I'd nearly made him crash the car. That would make her mad. The thought of me, putting him in danger. *Me*, putting *him* in danger! It was sick. Sick, sick, *sick*. And there wasn't a thing I could do to put it right. I couldn't tell Dee that it was him, her precious brother, leaning over me, opening the glove compartment. *Reaching for the screwdriver.* If I hadn't lurched sideways and thrown him off balance—

"Jo?"

Oh no, it was Mum calling up the stairs! She'd obviously got rid of the Handkerchief Lady. I sprang into bed, trying to make like I'd gone to sleep and forgotten to switch the light off, but Mum is almost never fooled by any of my ruses. She can see straight through me! I guess it's what comes of having a mum who's psychic.

"Jo?" She stuck her head round the door. "You still awake?"

Of course she knew I was! But I made this big production of suddenly waking up with a start.

"Oh," I said, "has it gone?"

"Miss Allardyce? Yes. She only needed a little pepping up. Now, then!" Mum folded her arms; a sure sign she meant business. "What happened, young lady?"

"Woman," I said.

"*Girl*," said Mum. "*Teenage* girl. Gave me her word she would be back by nine."

"I got back by twenty past," I bleated. "And I did ring you!"

"You think that makes it all right?" said Mum.

"I couldn't help it! I couldn't get through. I told you... they were engaged!"

"For half an hour?"

I blinked. "Well... y-yes."

"Rubbish! You're not telling me the line was busy right through from eight thirty till nine o'clock?"

"Maybe not qu-quite from eight thirty," I mumbled.

"Joanne, just be honest! You didn't even try ringing until nine o'clock, did you?"

I huddled down beneath the duvet, trying to escape the wrath that was to come. Mum is actually quite tolerant, but oh, boy! When she blows, she really blows. I braced myself for the tirade. *The last time I shall trust you, in future you'll be treated like a child, never allowed out by yourself at night again...*

"Oh, I can't be bothered!" said Mum. She threw her arms into the air, then pressed both hands on top of her head, as if to keep it from blasting off. "I've had a really tiring day. The last thing I need right now is my own daughter giving me a load of hassle."

I wriggled my way back out of the duvet. "I'm sorry, Mum! I am... really I am!"

"Bit late for that," grumbled Mum. But she was

softening, I could tell. I crept closer and stretched out a finger, trying to wipe away her frown lines.

"You won't get round me like that," said Mum. "You seem to think I'm just a stupid old fusspot, but the fact is, it's not safe out there for a young girl on her own at night. And don't start pulling faces at me!"

I wasn't pulling faces. I'd learnt my lesson! I wouldn't pull faces ever again.

"Mum." I settled myself, cross-legged in the bed. "You don't think you're working too hard, do you?"

"Well, of course I am," said Mum. "It's the only way I know how to make a living."

"But Dad pays you something!"

"Yes, your dad is quite generous."

"It's not like we're on the breadline, or anything."

"No; but I have to contribute my share."

"You don't have to wear yourself out!" I'd seen Mum at the end of some of her sessions; she would emerge looking absolutely drained. "I just don't know why you keep seeing that woman," I said.

"Who? Poor Miss Allardyce?"

"She's a neurotic!"

"She can't help it. She pays her money, the same as anyone else."

"Yes, and she wears you to a frazzle! She's like a *leech*. I can't understand why you bother with her."

"Someone has to bother. You can't ignore people's suffering."

"I can," I said. "When it's people like her, that latch on to you and take advantage of you and turn up at all hours of the day and night expecting you to just drop everything at a moment's notice and patch up their pathetic messy lives for them. It's just so *selfish*!"

"It is selfish," agreed Mum. "But that's all part and parcel of the condition."

I said, "What *condition*? I wouldn't get away with behaving like that!"

"No, you wouldn't," said Mum, "because you have no reason to." She said that Miss Allardyce was a "sad and troubled woman", but that things had happened in her life to make her as she was.

"Like what?" I said.

Mum wagged a finger. "Now, Jo! You know better than that."

I did, unfortunately. I was dying to hear what things had happened in the Handkerchief Lady's life, but I knew that Mum would never tell me. Everybody thinks of clairvoyants as being charlatans and frauds. They think it's all just play-acting, but Mum's gift is absolutely genuine, and Mum herself is one hundred per cent professional. She never gives away her clients' secrets. Maybe some day she'll write a book. Everybody in it would be anonymous, but I bet I'd be able to guess who some of them were! All she would say now was that I shouldn't make "superficial judgements".

"Things are not always what they seem. People are not always what they seem. The more you get to know a person, the more you understand – and the more you forgive."

I said, "Huh!"

"And what is that supposed to mean?" said Mum.

What it meant was, there were some people I didn't think could ever be forgiven. Some people I didn't think deserved to be forgiven. But I couldn't say this to Mum. She would immediately guess that I had someone particular in mind and would want to know who, and why, and what had happened. And even though, of course, I would deny it, Mum has an uncomfortable knack of ferreting out the truth.

"Do you forgive *me*?" I said. "For coming in late?"

"I'll have to think about that one," said Mum. "Ask me in the morning!"

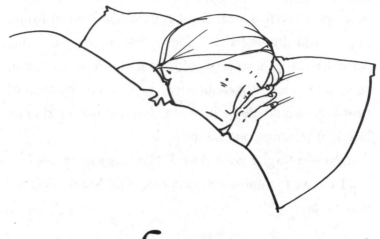

# four

I HAD THE most horrible night. It was full of scary dreams, all about gravel pits. But I wasn't asleep! I wasn't awake, either; I just lay, stiff and cold, like a corpse, in some kind of limbo, where Paul's face kept looming at me, mushroom pale with colourless eyes, out of a swirling yellow mist, and his voice kept urging me to "Ring your mum! Why don't you?" but every time I reached out for my mobile, it wasn't there. Paul said, "How careless! You've thrown away your chances. You'll never get home now." I cried, "But I must! I must get back to Mum!" So then he told me that there might be a phone in the glove compartment, and he reached across me to get at it, and I screamed, and the car veered across the road, and I struggled to open the door, but it wouldn't open, and Paul just laughed, this gloating laugh, and went on driving towards the gravel pits.

The dream never went any further; we never actually reached the gravel pits. But I knew all the time that they were there, waiting for me, at the bottom of the hill; and I knew that something evil was waiting there with them. If we ever did reach those gravel pits, I wouldn't be coming back.

Over and over, the dream repeated itself, like a loop of film, until I felt like I was going mad. In the end I must have fallen asleep, because at half past eight I woke up with a rude start when Mum came banging at the door wanting to know if I ever intended to get up. I was just so relieved when I heard her voice and realised that I was safe in my bed, and not trapped in Paul's car! I yelled at Mum that I was coming, and she said, "About time, too! Sleeping your life away."

I felt a whole lot stronger once I was up and dressed. I even began to wonder if perhaps I had exaggerated the whole incident. I am not one of those people (like Chloe, for example) who loves to dramatise everything, but maybe I had... overreacted. Maybe. At any rate, when Chloe rang me just after breakfast, saying had I got her text message and how about we go round to Dee's that afternoon, I didn't immediately fly into a panic and start burbling about dentist's appointments or having to go somewhere with Mum. I thought to myself that sooner or later I would have to go round to Dee's, because whatever her brother might be, Dee herself was still my friend, and the longer I left it the more difficult it would be to patch up our little disagreement. It wasn't a quarrel! But we had both been tetchy, and I didn't like being tetchy with Dee. So I told Chloe that after lunch would be fine, and we agreed to meet up at two o'clock, round Dee's place. Chloe said that she had already rung Dee to check it would be OK. I asked her what Dee had said.

"She said yes," said Chloe. "It'd be OK."

"Did you tell her we'd both be coming?"

"Course I did! I said I was going to ring you."

"What did she say when you said that?"

"She didn't say anything," said Chloe. "Why? What d'you think she should have said?"

"Oh! I dunno. I just wondered."

"Wondered what?"

"If she'd, like... said anything."

There was a pause. I  could picture Chloe holding the phone away from her and pulling one of her faces. She had this habit, when anyone said something she thought a bit weird, of crinkling her forehead and screwing her nose up, like a corkscrew. I suppose I was being a bit weird, only I had to check that Dee really did want me to go round. She'd been so cross on the phone! So angry with me for running out on her brother. But I couldn't go into the details with Chloe, so I just said again that I would see her at two and left her to go on pulling faces.

Usually when we went round to Dee's we shut ourselves up in her bedroom so we could be private, but Dee's bedroom is way up the top of the house, in what used to be the attic, and her mum said she wasn't yet well enough to "do stairs".

"But don't worry! You can have the front room all to yourselves. I won't come and pry."

Dee's mum is so lovely! It made me feel really bad, thinking all those dreadful thoughts about her son. Not that he was, actually, her son; he belonged to her husband. Dee's dad is heaps older than her mum. But that time when we'd been introduced to Paul, Dee's mum had been there, and she'd had her arm round his shoulders like she was really fond of him. It would be a terrible shock, if I were to reveal what he had done. She would be devastated to think that he might be a hideous prowling monster, preying on young girls, and her knowing nothing about it. Not even suspecting. I couldn't do it to her! Nor to Dee. It just confirmed my belief that it would be far the best thing for everyone, not only for me, but for Dee's family as well, if I didn't say anything. Which to be honest was a huge relief, as I thought that I would far rather just put it behind me and try to pretend that it had never happened.

Something else which was a huge relief: Dee seemed to have forgotten that she was upset with me. She was eager to hear how the celebration had gone, so for the next half hour we sat around cosily discussing it, with me and Chloe telling her what everyone had been wearing, and how utterly ghastly Mel Sanders had been, and what a complete idiot she'd made of herself.

"Trying to get it off with every guy that came anywhere near us!"

"She even tried it on with some old bloke behind the bar."

"Yes, and he must have been at least fifty!"

"It was just *so* degrading."

"Pathetic, if you ask me."

"And you should have seen what she was wearing! Those *boots*." Chloe sprang up and began tottering across the room on the tips of her toes with her knees bowed. "Tart boots!"

"Actually, they're glitter boots," I said.

"They're what?"

"Glitter boots!"

"Tart boots."

"Gl—"

"Never mind about the boots," said Dee. "Tell me about Danny!"

I subsided, glumly, into a nest of cushions on the sofa. "Nothing to tell."

"Why not? Didn't you see him?"

266

"She saw him, but he didn't see her," said Chloe. "All anyone could look at was Mel in her tart boots!"

"Really?" Dee gazed at me, sympathetically.

"It wasn't his fault," I said. "She hypnotises them!"

"So you didn't get to speak to him?"

I shook my head.

"Oh, Jo! And that was the whole point of it!"

"I know," I said. "But what can you do?"

"Buy a pair of tart boots!" said Chloe, and guffawed.

"Shut up," said Dee. "This is serious! I've got an idea... why don't we go there by ourselves? Just the three of us? Then he'll *have* to take notice."

Chloe said, "Brilliant! When shall we do it?"

"After Christmas?" said Dee.

"Yes, then we could tell our parents it was a going-back-to-school celebration. They'd like that... the thought we were all so eager to get back and start working again!"

"All right," said Dee. "Let's go for it!"

"Jo?" Chloe poked at me. "You on?"

"I am if Mum will let me," I said. "She doesn't really like me being out at night."

"Especially when you're late back," said Dee.

"*Late?*" said Chloe. "*Were* you?"

I said, "Only a little bit."

"But you left so early! You left loads before I did. I wondered where you'd gone, you just disappeared. I looked for you, and someone said you'd rushed off."

"I went to get the bus," I said.

"*Bus?*"

"Yes, you know," I said. "One of those red things with lots of seats inside? Maybe you've never been on one."

"Wouldn't want to go on one! Not at that time of night. Anyway, I thought you said your mum told you to get a cab? From *Albert.*"

Chloe knew all about Albert, and how he mother-henned me. So did Dee; they used to tease me about it.

"I couldn't get through," I said. I crossed my fingers as I said it. I certainly wasn't admitting to Chloe that I'd been trying to save money for a pair of glitter boots. As a matter of fact, I was fast going off the whole idea of glitter boots. I wished I'd never set eyes on the wretched things! If I hadn't known about them, I wouldn't have wanted them, and the nightmare of last night would never have happened.

"You should have waited for me," said Chloe. "My dad would've given you a lift. He wouldn't have minded!"

"Paul gave her one," said Dee. "He saw her standing there and he knew it wasn't safe, so he *very kindly*" – she glared at me – "out of the *goodness of his heart*, offered to take her all the way home."

She was still mad at me. Even though she seemed friendly enough on the surface, she was obviously seething underneath. It was so unfair! I felt like shouting at her. "Your precious brother tried to abduct me!" But I couldn't. I just couldn't do it to her. And, in any case, there was Mum.

Chloe was looking from one to the other of us. She has these antennae like a bat's radar, they pick up the least little thing.

"So what happened?" She leaned forward, eagerly.

"Nothing happened." I got in fast, ahead of Dee. "I just left my phone in the restaurant and had to go back and get it."

"He'd have *taken* you!" shrieked Dee. She was like one of those old gramophones, when the needle gets stuck. He'd have taken you, he'd have taken you, he'd have taken you. Chloe, by now, was all bright-eyed and alert, on the scent of some good gossip. She loves a bit of goss. I think it would be true to say that she thrives on it.

"Look," I said, "just don't keep on."

"But you were such an *idiot*!"

"Why? Why?" Chloe's ears were practically flapping in the breeze. "What did she do?"

"I didn't do anything! I just—"

"Just nearly went and gave Paul a heart attack! Jumping out of the car like that."

"You jumped out of the *car*?"

"We stopped at the lights," I said, "and there just happened to be a bus coming, so *to save him having to go all the way back*" – it was my turn to glare at Dee – "I rushed off and got it. OK? Simple!"

"You got the bus?"

"*Yes.*" I did wish she would stop repeating everything. It was beginning to get on my nerves. "What would you have done?"

"I'd have asked him to take me," said Chloe.

"Anyone would, that had any sense," said Dee. "I mean, honestly! How d'you think Paul would've felt, having to tell your mum you'd got run over?"

That was too much. That was more than I could take. I opened my mouth to yell the truth at her – and then promptly closed it again, just in time, as the door opened. I thought it was going to be Dee's mum, but it wasn't; it was *him*. Paul. He was really thrown when he saw me sitting there. I could tell, from the way he coloured up.

"Sorry," he said. "Sorry! I didn't realise."

"It's OK," said Dee. "You can come in."

Chloe giggled. "We're decent!"

"Actually, we were just going," I said.

Chloe did the corkscrew thing with her nose. "We were?"

I certainly was; I couldn't bear to be in the same room with him. "I've got to get home," I said. Reluctantly, Chloe unwrapped herself from the cushion she'd been hugging and scrambled to her feet.

"I suppose I'd better come."

"You don't have to go on my account," said Paul. "I only came to fetch something."

"'S OK," said Chloe. "I told Mum I'd be back by four."

He stood, holding the door for us. As I walked past he said, "I take it you got home all right in the end?"

Stiffly

272

I said, "Yes, thank you."

"And you got your phone?"

"Yes."

"Good!"

There was a pause. I knew Dee was waiting for me to apologise to him, to say how sorry I was for behaving like an idiot and nearly giving him a heart attack, but not even for the sake of our friendship was I prepared to do that. I just couldn't bring myself.

"Paul's really nice, isn't he?" said Chloe, as we set off down the road together. Fortunately, I was spared having to reply as she simply rushed straight on. "Wish I'd got a brother like that!"

It's true that Chloe's brother Jude, who is five years older than her, was like something out of the dark ages, when men were men and  women were doormats, and that his greatest delight in life was roaring round the estate on his motorbike, frightening old ladies and generally upsetting people; but at least he didn't abduct young girls.

"Could you fancy him?" She giggled. "I could."

Not me. No thank you! I supposed he wasn't bad looking if you happened to go for blond men (which I didn't, and never have). A bit like an older version of Dee, with the same silvery fair hair and blue eyes, except that Dee's eyes are bright, like the sky on a summer day, while his were pale and somehow wishy washy. I said this to Chloe, who said, "*I* could go for him!"

"I wouldn't, if I were you," I said.

"Why not?" Chloe was on it, immediately. What did I know that she didn't? "Is he married?"

I said, "No idea, but he's loads too old."

"Mm... kind of mysterious. Do you reckon he's got a past?"

I said, "Yes – he's probably been married six times and has a dozen kids. Listen, when you next see my mum, don't say anything about last night, will you? 'Cos if she knew I'd got the bus she'd never let me go anywhere, ever again!"

Chloe promised faithfully that she wouldn't breathe a word, and I knew that she meant it; but I also knew that she really couldn't be trusted. She makes these promises, thinking that she would die sooner than break them, and then at the first opportunity she goes and blabs. She is just totally incapable of keeping quiet. I decided that I would do my best to keep her and Mum well apart for at least the new few weeks...

# five

I HAVE ALWAYS thought of myself as quite a stolid sort of person. By which I mean that I am pretty grounded, not necessarily that I am boring and unimaginative. Though it is true that my imagination is nowhere near as vivid as Chloe's. Hers tends to splatter and splurge all over the place. "Running rampant", as one of our teachers once said, when Chloe terrified the life out of most of us by claiming to have seen a headless ghost lurking in the lower-school changing rooms.

"It wasn't just headless, it was knickerless, too!"

That was when Miss Mitchell accused her of letting her imagination "run rampant". My imagination does *not* run rampant. I have never seen any headless ghosts, with or without knickers. In fact, I have never seen a ghost of any kind, unless you count the time I saw my gran dancing with my grandad when they were young; but that was more of a recall. A vision from the past. As opposed to a *manifestation*. Gran wasn't actually there, in front of me. And far from finding it frightening, I laughed and felt happy.

What I'm saying is, I am definitely not a nervous type. I am not, for instance, scared of the dark, which I know a lot of people are; and when I went to the waxworks with my Auntie Sue and my cousin Posy and saw the Chamber of Horrors, it didn't bother me one little bit. Posy was all shaking, and clutching her mum's hand, but I was just, like, really interested. Same when Mum took us to a theme park and we went on the Ghost Ride. Posy screamed fit to bust! I screamed, too, but I only did it for fun. I'd have gone on it again, no problem. As for the London Dungeon... me and Chloe shrieked and giggled all the way round it.

So like I say, I am not a nervous type; but the events of that night continued to haunt me. I think it was the first time in my life that I had ever been truly frightened. It got so that I was reluctant to go to bed, for fear of what would happen when I closed my eyes. I started staying up later and later, watching telly into the small hours, until Mum caught me at it and demanded to know what I thought I was doing.

"Mum, it's holiday time!" I said.

Mum said holiday time or not, I ought to know better.

"Just taking advantage!" she said. "Your poor old mum crashes out at ten o'clock because she's totally shattered, and you sit here square-eyed half way through the night watching heaven knows what unsuitable rubbish!"

I hardly knew what I was watching, to tell the truth; I just didn't want to go to bed and have bad dreams. But after that I couldn't watch telly, because Mum made me promise – "No sneaking out of bed the minute my back's turned, do you hear me?" – so all I had was books, which are great for lying down and going to sleep with but no good at all for keeping awake as your eyelids very quickly grow heavy and start drooping, and before you know it you've gone and lost consciousness. And then the dreams begin, and there is nothing you can do about it.

Mum and me spent Christmas like we always do, with Auntie Sue and Uncle Frank, and my cousin Posy. I love Auntie Sue and Uncle Frank, but Posy is a bit of a trial. We are almost the same age, and so, of course, our mums expect us to do things together and be all cosy and chummy and talk girl talk in her bedroom. Well, sorry, I hate to ruin this idyllic picture, but the fact is she and I have absolutely nothing whatsoever in common. Not one single, solitary thing. How can you talk girl talk with someone who has *no* interest in boys, *no* interest in clothes, *no* interest in music – well, not what I would call music. To give you an example, she once went to a Cliff Richard concert with her mum and dad!!! She said he was just "so lovely"! Pardon me while I go away to recover myself.

Right. OK. Where was I? Saying about Posy. Her main passion in life, her *only* passion in life, is playing the harp. She started off with a teeny tiny little one, and now she has graduated to a great whopping thing almost bigger than she is. I suppose one day she will be 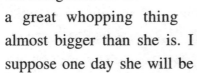 famous for her harp playing, and then I shall go round boasting to everyone that she is my cousin. In the meantime, if you happen to think, as I do, that the harp is an instrument the world could well do without, it does leave you a bit short of conversation. Mum says I should learn to be more tolerant.

"Live and let live. And don't you dare to sit there pulling faces while she's playing!"

To which I retort that a little plinking and plonking goes a long way, and why does it always, *always* have to be inflicted on us?

"Because her mum and dad are proud of her!" snaps Mum. "For goodness' sake, it's only once a year! Just put up with it."

Normally, as I am sure you will understand, I set out for Christmas with a glum and sinking feeling in the pit of my stomach. This Christmas – which just shows the state I was in – I was only too relieved to be getting away. Sooner Posy and her heavenly harp than run the risk of bumping into Paul every time I set foot outside the front door. I was also hoping that being in a totally different part of the world, down in Somerset, would put a stop to the bad dreams, and I have to say that it did help.

We came back home the day after Boxing Day and I thought that perhaps I was cured and could start living normally again, but it seems that when you have had a really bad fright it is not so easy to get over it. It's like there's a kind of aftershock. I wasn't having the dreams any more, and that was a relief, but when Dee rang up to check that I was going to the New Year firework display with her as usual, I desperately didn't want to go. Dee couldn't understand it, and neither could Mum. Mum said, "But you always go to the fireworks! What's the matter? You and Dee haven't fallen out, have you?"

I told her no, which was true. Dee had sounded her old self when she rang, not a hint of irritation. She had obviously forgiven me, and just wanted to be friends again.

"So why don't you want to go?" said Mum.

I hunched a shoulder and muttered that I didn't know. "I just don't."

"Oh, now, come on! There must be a reason. Something you're not telling me."

I sucked in my cheeks and looked down, hard, at the floor. It's fortunate that Mum made this vow, when I was little, that she would never, ever use her gift on me, a bit like doctors not treating members of their own family. She could have done it, quite easily. But she wouldn't, because that would have been like invading my privacy.

She tried coaxing me. She said, again, "Jo, you always go!"

"Twice," I said. "I've been *twice*."

"And you've enjoyed it. You've had fun!"

So why didn't Mum go if she thought it was so great? I muttered this under my breath, not intending Mum to hear. I didn't think she had, because she didn't pick up on it. Instead, in worried tones, she said, "You always *told* me you had fun."

282

"Yeah?" I said this in my best swaggering sort of voice. It seemed to me that a bit of bravado was called for, if I didn't want Mum probing too deeply. "So I've changed my mind. I've gone off the idea."

"Gone off the idea of fireworks?"

"Yeah. Right! You grow out of things, you know? I just happen to have grown out of fireworks."

It was a gross lie, 'cos I love those fireworks parties. But I was just so scared that *he* would be there. And it would be dark, and there would be crowds of people. It's all too easy to get lost in crowds of people. Worst of all, it was in Water Tower Park. Water Tower Park is right opposite the gravel pits, at the bottom of Gravelpit Hill. If there was one place in the world I didn't ever want to go to, that was it: Gravelpit Hill. Even just the sound of it made my insides start shaking.

One of the drawbacks of having a mum who is psychic is that you cannot get away with all the little fibs and evasions that most people take for granted. Mum always knows when I'm not telling her the truth.

"Something's happened," she said. "Something's upset you. It's all right, I'm not going to ask you what it is; I'm sure you'd tell me if you wanted me to know. Why don't we go along together?"

That stopped me *right* in my tracks. Go along together? To a fireworks display? Mum hates fireworks!

"You were absolutely right," she said. "I ought to go."

So she had heard me. Trust Mum! Ears like a lynx.

"What do you say? It's New Year's Eve! You can't sit at home all by yourself."

"You would have done," I said.

"Oh, well! Me. I'm old," said Mum.

She isn't old! Forty isn't old. But Mum is not a great one for going out and socialising; it was one of the things that she and Dad always used to fall out about. Dad just loves to party! Maybe it is being psychic that makes Mum such a home body. She gets too many... messages, too many emotions, when she is among people. But I am psychic, too, and I am certainly not a home body! Not as a rule, I'm not.

Mum obviously sensed that I was still dithering.

"You and me," she said. "We'll go together. It's time we did something together. We'll have fun!"

I couldn't help being apprehensive, even with Mum for company. I tried hard to relax, and laugh, and make like I was having a good time. I felt I owed it to Mum. I knew she had only come because she wanted me to enjoy myself, and that really she would have been far happier tucked up at home with a book and a glass of wine. So I grinned like mad, and waved at people I knew, and shouted "Hi!" and went *ooh* and *aaah* as the rockets exploded, but all the time I pressed close to Mum, like I used to when I was little and was scared she might suddenly disappear.

285

Dee was there with her mum and dad, and we all stood together for a bit and chatted.

"I thought you weren't going to come?" said Dee.

I said, "I wasn't. I was going to stay in with Mum."

"You can't stay in on New Year's Eve!" said Dee.

"I know, that's what Mum said."

"Chloe's around somewhere, but I haven't seen her. Have you?"

I shook my head. I did so hope she wasn't going to suggest we went off by ourselves to look for her. I wanted to ask if Paul was here, but I couldn't bring myself to say his name. In the end, Dee's mum and dad moved off to talk to someone else, and Dee went with them, leaving me still stuck like a limpet to Mum's side. I wished I'd had the courage to ask about her brother! Not knowing was even worse than knowing. I kept imagining him lingering and loitering, out in the darkness, at the edge of the crowd. I don't think I was ever more glad of anything than when the clock at last struck twelve, and we could sing Auld Lang Syne and go home. I felt safe at home; I hadn't felt safe in Water Tower Park. Mum asked me if I'd enjoyed myself, and of course I said yes. I don't think she altogether believed me, but she didn't say anything. Mum is *so* scrupulous about not prying. I guess it's because she knows she could probe my emotions any time she wanted, and there would be nothing I could do to stop her. The result is, I probably have more secrets from her than I would if she was just an ordinary mum.

Just occasionally I have wished that Mum *could* be a more ordinary mum, so that she would feel free to dig and delve and nag like they do. *What are you keeping from me? What aren't you telling me?* I think if she hadn't had her clairvoyant gift she might have got the truth out of me. And oh, in some ways, it would have been such a relief! To have been forced into telling her. It would have been like... handing over the burden. As it was, I kept it all to myself. Sometimes I thought it was growing easier; then something would happen to set it all off again.

The previous year, after Christmas, I'd gone up to Birmingham to stay with Dad and Irene for a few days, and Dad was expecting me to do same this year. I wanted to go, 'cos I wanted to see Dad, but suddenly I found I was having nightmares about getting there. I'd been so proud last year setting off on the train all by myself. I'd begged Mum to let me do it, so now, of course, she took it for granted that I'd want to do it again. But the bad dreams had come back, except that now it was a train I was trapped on. I kept trying to find the communication cord, and I couldn't, and it was just so scary!

I didn't say anything to Mum about it. I'd looked in her diary and seen that she had two bookings for the day

I was due to travel, and I knew I couldn't ask her to cancel them, just to drive me up to Birmingham. In the end I was glad that I didn't, in spite of the nightmares, because once I was actually on the train, and surrounded by people, all my fears fell away from me and I thought how silly and exaggerated they were.

It was lovely being with Dad again. It is quite a different experience from being with Mum, as they are almost exact opposites. Mum is quiet and serious, whereas Dad is very bright and extrovert. Also, he is a touchy-feely kind of person, which Mum is not. I am not sure that I am, either, to tell the truth, but I do like it when Dad envelops me in a big squeezy hug.

Me and Mum peck each other on the cheek occasionally, but that is about all. I don't know how she and Dad ever got it together! How did two people who are so entirely different ever think that they were soul mates? But they obviously were, once; and they are still good friends and care about each other.

I know lots of people whose mums and dads have split up and are really mean and vicious to each other and hardly even talk. I would just hate that! Mum and Dad speak quite often on the phone, and whenever I go to Birmingham Dad always wants to know how Mum is, just like when I get back the first thing Mum says is, "How's your Dad?" If people must split up, although I think it is terribly sad, then this is probably the way to do it.

It helps that Irene is a really nice person, very warm and friendly, so that I don't bear her any grudges for taking Mum's place. Unlike Mum, who enjoys her own company, Dad could not have survived by himself. He needs someone to kiss and cuddle and be there for him. Irene is rather billowy, with big soft wobbly bosoms, so I should think she cuddles really well!

I felt good when I got back home. I felt that at last I really had recovered myself; that from now on there would be no bad dreams, no more panics. I had learnt my lesson. Never again would I be stupid enough to get into a car with someone I didn't properly know. I'd been lucky to escape, but I *had* escaped, and now it was time to put it all behind me and move on. Yeah!

On our last Friday before the new term started, we had our going-back-to-school celebration in the Pizza Palace. Mum had said she was most impressed by my desire to get back to my lessons, but she would really rather I didn't go out by myself at night again.

"Not after last time. I don't want to seem like a harridan, but you were almost half an hour late. So if you don't mind, I think we'll keep it to a middle-of-the-day affair."

I didn't even try to argue with her. I told the others that it was lunch time or nothing, and they were quite happy.

"I know he works lunches," said Chloe. "I've seen him!"

"Yes, and there won't be so much competition at that time of day," said Dee.

One way and another, I'd had quite a lot of money for Christmas. Dad had given me a cheque and Irene had given me a really cool top, black with red swirls

291

(Mum said, "Hm! Rather sophisticated," in tones that weren't altogether approving, but personally I thought it was brilliant. Irene has great taste!). From Auntie Sue and Uncle Frank I'd had gift vouchers for the Body Shop; Gran-up-North had sent real money, by Special Delivery. I just love real money! Mum had told me that I could spend "up to £25" on her Beattie's store card, "Since clothes seem the only thing you care about."

Not true! I care about lots of things, such as, for example, protecting the environment and Save the Children. I am *always* putting money in collecting boxes. But obviously clothes are important and I did think I was entitled to a bit of a spending spree before going back to the daily grind of lessons and homework. I bought some black trousers, to go with my new black top, hesitated over a  miniskirt, decided against – Mum heaved a sigh of relief – tried on a couple of dresses, both unutterably hideous, went back and bought the miniskirt.

"You'd get away far cheaper just buying a scarf," said Mum.

I said, "What do I want a scarf for? I want a skirt!"

Mum said that if I tied a scarf round my waist, I would have a skirt.

"And it would probably cover up a great deal more of you than that thing does!"

Aha! She was just worried that people would be able to see my knickers.

"I'll only wear it for *parties*," I said.

"Like that makes it all right?" said Mum.

Sometimes I think that maybe forty is quite old, after all. I pointed out to Mum that when we had gone on holiday I'd worn a bikini.

"That didn't seem to bother you!"

"It did," said Mum, "but I knew I'd be fighting a losing battle. Can we go home now, or do you want to fritter more money away?"

I said that I wanted to fritter, so we ambled through the shopping centre, finally fetching up at the shop where I'd seen the glitter boots. They were still there, glittering away, but somehow they seemed to have lost their charm. They seemed a bit... tacky. So I bought a pair of PVC ones, instead. Bright red, with straps.

"Won't last five minutes," said Mum.

She says that about everything. She's always right, of course, but she misses the point. Who *needs* things to last five minutes? Mum has stuff in her wardrobe that she bought years ago. I don't know how she can bear to be seen in it!

It was fun, having our back-to-school celebration. Just the three of us – and gorgeous Danny! Without that idiotic Mel to distract him, he actually recognised me and remembered who I was.

"Oh!" he said. "You're the one who sold me the bunny!"

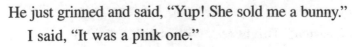

Chloe, needless to say, instantly dissolved into giggles. I felt like slapping her, but fortunately Danny didn't seem to be embarrassed by her ridiculous behaviour.

He just grinned and said, "Yup! She sold me a bunny."

I said, "It was a pink one."

"It was," said Danny. "It was a pink bunny."

Chloe said, "Wow!" and went off into yet another peal of mindless giggles.

"You can say wow," said Danny, "but it's not everybody that could sell me a pink bunny!"

I thought, *so there*, and kicked at Chloe under the table.

"Well!" Dee flopped herself against me, as Danny went off to take someone else's order. She let her head loll on my shoulder. "If that isn't cause for celebration, I don't know what is!"

I felt this big foolish beam spread across my face. Danny had remembered me! We had talked! We had had a conversation!

"Oh, boy," said Chloe. "She's got it really bad!"

I think I would have gone on foolishly beaming all the way home if the door of the restaurant hadn't suddenly swung open and Paul come walking in. I immediately froze. What was he doing here? It was Dee's mum who'd been going to collect us. She finished work at half past two, she'd said she'd be here to pick us up, I couldn't get into a car again with Paul!

"W-where's your m-mum?" I said.

"Oh, didn't I tell you?" said Dee. "Paul offered to come instead. We can give you a lift as well, if you like," she said to Chloe.

"It's OK," said Chloe. "Dad's coming."

That did it. I pushed back my chair and jumped up.

"I've suddenly remembered," I gabbled, "I told Mum I'd meet her in Beattie's. We're going to buy school stuff." I pulled a face. "*Boring*. But I'd better go, or she'll wonder where I am. See you Monday. Byeee!"

I flapped a hand and went rushing out, past a surprised-looking Paul, who said, "You're in a hurry!" Chloe came dashing after me, shrieking, "Jo! Your phone!" I'd gone and left it on the table again...

I snatched it from her, with muttered thanks, and ran like a hare all the way to the bus stop. I don't what I'd have done if Dee and Paul had driven past while I was waiting for the bus. Fortunately they didn't, as a bus came almost immediately; but I was shaking again, and that night the dreams came back. I began to wonder if I would ever be free of them, or whether they would haunt me for the rest of my life.

# Six

ON MONDAY WE went back to school. In spite of all our jokes about being *soooo* glad to start working again, and *soooo* glad to have mountains of homework – "Just *soooo* relieved I shan't have to sit watching telly all night" – I was actually quite happy to be back. With all its irritations (such as having to be in the same class as Mel Sanders, and play hockey in force ten gales), with all its silly little rules and regulations and its truly disgusting uniform (stripes!!! I ask you!), school was safe. School was *normal*. The worst that could happen to you at school was being sent to Mrs Jarvis (deputy head) for smoking in the games cupboard. Then, most probably, you would be suspended, as with any luck Mel Sanders would be before she was very much older. But since I almost threw up the only time I tried a fag, and since on the whole I am a reasonably law abiding sort of person, I really had nothing to worry about. Not even Paul.

I no longer froze at every corner, expecting him to be lurking there, nor jumped at every shadow. For a while I was nervous when out on the playing field because it is bordered by trees, and trees still made my knees turn to jelly, so that I did my best to stay safely in the middle, though this wasn't always possible, especially playing hockey. Miss Armstrong always liked to stick me way out on the wing, on account of me having these long gangly legs and her being of the mistaken opinion that this meant I enjoyed running. Unfortunately, having no aptitude *whatsoever* for the futile game of hockey, I generally managed to miss every pass that came my way, so that I was for ever cantering along by the side of the trees, with palpitating heart, in pursuit of that stupid little ball. And all the while, as I cantered, I would be thinking to myself how easily someone could be loitering there, in the shade of the

trees, waiting to spring; and how, if they had a car ready and waiting, they could bundle a person into it and be off and away and down Gravelpit Hill before Miss Armstrong had time to shout, "Jo! Move it!" (which she shouted quite a lot).

However, as the weeks passed by, and things jogged on just the same as always, too much homework, hockey in the freezing rain, Chloe told off a dozen times a day for talking, Mel Sanders sent home for customising her school uniform (i.e., hiking her skirt up practically to her navel), Dee being made class rep, me getting a D for a geography assignment – "Did you really expect to get away with this?" – quite honestly, in the end, I just didn't have the time to go on being neurotic. Little by little the bad dreams faded and I really did feel, at last, that I had come through my ordeal and could start living again.

Which I did!

We met up most Saturdays, the three of us, to mooch round the shopping centre. We had this thing where we pretended we were getting married, or going on holiday, or had a date with someone we really fancied, and we picked out all the clothes and accessories that we would buy. One Saturday we pretended we were pregnant and went to the Mother and Baby department, but Chloe kept getting these fits of the screaming giggles, which set me off, and even Dee, so that in the end we had to leave.

"Naked!" screeched Chloe. "We've got nothing to wear!"

Which, needless to say, set us off all over again. One Saturday we had a sleepover at Chloe's, where I was cajoled into playing The Game. I didn't really mind as we hadn't played it for ages. Not since that fateful night when we had decided to go for our end-of-term celebration. But it was all light-hearted. Chloe wanted me to do her and Dee.

"I can't remember when you last did us!"

So Chloe gave me her favourite silver bangle to hold, and Dee gave me her watch, and I did them both, sitting in torchlight in Chloe's bedroom. It was spooky, but it was fun. Whenever I did a session with Chloe it was like falling into a world made up of mad screen savers, all whirling and whizzing and scooting about. The inside of Chloe's mind never really stayed still long enough for me to make much sense of it. *Not* very restful. Dee, on the other hand, was more like the sea: calm on the surface, but waves building up below. I usually stayed on the surface as I really didn't want to probe too deeply; I didn't feel ready for that.

I had often wondered what I would say if, just by chance, I caught a glimpse of something really dark and disturbing. Would I tell them? Or would I keep quiet? I thought that I would probably keep quiet since, after all, it was only supposed to be a game. I suspected that Mum probably quite often saw things that were disturbing. I didn't know how she dealt with that as it wasn't something we had ever discussed, but I guessed that it must drain her and was one of the reasons she was so often worn out. It just added to my determination not to follow the same path that she had done. I mightn't mind helping people in some other kind of way, such as teaching handicapped children, say, or saving the rain forest, but no way was I going to plumb the depths of alien minds! I didn't even want to plumb the depths of my friends' minds.

"You never say anything bad, do you?" said Dee.

I replied, "Maybe that's because I don't see anything bad."

"That's right," said Chloe. "Because we're *happy*!"

We were happy, that term. We'd found our feet as Year 8s, and thought that we were pretty important; we'd got used to having Mrs Monahan as our class teacher, and had learnt all her little quirks and foibles. Like, for instance, the way she insisted that whenever she came into the room at the start of the day we all had to stand up and chant, "Good morning, Mrs Monahan!" Very weird, we thought; but a small price to pay for maintaining a good relationship.

Above all, of course, we had one another. Me and Chloe and Dee. We were so close, the three of us! Mel once sneeringly referred to us as "The Triplets". We didn't care. We were us, and she was no one. It is such a comfort, having friends! I was just so relieved that all the unpleasantness that had threatened us seemed to have blown over. More and more, it was like it had never been. I thought that we would be friends for ever.

And then it happened. The incident that shattered our lives: Gayle Gardiner went missing.

The news broke one Monday morning, the day we went back after half term. I first heard it on the radio (Mum won't let me watch breakfast TV. She's such a *puritan*.) As soon as they said the name Gayle Gardiner I just, like, froze.

"What's the matter?" said Mum.

I shrieked, "She's someone at school! She's in Year 12. Mum, put the telly on!"

I couldn't believe that it was *our* Gayle. But then Mum switched on to breakfast TV and I saw a picture of her, and all the familiar shivery darts of fear went zinging through my body as I heard them say how she had gone off clubbing on Saturday evening with a friend, Ruby Simpson (who is also at our school),

but they had somehow or other managed to have a terrific row on the bus on the way in to town, with the result that Ruby had turned round and gone back home, leaving Gayle to go on to the club by herself. The trouble was that nobody who was at the club that night could remember seeing her, so that it was now believed she had never reached it; in which case, something must have happened to her between Hindes Corner, where she would have got off the bus, and Valley Road, just five minutes away, where the club was.

Hindes Corner was the last stop before the bus station and people had come forward to say they remembered her getting off, but nobody had noticed where she had gone after that, whether she had taken the short cut to Valley Road up the side of Marks & Spencer and out through the multistorey (which I certainly wouldn't have done) or whether she had gone the long way round, via the High Street.

If she'd gone by the High Street, there must have been loads of people about, or so I would have thought. The multistorey would have been too scary for words, but I could see that if you'd just had a humongous row with your best friend and were still sizzling with fury, then the adrenalin would be pumping round your body at such a rate you might well go boldly marching into the bowels of darkness thinking you were immune. It's the sort of stupid, reckless thing I could have done myself, once upon a time. I wouldn't now, because I'd learnt my lesson; I'd been lucky. But I looked at the picture of Gayle on breakfast TV, happy and laughing and full of life, and I knew, with a sickening sensation of clamminess down in the pit of my stomach, that whatever had happened to her could all too easily have happened to me.

The police were appealing for witnesses to come forward. I thought that someone surely must remember seeing her. It wasn't like she was one of those frowsy, mouselike people. She was really striking, she had this startling red gold hair, all frizzed out like a halo, she'd been wearing (this is what they said on the TV) a bright orange-and-black checked coat with a tartan miniskirt and long red boots.

"She couldn't just disappear," I said. I could hear my voice, all plaintive and appealing. "Not in the middle of a town!"

"It's been thirty-six hours," said Mum.

"Yes, but they've only just announced it. Someone's bound to have seen her."

Mum shook her head. Not like she was contradicting me; more like... despairing.

"The first twenty-four hours are the crucial ones."

I wasn't brave enough to ask her why; in any case, I already knew the answer. If a person isn't found in the first twenty-four hours, it usually means it's too late. Unless, of course, she'd simply run away from home.

I suggested this to Mum, who agreed that it was a possibility.

"I mean, she's in Year 12," I said. "She could have gone off with a boyfriend."

Or she could have had a row with her parents. Mum agreed that that, too, was a possibility.

"But fancy letting a girl of that age go clubbing!"

"Mum, she's Year *12*," I said.

"Oh, I know, I know," said Mum. "You think I live in the dark ages, you think I'm just an old fusspot... but how do you imagine her mum and dad are feeling right now?"

Next day, we all knew how her mum and dad were feeling because they were on television, pleading for Gayle to come home. Or, if someone was holding her, to let her go and not hurt her. Both her mum and her dad were crying, and it made me cry, too. It brought it all back to me, how *my* mum might have cried and been on television, begging someone not to hurt me.

In the newspaper it said how the Gardiners were a "devoted family". Gayle and her mum and dad got on really well and never had rows, and Gayle had been looking forward to helping them celebrate their twenty-fifth wedding anniversary. They'd been going to have a big family gathering, but now it was probably going to be cancelled.

Our head teacher was interviewed and said how Gayle was a good student, popular with her classmates and not in any kind of trouble. Reporters had talked to Ruby, who'd told them how she and Gayle had had this massive row because Gayle thought Ruby had been going out behind her back with her boyfriend.

"But it wasn't true," sobbed Ruby.

The paper went and interviewed the boyfriend anyway and discovered that he'd actually been at another club on Saturday night, with a totally different girl, so that put paid to my romantic notion that maybe Gayle had eloped.

I still clung to the one shred of hope, which was something I'd once read somewhere, that by far the majority of young people who go missing have run off for reasons of their own. Like maybe they're deep into drugs and no one knows about it, or they've got a secret boyfriend, or they don't like their new stepdad, or – well, just anything, really. In other words, simply because someone has disappeared doesn't necessarily mean they've been abducted. This was what I kept telling myself, but I wasn't convinced. And all the feelings I had experienced after my close shave with Paul came flooding back.

Gayle's sister, Ellie, was in our class. She didn't come to school for the first couple of days, and then when she came back almost nobody was brave enough to talk to her. We didn't know what to say. We all felt really sorry for her and desperately wanted to show it, but we were scared in case we upset her and set her off crying. Her face was already white and pinched, and sodden with tears.

Her best friend, Tasha, kept giving us these reproachful glares, like she thought we were cold and heartless and didn't care; but the one time Chloe went bouncing up, full of good intentions, she snarled at her to "Just go away! Ellie doesn't want to be *bothered.*" It didn't exactly encourage the rest of us. Even Chloe, who as a rule is quite impervious to snubs, didn't go back for a second helping.

Every day we listened to the news, hoping that the police would have uncovered some clues, but nobody had come forward and they seemed as baffled as ever.

"Couldn't your mum help them?" said Dee. She said she'd once seen a film where a medium had been given something to hold that had belong to a girl who had disappeared, and the medium had "gone into a trance" and been able to tell the police that they would find the girl "buried in some woods by the side of a stream."

"And was she?" said Chloe.

Dee said she couldn't remember.

"Well, that was a lot of help," I said.

"Yes, but mediums *are* sometimes called in by the police," said Dee. "If we got something that belonged to Gayle and gave it to your mum—"

"Mum doesn't work that way," I said. "She has to have the person there, in front of her."

"*You* don't," said Chloe.

"Why don't we try it," urged Dee.

"Look, if Mum thought she could be of help, she'd go to the police herself," I said. "But she doesn't do that sort of thing."

"So what, exactly *does* she do?" said Chloe.

I explained that Mum tuned in to people's emotions. "Their hopes and fear. Dreams. Ambitions. Sort of... more psychological, I suppose."

I could tell from their silence that Dee and Chloe weren't too impressed.

"She really does help people get themselves sorted," I said. "She just doesn't do police-type stuff."

*

By Friday, it was almost a week since Gayle had disappeared. Still no one had come forward. The police had announced that they were going to stage a reconstruction on Saturday night, in the hope of jogging someone's memory. Dee and Chloe were coming to my place on Saturday for a sleepover. Last time we had gone to Chloe's, and next time would be at Dee's, which I was dreading as I didn't know how I would feel, sleeping under the same roof as her brother. I wasn't sure that I would be able to face it, and was already thinking up excuses why I couldn't go.

We sat upstairs in my bedroom that evening (Mum was in her consulting room with a client), wondering how the police reconstruction was going.

"There's got to be *someone* who remembers seeing her," I said. "I mean, how could you not notice someone like Gayle? She looks like a model!"

"Oh, do let's stop talking about it," begged Chloe. "It makes me feel all creepy. Let's play The Game!"

"We played it last time," I said.

"I know, but it'll take your mind off things." Chloe shot a glance at Dee. "What d'you reckon?"

"Yes, let's play it," said Dee. "It's better than just sitting here being morbid."

"But there's no point doing you two again," I said. "And I can't do anyone else 'cos you haven't brought anything."

"*I* have." Chloe plunged a hand into her bag and emerged triumphant with a gold locket on a chain. She dangled it before me. "See?"

"Who's it belong to?" I said.

"It's this girl my cousin knows. She's always asking me if you'll do her."

"We might as well," said Dee. "Otherwise we'll just spend all night glooming."

Between them, in the end, they talked me round. I was quite reluctant, and couldn't think why; but I took the locket and sat back on my heels on the bedroom floor while Dee and Chloe crouched on either side of me; Chloe cross-legged, Dee hugging her knees to her chest, waiting expectantly for me to perform.

I closed my eyes, letting the chain slip through my fingers. Concentrating. Focusing. Directing my energies. Something was there. Something...

Out of the ordinary. Something...

Powerful. Something—

And then it hit me. *Fear*. Wave upon wave of it. Cold, and gut-churning, drenching me in sweat; and somewhere a voice that screamed out in the darkness. *Help me! Help me!* But what could I do? Fear became panic. My mind thrashed in a frenzy, trying to find a way out, to break the connection.

"Jo? *Jo?*" Someone was shaking me. I dropped the chain and covered my face with my hands. I was trembling all over, and couldn't seem to stop.

"Jo!" Dee squatted in front of me, her face scrunched in concern. "What is it? What happened?"

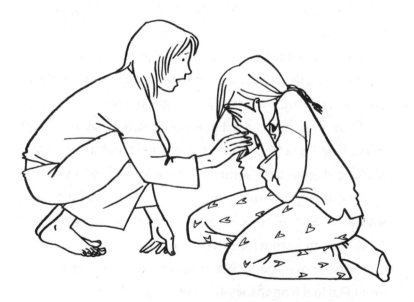

"I – don't know. Who is this person?" I turned angrily, on Chloe. "Where does she come from? What do you know about her?"

Chloe darted an anxious look at Dee.

"What's going on?" I cried. "What have you done?"

"It's my fault as much as Chloe's," said Dee.

"What is? What are you talking about? *Whose is it?*" I picked up the locket and hurled it as hard as I could across the room. *"Where did you get it from?"*

Then they told me. They confessed what they had done. They had gone to Ruby Simpson and asked her if she could lend them something that belonged to Gayle.

"We thought perhaps a... a book, or something. You know?"

A book might not have had so strong an impact; but Ruby had handed over the locket. It seemed she had borrowed it from Gayle the night they'd set out to go clubbing.

"What did you get from it?" whispered Dee.

I said, "Nothing. I don't know! I don't want to talk about it."

Chloe leaned in, closer. "Was it something scary?"

"*I don't want to talk about it!* You promised you'd never cheat me. You don't know what you're meddling with! I'm not ready for this sort of thing."

Dee looked downcast and said that she was sorry. Chloe muttered that they'd "just wanted to do something to help Gayle".

"Well, I can't help her!" I said. "What can I do? *I* don't know where she is!"

"But you think she's... in some sort of danger?" said Chloe.

That girl just never gives up.

"I think she's in trouble," I said. But everyone already knew that.

Dee picked up the locket and put it in her bag. "What shall we tell Ruby?"

"Just tell her I didn't see anything."

"But you did," said Chloe.

"I did not!" I snapped. "I *felt* things."

"So why don't we—"

"Oh, Chloe! Do shut up," said Dee. "Let's play some music and just forget about it."

We played some music, but I don't think any of us could forget. Certainly not me. I'd said that I hadn't seen anything, but it wasn't quite true. At the very moment that Dee had shaken me, and the link had been broken, I had had this sudden flash of being in someone else's body. Seeing through someone else's eyes. What I had seen was a car. I was in the car. And the car was familiar. I knew that I had been in it before – or one very like it. It was a Ka. A Ford Ka. A blue one...

What I couldn't work out, because I didn't have the experience, was whether I was really seeing through someone else's eyes – Gayle's eyes – or whether the waves of terror that had engulfed me had reactivated *my* terror and transported me back to that dreadful night, trapped in the car as we hammered towards the gravel pits.

There just seemed no way of knowing.

# seven

THAT NIGHT THE dreams came back. I kept waking, shivering and terrified; scared of going to sleep again. It was a comfort knowing that Dee and Chloe were there with me, curled up on the floor in their sleeping bags, yet at the same time I was just so angry with them for deceiving me. I knew they had acted from the best of motives, but they had no idea of the damage they could do, getting me to play around with forces that I hadn't yet learnt to control.

I guess part of the reason I was so angry was that I knew, deep down, it was more my fault than theirs. I should never have agreed to play The Game in the first place; Mum had warned me against it often enough. Dee and Chloe weren't to know. To them it was just a fun way of passing the time. On this occasion it had been more serious because they had genuinely wanted to help Gayle. But why put it all on to me? What was I supposed to do? I didn't know where she was!

Next morning I took Mum her breakfast in bed, so that the three of us could pig out by ourselves in the kitchen. We turned on the radio to hear if there was any news, but all they said was that the police had staged their reconstruction. They didn't mention if anyone had come forward.

"Maybe it's a bit too soon," I said.

"Or maybe they wouldn't announce it till they'd checked it out," suggested Dee.

We agreed that the police probably didn't pass on everything they knew.

"Stands to reason," said Chloe. "They'd have to keep something back... clues, and stuff."

Dee had to leave early as she was going off to visit her grandparents. Her mum and dad were supposed to stop by and pick her up on their way, but when I went to answer the door I found Paul standing there. My heart went clunking right down into the pit of my stomach. Why did it always have to be him? Why was *he* always the one who turned up? It was like he was doing it on purpose to taunt me.

"Hi," he said; and he smiled. "Is Dee ready?"

I said, "I'll get her!" and slammed the door in his face and went galloping back down the hall. "Dee! It's your brother!"

"Paul?" Her face lit up. "Oh, good! I didn't think he was coming."

She sounded really happy; she obviously adored him. It was just another reason why I couldn't say anything. I told myself that of course I *would*, if I were really sure. Even if it meant a furious lecture from Mum, I wouldn't hesitate. But how could I know, for certain? Dee was one of my two best friends! I would have hated to do anything to hurt her.

We watched as she drove off, sitting with Paul in the back of her parents' Volvo. I wondered if Paul still had his little blue Ka, or if he had got rid of it. "Disposing of the evidence," I thought.

"He's really nice, isn't he?" said Chloe, as we went back indoors. "Paul... he's so lovely!"

I muttered, "He's OK."

"Don't you like him?"

"He's creepy," I said.

"Mm..." Chloe crinkled her nose as she considered it. "I sort of see what you mean. He's kind of, like... *quiet*."

I said, "Creepy. Why does he keep smiling all the time?"

"Does he?"

"Yes." I stretched my lips. "He's always doing it."

Chloe said she hadn't noticed. "P'raps he's just being friendly."

"He doesn't have to keep doing it. It just looks stupid, keeping on doing it. And why's he still living at home? Why isn't he married?"

"Not everyone gets married," said Chloe. "He could be gay."

"More like *weird*."

"Dee practically worships him," said Chloe.

"Yes, and that's another thing." I closed the kitchen door, in case our voices carried up the stairwell (remembering Mum's phenomenal, lynxlike hearing).

"He wasn't there when we first knew Dee. She never even mentioned him. We never even knew she *had* a brother. He just suddenly, like, appeared one day out of nowhere."

"Actually..." Chloe hesitated.

"Actually what?" I said.

"Actually, I shouldn't be telling you this 'cos I'm not really supposed to know, but I heard he'd been in hospital."

"What, like you mean he's been ill?"

"Sort of," said Chloe.

"What d'you mean, *sort of*?"

"He's been in Arlington Park," said Chloe.

For the second time that morning my heart went into free fall. Arlington Park is a psychiatric hospital. People only go there if they're too sick to be let out into the community. I stared at Chloe. Her face had turned bright scarlet, so I guessed it was something she'd been sworn not to tell.

"Is that really true?" I said. Chloe nodded. "It's not just you, making it up?"

"I don't make things up!"

She does; all the time. But she said she'd actually been there when her mum was discussing it with a friend of hers who cleaned for Dee's mum. (Imagine having someone to do your cleaning for you! But Dee's mum is a solicitor, so I suppose she can afford it.)

"Mum didn't let me listen any more," said Chloe, "she sent me away, and afterwards she told me I wasn't to go gossiping about it to anyone. I'm only telling *you*," she said, "'cos we're friends."

I swallowed. "So... what was... wrong with him?"

"Dunno. Didn't get that far," said Chloe. "But you have to be pretty bad to be locked up!"

We agreed that you did; and that that was almost certainly why Dee had never mentioned to us that she had a brother.

"I mean, you wouldn't want to talk about it, would you?" said Chloe. "So we mustn't ever let on that we know."

"I wouldn't," I said. The last thing I wanted was to talk to Dee about her brother.

"He's obviously all right," said Chloe, "or they wouldn't have let him out. But it's probably why he sometimes seems a bit strange."

"Let's not discuss it," I said.

"No," said Chloe, "we probably shouldn't. Not behind Dee's back."

"Not any time," I said.

Later on, I listened to the news again, with Mum.

"Still nothing," I said.

Mum shook her head.

"You'd think *someone* would have seen her!"

325

"People don't always want to get involved," said Mum.

"You mean they wouldn't go to the police even if they had seen something? That is just so antisocial!" I said.

"I'm afraid people often are," said Mum.

"But why?"

"Oh, Jo! For all sorts of reasons."

I frowned, trying to think of some. "You mean, like... if someone mightn't want the police to know they were there? Like if they were committing a robbery, or something?"

"That could be one reason," agreed Mum.

"Even if someone's life was at stake?"

I just couldn't believe anybody would stay silent. Mum said, well, maybe they wouldn't.

"There's still time. Let's just hope someone's memory's been jogged."

"When would we know?" I said. "When would they tell us?"

"That's up to them," said Mum. And then she looked across at my plate and said, "What a mess you're making!"

We were sitting in the kitchen, having Sunday lunch, and I'd been slowly churning my cauliflower cheese into some kind of sculpture.

"Actually, I don't really want it," I said. "I'm not very hungry."

"Try," urged Mum. "I'm aware it's easier said than done, but honestly, sweetheart, worrying isn't going to help."

"No, I know." I heaved a sigh, and did a bit more sculpting. "You know those Ka things?" I said.

"What car things?" said Mum.

"*Ka.* K-A. Ka."

"Oh, those! Yes. What about them? Did you fancy one?"

"No," I said. "I think they're horrible."

"Cheap to run."

"Yes, but they're horrible."

"So why did you mention them?"

"I was just wondering whether... they were popular."

"I should think so. You see quite a lot of them about."

"Do you?" I said.

"Well, I do," said Mum. "Why, anyway?"

"Oh, it's a – a project we're doing," I said. "Environmental studies."

"Yes, well, I should think they're probably a good thing," said Mum.

Depends who's driving them, I thought; and I forced down the mashed remains of my cauli cheese.

"I might like to do environmental work some day," I said.

"Well, that would be a good thing, too," said Mum. "Certainly an easier way of earning a living than delving into the depths of other people's minds,"

"Do you ever have bad experiences?" I said. "Do you ever... see things that are... frightening?"

"Occasionally."

"*Really* frightening?"

"Like what?" said Mum.

"Well, like... like if someone had done something evil, like... murdered someone, or something."

"No," said Mum. "I've never had that."

"What would you do? If you thought someone had murdered someone?"

"Oh, Jo, what a question! It's never arisen, so I've never really given much thought to it. In any case, how would I know whether it was real, or just a fantasy?"

"Couldn't you tell?" I said.

"Not necessarily. People have the oddest things going on inside their heads. I think probably, unless the circumstances were quite exceptional, I would just have to... take no account of it."

I was so relieved when Mum said that. How would you know whether it was real or a fantasy? Not even Mum could be certain!

"What is all this, anyway?" she said. "Another project?"

"It's for a story," I said.

"A horror story?"

"Well – yes." I gave a little giggle, which even to my ears sounded somewhat hysterical.

"Wouldn't it be better just to write something about everyday life?" said Mum.

I thought, this *is* about everyday life; but to keep Mum happy, and set her mind at rest, I said that she was probably right.

"I'll try and think of something else."

But I couldn't. I was obsessed by thoughts of Gayle. Where she might be, what might be happening to her. All the stories I'd ever read about young girls being abducted came crowding and jostling into my mind. Had any of them ever had a happy ending? *Ever?* Had anyone ever been found alive?

It was like a nightmare, ongoing, without end. And I kept thinking, if it was like a nightmare for me, what must it be like for Gayle's mum and dad, and Ellie?

Monday morning, we heard on the news that two women had come forward as a result of the reconstruction. They said that they had seen Gayle talking to a man in a car, on the ground floor level of the car park.

They didn't know whether she had just got out of the car, or whether she was just about to get into the car, or whether she was just having a chat before going on her way. They were only passing through, and hadn't waited to find out.

"Why didn't they come forward earlier?" I cried. "If they're so sure it was Gayle?"

Mum said the whole point of a reconstruction was that it would jolt people into remembering things they might otherwise have forgotten, or not even realised they had seen.

"Doesn't seem to have jolted very many of them," I said, glumly.

At school, everybody was talking about "the latest development" (as they said on the news); but quietly, almost furtively, in corners or behind desk lids.

"Don't really see that it's going to be much help," I said, as I walked round the field with Dee and Chloe at first break. "I mean, they don't know whether she actually got *into* the car... they don't even know what sort of car it *was*."

"It says in the paper," said Chloe. "Least, it did in my mum's."

Chloe's mum read the *Daily Mail*, so later on, when I had a free period and was meant to be doing homework, I went to the library and had a look. It didn't actually say very much more. Neither of the women could remember anything about the car except that it been blue, and "small". Like a Mini, or a Micra, or a Ford Fiesta.

Or a Ka.

# eight

I PROBABLY SHOULDN'T have blurted everything out to
Chloe. Chloe, of all people! I knew how scatty she was.
Chloe has loads of good points – she is bright, she is
bubbly, she is a whole lot of fun. But she is such a
*blabbermouth*. Just because you are best friends with
someone doesn't mean that you are blind to their faults;
experience should have told me that confiding in Chloe
was not the wisest thing I had ever done. But I was in a
panic! I had found it difficult to believe when Mum had

told me how people "don't always want to get involved", how they wouldn't necessarily go to the police even if they had seen something. How could they *not*? How could they possibly stay silent when a girl's life was at stake? Now here I was, doing that very thing. Going to school, chatting to friends, moaning about double maths, grumbling about too much homework, when all the time I had information that could be important. I knew that I had to tell someone. So I told Chloe.

We were sitting on the terrace together at lunch time, in the usual howling gale which blows across from the playing field. Dee wasn't with us, she was at a meeting. Dee was always going off to meetings; she is a very public-spirited kind of person. If she had been there, I don't know what I would have done. Waited till I got home, perhaps. I would certainly never have said anything in front of Dee. But Chloe was giggling at the way I'd behaved in maths when Mr McFarlane, in his sarcastic way, had asked me if I intended "touching down on this planet any time soon" and I had stared at him, goggle-eyed, and said, "In a right-angled triangle?" which is somewhat, if not indeed totally, meaningless, but was all I could dredge up on the spur of the moment.

"I didn't hear him," I said to Chloe. "I didn't hear what he said!"

"In a right-angled triangle! It wasn't even geometry," gurgled Chloe.

Ha ha, hugely ha. I could see that it was probably quite amusing to small minds, and I would probably have laughed like a drain myself if it had happened to anyone else, but I thought it was quite uncalled for to suggest, as Mr McFarlane witheringly did, that my mind was "cluttered up with cheesy images of the opposite sex". He had some nerve! What did he know about my mind?

Needless to say, Mel Sanders had slewed round in her desk to look at me and contorted her features into prunelike disapproval.

"Naughty naughty!"

I'd felt like slapping her. I'd also felt like jumping up and rushing out of the room. My mind was in a torment – and *not* with cheesy thoughts of the opposite sex. Mr McFarlane and his stupid irritating maths was way down the scale of anything which might merit attention.

"I suppose you were thinking about *him*?" said Chloe. "Dreamboat Danny! *Swoon*."

"Actually," I said, "I was thinking about Gayle."

"Oh. Well! Yes." Chloe pulled a face. "I keep thinking about her, too. It must be so awful for poor Ellie!"

"And her mum and dad. Not *knowing*. That must be the most terrible part!"

Chloe agreed that it must. But surely, she said, Gayle wouldn't have gone off with a total stranger? I said that she might, if she'd just had a row with Ruby.

"You really think so?" said Chloe.

"I don't know! I don't know! But things happen – people do these things! You know what those women said about the car? A small blue car? You know they said they didn't know what make it was but it could have been a Ka – K-A, Ka! You know! Those little ones?"

"Y-yes." Chloe was eyeing me, uncertainly. I suppose I did sound slightly mad. It just suddenly all came spurting out of me.

"Well..." I took a breath. "I got into one of those."

"You mean, like... with a stranger?"

"Someone I didn't properly know."

Chloe chewed at her lower lip. She obviously sensed that this was something serious because for once she managed not to say anything; just waited, in silence, for me to continue.

"It was Paul."

"*Dee's* Paul?"

I nodded. "That night at the Pizza Palace... he gave me a lift."

"I remember! Dee was cross 'cos you'd jumped out of the car. You said – *oh*." Chloe clapped a hand to her mouth. "He didn't—"

"No. But he drove me the wrong way, he took me down Gravelpit Hill, it was really, really scary. And now there's all this about Gayle, and a blue car, and... you know on Saturday, we played The Game?"

"Yes," said Chloe, "and you went all peculiar."

337

"I didn't go peculiar, I saw something... I was in a car. It was a car I'd been in before. Or a car *like* one I'd been in before. Only I couldn't work out whether it was me, or whether it was Gayle, so that's why I didn't say anything, 'cos you can't always tell the difference. But now there's these women, and a blue car, and *I don't know what to do*!"

My voice came out in a self-pitying wail. Some Year 9 girls gave me these weird looks as they walked past.

"What do I do?" I said. "I don't know what to do!"

"There's only one thing you can do," said Chloe. "Go to the police. Jo, you've got to!"

"But suppose it wasn't really Gayle? Suppose it was just *me*?"

"It's the same car," said Chloe.

"It *might* be the same car."

"It's the same colour. And he did try to abduct you! I don't know why you didn't say something before!"

"I didn't want Mum knowing about it. And I didn't want to upset Dee. I still don't want to!"

"But if he's done something to Gayle, and he did something to you, he could do something to Dee, as well. She could be in danger!"

"Except he didn't actually *do* anything to me."

"No, 'cos you managed to escape! Think how you'd

feel," said Chloe, "if something happened to Dee and you could have stopped it."

She didn't say, think how you'll feel if something's happened to Gayle, but she didn't have to, because I was already feeling it. I knew that I should have gone to the police ages ago, or at least told Mum.

"Jo, you've got to report it," said Chloe. "I think you should go and see Miss Adams."

"She'll be so angry," I quavered.

Miss Adams is our head teacher, and is quite frightening at the best of times. But I couldn't really argue; Chloe was only telling me what I already knew.

"I'll come with you," she said. "I'll give you moral support."

She marched me back into school and along to the office, where she announced in ringing tones for everyone within a five mile radius to hear, that "Jo has to see Miss Adams. It's urgent!" Mrs Biswas, the school secretary, raised an eyebrow. She is probably not used to Year 8 pupils demanding to see the Head. It's usually the other way round, the Head demanding to see you. I was trembling now. I was probably looking like

I was in a bit of a state, because Mrs Biswas asked me quite gently, and not in her normal dragon tones, what the problem was. Chloe, all self-important, said, "She's got something to tell her. About Gayle."

Well, that was it; Mrs Biswas immediately went into action. Within seconds – it seemed like only seconds – I was in Miss Adams's room pouring out my story (Chloe having been sent packing, much to her indignation). Miss Adams listened to me in

grave silence, and at the end she said, "Is your mother at home?" Oh, God, she was going to ring Mum! But Mum would have had to hear sooner or later, so it was probably just as well.

While we were waiting for Mum to arrive, Miss Adams asked me lots of questions, which I did my best to answer truthfully and in as much detail as possible; then when Mum appeared, looking worried and flustered, and obviously wondering what kind of ghastly trouble I had got myself into, we had to go through it all again for her benefit, only this time, thank goodness, Miss Adams did most of the talking. Every now and again she would say, "Is that right, Joanne? Is that what happened?" and I would mutter "Yes" and do my best not to catch Mum's eye.

Neither of them lectured me, or told me how criminally stupid I'd been. The lectures came later. And how! But that day, in Miss Adams's study, they were mainly concerned about Gayle. Miss Adams rang the police, and two CID people came round, like, at the double. So then it all had to be told for the third time, and the more I heard it the more guilty I felt at having kept quiet for so long.

Nobody actually blamed me for not saying anything, though one of the CID officers, the female one, did ask me why I hadn't. I went scarlet and mumbled that I hadn't wanted to upset Dee. Mum looked at me rather hard, as if she knew that that was only part of the reason. Her look seemed to say, "I'll speak to you later, my girl." (Which she did, but I think I will draw a veil over that.)

After I had been thoroughly grilled – I believe that is the correct word for when someone is being questioned by the police – Mum and I had to go down to the police station. In a police car! (They brought us back later to pick up our own car.)

I felt very self-conscious, walking out of school with two CID people. Even though they were in plain clothes I felt that everyone who saw them would guess they were police, and would wonder what I had done. As it happened, it was the middle of the first period after lunch, so lessons were in progress and I don't think anybody did see me, but I still didn't like it. I felt like I had committed some crime and was under arrest. Mum was grim the whole time, and I knew she was saving up things to say to me.

Once at the police station I was taken to an interview room, where I had to give a statement. It should have been easy, because by now I had told the story at least three times, but I kept worrying that I wasn't remembering properly, or wasn't saying it right. Like when the police wanted to know – *again*, 'cos they had already asked me once – whether Paul had done anything to me, and I said he hadn't; but then I suddenly remembered how he had leaned across me to get to the glove compartment and how there had been a screwdriver in there, and I had screamed and jerked away, and he had almost lost control of the wheel. That was something I hadn't said first time round, because it didn't really count as "doing anything", and it had

somehow just slipped my memory. But as soon as I said it, they pounced, and wanted to know more, like did I think he was actually reaching for the screwdriver; to which I had to say that I didn't know. All I knew was that he had driven me down Gravelpit Hill and I had been terrified.

There was one thing I didn't tell the police and hadn't told Miss Adams, either. I didn't say anything about my session with Dee and Chloe, when they had given me Gayle's chain to hold. I didn't think that they would understand; and, besides, it didn't really seem relevant. But I did tell Mum about it, when we finally arrived back home. I'm not sure what prompted me, except perhaps that I needed to get it off my chest. And oh, it was such a relief! I realised that I had felt really guilty about it.

I thought Mum would be angry, but she said that what concerned her far more was that I had accepted a lift from a virtual stranger, rather than that I had "misused my gift".

"I know the temptation. Believe me, I do!"

"Did *you* ever misuse your gift?" I said.

Mum said she was ashamed to admit that she did. Mum had grown up in ignorance of the fact that she had psychic powers. Her gran – my great gran, that I never knew – had been reputed to "see things", and her mum – my gran – had once predicted that her next door neighbour would find her missing wedding ring "down the side of the sofa", and she had.

"But everyone just put that down to a lucky guess."

Nobody ever warned Mum about misusing her gift, because nobody ever realised that she had it. Mum herself only knew that sometimes, when she was with someone, she would get these "feelings". One day at school she borrowed a pen from her best friend, Liz, and she got really strong feelings.

345

"Of excitement," said Mum. "So I asked Liz and she said it was true, she *was* excited. She was going up to London, to the ballet. So then I started doing it deliberately... borrowing things from people. Pens, rubbers, rulers, seeing what feelings they gave me. It was just a game – except in the end it wasn't, as you've discovered."

I asked Mum what had happened, and she said that even after all these years she didn't really like to talk about it.

"Which is why I've never told you before. It still makes me feel bad. I borrowed something from a girl called Janice Baker. She was one of those girls... we all used to gang up on her. I suppose today you'd call her a nerd, or a wimp. We just thought she was wet. Anyway, I had these really dark feelings come over me, like someone was walking across my grave. A few days later we learnt that she'd been taken to hospital... she'd been in a car crash."

"Did she die?" I said.

"Yes." Mum nodded. "I know it wasn't anything I did, and there was probably nothing I could have done to stop it, but after that I didn't play the game any more."

"I'm not going to play it, either!" I said.

"Well, I'm glad about that," said Mum. "But, Jo, I'm really horrified that at your age, after all the times we've talked about it, you could be so foolish as to get into a car with someone you don't know. How could you do such a thing? What were you thinking of? No! Don't tell me." She held up a hand. "I remember... what was it? Glitter boots! All for a pair of tacky fashion items that wouldn't last five minutes, you go and put your life in jeopardy! I'm at a loss. It hardly bears thinking about!"

She went on this vein for quite some time. This is the part I'm drawing a veil over, as it was rather uncomfortable. I didn't try defending myself because I knew that I couldn't.

"All I can say," said Mum, "is that I hope to goodness you've learnt your lesson."

I said, "Mum, I have!"

"Even I," said Mum, "have never done anything quite as stupid as that. And heaven knows," she said, "I've done some stupid things in my time!"

"It's just that he was Dee's brother," I pleaded.

"I hear you," said Mum. "But has it never occurred to you that people are always someone's brother? Someone's father? Someone's husband?"

I hung my head.

"Anyway," she said, "you did the right thing in the end. It's a pity you didn't do it sooner, but—"

"Dee's going to hate me!" I said.

"It won't be easy," agreed Mum, "for either of you. But she's a sensible girl, I'm sure she'll understand. She couldn't expect you to keep quiet indefinitely. You had to speak out, Jo. I know Dee's your friend, but if there's any danger at all of him doing to other girls what he might have done to you... even Dee herself could be at risk."

"I know." I heaved a sigh. "That's what Chloe said."

"Well, Chloe talked sense for once."

"But suppose Paul isn't anything to do with it?" I said.

"In that case, there's no harm done. At least the police will be able to eliminate him from their enquiries. Even so," said Mum, "we still have to ask ourselves why he was taking you down Gravelpit Hill."

"He said he liked it better than the other way."

"Even though the other way is half again as short?"

"Yes, and why did he have a screwdriver?" I said.

Mum said she wasn't so bothered about that. "People might have a screwdriver for all sorts of legitimate reasons. But to take you off in the wrong direction... that needs some explaining."

A few minutes after I'd had this conversation with Mum, the phone rang. It was Dee.

"Where were you?" she demanded. "What happened?"

I said, "I—"

"What?"

"I had to—"

"*What?*"

"Had to—"

"Chloe said something about you going to see Miss Adams."

"Yes," I said. "I had to go and see Miss Adams."

"About Gayle?"

"Yes. I had to – had to – tell her something."

"What?"

"I c-can't s-say, it's..."

"Does Chloe know?"

"Ch-Chloe?" I said.

"She's got that look. You know that look she gets? When she's hiding something?"

I swallowed.

"If you could tell her, I should have thought you could've told me," said Dee.

She was obviously feeling hurt. I could understand it; I would have felt hurt in her place. How could I tell Chloe something and not tell Dee? I muttered that I had told Chloe before I had been warned by Miss Adams "not to go talking about it".

"You weren't there," I said. "You'd gone off somewhere."

"I was at a meeting," said Dee.

"Yes. Well... this is what I'm saying. You weren't there! If you had have b—"

"Hang on," said Dee. "Something's happening. I'll ring you back."

As I put the phone down, I found my hand was shaking. What did she mean, something was happening? Was it the police? Had they gone round there? I had these visions of Paul, being dragged from the house in

handcuffs. Except that surely they wouldn't do that until they knew for certain? Surely they would just ask him – politely – to accompany them to the police station for questioning. That was what they did. They didn't go round arresting people before they had proof. Did they?

Before I could consult Mum, the phone had rung again. This time it was Chloe, in a state of barely suppressed excitement.

"Hi! What happened? Did you go to the police?"

I said, "I don't want to talk about it. Dee's just rung me. It was awful!"

I heard a little gasp from Chloe's end. "Does she know? Have they taken him away?"

I said, "*I don't know.* We shouldn't be talking about it!"

"I didn't tell her anything," said Chloe, virtuously.

"You told her I'd gone to Miss Adams about Gayle!"

"Oh. Yes – well. I had to tell her *something.*"

I didn't see why she had to, but I wasn't about to get into an argument.

"Look, I have to go," I said. "Tea's ready, and I'm expecting Dee to ring back."

"OK." Chloe said it quite amiably. She's always very good-natured, which is just as well since she spends a large part of her life putting her foot in things, upsetting people and being yelled at. *Chloe, for goodness' sake! Chloe, you IDIOT! Chloe, how COULD you?* She never takes offence.

"See you tomorrow," she said.

"Yeah," I said. "See you."

I spent the rest of the evening waiting in a kind of dread for Dee to ring back, but she never did; and on the news next morning they announced that there had been "fresh developments in the case of missing teenager Gayle Gardiner".

A local man was helping police with their inquiries.

# nine

IT HAD NEVER occurred to me to swear Chloe to secrecy;
I mean, I just never thought. I knew she was a
blabbermouth, I knew the only way you could rely on her
to keep a secret was if you sealed her lips with sticky tape
and tied her hands behind her back. But this was more
than just a secret. It was more than just our usual girly
chitchat about who was going out with whom and who
had stolen someone else's boy friend. It was something I
had told her in strictest confidence. I never for one

moment imagined she would go and blurt it out – and especially not to Gayle's sister.

I could sense the minute I walked into the classroom that the atmosphere was tense. Ellie was huddled in a corner with two of her friends; she was crying, and they both had their arms round her. Other people were standing around in little groups, looking shocked and not talking. I saw Dee, sitting at her desk, with her head bent over a book; and Chloe, hovering on the fringe of Ellie and her friends.

I was about to go over to Dee when Mr McFarlane breezed in, brisk and ill-tempered as usual, to start on the first lesson of the day. Maths, heaven help us! Dee, being some kind of genius, was in the A group for maths, which meant she took herself off to a different classroom and thus I didn't get a chance to speak to her; for which, to be honest, I was profoundly grateful. I just didn't know what I would find to say. Or if she would even let me.

After maths we had French. Dee and I were in the same group for French and normally sat next to each other, but that morning Dee deliberately chose a desk as far away from me as it was possible to get. As far away from everyone else, as well. I could understand why *I* was being shunned – if I had had a brother and my best friend had shopped him to the police, I probably wouldn't want to talk to them, either; but what had the others done to upset her?

Shayna Phillips, who was sitting near me, leant across to whisper.

"It must be so awful for her!"

I said, "W-what must?"

355

"Well – you know! Her brother."

I obviously looked confused. Which I was.

"Being arrested," mouthed Shayna.

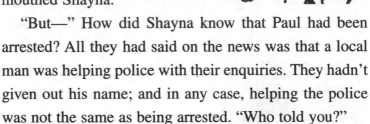

"But—" How did Shayna know that Paul had been arrested? All they had said on the news was that a local man was helping police with their enquiries. They hadn't given out his name; and in any case, helping the police was not the same as being arrested. "Who told you?"

Mrs Armstrong came in at that point. Shayna had just the time to whisper the one word, "Chloe."

"*Chloe?*" I couldn't believe it. I just couldn't believe that even Chloe could be that... untrustworthy. That *disloyal*. How could she do such a thing?

"She told Ellie."

I opened my mouth to say, "*Ellie?*" but Mrs Armstrong got in ahead of me.

"Joanne, I cannot believe that my somewhat ample presence has escaped your attention?"

Mrs Armstrong is rather plump, hence her reference to ample presence, which would normally have made everyone laugh. Today people just gave nervous smiles. I gazed across at Dee, willing her to look in my direction, but she kept her head down the whole lesson. I felt so bad! She must have thought that Chloe and I had ganged up on her, gone behind her back – which of course, in a way, we had. I wished with all my heart that I had never confided in Chloe. Dee would probably still have hated me, for going to the police, but at least no one else would have known about it. Now, thanks to Chloe – thanks to me – it seemed that the entire school knew. Certainly everybody in our class.

"But I only told Ellie!" wailed Chloe, when we met up at break.

"You shouldn't have told *anyone*," I said.

"You didn't say not to!"

"I shouldn't have had to say not to. You should have known! How do you think Dee feels, everyone going round talking about her?"

"They're not talking about her, they're talking about her brother!"

"Oh, for goodness' *sake*." I think I actually stamped my foot. I was just so angry with her!

"Look, I'm sorry," said Chloe. "I'm sorry, I'm sorry! I can't say more than that, can I?"

"I don't know why you ever said anything to begin with!"

"I didn't mean to, it just kind of... slipped out. I was talking to Ellie."

"*So?*"

"So – I don't know! It just happened. So what? It's no big deal. It'll be in all the newspapers soon, anyway."

"Only if they actually arrest him, which they haven't done yet. Not as far as I know. Why did you have to go and say they'd *arrested* him?"

"'Cos I thought they had." Chloe said it sullenly. "I thought it was the same thing."

"Well, it's not! They're just talking to him. He's *helping* them. He could be innocent!"

"You said—"

"I said I'd got into his car and he'd driven me the wrong way."

"Well, there you are! Even if he didn't take Gayle, he tried to take you, so he's *not* innocent. What I don't understand," said Chloe, suddenly jumping on some grievance of her own, "is why you couldn't tell? When

358

he offered you a lift... you're supposed to be psychic! Why couldn't you *tell*?"

I snapped, "It doesn't work that way!"

"Seems to me it doesn't work any way," muttered Chloe. "First you say you've seen him in a car with Gayle, then you say you're not sure, then—"

"Oh, shut up," I said, "and don't be stupid!"

Not very clever, I admit; but there were times when Chloe just got me *so livid*.

We didn't see Dee all during break, and she kept well away from us – and from everyone else – at lunch time, too. It wasn't till school let out at 3.30 that we came face to face. We arrived at the gates at the same moment, and couldn't really avoid each other. Before I could say anything, Dee had put her face up close to mine and hissed, "I'll never forgive you, Joanne Daley! Never, never, never, as long as I live!"

When I got home, I burst into tears. I hardly ever cry, I am just not a crying sort of person; but Dee was my best friend! My *very* best friend.

"She hates me!" I wept. "She's never going to forgive me!"

"Oh, Jo, I'm sure she will, in time," said Mum. "Don't forget, this must have come as a terrible shock to her."

"It's Chloe's fault," I said. "Going and telling everyone!"

"That certainly can't have helped," agreed Mum.

"But I was the one who went to the police! I'm the one she hates! I don't know how she found out it was me," I wailed. "Why did they have to tell her?"

Mum said they might have asked her questions, trying to see if I had ever mentioned anything to her.

"I wish I'd never mentioned it to anyone," I sobbed. "I wish I'd never gone to the police in the first place!"

"Jo, you had to," said Mum. "You know you had to. You did the right thing."

I may have done the right thing – but I had lost my best friend. I also had this feeling that Chloe and I wouldn't ever get back to being close again. We'd sort of made up after our breaktime spat, but without Dee to complete the threesome, things just weren't the same. We needed Dee to give us substance. Without her, our relationship was so flimsy I felt that sooner or later we were just going to float apart.

Chloe rang me that evening. Aggressively she said, "Look, I'm *sorry*. OK?"

"No," I shouted, "it's not OK! Think how Dee must be feeling."

"Pity you  didn't think of that before you went to the police," said Chloe.

We rang off in a huff, but then I thought about it, and I thought perhaps I'd been ungracious, because after all Chloe had said she was sorry, so after a bit I rang her back and said that *I* was sorry.

"I shouldn't have snapped at you."

"It's all right, it doesn't matter now," said Chloe. "They've found her! Gayle. She's alive! It's on the news, go and see."

I rushed off immediately to put the television on. I was just in time to hear that "The missing teenager, Gayle Gardiner, has been found by a man out walking his dog in Tanfield Woods, only a few miles away from where she was last seen before she disappeared, over a week ago."

At first when I heard it, my blood ran cold and I thought Chloe had got it wrong, because almost always when they say "found by someone walking their dog" they mean that a body has been found. Also, it has to be said, Chloe is not the most reliable informant. She once told me that I had got "eighty-six per cent" for a maths exam. Un-be-lieve-able! But she swore that she had seen it.

"With my own eyes! It was there... Joanne Daley, eighty-six per cent."

Well, it turned out to be *twenty*-six, and ever since then I have always taken whatever she says with a large pinch of salt. So when I heard the words "a man walking his dog" my heart just went *thunk*, and for the first time in my life I thought I might actually be going to faint. I had to sink into a chair to stop myself from falling. I almost missed the bit that came next. Mum wasn't there (she was in her room, doing a consultation), so I snatched up the phone and rang Chloe back and shrieked, "What did they say, what did they say? Did they say she's all right?"

"Yes, she's in hospital. They think she was being held prisoner and managed to escape."

"Did anything, like – uh! You know. Happen to her?"

"Dunno," said Chloe. "They didn't say. They just said she'd been found."

"So they didn't say who'd taken her?"

"No, but if it's him," said Chloe, "she'll be able to tell them."

One part of me almost wanted it to be Paul, because then I could stop feeling guilty. If he'd really been holding Gayle against her will, not even Dee could blame me for going to the police. But there was another part of me which desperately *didn't* want it to be him, because I thought that it would break Dee's heart, and she was still my best friend even if she had stopped talking to me.

Next morning, I watched the news with Mum. By this time they had a few more details, which I think Mum would rather I hadn't heard, and perhaps I would rather not have heard, too, but you can't hide your head in the sand. These things happen, and it is no use going through life thinking that everything is wonderful, because lots of things just aren't. Lots of things are horrible and frightening and make you feel sick.

"I just thank heaven she managed to get away," said Mum. "Goodness only knows what the poor girl went through, but at any rate they'll be able to do DNA testing, and that will put paid to all the uncertainty."

She meant about Paul, of course. There was still this big question mark hanging over him.

"Don't worry," said Mum. "I'm sure it will be resolved very quickly."

In spite of not being at all convinced that I really wanted to know, I couldn't stop myself buying a newspaper on the way in to school and reading about what had happened to Gayle. How she had got into a car in the car park with someone she just knew vaguely, by sight. She had "seen him around" a few times, at clubs and discos; he was "sort of" familiar. Most probably (this was what I thought when I read it) she had been in a state after her big row with Ruby, because having a row with your best friend *does* get you into a state, and she just hadn't been thinking clearly.

There were some people who might say she had been stupid and old enough to know better, but I knew how easy it was, even when you have been warned over and over by your mum, by your teachers, by just about everybody.

All the time that I was reading about Gayle, I kept thinking how it could have been me. It could have been me who was abducted. It could have been me who was kept prisoner. It could have been me who was assaulted. I had been lucky: Gayle hadn't. Chloe seemed to think that she had. She pointed out that she had *got away*; but I remembered all the nightmares I had had after just nearly being abducted – or thinking that I was being abducted, because by now, after all this while, I felt that I could no longer be sure. Had Paul really been going to take me to the gravel pits? Or had I just imagined it? Chloe, when I told her my doubts, scoffed at the idea.

"Why did he take you down that road if he wasn't going to the gravel pits?"

"He might just have been going the long way round," I said.

"But *why*?" said Chloe. "What would be the point?"

I didn't have any answer to that. I just knew that the panic had stayed with me for weeks, and I couldn't help wondering how Gayle was going to cope.

Dee wasn't in school that morning, and neither was Ellie. Even if Dee had been, I probably wouldn't have found the courage to go and talk to her, however much I felt the need to unburden myself. To explain why I had done what I had done: to try and make her understand. In lots of ways, I am the most terrible coward. It would have shrivelled me completely if Dee had refused to listen; or worse yet, had told me that she hated me.

That evening, we heard that a twenty-three-year-old man was in police custody, charged with "the kidnapping of schoolgirl Gayle Gardiner".

It wasn't Paul.

# ten

"THANK GOODNESS FOR that!" said Mum, when she heard the news. "Those poor parents! What they must have been through. Not to mention Gayle."

She said that she was immensely relieved that Dee's brother had been cleared – "but it does leave questions unanswered. We still don't know, for instance, why he took you all the way down Gravelpit Hill."

Of course this was true, but I almost didn't care any more; it seemed so long ago. So much had happened since then. Now I just wanted to make things right again with Dee.

She was back in school next day, and so was Ellie. Ellie was subdued, and we were all shy of asking her how Gayle was, but we smiled at her and she managed to smile back, even if it was a bit tremulous. Dee walked round looking stiff and defiant, with her head held high. She still wasn't speaking to us.

"I don't know what she's got against *me*," said Chloe, sounding indignant. "I wasn't the one that went to the police!"

I said, "No, but you were the one that blabbed to Ellie."

"I didn't *blab*."

"You told her about Paul!"

"I didn't tell her, it just slipped out. And anyway, how was I to know?"

I felt like slapping her. We'd already been through all this! "Know *what*, for goodness' sake?"

"Know anything! I'm not a mind reader! If you don't want people to say things then you have to *tell* them, not just leave them to work it out and then start snapping at them when they go and do it. Not being *mind readers*," said Chloe.

"Now you're blathering," I said. "You're obviously feeling guilty, so you're *blathering*."

"I don't feel guilty! Why should I feel guilty?"

"*For telling people!*" I yelled.

"I didn't tell people. I told *Ellie*. She was the one that told people!"

"That's right," I said, "blame someone else!"

"Well, it's no use blaming me," said Chloe. "If you hadn't gone to the police—"

"Pardon me," I said. "You were the one that told me to!"

"Only because you said he'd tried to abduct you. Then you went and changed your mind and said it was a mistake."

"I never said it was a mistake! I said I couldn't be *certain*."

"Well, ho!" said Chloe. "Fancy getting someone arrested when you can't even be certain! How'd you like to be arrested when someone couldn't even be certain?"

Through gritted teeth I said, "He was not *arrested*. I told you this before! He was helping police with their enquiries."

"Same thing," muttered Chloe.

How many more times???

"It is *not*! If you'd just kept your mouth shut for once, none of this would ever have happened."

"I've got as much right to talk as anyone else," said Chloe. "And even if I hadn't said anything to Ellie, Dee still wouldn't be speaking to you 'cos you were the one who shopped her brother!"

This, unfortunately, was quite true. I fell silent, not knowing how to respond. I still had this feeling that I had been right and Chloe had been wrong, but you couldn't ever discuss things sensibly with her. She was, I decided, very immature; one of those people who couldn't take criticism. But I didn't want to quarrel with her! I was still trying to think of some way to put an end to it – without actually saying yet again that I was sorry, since I didn't see why I should have to – when Chloe did it for me.

"Oh, don't let's fight," she begged. "It's so horrid! I'm sorry if I told Ellie when you didn't want me to, but I didn't *realise*. I wouldn't have done it if you'd said not to. Read my lips... I – AM – SOR – REE. *Sorreeeee*. Look, look!" She suddenly fell to her knees and clutched me round the legs. "I'm grovelling! Hard as I can... grovel, grovel!"

One of the best things about Chloe is that she never bears grudges – and she makes me laugh. So of course I had to say that I was sorry, too.

"I didn't mean to yell at you."

After that, it was easy enough to hug each other and make up; but it didn't solve the problem of what to do about Dee. Come Monday morning, she still wasn't talking. Chloe, who in lots of ways is braver than I am (although sometimes she is just foolhardy) actually tried speaking to her. She said, "Dee! Hi. Come and sit with us." Dee resolutely took no notice; simply sailed straight on across the room like we didn't even exist.

"Well, all right," said Chloe, at breaktime, "if she doesn't want to be friends any more we'll just be friends with each other. We don't need her."

But I knew that we did; and you can't let friendships just fizzle away to nothing without doing something to try and save them.

"We'll have to apologise," I said.

"To Dee?"

"Yes," I said, "to Dee."

"What for? We have *we* done?"

Oh, Chloe, I thought, don't start that again!

"P'raps *I* might apologise," said Chloe, thoughtfully,

"but I don't see why you should." Well! Chloe is capable, at times, of really taking you by surprise. "You *had* to go to the police," she said. "There wasn't anything else you could have done."

"No, but I didn't have to discuss it behind her back. It was my fault," I said. "If I hadn't talked to you, you couldn't have talked to Ellie, and nobody would ever have known."

"So when shall we do it?" said Chloe. "When shall we go and grovel?"

We decided that we would grab hold of Dee at lunch time and insist that she listened to us.

"We can't go on like this," I said.

I said it to Dee, as well, when she tried to break away from us. "We've got to have things out!"

"I have nothing to say to you," hissed Dee. "I don't ever want to speak to you again. Either of you!"

"Oh, stop being so *childish*," said Chloe.

Well! I think that really took the wind out of Dee's sails. Chloe, of all people... telling her not to be childish! At any rate, she stopped fighting us and let us walk her round the playing field until we came to a secluded spot.

"OK," said Chloe. "Now we're going to grovel. I'm going to grovel for talking to Ellie when I shouldn't have done—"

"And I'm going to grovel for discussing things with Chloe when I ought to have discussed them with you," I said.

Dee just tossed her head.

"Honestly, we're *sorry*," said Chloe.

"Fat lot of good being sorry is," muttered Dee.

"We don't know what else to do," I said.

"You should have thought of that before. Paul's had enough unhappiness in his life without you going and adding to it!"

I stammered again that I was sorry, and to my horror Dee then broke down in tears. I'd never seen her cry before; like me, she is not a crying sort of person. Chloe is what Mum calls "volatile", she can burst into loud sobs or uncontrollable giggles at the least little thing. But Dee is always so contained.

.

"He was just starting to get better," she sobbed. "He was just getting his confidence back."

Chloe and I exchanged nervous glances. I guess we were both remembering what Chloe had said about Paul being in Arlington Park.

"It's been terrible for him." Dee fished a paper handkerchief out of her bag and mopped at her eyes. Between fresh bursts of tears she told us how after uni Paul had gone to work in America, and while he was

there he had got married and had a little boy. "Jimmy. He was so s-sweet!" Then two years ago Paul and his wife had come over on a visit, with Jimmy, and this appalling thing had happened.

Paul's wife and the little boy had been mown down by a hit-and-run driver. Dee said that Paul had been so traumatised that he'd had a breakdown.

"He had to go into hospital. He was there for ages. He just came out, a few months ago. He was doing so well! He was really managing to cope. And then *this*." She glared at me, suddenly ferocious. "You don't know what you've done to him!"

Chloe and I had been listening in a kind of stricken silence. Chloe now started shuffling her feet. It was one of those moments when you just feel like digging a hole and burying yourself. Everything which had previously seemed so strange, even sinister – Paul's manner, his hesitancy, the way he kept smiling – as if, perhaps, to reassure himself? – were all now totally explicable. Except just for that one thing. Why had he driven me down Gravelpit Hill?

I don't think even then I would have asked, but then Dee started laying into me.

"How *could* you? How could you do such a thing? How could you even *think* of it? Accusing him like that!"

And then it just burst out of me. *"But why did he take me on the wrong road?"*

"Would you want to drive past the spot where the two people you loved most in the whole world had been killed?" shouted Dee.

Dee never shouts. *Never*. I found that I was trembling.

"If only he'd turned round..." The words came out in an apologetic whisper. "If only he'd turned round when I asked him!"

"How could he *turn round*? How can you *turn round* when you're going down Gravelpit Hill? It's crazy. He would have turned round at the roundabout, if you'd just given him a chance!"

Suddenly, I was back on that dreadful night. I was falling out of the car, stumbling across the road. Paul's voice was calling after me: "Joanne! I'd have taken you! I was going to go round the roundabout!"

It was true: you can't turn on Gravelpit Hill. At the time I had been in too much of a panic to think straight. I realised now that Paul *would* have taken me back into town, if I'd just waited.

I told Mum about it when I got home. I said that I had upset Dee, I had upset Paul, and Dee was never going to forgive me. Mum tried her best to comfort me. She kept

376

saying things like "You weren't to know" and "It was just unfortunate." But I felt that I had lost Dee for ever.

"She'll never be friends with me again!"

"Give her time," said Mum. "I'm sure she will."

Mum was right, of course; she always is. The very next day, Dee slipped her arm through mine and said, "Truce?" We got together that weekend, the three of us, and started unravelling, tugging at all the threads. Dee said that Paul blamed himself, for not being brave enough to take me home on the Tanfield Road or trying to explain why he was going the long way round. Then I said that I blamed *myself*, for "misusing my gift".

"Mum's always warning me not to play around with things I can't properly control."

"Yes, but that was our fault," said Dee. "We tricked you."

"Actually, it was my idea," said Chloe.

"But I went along with it," said Dee.

"So did I," I said.

"You didn't know," said Dee.

"But I shouldn't have been playing The Game anyway!"

"Well..." Dee shrugged. "We shouldn't have encouraged you."

"And I shouldn't have talked to Ellie." Chloe sat back on her heels and looked at us, challengingly. It was like she was saying, There! I've admitted it.

I wasn't about to contradict her. "But if I hadn't been saving up for a pair of stupid glitter boots, I'd have got a cab back like I was supposed to, and Paul wouldn't ever have offered me a lift in the first place."

"*Glitter* boots?" said Chloe. "Is that what you were saving for?"

Somewhat shamefaced, I nodded. "I wanted to impress Danny."

"Oh! Well." Chloe bounced back upright. "That's understandable!"

"Absolutely," said Dee.

"But they were hideous!" I wailed.

"Yes, they were," said Chloe.

"So why did you want them?" said Dee. "If you thought they were so hideous?"

"'Cos at the time I thought they were funky."

"*Funky?*" Chloe crinkled her nose. "You've got to be joking! You know who had a pair, don't you? *Mel*."

"Yes, and you know who Danny spent all evening talking to?" I said.

"*MEL!*" We all chorused it together.

"Boys are so rubbish," said Chloe.

We were back at our usual girly chitchat – that is what my dad calls it. Situation normal: we were friends again!

But somehow or other, and I am not really sure why, things were never quite the same as they had been. We laughed and joked and gossiped, we were still a threesome; but over the coming months, almost without our realising it, we slowly began to drift apart. I guess it might have happened anyway, as we moved up the school. We're Year 10, now, and we're all in different classes. Looking back on those early days, I can see that we didn't really have all that much in common. Dee's into science in a big way, I'm more into languages.

379

Chloe's not really into anything, except boys. Her period of thinking they were rubbish was quite short-lived. She's as scatty as ever!

She mainly hangs out with Mel, and they go boy hunting together.

Dee and I are still friends; just not as close as we were before. My best friend at the moment is this really sweet girl called Grace, who comes from Hong Kong and only

joined the school last term. She has inspired me with the desire to travel! That is why I am working really hard at my languages.

As for Dee, she goes round with a group of fellow boffins. All very earnest and totally brilliant. You know the sort of thing. They claim to like *opera* and play *bridge*. Well, some of them do. They tend to look down on the rest of us; to them, we are just riff raff. But Dee and I respect each other. I think that respect is important. I have even learnt to respect my gift. I certainly don't mess with it any more. To be honest, I try not to even think about it. Grace, for instance, has no idea that I have a gift. That's the way I want to keep it! Maybe one day I'll be like Mum and put it to some sort of use, but for the moment I'm just trying to concentrate on being a normal, ordinary person the same as everyone else. Life's a whole lot less complicated that way. I don't feel ready to cope with school, *and* boys, *and* growing up, *and* the clairvoyant thing. Treating it like I did, like some kind of party game, I caused so much unhappiness to the one person who certainly didn't deserve it. I mean Paul, of course.

I bumped into Paul a few weeks ago. I was in the shopping mall and he was coming out of one of the stores. My instinct was to turn and run. I mean, I really thought that I would be the last person on earth he would want to see. But there were people all round me, and I left it too late. We were face to face before I had a chance to take avoiding action. My only hope was that he wouldn't recognise me, but he did. And he stopped. And he smiled.

"Joanne," he said.
"How are you?"

I said, "I'm f-fine.
H-how are you?"

"I'm well," he said.

And he really seemed
it. He really seemed
happy and relaxed. I
was so grateful to him for
talking to me! Dee had
told me ages ago, when I stammered out my apologies,
that according to Paul there was "nothing to apologise
for". But I never, ever thought that he would stop and
speak to me. I have been walking on air ever since! I
believe now that he is a very special sort of person, and I
am just so thankful that I didn't destroy him – which I so
easily could have done.

When I spoke about this to Mum, she said, "Maybe in
future you'll listen to me!" She said it sort of half joking,
but I wasn't joking when I promised her that I would.

"Honestly, Mum! I mean it."

"Until next time," said Mum.

She's wrong. For once she is *definitely wrong*. There
isn't going to be any next time. No way!

# Sugar and Spice

# JEAN URE

Illustrated by Karen Donnelly

for Mariam

# one

"Ruth! Time to get up."

*Time to get up. Get yourself dressed. I'm not telling you again!* Every morning, same old thing.

"Did you hear me? Ruth?"

Yes, I did! I heard you.

"I'd like some kind of response, please!"

And then she'll go, *I hope you haven't gone back to sleep?*

"I hope you haven't gone back to sleep?"

*Get up, get dressed. How many more times?*

Why doesn't she just give it a rest?

"Do I have to shout myself hoarse? Get yourself up this instant!" Mum suddenly appeared like a tornado at the bedroom door. "And get your sisters up, as well. For goodness' sake! It's gone seven o'clock."

Boo hoo! So what?

"Do you want to be late for school? Because you will be!"

Don't care if I am. Sooner be late than get there early.

"All this big talk," said Mum. "Going to be a *doctor*. Going to pass *exams*. You'll be lucky to get a job in Tesco's if you don't shift yourself and make a bit of an effort!"

Mum had no idea. She didn't know what it was like. She didn't know how much I hated it. Hated, hated, HATED it!

"Ruth, I'm warning you." Mum marched across to the window and yanked back the curtains. I could tell she was in a mood. "I can't take much more of this! I'm running out of patience."

So why couldn't she just go away and leave me alone? I burrowed further down the bed, wrapping myself up in the duvet. I was safe in the duvet. In bed, in the bedroom. At home. I'd have liked to stay there for always. Never go out again anywhere, ever. And specially not to *school*.

"I mean it," said Mum. "I can't be doing with this battle every morning. I've got your dad to see to, I've got your brother to see to... now, come along! Shift yourself! I don't have all day." And with one tug she hauled the duvet right off me.

"*Mu-u-um!*" I squealed in protest, curling myself up into a tight little ball and clinging to the pillow with both hands. "Mum, *please!*"

"Enough," said Mum. "Just get yourself up. And don't forget your sisters!"

*They* were still asleep. They'd sleep through an earthquake, those two. All snuggled up together, Kez

with her thumb in her mouth, Lisa on her back, blowing bubbles. Ah! Bless. Like a pair of little angels. *I don't think.* Actually, I suppose, they're not too bad, as sisters go.

They can sometimes be quite sweet, like when Kez climbs on to your lap for a cuddle, or Lisa does her show-off dancing, very solemn, with her fingers splayed out and her face all scrunched up with the effort she's putting into it. She's really cute when she does her dancing! Other times, though, they can be a total pain. This is because Mum lets them get away with just about everything. Dad too. He's even worse! *Spare the rod and spoil the child* is what one of my nans says. I know you're not allowed to beat your children these days (Nan was beaten with a *cane* when she was young) but I do think Mum and Dad ought to exercise a little bit more discipline. I try to, but it's a losing battle. They just cheek me or go running off to Dad.

"Dad! Ruth's being mean!"

Then I'm the one who gets the blame, cos I'm twelve years old and they're only little, except I don't personally think nine is as little as all that. I'm sure I wouldn't have been rude to my older sister when I was nine. If I'd had an older sister. I certainly wouldn't have helped myself to her things without asking, which is what Lisa is always doing and which drives me completely *nuts*. Kezzy is only six, so maybe there is a bit of an excuse for her. Maybe.

Anyway, I wasn't wasting my breath pleading with them. I just got hold of the pillows and yanked. That got their attention! Kez blinked at me like a baby owl. Lisa started wailing.

"Get up!" I said, and kicked the bed. Unlike Mum, I don't stand for any nonsense. You have to be firm. "Go on! Get up!"

"Don't want to get up," grumbled Lisa. "Haven't finished sleeping."

"Can't help that," I said. "You have to go to school." When I was nine, I loved going to school. I couldn't get there fast enough. "Who've you got this term?" I said.

Lisa sniffed and said, "Mrs Henson."

I felt this great well of envy. Lisa didn't know how

lucky she was! Mrs Henson was just the best teacher I ever had. *The best.* When I told Mrs Henson I wanted to be a doctor she didn't laugh or say that I'd better not set my sights too high. She said, "Well, and why not? I'm sure that would be possible, if you work hard enough." She made you feel like you could do anything you wanted. You could be a doctor or a teacher. You could even be Prime Minister!

"Mrs Henson is just so lovely," I said.

Lisa said she wasn't lovely. "She tells me off."

"In that case, you're obviously doing something wrong," I said.

"I'm not doing anything wrong. She just picks on me!"

"Mrs Henson doesn't *pick* on people," I said. I felt quite cross with my stupid little sister. Fancy having a wonderful teacher like Mrs Henson and not appreciating her! If I still had Mrs Henson, Mum wouldn't have to bawl and bellow at me every morning. I'd be out of bed like a shot! "You just get dressed," I said. "And stop whining!"

I dragged on my school clothes, which I hated almost as much as I hated school. *Black skirt, grey jumper.* Ugh! It made me feel miserable before I even got there. I'd always looked forward to having a school uniform as I thought it would be something to be, like, proud of, but nobody could be proud of going to

Parkfield High. (Or Krapfilled High, as some of the boys called it. I know it sounds rather rude, but I think it's more suited than Parkfield since there isn't any park and there isn't any field and it's absolutely *crud*. Which is why I hated it.)

Lisa was now complaining that she couldn't find her knickers and Kez had gone and put her top on inside out, so I had to stop and grovel on the floor, all covered in shoes and socks and toys and books and dirty spoons

and empty pots. I found the missing knickers, which Lisa then screamed she couldn't wear on account of someone having gone and trodden on them and left a muddy footprint; so we had a bit of an argument about that, with me telling her that no one was going to see them, and her saying that they might, and me saying how? – I mean, *how*? "Boys peek when you go upstairs," she said, which meant in the end we had to get out a clean pair, by which time Kez had not only got her top on inside out but had put both feet down the same leg of her trousers and couldn't work out what to do about it. Honestly! My sisters! Was it any wonder I was always late for school? Not that I cared. Nobody ever noticed, anyway.

In the kitchen, Mum was putting on her make-up, filling lunch boxes, getting breakfast, dressing Sammy. Sammy is my little brother. He's four years old and is even more spoilt than Kez and Lisa. This is because he's a *boy*. There is a lot of sexism going on in my family.

Mum said, "Ah, Ruth! There you are. About time! Just keep an eye on the toast for me, love. Oh, and lay the table, will you, there's a good girl."

So I kept an eye on the toast and laid the table and finished dressing Sammy and removed the raw carrot from my lunch box as I'm *not a rabbit*, whatever Mum may think, and put some more peanut butter in my sandwiches when she wasn't looking, and got out the Sugar Puffs, and got out the milk, and finally took Dad's breakfast tray in to him, being careful not to spill his mug of tea. Dad always has his breakfast in bed, then Mum helps him get up and settles him comfortably for the day before rushing off to work, dropping Sammy off at Reception and Kez and Lisa at Juniors. I have to make my own way, by bus, but that's all right; I'm quite good at getting around London. It's easy when you know how. Also it means that I can d-a-w-d-l-e and not get into school too early. If there is any danger of getting in too early I wander round the back streets until I can be sure that the first bell will have gone.

It's quite scary in the playground, even in the girls' part, as there are all these different gangs that have their special areas where you're not allowed to go. Unless, of course, you happen to belong to them. I do not belong to any of them, so I have to be really careful where I tread. It's like picking your way through a minefield. Any minute you can stray into someone else's territory, and then it's like, "Where d'you think you're going?"

I don't know why I never belonged to a gang. Cos nobody ever asked me, I guess. When we were at Juniors we all mixed together. My best friend was Millie and my second best friend was Mariam. I thought that when we went to senior school we'd all go on being friends. But almost the minute we arrived at Parkfield, they got swallowed up into gangs. The gangs were, like, really exclusive – *if you're not one of us, we don't want to know you*. It meant that when we were at school, all the people I'd been juniors with almost didn't talk to me any more. There was a gang of white girls I could have joined, maybe, if I'd wanted, but there was this girl, Julia Bone, who was their leader, and she said to me one day that I looked really geeky.

"D'you know that? You look like a total nerd. *Are* you a nerd?"

I suppose I probably am, cos instead of saying something back to her, such as, "You look like a horse" (which she does, with those huge great teeth of hers), I just went bright red and didn't say anything, so that everyone tittered and started calling me Nerd or Geek.

I *know* if I'd told her she looked like a horse they would've respected me a bit, and might even have let me into their gang, but I always think of these things too late. At the time my mind just goes blank.

It was way back at the start of Year 7 when Julia Bone told me I looked like a nerd. All that term they called me names. Another one was Boffin. The Geek. The Nerd. The Boffin. I'd hoped they'd forget about it during the holiday, but we'd just gone back after Christmas and they were still at it. Yesterday I'd made a big mistake, I'd arrived before the bell had gone, and practically the first thing I'd heard as I crept into the playground was, "Watch it, Geek! You looking for trouble?"

I never look for trouble. I know they say you should stand up to bullies, but how can you when there's loads of them and only one of you? I think it's best just to keep out of the way.

I reached Mum and Dad's bedroom safely, without spilling any of Dad's tea, and pushed the door open with my bottom. Dad was propped up against the pillows, all ready and waiting. He said, "Thanks, Ruthie. That's my girl! How's school?" He talks in little bursts, all puffy and wheezy. He has this thing where he's short of breath. "School OK?"

I said that it was, because Mum is always careful to remind us that Dad mustn't be upset; and in any case, what would be the point? Dad couldn't do anything. You had to go where you were sent, and I'd been sent to Parkfield High.

"Lessons OK?" said Dad.

I smiled, brightly, and nodded.

"Learning how to be a doctor?"

I nodded again and smiled even more brightly. It's a kind of joke with Mum and Dad, me wanting to become a doctor.

"That's the ticket," said Dad. "Keep at it!"

Back in the kitchen, Sammy had poured milk all over himself and Kez was making a fuss because she said her toast was "burnded". She'll only eat it if it's, like, *blond*. Lisa was snuffling and wiping her nose on her sleeve. She's always snuffling – she can't help it. She has what Nan calls "a weak chest". But she doesn't have to wipe the snot off on her sleeve – that's disgusting! At the *breakfast* table.

"Where's your hanky?" I said.

"Haven't got one."

"Well, get one!"

"Don't know where they are."

"What d'you mean, you don't know where they are? They're where they always are! Th—"

"Oh, Ruth, just go and get her one!" said Mum. "And scrape Kez's toast for her while you're at it."

I'm frequently surprised that my legs aren't worn to stumps. I know Mum can't do everything, but I do occasionally wish that I could have been Child Number Two instead of Child Number One. I don't think that being Child Number One has very much going for it.

In spite of fetching hankies and scraping toast and collecting Dad's breakfast tray and getting the tiresome trio into their shoes and coats while Mum saw to Dad, I still managed to reach school before the bell. My stomach did this clenching thing as I turned into Parkfield Road and saw it there, waiting for me, like a great grey prison.

397

There's this wire mesh stuff over the windows, to stop them from being broken, and the walls are always covered in graffiti. Every term the graffiti's removed and every term it comes back again. I think some graffiti's quite pretty and I don't know why people object to it. But the stuff on our school walls is mostly just ugly, same as on our block of flats. If Mum'd seen them she would've known why I hated school so much, but Mum had enough to cope with, what with Dad, and work, and the tiresome trio, so she hardly ever went to parents' evenings. Actually, I don't think many other parents did, either. They would've found it too depressing, not to mention a total waste of time. You know those tables that they print, saying which schools have done best and which have done worst? Well, my school was one of the ones that did worst. It always did worst. It was the *pits*.

I was about to go slinking off down a side street and give the playground time to clear when someone called out, "Hi, Ruth! Wait for me!" and Karina Koh came huffing up the road. I obediently stopped and waited, cos it would've been rude not to, and also I wouldn't have wanted her to feel hurt, but I can't say that my heart exactly leapt for joy. Out of the whole year, Karina was the only one who called me Ruth (rather than Geek or Nerd) and the only one that ever wanted to hang out with me, so you might have thought I'd be a little bit grateful to her; maybe just at the beginning I was, when she first, like, came up to me in the playground and sat next to me in class. It's horrid being on your own and I did think that Karina would be better than no one. I even hoped we might become proper friends, but the truth is, I didn't really terribly like her. She'd been thrown out of Julia Bone's gang, which was why she'd latched on to me. She said we could be a gang all by ourselves.

"Just the two of us! OK? And we'll take no notice of the others cos they're just garbage. They're all garbage, and we hate them! Don't we?"

She was always wanting me to hate people. Usually I agreed that I did, just to keep her happy, but it was a lie, cos I didn't. Not really. I hated *school*. I think perhaps I hated school so much that I didn't have any hate left over for actual people. Not even Julia Bone, who Karina hated more than anyone. She told me all sorts of things about Julia Bone.

"She *smells*. Have you noticed? I always hold my breath when I have to go near her. I don't think she ever has a bath. I don't think she even knows what a bath is for. She doesn't ever wash her hands when she's been to the toilet. I've seen her! She's *rancid*. She lives in a bed and breakfast. Did you know that? She has to live there cos her dad ran off. Her mum's, like, on drugs? She's a real junkie! And her sister's a retard. The whole family's just garbage."

Karina knew everything about everybody. But only *bad* things; that was all she ever told me. Like that morning, on the way in to school, when she told me that "Jenice Berry's mum's gone into the nut house." Jenice Berry was best friends with Julia Bone, so naturally Karina hated her almost as much as she hated Julia.

"They took her off last night. Came to collect her. She was raving! I know this cos we live in the same block."

She sounded really pleased about it. I said that it must be frightening, having your mum taken away, but Karina said that Jenice deserved it.

"They're all mad, anyway. The whole family."

Sometimes I thought that Karina wasn't really a very nice person. Then I'd get scared and think that maybe I wasn't a very nice person, either, and that was why nobody wanted me in any of their gangs, which would mean that I was even *less* of a nice person than Karina, since she'd at least started off in a gang. I hadn't even done that.

Other times I thought maybe Karina had only become not very nice because of everyone rejecting her, in which case I ought to be more understanding and sympathetic. So I tried; I really tried. I *wanted* us to be friends and she kept saying that we were, but every time I felt a bit of sympathy she went and ruined it. Like now when she said in these gloating tones that "People like Jenice Berry always get what's coming to them. Her and Julia Bone… they'll get theirs! It's only a question of time."

We walked through to the playground just as first

bell was going. Julia caught sight of us and yelled, "Watch it, Geek! We're out to get you! And you, Slugface!" I won't say what Karina shouted back as it was a four-letter word, which I didn't actually blame her for as it's quite nasty to refer to a person as a slugface, even if they're not that pretty (which

401

Karina is not!). And I wasn't really shocked, which I would've been once. Everybody used four-letter words at Parkfield. All the same, I did wish Karina wouldn't answer back; it only made matters worse. Although maybe that's just me being a wimp. I suppose it was quite brave of her, really.

As we set off across the playground I caught sight of Millie, who used to be my best friend. I waved at her and she twitched her lips in a sort of smile but she didn't say hallo or anything. Her gang was one of the toughest. They weren't as mean as Julia's lot, but only because they would've thought it beneath them. They were, like, really superior. Like anyone that wasn't black wasn't worth wasting your breath on. It was hard to remember that this time last year me and Millie had been sharing secrets and going for sleepovers with each other. She wouldn't even give me the time of day, now. Nor would

Mariam, though I think Mariam would've liked to, if it hadn't been against the rules.

All the gangs had rules. The main one was that you didn't go round with anyone who didn't belong, which was why nobody went round with me – except Karina. Even the people that just hung out in little groups kept away from us; I dunno why. Karina said it was because I was a boffin. But I didn't mean to be!

The bell rang again. By now, the playground was almost empty.

"I s'ppose we'd better go in," I said. I didn't want to, but when it came to it I wasn't actually brave enough to do what some of the kids did and bunk off school. I think I still believed that school was a place where you might be able to learn something.

We trailed together across the playground and up the steps, keeping as far away from the rest of our year as we could.

The main corridor was full of bodies, all bumping and banging, and everybody shouting at the top of their voice. One of the teachers appeared at a classroom door and bawled, "Stop that confounded racket!" but nobody took any notice. A couple of boys barged into us from behind and a big yob called Brett Thomas caught my glasses with his elbow as he belted past. I went, "*Ow!*" I felt the tears spring into my eyes. It's really painful when someone smashes your glasses into your face. "That hurt!" I said. But I didn't say it loud enough for Brett to hear.

Karina said, "They're *animals*." But she didn't say it loud enough for Brett to hear, either. Not even Karina was brave enough to say anything to Brett Thomas. He'd told Mr Kirk, our class teacher, only yesterday, "No one messes with me, man!" and even Mr Kirk had backed down. Brett Thomas did pretty well whatever he wanted.

"He's on drugs," said Karina. "And his mother's a—" She put her mouth close to my ear. "*She goes with men.*"

I felt like yelling, "SHUT UP!" I didn't want to hear these things – not even about Brett Thomas. I didn't even know whether they were true. According to Karina, practically the whole of Year 7 was either on drugs or had mothers who were loopy or locked up or going with men, or fathers who had run away or drank too much or beat them. Some of them (according to

Karina) had fathers that were in prison. I wasn't sure that I always believed her. On the other hand…

Well, on the other hand, maybe she really did know these things. Maybe they were true and the whole of Year 7 was mad and dysfunctional, and that was why they behaved the way they did. It was a truly glum and gloomy thought and it filled me with despair. Sometimes I just couldn't see how I was ever going to survive another five years of Parkfield High.

But that was before Shay came into my life.

# two

It was that same morning, when Julia yelled "Slugface!" at Karina, and Brett Thomas mashed my glasses into my face, that Shay arrived at Parkfield High.

Mr Kirk was at his desk, bellowing out names and trying to mark the register, which wasn't easy with all the hubbub going on. Brett Thomas and another boy were bashing each other in the back row, and some of the girls were shrieking encouragement. Mr Kirk would bawl, *"Alan Ashworth?"* at the top of his voice and someone thinking they were being funny would yell, "Gone to China!" or "Been nicked!" and everyone would start screeching and hammering on their desk lids.

Karina had told me last term that sometimes the teachers at Parkfield High went mad and had to be taken away in straitjackets, and for once I believed her. Well, almost. I didn't think, probably, that they went actually *mad*, but you could definitely see them getting all nervous and twitchy. Some of them got twitchy cos they were scared, like Mrs Saeed who taught us maths. She was so tiny and pretty looking, and Brett Thomas was like this huge great ugly hulk looming over her. I used to feel really sorry for Mrs Saeed.

But Mr Kirk, he twitched cos he was frustrated. What he'd really have liked, I reckon, was to hurl things. Books and chairs and lumps of chalk. Only he knew that he couldn't – he could only hurl his voice, and nobody took any notice of voices, least of all Brett Thomas. Karina said that Mr Kirk went home and beat his wife instead, but I think she may just have been making that up.

Anyway. The door opened and Mrs Millchip from Reception came in. She had this girl with her and everyone suddenly broke off yelling and hammering and turned to look. Even Brett Thomas stopped bashing, just for a moment. Mrs Millchip walked over to Mr Kirk, but the girl stayed where she was, leaning inside the door, with her hands behind her back, and this kind of, like, *bored* expression on her face.

If she hadn't looked so bored and so... supercilious, I think that's the word, meaning above all the rest of us, like we were rubbish and she was the Queen of England (except the Queen would be more gracious, having been properly brought up). Even as it was, with this scowly kind of sulk, you could tell she was totally drop dead gorgeous.

She looked the way I look in my daydreams. Tall. (I'm short.) Slim. (I'm weedy.) Heavenly black hair, very thick and glossy. (Mine is mouse-coloured and limp.) Creamy brown skin and a face that has cheekbones, like a model, and these huge dark eyes. (My skin is like skimmed milk, plus I wear braces, not to mention *glasses*.)

Mrs Millchip left the room, but the girl just went on leaning against the wall. Into the silence, Mr Kirk bellowed, "This is Shayanne Sugar, who's just joined us. I'd like you to make her feel welcome." Just for once there wasn't any need for him to bellow, but I expect by now he'd forgotten how to talk normally. I didn't really believe that he beat his wife when he got home, but he probably did bawl at her. She'd say, "You don't have to shout, dear, I'm not deaf," and Mr Kirk would bellow, "**I AM NOT SHOUTING!**" Well, that's what I like to imagine.

He told Shay to find herself a seat, while he went on with the register. Immediately everyone lost interest and went back to what they were doing, which was having private conversations and rooting about under their desk lids, eating things, or, in Brett Thomas's case, bashing. Shay stood there, letting her gaze move slowly about the classroom, like she was summing people up, deciding which would be the best person to sit next to.

There were several spare seats as it was the second week of term and the people who usually bunked off had already started. There was a spare seat next to me, but I knew she wouldn't choose that one. Why would a person who looked like a model want to sit next to an insignificant weed with braces on her teeth? *And* glasses.

"Talk about picky," muttered Karina. (She was sitting next to me on the other side.) "What's her game?"

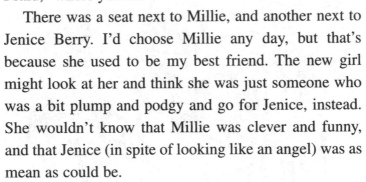

"It's important," I said, "where you sit."

There was a seat next to Millie, and another next to Jenice Berry. I'd choose Millie any day, but that's because she used to be my best friend. The new girl might look at her and think she was just someone who was a bit plump and podgy and go for Jenice, instead. She wouldn't know that Millie was clever and funny, and that Jenice (in spite of looking like an angel) was as mean as could be.

Karina was still buzzing in my ear. "Why's she started so late, anyway? Why didn't she come at the beginning of term?"

I never really found out why Shay started so late. There were lots of things about Shay I never found out. Of course, she *might* go and sit next to one of the boys, if she wanted to be different. I wouldn't! But then I spend my life trying not to be different. Unfortunately it seems that I just am. I hate it! All I want is to blend in and be the same as everyone else. I don't know why I can't be, but it's always like there are people going, "Oh, *her*," or, "Well, of course, *Ruth Spicer*." Like, *she would, wouldn't she?* You have to be bold to enjoy being different. Like Shay. Shay was the boldest person I've ever known.

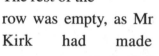 Just for a second, her eyes met mine and my heart went bomp! inside my ribcage. I really thought she was going to come over and sit by me. But she didn't. Instead, she stalked off to the back row and settled herself in solitary splendour, not next to anybody. The nearest person was Brett Thomas, right at the far end. The rest of the row was empty, as Mr Kirk had made  everyone move further down to the front. (Everyone except Brett Thomas. Nobody moved him anywhere.)

I waited for Mr Kirk to tell Shay to come closer, but he was still busy bawling his way through the register and didn't seem to notice. Karina sniffed and went, "Huh! Who's she think she is?" I didn't bother answering. I was thinking to myself that once Shay got put in the register we *would* be next to each other... Ruth Spicer, Shayanne Sugar. I wondered if Shay would

413

notice this and think it was neat. Sugar, Spicer: Sugar and Spice! It made us sound like a TV programme!

Our first class that day was English, with Mr Kirk. After he'd banged on his desk with a book and got a bit of peace and quiet, he started handing back last week's homework, which was an essay on "The Night Sky". As usual, most people hadn't actually done it. When Mr Kirk demanded to know why, one of the boys said he couldn't be bothered, another said it was a waste of time, and Arlon Phillips, the boy who'd been fighting with Brett Thomas, said what was the point? Brett agreed with him. He said that it was a girl's subject, anyway.

"What's to write about? *The night sky is black. Wiv stars. And sometimes the moon, when it ain't cloudy.* That's about all there is to say."

"So why didn't you say it?" said Mr Kirk.

"Just have," said Brett.

"Would it have been too much trouble to write it down?"

Brett said yeah, it would. "I don't do homework, man."

"Well, I'm happy to tell you," said Mr Kirk, "that some people do. And that some people have found rather more to say on the subject than you have. For instance, how about this from Ruth Spicer—"

Oh, horrors! He was going to read it out! This is

what I mean about being different. I don't *ask* for my essays to be read out. I don't want them read out! Already I could hear the sounds of groaning. *That Ruth Spicer! There she goes again.* I knew if I turned round I'd see hostile eyes boring into me.

"Ruth has very creditably managed to write two whole pages," said Mr Kirk.

Oh, no! *Please.* I felt myself cringing, doing my best to burrow down into the depths of my prickly school sweater.

"I'll give you just two examples of imaginative imagery... *the clouds drifted past, like flocks of fluffy sheep.*"

Behind me, Julia made a vomiting sound. *Pleeurgh!* Jenice Berry immediately did the same thing. I could feel my cheeks burning up, bright red and hot as fire. Please let him stop! Why did he have to do this to me?

"The other example," shouted Mr Kirk, above the rising din of sniggers and vomits, "**ARE YOU LISTENING?** *The moon hung in the sky, like a big banana*."

It sounded completely stupid, even to me. I'd been so proud of it when I wrote it! I'd thought it was really poetic. Now I just wanted to curl up and die.

"Moon's not a *banana*," yelled Julia.

"Can be."

Heads all over the room turned, in outrage. Who would ever dare contradict the great Julia Bone?

"Crescent moon," said Shay. "That's a banana."

Julia glared and muttered. Mr Kirk said, "Precisely! Very nice piece of writing, Ruth." (Cringe, cringe.) "As for the moron who wrote this—" He held out a sheet of paper with just the one line on it. "*The night sky is too dark to see*." He scrunched the paper into a ball. "I have only one thing to say to you, and that is, *grow up*!" And then he handed me back my essay and said, "Excellent!"

When I was at juniors I would've prinked and preened all day if Mrs Henson had said excellent. But at Parkfield High it wasn't clever to be clever. It was just *stupid*. Now they would call me names even worse then before. I could already hear the two Js, sitting behind me, making bleating sounds under their breath.

"Ba-a-aa, ba-a-aa!"

I did my best to ignore them, but I'm not very good at blotting things out, I always let them get to me, and then I want to run away and cry. Fortunately I do have a little bit of pride. Not very much; just enough to pretend that I don't care, or haven't noticed. I'd be too ashamed to let my true feelings show in front of people.

At the end of the lesson Mr Kirk set us some more homework. The subject was: My Family. He said he wanted it in by the day after tomorrow.

"Thursday. OK? I will accept no excuses! Anyone says they forgot and I shall send them for a brain scan. You have been warned!"

I muttered, "Send some people for a brain scan and you wouldn't find any brain."

I know it wasn't very nice of me, since people can't help not having any brain, any more than I can help having to wear glasses, but I don't think it's very nice to make fun of someone who's just trying to fit in and be ordinary. I didn't *ask* Mr Kirk to read out my essay. Unfortunately, Karina caught what I'd muttered. She gave this huge shriek and swung round in her desk.

"D'you hear what she said? *Send some people for a brain scan and you wouldn't find any brain!*"

If looks could have killed... well, I'd be dead, and that's all there is to it.

"Big banana moon!" said Julia.

"Ba-a-aa," went Jenice.

They carried on all through break.

"Why d'you have to go and tell them?" I said.

Karina tossed her head. She hates anything that she thinks is criticism.

"Not much point saying things if you don't say them to their faces!"

I expect she was probably right; I just wasn't brave enough.

"Look," said Karina, "there's the new girl."

Shay was leaning against the wire mesh that fenced us in. As well as wire mesh we had big gates with padlocks and brick walls with bits of broken glass on top. Most schools have security to keep people from getting in, but at Parkfield they had it to keep us from getting out. Well, that's my theory.

"Look at her! What's she doing?"

Shay was just watching. I saw her eyes slowly swivelling to and fro, same as they had in the classroom. She caught me looking at her and I very hastily turned the other way and began to study some interesting clouds that were drifting across the sky. They did look like sheep. *Flocks of fluffy sheep.* I felt my cheeks begin to burn all over again. If Mr Kirk was going to keep singling me out I'd just have to stop doing his stupid homework. Either that or do it so badly-on-purpose that he'd be rude about it and treat me the same as everyone else. One or the other. But I couldn't go on being humiliated!

The bell rang and we trundled back into school. First lesson after break was maths, which isn't one of my favourite subjects, though I do work quite hard at it, as far as you *can* work hard at Parkfield High. I used to think that I'd need it if I was going to be a doctor, cos of having to measure things out and knowing how much medicine to give people; but in fact, after one term at Parkfield I'd pretty well given up on the idea of being a doctor. I could understand a bit better why Mum and Dad had laughed when I'd first told them. Dad had said, "Well, and why not be a brain surgeon while you're about it?" Mum had said that I could always be a nurse. But I didn't want to be a nurse! I wanted to be a doctor. Well, I *had* wanted to be a doctor. Now it seemed more likely I'd end up in Tesco's, with Mum. But I still struggled and did my maths homework.

At least Mrs Saeed never embarrassed me by making comments in front of the class. Even when I'd once – wonder of wonders! – got an A-, she just quietly wrote "Good work!" at the bottom and left me to gloat over it in private.

Most people crammed as far back as possible for maths classes because Mrs Saeed was too nervous to make them move closer. Me and Karina were the only people in the front row. We didn't *have* to sit in the front row; there were empty desks in the row behind. But I liked Mrs Saeed and it seemed really rude if nobody wanted to sit near her. She might wonder why not and start to think that there was something wrong with her. It's what I would think, if it happened to me.

Shay didn't arrive until the last minute. This was probably because no one had bothered speaking to her, or told her where to go. *Including me.* I told myself that it was because she looked so superior and, like, forbidding, but really it was because it had never occurred to me. Even if it had, I still wouldn't have done it because I'd have thought to myself that I was too lowly and unimportant to go up and start talking.

"Here's Miss High and Mighty," hissed Karina. "D'you think she's looking for her throne?"

She was looking for somewhere to sit. Her eyes

flickered about the room, as they had before. And then, to my surprise and confusion, they came to rest on *me*. Next thing I know, she's plonking herself down at the desk next to mine. She said,

"Maths, yeah?"

I said, "Y-yeah."

"My favourite subject, I don't think!"

"Mine neither," I said.

"Well, there you go," said Shay. "That's one thing we got in common."

I was, like, really flattered when she said that. I couldn't have imagined having *anything* in common with someone as bright and bold as Shay.

After maths we had PE, in the gym. PE was one of those lessons that I absolutely dreaded, the reason being I'm just *so bad* at it. Karina was every bit as bad as I was, which meant we usually spent our time skulking in the corner, trying not to be picked on, while people like the two Js barged madly about, swinging to and fro on

the ends of ropes and
hanging off the wall
bars, shrieking. Today,
Miss Southgate, our
big beefy PE
teacher, made us
all jump over
the horse
thingy. Oh,
I hate
that!
I really
hate
it!

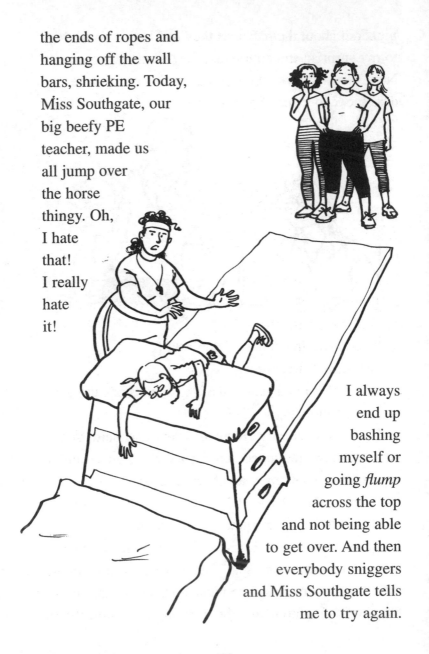

I always
end up
bashing
myself or
going *flump*
across the top
and not being able
to get over. And then
everybody sniggers
and Miss Southgate tells
me to try again.

422

"And this time, take a real run at it!"

So I do, but it isn't any use cos I still can't get over. Most probably what I do is catch my foot in the edge of the coconut matting and go sprawling on my face.

And then my glasses fall off and I hear them go *scrunch* underneath me, and Miss Southgate sighs and says, "All right! Next person." If the next person is Karina, she'll go flump just like I did. But if it's the two Js, they'll go hurtling over with about ten metres to spare *and* land on their feet the other side.

Until now they'd always been the star performers when it came to PE; them and a girl called Carlie who was in Millie's gang. They all belonged to the junior gym team and could bend themselves double and walk on their hands and balance without any signs of wobble on the parallel bars. Karina, in her sniffy way, said who'd want to?

"It's just stupid! Just showing off."

I didn't say anything to Karina, cos she'd only have got the hump with me, but I'd have given anything to be able to show off. Sometimes I had these dreams of hanging at the top of a rope, right up near the ceiling, and everybody being madly impressed and going, "Look! Look at Ruth!" Unfortunately I'm scared of heights, so it wasn't really very likely to happen. All I could do was watch, in a kind of awe. I wouldn't have minded if I never got an A- again, if I could only have whizzed up a rope or done the splits, like Julia. Cos she was absolutely THE BEST, it has to be said.

Until now. I couldn't believe it when Shay started up. She'd been doing her leaning thing, against the wall bars, silently observing everyone. And then it was her turn to run at the horse and she just, kind of, loped up to it, sailed over like it wasn't even there, and did a somersault with a handspring on the other side to finish off.

Everyone gaped, including the two Js. Karina muttered, "Who's she think she's impressing?" but it wasn't like Shay had done it to impress; more like it was just something that came naturally to her. "This is the way you jump over a horse." I got the feeling she didn't care one way or the other what anyone thought of her. She was Shay, and that was how she was, and they could take it or leave it. Which is the way that I'd love to be!

Afterwards, as we were leaving the gym, I heard Miss Southgate talking to her.

"Well," she said, "it looks as if we have a new recruit for the gym team! How about it? Would you like to join us?"

To my utter astonishment, Shay shook her head and said no. I couldn't believe it! How could she say *no*, just like that? To a teacher! I could tell Miss Southgate wasn't pleased. She said, "Well! That sounded pretty definite," and her voice was all sharp and prickly. I thought Shay would apologise, but she didn't; she didn't say anything. I asked her later – I mean, like, weeks later – why she hadn't wanted to join, and she just said, "Not worth it." She was such a mystery!

That evening, after tea, I shut myself away in the
kitchen to do my homework. The kitchen was the only
place that was warm enough since the central heating
had been turned off. Mum said we couldn't afford to
heat the whole flat, so now we just had it on in the front
room, but I was allowed to have the oven on low in the
kitchen. It wasn't exactly quiet out there cos I could
hear the television blaring in the next room, and the
person in the flat that joined ours had music on, really
loud, but I didn't mind that so much as the way Sammy
and the girls kept crashing in and out.

"We're playing!" yelled Lisa.

When I complained to Mum she said that it was nice the girls played with their little brother, and then she sat herself down at the kitchen table to ring one of my nans on her mobile. They started to talk and I really couldn't concentrate cos of listening to what they were saying. After a bit Mum put her hand over the mouthpiece and whispered, "Get Sammy off to bed for me, will you? There's a good girl!"

*Well.* That was easier said than done. It wasn't a question of "just getting him off to bed". First you had to catch him. Then when you'd caught him you had to fight to get him out of his clothes and into his pyjamas, and then another fight to get him to clean his teeth, and another fight to actually persuade him into the bedroom. (Actually Mum and Dad's bedroom, as we only have the two.) I finally got back to the kitchen to find that Mum was now working her way through a mound of ironing.

"If you did that in the other room," I said, "you could watch television at the same time."

"Too much hassle," said Mum. "Go on, you can work, I won't interfere with you."

I took out a sheet of paper and wrote MY FAMILY in big letters across the top. What could I write about my family?

"Look at this!" Mum was holding up one of Lisa's school blouses. "What on earth does she get up to?"

I nibbled the top of my pen, searching for inspiration. (*Bang*, went Mum, with the iron.) Maybe I could just write one line, like the person that wrote about the night sky.

*"My family is so ordinary I cannot think of anything to say about them."*

Then Mr Kirk (*bang, thud*) would read it out and tell me to grow up and everyone would laugh, only they wouldn't be laughing because I was a geek or a boffin, they would be laughing because I'd dared to be cheeky. They might even start to respect me a little.

What if I did the spelling all wrong, as well?

*"My famly is so ornry I cannot thing of anythink to say abowt them."*

Yess!!!!

"Know what?" said Mum. "This iron's giving out."

*"They are jest to bawrin for wurds. Wurds canot discribe how bawrin they are."*

I was really getting carried away, now.

*"My mum is bawrin my dad is bawrin my sistus is bawrin my b—"*

"Well, that's it," said Mum. "That's the iron gone."

*"—my bruthr is bawrin. This is an eggsample of the bawrin things that happen in my famly. My mum has*

*jest sed to me that the ion has gon but she duz not say*
*were it have gon. Maybe it have gon to the Nawth Powl.*
*Maybe it have gon to Erslasker. I wil aks her. Were has*
*the ion gon, I wil say."*

"What are you talking about?" said Mum.

"The iron," I said. "Where's it gone?"

"What d'you mean, where's it gone? It's broke! Why
don't you make us a cup of tea and bring it in the other
room? You've done enough scribbling for one night."

I made the tea, but I didn't go into the other room. I
stayed in the kitchen, writing my essay. I found that
once I'd got going, my pen seemed to carry on all by
itself and I just wrote and wrote, making up all these
funny spellings. *Tellervijun* and *sentrel heetin* and
*emferseema*, which is what my dad has got that makes
him run out of breath. (It's really spelt *emphysema*. I
learnt it, specially.) In the end, I wrote five whole pages!
Even longer than my essay about the sheep and the
bananas. I felt quite proud of it.

But then, guess what? I got cold feet! I woke up in
the middle of the night and I knew I couldn't really
hand in five pages of silly spelling. I just wasn't brave
enough. But it was too late to write anything else, and
even if it wasn't I couldn't bear the thought of Mr Kirk
singling me out again. Specially not if it was about my
family. I'd just die of shame! So I tore up my five pages,
even though I thought they were funny, and on the bus

next morning, on the way to school, I wrote down my original sentence: "My family is too ordinary for me to say anything about them."

I wondered, as I got off the bus, whether Shay would sit next to me again. I did hope she would! It had made me feel a bit special, when Shay sat next to me. But I really couldn't think of any reason why she'd want to.

# The Secret Writings of Shayanne Sugar

## They are <u>PRIVATE</u>

## KEEP OUT

This means you!!!

This school is a DUMP. The kids are RUBBISH. The teachers are PATHETIC. It is all GARBAGE.

Well it's OK, I won't be there for long. Not if I can help it! They're all a load of drivellers. Some stupid woman wanted me to join the gym team. Purlease! I'm not joining any of their ridiculous little teams, I'm not joining anything at all, NO WAY, full stop, finish. THE END. Sooner I get moved on the better. And I will! They'll soon get sick of me. BUT NOT HALF AS SICK AS I ALREADY AM OF THEM.

There's only one girl out of the whole stupid lot that's not a total thicko. Her name's Ruth and she looks like she's made of matchsticks.

Anything but a thicko! Ha ha. All the dorks and drivellers gang up against her, so I might kind of cultivate her and see what happens. Just out of interest. I certainly don't want her as a friend! Don't want ANYONE as a friend. I can manage on my own, I can! I don't need anyone. So I might not bother. I'll think about it.

Thinks...

I s'ppose it might give me something to do. Take away some of the boredom. WHILE I'M THERE. She hangs out with this girl that's a real slimeball. A right maggot mouth. But that's no problem! I can deal with her. She's just scum, like all the rest of them. Old Matchsticks has at least got a brain; sort of person

I could do something with. P'raps I'll give it a go. See what happens. If she's not interesting, I can always drop her.

The creep that takes English said to write an essay on My Family. What a stupid subject! My mum's a vampire. She sucks blood... yeah, and my dad's the invisible man!

One term. That's all I give it. After that — who knows? Maybe they'll just give up on me. Save us all a lot of grief.

Gonna write my essay now, about the vampire. Har har!

# three

On my way into school next morning, I was ambushed by Brett Thomas. He must have seen me coming and laid in wait, cos he sprang out from behind a tree as I walked into the playground. It was quite scary. I jumped and gave this little pathetic bleat. Brett said, "Where ya goin', Goofball?"

I said, "Going into s-school."

I mean, where else would I be going?

"Wotcha got in yer bag?"

"N-nothing!" I clutched my bag very tightly with

both hands. "I haven't got anything in it!"

"Wotcha mean, you ain't got anyfink in it? Wotcha carryin' it for?"

"It's just *s-school* stuff." I cast round, desperately, but the playground was empty. I'd done my usual trick of arriving late, after the bell. It was just me and Brett Thomas!

"Give it us." He reached out and grabbed the bag from me. There wasn't anything I could do; I had to let him have it. Brett Thomas was a real hard nut, he'd bash your head in soon as look at you. Even Karina, who didn't mind giving a load of bad mouth to Julia Bone, wasn't bold enough to stand up to Brett Thomas. Nor was Julia, come to that. Nobody was.

"Wossis?" He'd pulled out my lunch-box and flipped off the lid. I watched as he prised up a corner of one of my sandwiches and sniffed at it. "Peanut butter? Man, that's some repulsive crap!"

All the food that Mum had put in my lunch-box went hurtling across the playground.

"What else yer got?"

"Nothing," I said. "It's just homework."

"*Homework?*" He upended the bag and shook out the contents. "Only nerds do homework!"

He was about to mash all my books and papers into the ground when a voice yelled, "You do that and I'll beat you to a pulp!"

It was Shay. I couldn't believe it! Shay, daring to
threaten Brett Thomas... I felt like snatching up
my stuff and making a run for it, but I
knew I couldn't leave her there.
She didn't know what Brett
Thomas was like; she
didn't know what
she was letting
herself in
for.

"Honestly, it's all right," I said, "it doesn't matter, it's
not important, it—"

"Course it's important!" She turned on me, fiercely.
"Can't let people get away with this sort of thing!"

"So who's gonna stop us?" Brett brought his foot
down on top of my maths book and began grinding it
into the mud.

"I am," said Shay.

"Oh, yeah? You an' whose army?"

"Don't need any army!"

Shay launched herself at him. He was bigger and stronger than she was, but she caught him by surprise and managed to throw him off balance. I hastily scooped up my papers and rescued my maths book.

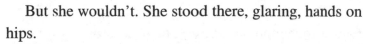

"Come on," I said, "let's go! Shay... *let's go!*"

But she wouldn't. She stood there, glaring, hands on hips.

"That is such *bad* behaviour," she said. "What are you? Some kind of throwback?"

"*Please!*" I was hopping from foot to foot. There still wasn't anyone else in the playground. "Leave him!"

"Next time," said Shay, "just pick on someone your own size."

We turned, and walked off across the playground. Brett came after us. He didn't actually do anything, just fell in behind us, breathing over our shoulders and uttering threats.

"I'll get you for this, bitch! You don't know who you're dealing with!"

Even now, Shay couldn't resist answering him back. "I know *what* I'm dealing with," she said. "Stone Age moron's what I'm dealing with!"

By the time we reached our classroom I had this great big tremble running through me, from top to bottom, making my whole body shake. I sank into my desk, next to Karina.

"You look really freaked out," said Karina. "Like you've been chased down the street by a horde of headless ghosts."

I told her it was worse than that. "Brett Thomas snatched my bag and Shay said she'd beat him to a pulp and he was a S-Stone Age moron!"

"What a total idiot." Karina craned her head to give Shay a contemptuous glare. (Shay had chosen to sit next to me, on the other side.) "Stupid thing to do!"

"Pardon me?" said Shay. She also craned her head. "You don't think it's right someone stands up to him?"

"Not unless they want to get themselves knifed," said Karina.

"He'd just better try it!" said Shay.

"You wait. You'll see! He'll get you."

"You shouldn't have done it," I said. "He's a horrible boy! He's been excluded once."

"Really?" said Shay, but she didn't sound too impressed.

"Yes, and then they went and let him back, and now he terrorises everyone."

Shay tossed her head. "Doesn't terrorise me!"

"But he's dangerous," I said. "He's really mean."

"So'm I," said Shay. "I'm meaner than a hyena! He's not gonna get me."

And he never did. I don't know what it was, whether he was scared of her, or whether he respected her, but after that he never came anywhere near her. He never came near me again, either, thanks to Shay. I don't know how it is that some people can stand up for themselves and beat the bullies and others can't. If I'd told Brett he was a Stone Age moron, I dread to think what he would have done. There was just something about Shay that warned people off.

When it came to lunchtime I didn't have anything to eat, on account of all my food being scattered over the playground. Karina, who also brought packed lunches, said that I could have half of one of her sandwiches, if I wanted, and a mouthful of yoghurt.

"But that's all, otherwise I'll get hungry, and if I get hungry I'll feel faint."

Shay then came over to sit with us, bringing a trayful of chips and curry, and a slice of cake.

"I tried to get two dinners but they wouldn't let me, but that's OK, we can share... look, I'll divide it up."

She actually drew a line with her knife down the middle of the plate and said that one half was for her, and the other half was for me. When I tried to thank her, she said I didn't have to do that.

"We're Sugar and Spice, right?"

She'd noticed! All by herself, without me telling her. Karina said, "What's that s'pposed to mean?"

"Means we share," said Shay.

"Why?" said Karina.

"Cos we do. Yeah?" Shay glanced at me for confirmation, and I beamed and nodded. I could see Karina was cross as hornets and didn't want Shay sitting with us, but it wasn't like her and me had sworn eternal friendship. We hadn't sworn any sort of friendship. We'd just drifted together out of convenience, cos being together had seemed better than being on our own. Maybe the three of us could form a gang. The Sugar and Spice gang!

It was a cosy idea, but I think I already knew that Shay wasn't a cosy sort of person.

We had two lots of homework that night: French and biology. I'm not terribly good at French, but I am good at biology! I love to find out about the body and the way it works, even though some of it is gruesome. The intestines, for example. All those metres of tubing, all pulsating away like crazy, gulping and squeeeeeeeeeezing, like a big sausage machine, as they move stuff along. It's really pretty disgusting if you stop and think about it. I mean, if all the time you're imagining to yourself what's going on inside you, all the gulping and the squeeeeeeeeeezing and the sausage-making. After we'd learnt about it that morning I'd looked at Brett Thomas and wanted to giggle. The thought of Brett Thomas's innards! All churning about. Slurping and slopping and squirming like maggots. Ugh. Yuck. Totally gross!

441

I said this to Karina and she squealed at me to shut up. She said if that was what went on inside us, she'd rather not know. But in its way it is actually quite fascinating, and especially if you're thinking that maybe one day you'll become a doctor.

Not that I was; not any more. People like me don't get to be doctors. Still, it didn't stop me being interested, and I'd been looking forward all afternoon to drawing my picture of the human digestive tract, which was what Mrs Winslow had set us. I sat down at the kitchen table with my felt-tip pens and began carefully to copy out the picture from the sheet she'd given us.

First there was the stomach, looking like a set of bagpipes. I did the stomach in yellow, cos I knew it was full of acid and yellow seemed like the right colour. Then a wiggly bit, which was the *duodenum*, which became the *jejunum*, which became the *ileum*, which all together made up the *small intestine*. I did those in green, as I thought that all the food that had been churned up by the acid might probably turn a bit greenish as it slurped on its way.

Next there came the *large intestine*, looping up one side and down the other, with a band across the middle. I made the large intestine big and bulgy, and I used a brown felt-tip pen for filling it in.

By now, my drawing was looking quite colourful; I just needed to say what everything was. I found a spider-tip pen and began to draw arrows and print duodenum and jejunum in tiny neat letters, being sure to check that I had the spelling right.

I'd just drawn an arrow pointing to the up bit of the large intestine and was about to write *ascending colon* when the kitchen door crashed open and Sammy burst through, shrieking, followed by Lisa and Kez. You'll never guess what! He went slamming straight into me, so that my pen scraped across the page, tearing up the paper and leaving a great furrow right through the middle of my beautiful drawing that I'd taken such care over. Oh, I was so angry! I bellowed at him.

"You stupid blithering idiot! Look what you've done!"

Sammy stopped and put his thumb in his mouth.

"*Look!*" I snatched up the page and thrust it in his face. "See that? See what you've done? You've gone and ruined it! You stupid, thoughtless—"

"What's the matter?" said Mum, appearing at the door.

443

Sammy at once ran to her, sobbing. "What have you done to him?"

I said, "It's not what I've done, it's what he's done!"

"She yelled at him," said Lisa.

"Poor little mite! You've scared the life out of him."

"But he's ruined it! He's ruined my homework!" I was almost sobbing myself. My lovely intestines! I'd worked so hard at them. "It's taken me ages!"

"I'm sure he didn't do it on purpose," said Mum.

"They shouldn't be allowed out here when I'm doing my homework! Why can't they stay in the other room and watch television?"

"Don't want to watch television!" screeched Lisa.

"We've already watched it," said Kez.

Mum was peering over my shoulder at my poor mangled drawing. "Oh, dear! What a shame. Can't you do it again?"

"No! I haven't got time, I've still got my French to do."

"Why not use that one?" Mum nodded at the sheet Mrs Winslow had given us. "Why not just cut it out and stick in on the page, and then colour it?"

"Cos we're supposed to *copy* it!"

"That's a bit daft," said Mum. "That's a proper drawing, that is. Better than anything you could do. What's the point wasting your time trying to copy it?"

I said, "Why ask me?" And I crumpled up my spoilt drawing and hurled it across the room. I knew that Mum

was right, the drawing on the printed sheet was oceans better than the one I'd done, even with all my lovely bright colours and my little arrows. How should I know why Mrs Winslow wanted us to copy it? All I knew was that I'd enjoyed doing it and I'd been really pleased with the result and secretly hoping that perhaps I might get an A, or even an A+, and now it was totally ruined and I just felt *sick*.

"I'll take him away," said Mum. "Come on, Sammy! You come with your mum. Leave Ruth to get on with her studies."

I said, "It doesn't matter now, I've given up. I'm not going to bother any more."

"Well, I must say," said Mum, "I've never really seen why they have to give you all this extra work. You're at school seven hours a day. Isn't that enough?"

Mum went off, taking Sammy and the Terrible Two with her. I pulled my French book out of my bag and looked at it and put it back again. I'd given up! I wasn't bothering any more. Other people didn't bother; why should I? Nobody ever got into trouble. Now and again the teachers would mutter about "staying after school", but nothing ever came of it. I thought probably they preferred it if they didn't have too much homework to mark. I wasn't ever going to bother with homework again! What was the point, if I was just going to end up in Tesco's? I bet they'd never asked Mum if she'd got any GCSEs, and *she* was allowed to work on the *checkout*. I could do that! No problem. In any case, as Brett Thomas had said, only geeks did homework. I was through with being a geek!

Next day I told Karina that I wasn't bothering with homework any more. Karina said that she was glad. She said it was a great relief.

"It's not good if you keep getting things read out and teachers saying all the time how you've written loads more than anyone else and how you're just so *brilliant* and *wonderful* and—"

"No one's ever said I'm brilliant and wonderful!"

"No, but they keep going on about you... listen to

what *Ruth's* written, look what *Ruth's* done. It's not good," said Karina. "It just puts everyone's back up."

"Well, look at this," I said, and I showed her what I'd written for Mr Kirk. Karina read it and giggled.

"Hey!" She turned and grabbed at someone. It was a girl called Dulcie Tucker who was in Millie's gang. "Listen to what Ruth's written for Mr Kirk... *My family is so boring that I can't think of anything to say about them!*"

"Yeah. Right on," said Dulcie, like she couldn't have cared less.

I snatched the page back from Karina. "You don't have to go telling everyone," I said.

"Why not? It's funny! I hope he reads it out."

"So anyway, what about you?" I said. "Are you still going to do homework?"

Karina pulled a face. "I've got to. My dad'd bash me if I didn't."

"How would he know?" The teachers never sent notes home, or asked to speak to your parents. Not that I'd ever heard.

"He checks on me," said Karina. "He says he pays all

these huge amounts of tax so that I can get an education and he's going to make sure that I get one."

"Some hope at this school," I muttered.

"Yeah, well, I don't want one anyhow," said Karina. "Soon as I can, I'm getting out."

I asked her what she was going to do, but she said she didn't know.

"Don't know, don't care. Just so long as I can leave this dump."

I wondered what I'd do if my dad were like Karina's. Well, or my mum, since my dad doesn't pay any tax. He's on disability allowance. Mum pays! She's always going on about it. "All this money they take off me." Didn't she realise it was for me to get an education?

"Besides," said Karina, "it doesn't matter about me, cos I don't get up people's noses like you do."

"I don't mean to," I said.

"I know you don't *mean* to, but that's how it comes across. Always getting things right and knowing all the answers and sticking your hand up and doing your homework and – just everything!"

Humbly, I said, "I'll try and stop."

"Well, it'd be good," said Karina. "Cos then people wouldn't hate you quite so much and we might be able to join Amie Phillips and her lot. I could probably join them right now, if I wanted, but I wouldn't do it without you. It'd be nicer if we were together, wouldn't it?"

I said that it would, but really and truly I wasn't sure that I wanted to join Amie Phillips' lot. They were all remnants: all the leftovers that no one else wanted.

I didn't want to be a remnant! At the beginning of term I might have been desperate enough, but now there was Shay, as well as Karina, and I didn't feel quite so alone. I wasn't sure whether I could actually call Shay my friend, but she always chose to sit next to me, and sometimes she hung out with us in the playground (much to Karina's disgust). I don't know if she was jealous, or what, but she really didn't like Shay.

She used to hiss at me, like an angry snake. "Look at her! She's coming over – she's going to tag on to us. Get rid of her! Tell her to go away, we don't want her!"

I might have said, "Tell her yourself," but I didn't, just in case she took me up on it. I didn't want Shay to go away, I liked having her around – it made me feel safe and protected. I knew that all the time Shay was there, nobody would pick on me. Maybe after a bit, if I stopped showing off and sticking my hand up and being too much of a smart mouth, school might almost become bearable. Well, that's what I liked to think.

That weekend I helped Mum round the flat and played with Sammy and watched some television and didn't do any homework at all. Mum never said anything, like, "Don't you have any homework to do?" She never asked me about school; she was too busy working and looking after Dad. Dad sometimes asked me. He'd say, "How's school, then?" but I don't think he really wanted me to tell him. I usually just said, "'s OK," and left it at that.

I never saw Karina out of school. I could have done, cos she didn't live all that far away, but we weren't real proper friends. Not like me and Millie had been, or me and Mariam. I bumped into Mariam that weekend, when I went up the corner shop to get Dad's paper. We almost never spoke at school, but if we met outside we'd stop and chat. Mariam told me that her mum and dad were sending her away to live with her auntie. I said, "Oh, that's awful! Why are they doing that?" I mean, I love my aunties, all three of them, but I couldn't bear not to be with my mum and dad. I'd even miss Sammy and the Terrible Two!

I was all ready to sympathise, when Mariam said she was glad she was going to live with her auntie because it meant she wouldn't have to go to Parkfield any more. She said she'd be going to a much nicer school where there weren't any gangs and she wouldn't be bullied. I hadn't realised that she'd been bullied. I told her about Brett Thomas chucking my lunch across the playground, and the two Js calling me names, and she said that she hadn't realised that, either.

"If we'd all stuck together," I said, "it would've been all right."

Mariam told me that she'd only joined a gang because they'd threatened her.

"They said if I didn't join them I'd be one of the enemy... they said bad things would happen to me."

She promised that she'd call round when she came home for the half-term break, and we wished each other good luck. I went on my way feeling really depressed, even though I was happy for Mariam that she was going to a nicer school. She was such a sweet, gentle person. Not like me, always muttering cross things and frightening my poor little  brother and yelling at my sisters. I'd never heard Mariam yell, and I really hated the thought of her being bullied all this time and me knowing nothing about it. I did envy her, though, getting away from Krapfilled High.

On Monday, we had some of our homework back from the week before. I don't think Mr Abrahams even noticed that I hadn't done my French, but Mrs Winslow seemed a bit upset about not having any biology from me. She said, "I'm surprised at you, Ruth! What happened?" I mumbled something about my brother going and ruining my picture of the intestines and she said that was a pity but she really would like me to try and do it.

"It seems such a shame when your work is so good!"

Karina jabbed me with her elbow and pulled down the corners of her mouth. She herself had stuck the printed drawing into her biology book, like Mum had suggested I should do. At the  bottom Mrs Winslow had written, "This is not what I asked for." But she didn't suggest that Karina should do it again.

Next day, Mr Kirk handed back our essays on "My Family". I waited with bated breath to hear whether he'd read out what I'd written. I *wanted* him to read it out, to show people that I wasn't being a goody-goody any more. But he didn't! He didn't even comment. Not out loud. He commented on all the other essays that people had written. (*Some* people. A few people. There were only about ten.)

"Karina, I do think it would be rather nice if you were to consult a dictionary occasionally. All this fancy spelling makes it rather difficult to interpret. Or were you attempting a foreign language?"

"English," said Karina. (She has *no* sense of humour.)

"Really? Well, you had me fooled!" said Mr Kirk. "Shayanne... Your mother is a vampire and your father is the Invisible Man. Yes! Well. What can one say?" He

453

tossed a wodge of pages on to Shay's desk. I stared at them in amazement. Shay's writing was very big and black and angry-looking. It was so big she hardly got more than about six words on a page. "Next time, perhaps, you might try using up a few less trees."

Shay said, "It all comes from sustainable sources."

"That may be, but the school still has to pay for the paper, so just concentrate on being a bit more economical. *Ruth*." He held out my one page; I took it. "This is disappointing. Please don't do it again."

That was all he said. I felt my cheeks burn just as fiercely as they had last week when he'd read out about the moon being a banana and the flocks of sheep. I felt so ashamed! Karina instantly slewed round in her desk and hissed, "Did you see what she wrote? *My family is so boring I can't think of anything to write about them!*"

She didn't impress anyone; the two Js just stared, stonily. And Shay was frowning. She was looking really ferocious. What was she so angry about? Who was she so angry *with*? I thought at first it was with Mr Kirk, because of what he'd said about using up less trees, but Shay never cared a fig what anyone said, least of all teachers. It was me! I was the one she was angry with! She was glaring at me like daggers might suddenly come shooting out of her eyes and make straight for me. I said, "W-what's the matter?"

"You," said Shay. "You're what's the matter!"

I said, "W-why? What have I done?"

"You know what you've done!"

I said, "What, what?"

Shay said that we'd "talk later". She said, "You've gotta get a hold of yourself... you can't carry on like this."

I just hadn't the faintest idea what she was talking about.

# four

As soon as we got into the playground at break, Shay grabbed hold of me.

"OK! Time to talk."

"Bout what?" said Karina.

"Nothing to do with you! This is between me an' Ruth."

Karina tossed her head. "So what are you waiting for? Talk!"

"Excuse me," said Shay, "it happens to be private."

"Why?" I could see that Karina was working herself

up into a fit of jealousy. I could sort of understand it. Shay was a bit... well! In your face, I suppose. "What's private about it?"

"None of your business," said Shay.

Karina stuck out her lower lip. She could be really stubborn! Also, she's quite thick-skinned, like she was obviously determined to stay even though Shay had made it as plain as could be that she wasn't wanted. I'd rush off immediately if I thought I wasn't wanted; I'd be too ashamed to hang around. But Karina wouldn't budge for anyone.

"It's rude to have secrets," she said.

"Yeah? Well, it's rude to pry into other people's business. Just go away!"

"Won't!"

"You'd better," said Shay.

Karina gave a little swagger. "Or what?"

"You'll regret it, is what!"

Karina said, "Huh!" but I could tell she was starting to have second thoughts. "I could go and join Amie's lot," she said, "if I wanted."

"So join!" snapped Shay.

"I will, if you're not careful." Karina looked at me as she said it. "Is that what you want? You want me to go and join Amie's lot?"

I was beginning to feel a bit desperate. I didn't know what all this was about! "I'm sure we won't be long," I said. "Will we?" I turned, hopefully, to Shay, who still had hold of me. "We won't be long?"

"Dunno," said Shay. "Depends." She glared at Karina. "If some people would just let us get on with it—"

"Oh, don't worry! I'm going," said Karina. "I wouldn't stay here if you went on your bended knees and begged me!" And she flounced off across the playground to where Amie Phillips and her cronies were standing in a little huddle.

I wondered whether I'd mind if Karina joined them. I couldn't decide. I was too busy worrying about Shay and what she wanted to talk to me about. Why was she being so fierce? And what was so private?

"Right!" She gave me a little push. "What was all that with your homework?"

Stupidly, I said, "W-what homework?"

"Yeah, well, this is it," said Shay. "*What* homework? You never did any, did you?"

"I d-did my English," I said.

"One line! Call that an essay?"

"I couldn't think what else to write!"

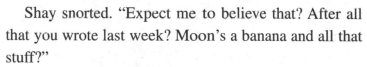

Shay snorted. "Expect me to believe that? After all that you wrote last week? Moon's a banana and all that stuff?"

I hung my head, ashamed. "That was just stupid."

"It wasn't stupid, you mongo! It was clever. That's why he read it out."

"But I don't want him to read things out!"

"Why not?"

I mumbled, "Cos it makes people hate me."

"What *people*?" Shay's voice was full of scorn. "These people?" She waved a contemptuous hand at all the various groups and huddles in the playground. "Call that lot *people*? They're just mindless blobs!"

They might have been just mindless blobs, but they still called me names and made fun of me. And what did it matter to Shay, anyhow? I hadn't noticed her being so brilliant, what with calling her mum a vampire and using up all that great wodge of paper with hardly anything written on it. She hadn't even bothered to do her French, or draw the intestines.

I said this to her and she snarled, "We're not talking about me, we're talking about you!"

"But what does it matter?" I cried. "Nobody cares! What's the point?"

"I'll *tell* you—" Shay stabbed a finger into my breast bone "—what the *point* is." Jab, stab. "The *point*—"

I went, "Ow! Stop it!" She was really hurting me.

"Well, then, just shut up," said Shay, "and listen!"

I said, "I'm listening."

"Right, then! You've got a brain. Yeah?"

I nodded, humbly. I knew I had a *bit* of brain, cos

Mrs Henson had told me so. Mrs Henson had said, if I worked hard enough I could pass exams, I could get to uni, I could be a doctor.

"So if you've got a brain, why not use it!" bellowed Shay.

I shrivelled. I did wish she wouldn't shout quite so loud.

"You want to end up like that lot?" Again, she waved a hand about the playground. "You wanna be pushed around for the rest of your life? Cos that's what'll happen. You let 'em get to you an' you'll be just another gawker like all the rest of 'em. Probably end up working in Tesco's."

I bristled at that. "What's wrong with working in Tesco's?" I wasn't going to tell her that my mum worked there.

"There isn't anything wrong with it," said Shay, "if that's what you wanna do."

"Well, maybe it is," I said.

"Yeah, and maybe it isn't," said Shay.

She had some nerve! "I don't see why you're going on at me," I muttered. "What about you?"

"Doesn't matter about me! I can look after myself. Don't see anyone pushing me around, do you?"

Humbly, I shook my head.

"So that's the difference between us. Yeah? It's why I can get away with it and you can't."

I thought, get away with what? But I sort of knew what she meant. Shay did her own thing, no matter what anyone said. When I tried doing my own thing, everyone jumped on me. What I couldn't work out was why it bothered her. Why should she care if I ended up in Tesco's? Why should I care, if it came to that? Mum was happy there. She had all her girlfriends, and they laughed and had fun. Of course it wasn't the same as being a doctor, but that was just a daydream.

"Oi!" Shay poked at me again with her finger. "You listening?"

I said, "Yes!"

"So you gonna do what I tell you?"

I sighed. "I s'ppose so."

"You better had!" said Shay.

I went back into class that day wondering how I felt about Shay bullying and bossing me. I decided that I didn't really mind. Which was strange, in a way, cos as a rule I get a bit stroppy if anyone tries telling me what to do, like with Millie and Mariam we never laid down rules or bossed one another. We got on really well! But with Shay it was like she'd set herself up as my own personal bodyguard. My minder! So long as I did what she told me, I'd be safe. I know it was a bit wimpish of me, but it did feel good to have someone on my side for once.

As soon as we were sitting at our desks, Karina turned to me and hissed, "What was all that about?"

I said, "Oh! Nothing, really. Just homework."

"What d'you mean, just homework?"

I smiled; a bit shamefaced. "Shay says I ought to do it."

"Why?" Karina's eyes narrowed to slits. "What's it got to do with her? I thought you were going to stop all the goody-goody boffin stuff?"

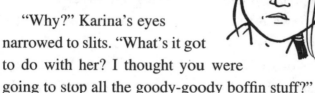

I said, "Y-yes. Well – maybe. I don't know!" I felt like a puppet, being jerked about in all different directions. "It's difficult," I said.

"You're just *weak*," said Karina. Fortunately everyone else was yelling at the top of their voice, so no one but me could hear her. "You just let her push you around! Don't blame *me* when everyone turns against you. I could join Amie's lot tomorrow, if I wanted. It's what I'll do," she said. "I will! I'll tell Amie we're not together any more."

We never had been together; not really. All the same, I hate upsetting people and I didn't want Karina to feel like I'd driven her away. I whispered, "I'll do my homework but I won't write stuff that's going to be read out."

"You'd just better *not*," said Karina.

"Well, I won't," I said. "Least, I'll try not to."

I added that bit to myself, very low, so Karina couldn't hear. I wasn't sure, if Mr Kirk set us an essay on something really interesting, that I'd be able to stop myself. Sometimes when I start writing I get, like, carried away, and that's when the flocks of sheep start appearing, and moons start turning into bananas.

There wasn't any problem with that night's homework cos all we'd had to do for Mr Kirk was read ten pages of *The Diary of Anne Frank*, and I'd already done that. I'd not only read ten pages, I'd read the whole book. I'd sat up in bed and finished it by torchlight, while the Terrible Two grunted and groaned and snuffled in their sleep. It was so funny in places, and so sad in others, that I couldn't tear myself away from it.

Even when I'd come to the end, I couldn't get to sleep for thinking about it. Imagining how it must have been, when the Nazis came. Imagining how it might have been, if they hadn't come. If Anne Frank had grown up and got married and had children of her own.

Karina said it was just utterly boring and she didn't know what people saw in it. According to Karina, if Anne Frank hadn't been discovered by the Nazis and sent to a concentration camp, no one would ever have bothered reading her stupid diary.

It was when Karina said things like that that I knew we couldn't ever be friends. I knew that if Mr Kirk had set us an essay on Anne Frank, I'd have dashed off ten pages of my own, just like that, and wouldn't have cared if Karina *had* gone off to join Amie Phillips. However, all we had for homework that night was maths. Oh, dear! I really have to concentrate *so* hard on maths. But I decided that I would. I'd make a determined effort, because dear Mrs Saeed never embarrassed me, or singled me out, even when I did get good marks. Also, of course, Shay would be pleased with me. I wanted Shay to be pleased. At any rate, I certainly didn't want her to be cross!

So after tea I cleared a space on the kitchen table and sat down with my maths book and started to concentrate. It was fractions, at which I'm quite hopeless. Especially *decimal* fractions. But I remembered Mrs Henson telling me: "You can do it, Ruth, if you just put your mind to it." That was fractions, too. I seem to have a big black hole in my brain when it comes to numbers. But I could do it!

I chewed the top of my pen. 0.35 + 0.712 + 0.9... I couldn't even use a calculator, cos my dear little brother had gone and ruined the only one we had. He'd dropped it in the bath! Can you imagine? Mum said she'd see if there was another one on offer somewhere, like with a packet of crisps or something, but in the meantime I was having to work everything out *on paper*. In fact, that was what we were supposed to do anyway, but I bet nobody else did.

I'd just worked out the answer and was feeling rather pleased with myself, when Mum came bursting into the kitchen and cried, "Ruth, I've just remembered... it's Lisa's Home Bake day tomorrow and I promised her I'd make something for her to take in. I'd clean forgotten about it! Just pop down the corner shop, there's a good girl, and get me some pastry. I haven't got time to make any."

*I* hadn't got time to go down the corner shop. "I'm doing my homework!" I said.

"Oh, now, come on, it'll only take you five minutes!"

"So why can't Lisa go?" She was the one that wanted the stupid pie, not me.

"I'm not sending a nine year old out in the dark. Just get yourself down there and stop being so stroppy."

I went off, grumbling. How ridiculous, going to the corner shop for pastry when I had a mum who worked in Tesco's! Needless to say, there was a queue a mile long at the checkout. There would be, wouldn't there?

Everyone picking up fish fingers and TV dinners on their way home from work. Angrily I snatched a packet of pastry out of the freezer and stamped about at the back of the queue. Why did Mum do this to me? What about my education? I knew she had a lot to cope with, what with working all day and having to look after Dad, not to mention Sammy and the Terrible Two. But I was trying to do my maths homework!

Anyway, guess what? When I finally raced home with the pastry, it was THE WRONG SORT. She hadn't wanted *frozen* pastry.

"How can I roll it out if it's frozen?"

She sent me all the way back again. This time, for *chilled* pastry.

"Short crust, mind, not puff!"

So then I had a bit of an argument with the man at the checkout cos he said the frozen pastry wasn't properly frozen any more and he didn't want to take it back. But Mum hadn't given me any more money and I was practically in tears, cos I just couldn't stand the thought of going all the way home and all the way back for the second time, but in the end a nice lady standing behind me said it was all right, she'd take the frozen stuff, and I was just *so* grateful to her.

"That's better," said Mum, when I'd panted up six flights of stairs and back into the kitchen. (The reason I'd had to pant up the stairs was cos the lifts weren't working. *Again*.)

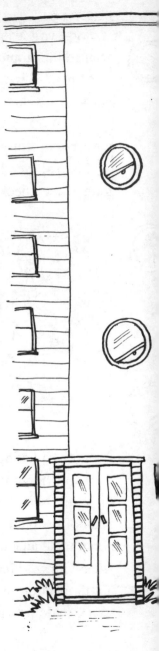

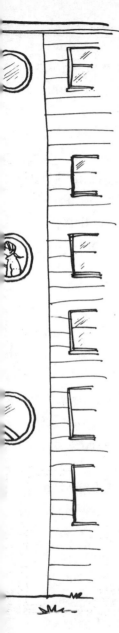

"Now, look, just pop across the hall and ask Mrs Kenny if she's got a tin of cherries I could have. Here! You can give her this in exchange." She tossed a tin of fruit salad at me. "Go on! I can't make a pie out of fruit salad."

I *hate* having to go and ask Mrs Kenny for things. Mum's always making me do it. I just find it so degrading! Anyway, Mrs Kenny didn't have a tin of cherries. I told her Mum wanted to make a pie for Lisa's Home Bake, so she gave me some sticks of rhubarb instead. I loathe rhubarb; so does Lisa. Tee hee! I should care. Mum did, though. She said, "What's this? Rhubarb? That's no good! I wanted cherries. You know Lisa won't eat rhubarb!"

"That's all she had," I said.

Mum made an impatient tutting sound, like it was my fault Mrs Kenny didn't have spare tins of cherries in her cupboard. Why didn't Mum, if it came to that? What's the point of working in Tesco's if you can't stock up with things?

"We'll have to cook it," said Mum. "Get me a saucepan. Well, go on! Don't just stand there. Do something!"

So before I know it, I'm over at the sink scrubbing rhubarb and chopping it into little pieces and pulling off the stringy bits, and dumping it in the pan and showering sugar over it.

"Not that much!" screamed Mum. "God in heaven, your dad won't have any left for his tea!"

I sometimes think that my mum is *seriously* disorganised. Me, myself, I like things to be orderly. I'm always tidying my desk and making out lists of Things to be Done. But it seems like I'm the only one in my family.

After I'd helped with the pie and done the washing up, including all the stuff left over from earlier, Mum said we might as well get the lunch-boxes ready for tomorrow.

"Save the rush in the morning."

I said, "*Mu-u-um*, I'm trying to do my homework!"

"Oh, very well," said Mum. "If you don't want to help. As if I don't have enough to do! I'd *hoped* to be able to put my feet up at some stage."

I looked at Mum and she did look frazzled. I know it wears her out, all the work she has to do. So we made up the lunch-boxes and I did some more washing up, and then, because poor Mum was obviously worn out, I told her to go and sit down and I'd make her a cup of tea; but when I took the tea into the other room I found her struggling with Dad's oxygen cylinder, trying to

drag it out from the bedroom. I ran straight over to help her. Dad's oxygen cylinder, which he has to use if his breathing gets extra bad, is really really heavy. Between us, we managed to lug it across the hall and into the lounge. We were both panting, though not as much as Dad. I suppose I ought to be used to it by now, but I'm always secretly terrified that maybe one day he just won't be able to breathe at all.

Naturally, with all the racket going on, Sammy woke up. He came pattering out in his pyjamas, wanting to know what was happening. Seconds later, the Terrible Two appeared. By the time I'd got them all back to bed, and Dad was breathing better with his oxygen mask, it was nearly ten o'clock and I was just feeling too tired to concentrate on fractions. The homework had to be handed in next morning. What was I going to tell Shay???

# Secret Writings of Shayanne Sugar

Today I told that Karina girl where to get off. Some people just can't take a hint, I had to yell at her in the end. Then you should have seen her go! But really she must have a hide like an elephant. You tell a person to shove off, you can't make it much plainer.

SHOVE OFF YOU DORK YOU'RE NOT WANTED!

She's still hanging around, but I reckon she's starting to get the message. If she hasn't gone by the end of next week — well! She'll get what's coming to her.

Had a long talk with Spice. Told her to pull her finger out and stop trying to bring herself down to the same level as the rest of the morons. What's it matter if they call her names? Names can't hurt you.

Anyway, they won't be calling her anything so long as I'm here. Anyone calls her names while I'm there, they'll get my fist in their gob. Yeah, and that includes Brett Thomas. What a gorilla! And that stupid

Joolyer and her sappy little friend. Prinking and prancing. I told Spice, they're just a load of dumbos. She's gotta get her act together! She said she would, but she's not gotta lotta bottle. God knows what'll happen when I'm not there. Still, that's her problem. She'll have to learn to fight her own battles — I can't be around all the time.

I dunno why I bother, really. What's it to me if she ends up like the rest of 'em? Be easier just to let her get on with it. She's nothing to me! This time next year I won't even remember who she was. But I just CAN'T STAND IT when a load of mindless blobs go round guzzling and slurping and GOBBLING UP anyone that's got a bit of brain. It DISGUSTS me, to tell the truth. That's why the Karina girl has gotta go. Not just cos she's in the way, though she is in the way (but not for long. I got her number!) but because

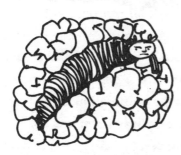

she's like a leech. Except instead of sucking blood, she sucks brain. I've watched her! She thinks it's really funny when Spice turns in one line of homework and calls it an essay. Yay! That's great! That's really amusing, that is. Another bit of brain down the toilet. If she had her way, she wouldn't stop till she'd sucked the lot out, and then there'd be one more mindless blob cluttering the place up and thinking it's clever to be stupid.

GOD THEY MAKE ME SICK.

The Vampire's gone off for three days on a training course. She says it's to do with cosmetics. Oh, yeah? More likely a course on How to Put your Fangs to Good Use, or How to Avoid Garlic. In other words, a vampire convention! That's what I reckon. There'll be all these other vampires there, all sharpening their fangs and thirsting for fresh glasses of blood. I asked her if she was taking her coffin with her and she said, "What on earth are you talking about?" She said I had a very morbid sense of humour. "If it is a sense of humour. Honestly, Shay! Do you have to be so ghoulish?"

Yup! I have to be. It's the only way I can get by.

The Vampire went off yesterday. She thinks the Invisible Man is then here keeping an eye on me, but if he is I can't see him.

"Hi, Dad! You there? Anyone at ho-o-o-o-me?"

No reply. I don't think he came back last night. At any rate, his bed wasn't slept in. I've checked the answerphone, but there's no messages. Nothing on the email. I've tried ringing his mobile, I've rung it several times, but it always seems to be switched off. Maybe he's gone on a training course, too. How would the Vampire know? They never talk.

I remember the first time they left me, I was scared. I stayed in my bedroom and cried. Boo hoo! So pathetic. Course, I was only nine years old. I couldn't give a toss now. What do I care?

It's odd he hasn't even left a message. I s'ppose he's all right. I s'ppose he hasn't had a car crash or anything. Nah! Course he hasn't. The police would have been round. It's what they do, they come and tell you. He probably thinks the Vampire's here. He thinks she's here, she thinks he's here.

GOD THEY'RE SO USELESS!

# five

I desperately didn't want to wake up next morning.
Mum had to come and bawl at me three times. *"Ruth,
I'm not telling you again!* Get out of that bed! And get
your sisters up. Do you want to be late for school?"

I didn't just want to be late. Being late wasn't
enough. I didn't want to go *at all*. I was just so scared
that Shay was going to be angry with me! It wasn't that
I thought she'd bash me or anything. But she'd give me
that *look*, like I was lower than an earthworm. Like she
didn't know why she'd ever bothered.

"Just a mindless blob!"

Shay despised mindless blobs. I didn't want to be one of them. I didn't want her to despise me – I wanted to be someone worth bothering with!

I crept into class just as Mrs Saeed was collecting homework.

"Ruth," she said, "just in time!" And she smiled at me and held out her hand, with this really happy expression on her face. "Homework?"

I mumbled that I was sorry, but I hadn't done it. Poor Mrs Saeed! She looked so disappointed, like I'd really let her down. She said, "That's not like you, Ruth." I hung my head and didn't dare look at Shay. As I slipped into my seat, Karina nudged me, like she was gloating, and went, "Hah!"

It was like she thought she'd scored some kind of victory. I wanted to turn my back on her, but that meant I'd be facing Shay. I grabbed my rough book and shielding it with my hand, cos Karina was really nosy, she always wanted to be in on absolutely everything, I wrote, "I couldn't help it, I had to do things for my mum," and pushed it across to Shay. Would she write back to me???

She did! She wrote, "**WHAT THINGS?**"

I waited till Mrs Saeed was chalking stuff on the board, then whispered, "She made me go down the shops, *twice*, and then she made me go and borrow some rhubarb from Mrs Kenny, and then I had to help her make a pie, and then—"

Mrs Saeed turned round and I immediately stopped. I don't know why, since most everyone else was talking. People just talked all the time. If they weren't talking they were playing games or reading magazines. Brett Thomas was chucking things about the room, Dulcie Tucker was plaiting someone's hair, a girl called Livvy Briggs was painting her nails. But I guess I felt I'd already upset Mrs Saeed quite enough.

"Then what?" hissed Shay.

"Then... we had to get the lunch-boxes, and then I

did the washing up and made a cup of tea, and then Dad was taken bad and I had to help Mum with his oxygen, and then – then I had to see to the others, and – and by then it was time for bed!"

Shay went, "Hm!" She was looking at me, frowning, but not like I was an earthworm. More like I was... some kind of problem that had to be solved.

"Gotta get things sorted," she said.

At breaktime she told Karina to "Just go away and do something else. All right?" Karina turned an odd mottled colour, all red and blotchy, and shrieked, "Who d'you think you are, telling me what to do?"

Shay, in this really bored tone, said, "We've been through all this before."

"Yes, we have!" shrilled Karina.

"Well, then... just go away and leave us alone! This is between me and Spice."

I wanted to say that it didn't really matter if Karina stayed, but I knew that it did. It wasn't that we were having secrets, but it was definitely something private. Just between the two of us.

"You'll regret this!" Karina hurled it venomously over her shoulder as she stalked off. "You'll be sorry!"

It was me she was saying it to, not Shay. She knew Shay wouldn't care.

"Forget about her," said Shay. "She's rubbish! Tell me again why you couldn't do your homework."

I sighed. "Well, there was this Home Bake day at my sister's school—"

I went through it all, from the beginning. The pastry, the rhubarb, the pie, the lunch boxes, the tea, Dad's oxygen. It all sounded completely mad! Well, it did to my ears. But Shay just listened, without saying a word.

"So then it was, like, ten o'clock," I said, "and I was just too tired!"

"Not surprised," said Shay. "Anyone'd be too tired."

I looked at her, gratefully. She wasn't mad at me!

"Does this sort of thing happen all the time?" she said.

I nodded. "Most of the time. See, my dad's got this thing where he can't breathe properly. Sometimes he has to have oxygen, and the oxygen cylinder's, like, really heavy? And Mum can't manage it on her own, so I have to help her, and then there's Sammy, he's my little brother, and Kez and Lisa, they're my sisters, and I have to help her with them cos she's got Dad to take care of, plus she goes out to work all day, so—"

"This is crazy!" cried Shay. "You ought to tell your mum that you've got homework to do."

"I have! But Mum doesn't believe in homework. She says we get too much of it. It's not her fault!" I was anxious that Shay shouldn't think badly of Mum. "It's just that she's so worn out, you know? She really needs me to help her."

"Yeah, but you really need to do your homework," said Shay. "Know what?"

I said, "What?"

"You oughta go to the library and do it."

I looked at her, doubtfully. Before Karina latched on to me I used to spend every lunch break in the library (except that it's actually called the Resource Centre and has more people using the computers than reading books) but no way did I want to stay on at school at the end of the day. I didn't want to stay on at school a minute longer than I had to! I said this to Shay and she said she wasn't talking about Krapfilled's library, she was talking about the *public* library.

Surprised, I said, "Do they let you?"

"Course they let you! What d'you think?"

I didn't know. I'd only ever been to the public library once, and that was at juniors, when Mrs Henson had taken us all on a class visit and had shown us how to borrow books. I'd asked Mum if I could have a ticket, but somehow we'd never got around to doing it.

"It's not right," said Shay, "not even having half an hour to do your homework. And look, just stop worrying about that stupid Karina." She'd obviously noticed my eyes straying across the playground, to where Karina was hovering on the outskirts of Amie Phillips and her gang. "She's not good for you – she'll just drag you down."

I said, "I know, but I wouldn't want her feelings to be hurt."

"You don't actually *like* her?" said Shay.

I wrestled with my conscience. I think it was my conscience. I felt that I ought to like Karina, seeing as we'd been sort of sticking together ever since half way through last term; but I kept remembering stuff she'd said, like for instance about Anne Frank, and I knew that I didn't really.

"You don't, do you?" said Shay. "You just put up with her. But she's a blob, same as the rest of 'em, and that's what you'll be if you don't junk her. You gotta think of yourself," urged Shay. "Won't get anywhere, otherwise."

I knew that Shay was right, though I still didn't want Karina's feelings to be hurt. She deliberately went to sit somewhere else for our first class after break and I must say it was a huge relief not to have her nudging and poking at me all the time, but she wasn't sitting anywhere near Amie, and that was a bit of a worry because what would she do if Amie wouldn't let her be part of her gang? She'd be on her own and then I'd feel dreadful.

I did my best to harden my heart, but it wasn't easy. Not even when I was leaving school that afternoon and Karina came up to me and hissed, "I hate you, Ruth Spicer! The only reason I ever hung out with you in the first place was cos I felt sorry for you, cos you're such a pathetic nerd!" I suppose I should have hated her back, but I knew what she was saying wasn't true. I don't mean about me being a nerd, but about that being the reason she'd hung out with me. She'd hung out with me because we were both on our own. Nobody wanted Karina any more than they wanted me. And now I had Shay and Karina didn't have anyone and I felt quite bad about it.

Next morning she still wasn't talking to me, and she didn't seem to be talking to anyone else, either. I did so wish Amie Phillips would let her join her lot! I didn't want to have her on my conscience.

I'd thought Shay might have forgotten her idea of me going to the library. I might have known she wouldn't. She said she'd been thinking about it and she'd decided I ought to go there straight away, after school, and get started.

"No time like the present," she said, in this bossy, grown-up way.

I told her, apologetically, that I couldn't do it that day cos my dad would be worried where I was. I always get home an hour before Mum and if I didn't arrive he'd think something had happened. Dad gets very wound up. I suppose it's because of not being well. Shay said, "Phone him!"

"I can't," I said. "I haven't got a phone!"

I'd once said this to Karina and she'd stared at me like I was something that had just crawled out of a pond. "You haven't got a *mobile*?"

I was so ashamed! I thought that Shay would stare at me as well, but she just shook her head, like "Stop making excuses!" and said, "Use mine. Here!" She thrust one at me. "Ring your dad and tell him."

"What, n-now?" I said.

"Why not?" said Shay.

I thought that Dad might be snoozing, or watching telly, but I wasn't brave enough to argue. Meekly I took the phone and dialled our number. Dad sounded puzzled when I said that I was going to the library to do my homework. He said,
"Why? What's in the library?" I explained that it was somewhere you could sit and work. Dad wanted to know what was wrong with sitting at home, so I mumbled something about the library being more peaceful, cos you weren't allowed to talk in there. That was what Shay had said.

"No one's allowed to talk, so you can just get on with things."

"Well, suit yourself," said Dad. "I don't know what your mum's going to say."

We had maths and French to do that night. I was quite nervous about going to the library. I kept asking Shay what you had to do. She said, "You don't have to do anything! Just go in and sit down."

She could obviously see that I was anxious, and maybe she thought that left to myself I mightn't ever get there, so in the end she said that she'd come with me.

"Just this one time."

I was humbly grateful as I knew that Shay lived way over the other side of town and it would take her for ever to get home.

"You'll be really late getting back," I said.

"So who cares?" said Shay.

"Well... your mum?" I said. "Won't your mum be worried?"

Shay tossed her head. "My mum never worries. She's not there, anyway."

"What, you mean... when you get back the flat is empty?"

"House. Yeah. 's empty."

I couldn't imagine getting back to an empty house. Well, I couldn't imagine getting back to a *house*, cos I've always lived in a flat. And there's always been someone there. When I was little it was Mum and now, of course, there's Dad. I asked Shay if she minded and she said no, why should she? She sounded a bit aggressive, like she thought I was being nosy, or criticising the way she lived, so after that I didn't say any more. I'd learnt that if Shay wanted me to know things, she'd tell me. If she didn't, there was no point in asking. She wasn't exactly secretive. Just, like, what she did was her business and no one else's, not even mine. She was looking out for me, but we still weren't proper friends. Not like I'd been with Millie and Mariam, when we'd all exchanged confidences and knew everything there was to know about each other.

Anyway, I was really glad that Shay had come with me as the library is this huge, important-looking building with great wide steps going up to it and a big green dome on top, so that if I'd been on my own I'd probably just have turned round and run away. But Shay marched in there as

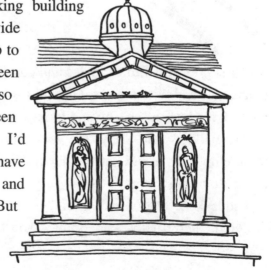

487

bold as could be, with me creeping behind her, and nobody stopped us or asked us what we thought we were doing. Shay consulted a board which said *Ground Floor, 1ˢᵗ Floor, 2ⁿᵈ Floor*, etc.

"Children's," she said. "You don't want that! It'll be full of kids. We'll go up to the Adults."

I wasn't sure that I wanted to go up to the Adults, but she didn't give me any choice, just dragged me on to the escalator.

The first floor was full of tables and chairs, and racks of magazines and newspapers. Grown-ups were sitting all around, reading or writing and looking solemn.

"This'll do," said Shay. She very firmly led me over to an empty table and sat me down. "There! Now you can get on with things."

I squeaked, "You're not going?"

"Gotta get back," said Shay. "You'll be all right here."

And she waltzed off to the escalator, leaving me on my own. It was a really bad moment. I was still expecting someone to come over and tell me that I wasn't allowed in the library all by myself, without a grown-up, and that I must go away *immediately*, but nobody did. Nobody took any notice of me at all. After a while I started to relax and concentrate on my homework, and oh, it was so lovely sitting there! I'd never been anywhere without noise or bustle. Without music or the telly, or Mum nagging at me to do things, or Sammy and the Terrible Two roaring in and out. I mean, just at first it was, like, a bit weird; I kept listening to the silence and wondering what was wrong, but once I'd got used to it I thought that this was how

I'd like to live. I'd have one room all of my own, with a table and chair and lots of bookshelves, where no one could come in without being invited, or at any rate asking permission. In other words, it would be totally, utterly and completely PRIVATE. And I'd get all my homework done with no trouble at all. Even maths. Even decimal fractions. Hooray!

Mum wasn't too pleased when I got home. She said, "Where have you been?"

I said, "In the library! I told Dad, I—"

"I know you've been *in the library*, but what for?"

"Doing my homework! It's quiet in there, I can get on with things."

Mum said, "I could've done with you getting on with a few things here!" She said how was Dad expected to cope, all by himself, when the Terrible Two got back and I wasn't there? "Seems to me your dad's health is more important than your homework! Who told you to go to the library, anyway?"

I said, "A girl at school."

"What girl?"

"New girl. Shay. She said the library was a good place to work in, and it is, cos I've done *all* my homework," I said, proudly, "and now I can help you!"

"Bit late for that," grumbled Mum, but she agreed that I could go to the library if I had to, so long as I was home by quarter to five. She still wasn't happy about it. She still didn't really see why I should want to go and shut myself away in "a stuffy old place like that" when I could be sitting here in the kitchen at home.

I said, "Mum, it's not stuffy! They've got computers and CDs and a coffee bar. And books, and newspapers, and—"

"Yeah, yeah," said Mum. "So who is this girl? *Shay?* What kind of a name is Shay?"

I said, "It's short for Shayanne."

"What, like she's a Red Indian or something?"

Shocked, I told Mum that people didn't refer to Red Indians any more. "They're Native Americans!" We'd learnt that in Juniors.

Mum said, "Whatever! Is that what she is?"

I said, "I don't think so."

"Well, whoever she is," said Mum, "she sounds like she's really pushing you around."

"I only do what I want to do," I said.

"Huh!" Mum obviously wasn't convinced. She said that Shay sounded like a bit of a bully. "Perhaps I'd better meet her. Why don't you ask her over?"

*Me?* Ask *Shay?*

"Well why not?" said Mum. "It's time I met some of your new friends."

"Yes, but—" Shay wasn't that sort of friend. "She lives in Westfield."

"So? If you're saying we're not grand enough for her—"

"It's not that!"

"She goes to the same school as you even if she does live in Westfield. What's she got to be snotty about?"

"She's not snotty," I said, but even as I said it, I thought to myself that I didn't actually know. I didn't actually *know* very much at all. But I did know that Westfield was posh, cos Mum always said it was. It was where Mum dreamt of moving to if ever she had a big win on the lottery. And if Westfield was posh, Ennis Road, where we lived, was the pits. How could I invite Shay to Ennis Road?

"It's been a long time since you had anyone over," said Mum.

Not since Juniors. But that had been different cos we all lived on the same estate. Millie lived in Archer Court, which was the big block of flats right opposite, and Mariam lived round the block, just five minutes away.

"Dunno how she'd get here," I said.

"Trust me," said Mum, "if they live in Westfield, they'll have a car. You ask her over for Saturday. I'll get something in for tea."

I really didn't think that Shay would want to come. I plucked up my courage and asked her in the playground

at break next day. I said,
"My mum said to invite
you to tea, Saturday, but
it's all right if you'd rather
not." I knew she wouldn't
just make an excuse, like
anyone else would. She
wouldn't pretend she was

going somewhere or had to see her nan or her auntie.
She'd say, straight out, if she didn't want to come. I was
just so surprised when she said yes!

"I'll get the Vampire to drop me off." She always
called her mum the Vampire; I didn't like to ask why.
"What time d'you want me there?"

That threw me into a fluster as I hadn't thought that
far ahead. I said, "Um... 'bout two o'clock?"

And then immediately wished I'd made it later
because what were we going to do from two o'clock
until tea time? Shay wasn't the sort of person you could
have cosy conversations with and I didn't fancy sitting
down to watch TV. I hardly ever watch telly, as a matter
of fact; only if there are hospital programmes. I like
those! Unfortunately Dad says they "turn him up" so I
can only watch if he's doing something else, which
usually he isn't.

I told Mum I'd asked Shay for two o'clock and Mum
said that was fine. "You can take the kids up the park."

"Mu-u-u-m!" I was horrified. I couldn't expect Shay to trail up the park with a bunch of snotty kids! But Shay totally astonished me, cos when she arrived and Mum said, "Well, now, how about you all getting out from under my feet for a bit?" she seemed to think it was quite a good idea.

And in fact it wasn't so bad as it at least gave us something to do. We went to the adventure playground and me and Shay sat on the swings while the others went on the kiddy slide and the roundabout and the dotty little climbing frame and kept out of our hair, except for Sammy falling over and hurting himself and bursting into loud bawling sobs, and then it was Shay who went over and picked him up and kissed him better.

"He's kind of cute," she said, as she came back.

"He's all right," I said. "But he's spoilt rotten cos he's the only boy. Are your mum and dad like that?"

"Like what?" said Shay.

"*Sexist*."

Shay said, "Dunno. I expect so. Prob'ly. Most people are."

I don't quite know what we talked about as we sat on the swings. Shay didn't ask me any questions about myself and I didn't ask any about her, cos I had this feeling she mightn't like it, plus we weren't really what I'd call friends, at any rate not yet, though I hoped that we might be one day. We certainly weren't at the stage of swapping secrets or anything like that. Mostly at school I still hung out with Karina, except when Shay decided she wanted to talk to me, and then Karina would go off in a sulk. But you can't invite someone to tea and then spend the time in total silence, so I think most probably I just burbled. It's what I do when I get embarrassed. I open my mouth and words come streaming out, all hustling and jostling and banging and bumping, and I just don't seem to have any control over what I'm saying. I mean, I didn't particularly *want* Shay knowing all my great plans for being a doctor and how Mrs Henson had told me that I could do whatever I wanted if I put my mind to it. The idea of being a doctor now struck me as utterly pathetic, and telling her about Mrs Henson just seemed like boasting.

When we got home, tea was ready. Mum had made this huge effort and bought cakes and buns and biscuits, and sausage rolls and crisps and toffee pudding. Almost like a birthday party! She'd never laid on such a spread for Millie and Mariam. We all sat round the kitchen table, including Dad, and Sammy behaved really badly, snatching at food and upsetting his drink, and nobody doing anything to stop him, so that I felt really angry.

It wasn't fair! Just because he was a boy. At one point he picked up a sausage roll and chucked it at Shay, across the table. Even Mum thought that was going a bit too far. She said, "Sammy! Stop it!" but Shay just caught the sausage roll and chucked it straight back at him.

"Well!" said Mum, beaming. "You've obviously got a brother of your own!"

"*Have* you?" I said.

Shay shook her head. "Nope!"

"Sisters?" said Mum.

"Nope."

"Only child? Oh, dear! This lot must seem like a right handful."

Mum wasn't in the least bit shy of asking questions. Not even if Shay did live in Westfield. She even asked her what her mum and dad did. Shay said that her mum was a beauty consultant and her dad ran his own company.

"Ooh! That sounds important," said Mum.

"He sells *plastic boxes*," said Shay. She said it like he was selling maggots, or drain covers.

"But his own company!" Mum was impressed, I could tell. Dad asked how many people Shay's dad employed. Shay said, "Two."

"Well – still. He's his own boss," said Dad. "No one to tell him what to do."

Before he got his emphysema, Dad used to work on the buses. He was always complaining of people telling him what to do.

After we'd finished tea, Shay thanked Mum for inviting her and said that she'd be going now. I was relieved, in a way, cos although I'd quite enjoyed her being there I couldn't think what we'd have done next. I really didn't want to take her into my bedroom. It was just such a mess, what with Kez and Lisa's stuff all over the place. I would've been too ashamed. I try very hard to keep my bit clean and tidy, but it's quite disheartening. Sometimes I'm tempted to just give up. But if we didn't go into the bedroom we'd either have to sit in the kitchen, which would be boring, or sit in the other room and watch television, which would probably also be boring. I just *so* didn't want Shay to be bored!

Mum asked her how she was getting home. "Do you want to ring your parents and tell them to come and fetch you?" Shay said no, that was OK, she could find her own way.

"But it's going to be dark any minute," said Mum. "I really think you should ring."

But Shay wouldn't. I went down to see her off, and I thought that I'd be a bit scared going back across town in the dark.

"I do it all the time," said Shay.

I was about to ask her if her mum didn't worry, when

I remembered what she'd said, that her mum never worried. I said this to Mum when I went back upstairs.

"She's very independent," I said.

"Very self-possessed," said Mum, like being self-possessed wasn't a good thing. "I just hope she wasn't angling for us to take her home."

"She wasn't," I said.

"Well, too bad if she was. It's time she learnt that we can't all afford to run cars. I'm just surprised her parents are so irresponsible. Letting a girl of that age roam about by herself! And you needn't think you're going to start doing it."

"Mum, didn't you like her?"

"Not my cup of tea. Too sure of herself by half."

"She was nice to Sammy," I said.

Grudgingly, Mum agreed that she was.

"And she thanked you for inviting her!"

"Oh, yes, she remembered her manners," said Mum. "But there's just something about her... what happened to Millie? Why aren't you seeing her any more?"

"She's got other friends," I said.

"Well." Mum sighed. "Just don't let that Shay push you around, all right? Be careful! I'm not at all sure she's a good influence."

When I'm a mum, I'll *never* say that about my children's friends.

# Secret Writings of Shayanne Sugar

The Vampire's back. So's the Invisible Man. They had a right slanging match when they discovered they'd both been away at the same time. It was like, "What is the MATTER with you? Why can't you ever comMUNICATE?"

"ME communicate? What about YOU?"

"I'd had that conference arranged for MONTHS!"

"So why the [swear words, swear words] didn't you [swear words] TELL me?"

"I did [swear words] tell you! You just never [swear words] LISTEN!"

After which we had a whole string of swear words. If I was putting little stars instead of actual words, the conversation would look like this:

**************** ******* **********!

***** ******* ****!

**** **** **************** *****!

*** *****!

There isn't any point writing the actual words. They were mostly all the same and really VERY boring. Especially when you've heard them as often as I have.

I mean, they just *do* it all the time. After a bit I shouted, at the top of my voice: "Just SHUT UP, I'm SICK OF IT!"

So then they both spun round to look at me, like, "Who's this telling us to shut up? Where has she  come from?" And then they remembered that I lived there, and that I was their daughter – well, supposedly – and the Vampire said, "You should've rung me! Why didn't you ring me?"

"Didn't think you'd be interested," I said.

She didn't like it when I said that. She did this flinching thing, like I'd made the sign of the cross or breathed garlic over her.

"Well, of course I'd have been interested!"

Dunno why. She wasn't interested before, when she was away doing something and I rang to ask what I was supposed to have for supper. She got quite stroppy and said, "Oh, for goodness' sake! Can't I even go away for one night? Just look in the fridge and help yourself!" In other words, LEAVE ME ALONE. I don't want to be PESTERED.

I didn't bother reminding her. I mean, really, why bother?

"I thought you'd be too busy," I said.

The Vampire said well, yes, she had been busy. "But you could've always rung your dad."

I told her that I'd tried. "He didn't answer."

At this the Vampire narrowed her eyes and breathed very deeply and said, "I see!" To which the Invisible Man immediately barked, "See what?"

"That you obviously had no desire to be contacted!" snarled the Vampire. "I wonder why not?"

Which set them off, all over again. I just left them to it. They're as bad as each other and it drives me nuts. I wouldn't care if they both went off and never came back. I can manage on my own. I've proved that! Course, I'd need some money, but there's plenty of stuff here I could flog. Either that, or you know what. Well, I know what! Anyone else that might be reading this, ON PAIN OF DEATH, won't have the least idea what I'm talking about. Which is fine by me! I don't intend to spell it out. There's ways; that's all I'm gonna say. I WOULD NOT GO HUNGRY! You have to look out for yourself in this world and that's what I aim to do. Gotta be prepared. I've been preparing since I was nine years old. No way am I just gonna sit in my bedroom and cry. Not again. Not ever.

They're still at it, down there. Still carrying on. Probably one day they'll split up and then they'll be quarrelling over which one's gotta be responsible for me. SHE won't wanna be, HE won't wanna be.

WHO CARES???

Went round to Spice's on Saturday for tea. We had all stuff that the Vampire won't buy. Crisps and cakes and sticky puds. Pretty cool! The Vampire says it's junk food and will make you F.A.T. She's more terrified of F.A.T than anything else. I bet she'd sooner have a brain tumour than suffer F.A.T. I'm gonna buy her a trick tape measure for her birthday, so when she measures herself, like she does practically every week, she'll think her waist's expanded by about five centimetres and then won't she SHRIEEEEEEK!

I reckon a bit of junk food would do her good – she looks like one of those wire coat hangers with clothes

hung on it. I think I'm gonna start eating junk food. I'm gonna get as fat as fat can be, so fat I can't move. I'll just, like, lie there, in a big jellified heap on the floor, and she'll keep tripping over me, until in the end she has to stop and look, and see what it is, and she'll discover that it's ME. Her DAUGHTER. Shock horror! The shame of it. That'll show her!

It was OK round Spice's. Don't think her mum likes me too much, but so what? I'm used to it. In any case, who needs to be liked? Not me! I can't stand people that creep and crawl and are willing to do just ANYTHING to gain approval.

Spice's little brother is quite cute. I guess I wouldn't mind having a brother. I wouldn't want a sister. NO THANK YOU! But a brother would be neat, so long as he was little, and then when the Vampire went off and the Invisible Man disappeared we'd be left by ourselves and I'd look out for him, see he was all right. I wouldn't ever let him go hungry, or be frightened. He'd know there was nothing to worry about so long as I was there. But fat chance of the Vampire ever having another kid! She made one BIG MISTAKE having me – she's not likely to do it again.

Dunno how Spice manages, though, not having her own space. Drive me bonkers that would. People around me all the time. Just ONE person's all I'd want. But not the Vampire or the Invisible Man. Gotta be someone that really wants me.

Yeah! SOME HOPE.

# six

On Monday, at school, Shay said to me, "Now that I've been round your place, I s'ppose you'd better come round mine."

I was quite shocked! I was really surprised that she'd want to see me out of school. It had to mean she looked on me as a real proper friend. After all, you don't invite just anyone back. It has to be someone you like.

"What d'you reckon?" She was looking at me in that way that she did, like really *piercing*. If you were someone she didn't rate, like one of the mindless blobs, it could practically shrivel you on the spot. "This Saturday? Wanna come?"

I beamed and nodded and said, "Yes, please!"

"Won't be anything special," said Shay. "Not like round your place."

She really thought my place was *special*?

"All that stuff your mum got in... won't be anything like that."

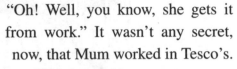

"Oh! Well, you know, she gets it from work." It wasn't any secret, now, that Mum worked in Tesco's.

"Think she'd get you some garlic?" said Shay.

I said, "*Garlic?* What'd I want garlic for?"

"Protect yourself. Told you my mum was a vampire, didn't I?"

I thought this was meant to be funny, so I laughed and waited for Shay to laugh, too. Instead, very solemnly, she said, "Best come prepared... don't s'ppose you've got a crucifix by any chance?"

Bewildered, I said, "N-no."

"Looks like it'll have to be the garlic, then... they don't like garlic.

Garlic and crucifixes. They're the only protection –
apart from a stake through the heart."

I swallowed; I was getting a bit nervous. Not that I
really thought Shay's mum was a vampire, of course I
didn't! There aren't such things as vampires. But what
sort of woman was she?

"Oh, don't worry," said Shay. "She won't get you.
Doesn't usually come out of her coffin till about five
o'clock. But you'd better bring some garlic, just in
case!"

Shay had this really wicked sense of humour. Like
really ghoulish. The only trouble was I couldn't always
be sure when she was joking and when she was being
serious. Sometimes it seemed like she was being both
together.

Anyway, I said that I'd love to go round, and we
agreed that we'd meet up at three o'clock in the
shopping centre, on Saturday afternoon, and I'd go back
with her. When I asked Mum, that evening, if it would
be all right, Mum said, "Oh! Visiting the nobs, are we?"

I didn't understand what she was talking about. I
thought she meant *knobs*, like door knobs. Apparently
she meant "nobs" as in posh people.

"Dunno what you're going to wear," said Mum. "I
can't afford to buy you new clothes."

I said, "Why can't I wear what I always wear?"

"Doesn't look like you've got much choice."

She'd noticed that when Shay came to visit, her clothes had been what Mum called "quality". I hadn't noticed cos I don't think I've got much fashion sense, but Mum has an eye for these things. She said Shay's gear was "all designer labels... ridiculous on a girl her age!" To me it had just been a black jacket and black jeans and black boots. Everything black!

"Yes, and everything costing a bomb," said Mum. "Take it from me, she didn't pick that lot up from British Home Stores. Well, I'm sorry! We just can't afford to compete."

I didn't want to compete. I knew that I couldn't, anyway; not with Shay. But Mum had gone and made me self-conscious, so that I looked at my clothes in the wardrobe, which I had to share with the Terrible Two, and for the first time thought how horrible and shabby they were. What had I worn last Saturday, when Shay came? A shapeless old coat that had once been quilted and was now sagging and flat. And *grey*. And *torn*.

Boring blue joggers, all thin and baggy from too much washing. Ancient trainers, which had never been new in the first place. Well, they obviously had for someone, but not for me. We'd got them at a jumble sale in the church hall, which is where we get most of our clothes. It had never bothered me before, but suddenly I wanted designer labels, like Shay. Or if not designer labels, at least things that were *new*, and which I'd been able to choose for myself. Not all this stinky old stuff that had been worn by other people!

In spite of what she'd said, Mum was obviously anxious for me to make a good impression cos she came home the very next evening with a brand new top that she'd got from Tesco's.

"I thought it would go quite well with your tartan skirt."

Mum was right – it did. I just wished that I could be more grateful, cos I knew that money didn't grow on trees and we had to count every penny, and the Terrible Two needed new shoes, and Mum and Dad hadn't had a holiday in simply years, but oh, I'd have so loved to have had a new skirt as well! *And* to have chosen for myself.

Mum must have sensed that I wasn't as enthusiastic as I should have been, cos quite sharply she said, "Well,

I'm sorry, it's the best I can do. If you will choose friends that are out of your league..."

But I hadn't! I hadn't chosen Shay any more than I'd chosen my new top. Shay was the one who'd done the choosing. I said this to Mum, who said, "I can't imagine what she picked on you for. You've got nothing in common! What have you got in common?"

That was something that had puzzled me. Shay was so sure of herself, so up-front, so... well! Independent. I was just plain ordinary Ruth, who wouldn't say boo to a beetle. Why had she chosen *me*?

I didn't know, but I was very glad that she had. Things were so much better, now that Shay was looking out for me. Nobody bullied me and nobody bothered me. I almost, even, quite enjoyed going to school, which meant Mum didn't have to bellow and bawl at me every morning to get out of bed. Karina was still a bit of a problem as Amie Phillips didn't seem to want anything to do with her and I felt bad when I saw her hanging out by herself, so that sometimes, when Shay wasn't around, I tried talking to her. But I always ended up wishing that I hadn't as she was so nasty and said such hateful things. Like one day it was, "I see she's still got you in her clutches, then," and another day, "Did she give you her *permission*?"

When she said that I got cross and snapped, "I don't need permission! I can talk to whoever I like."

Karina, looking sly, said, "Oh, yeah?"

I said, "Yeah!" And it was true. I didn't need Shay's permission to talk to her. I only waited till Shay wasn't around cos I wanted to avoid unpleasantness. For Karina's sake. I did it for Karina! But I was fast coming to the conclusion that it wasn't worth it. I mean, I was going out of my way to be polite and friendly and she was just, like, sneering at me all the time. I decided that I wouldn't bother any more.

On Saturday, when I set off to meet Shay in my nice new Tesco top – covered up, alas, by the same old tatty coat – Mum said, "How are you going to get back? I don't want you crossing town by yourself in the dark!"

I'd been wondering about this, but I didn't want Mum getting fussed and suddenly telling me I couldn't go, so I brightly said that Shay's mum or dad would bring me back and scooted off, quickly, towards the lift before Mum could ask any more awkward questions.

Shay was waiting for me in the shopping centre, perched on the rim of one of the big flower tubs outside WHSmith. She was wearing her black outfit again and this time I looked more closely and I saw that Mum was right, it was dead classy! And it really suited her. Mum, being a bit sniffy, had said that black was "no colour for a young girl", but it wasn't *all* black, cos the trousers had little flared bits with bright red flowers, and the top had red piping all round it, and in any case Shay didn't look like a young girl, she looked more like about fifteen. She made me feel really babyish.

"Get a load of this," she said, holding out a carrier bag. "I've been round the stores, getting stuff for our tea. What d'you reckon?"

I took one look in the bag and went, "Wow!"

"Is it enough?"

"That'd feed an army," I said.

It looked like she'd visited every food shop in the centre. There was stuff from Sainsbury's, stuff from  Marks, stuff from the cake shop in the Arcade, stuff from the chocolate shop on the top level, even stuff from the health food shop.

"Yeah, I dunno about that," said Shay. "I'm actually getting into junk food right now. It's just they had this lying about, so I took some. Oh, and look! I got this for you." She thrust her hand into the bag and pulled something out. Garlic! "Remember, if the Vampire appears, just hold it up, like this, then she can't get you."

I giggled, but a bit uncertainly. I said, "That's a joke, right?"

"Best not take any chances," said Shay.

We caught the bus to Shay's place. She lived up on the hill, just out of town, in an actual real house with its own grass outside, and a proper bit of garden at the back.

Shay said, "Stupid if you ask me! Why can't we all live in flats? Wouldn't take up nearly as much space."

I expect that is true, but I don't care! I have decided that when I am grown up and can afford it, that is when I am a doctor – if I get to pass my exams – I am going to have a house *just like Shay's*. Shay said, "It's not anything special. There's houses heaps bigger than this. This is just a titchy little thing."

Well! It may have seemed titchy to her, but I could hardly believe it. It had three floors, with different sorts of rooms on each floor, like a special room for watching

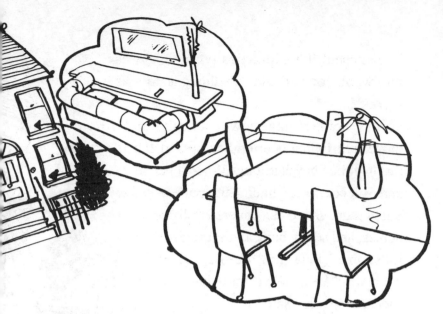

television in and a special room for eating in and a basement where the kitchen was. Shay said we'd go down to the kitchen first of all and dump our junk food ready for later. The way she said it, "our junk food", she made it sound like it was some sort of gormy dish that you might get in a restaurant. Except that I don't think it's spelt gormy, cos I think it's French. I think it might be *gourmet*.

"Bacon-flavoured crisps," said Shay, lovingly. "Chocolate-covered jelly babies... fudge ice cream. This is going to be good!"

She led the way down some steps and into this huge great room like an underground cavern. There was a long counter running down the middle and rows of pots and pans, and strings of onions hanging off the walls.

The kitchen! It was practically as big as the whole of our flat. I thought to myself how Mum would love it; she's always complaining how she can't move for tripping over bodies.

"Right." Shay laid out all her bits and pieces, her bacon-flavoured crisps and chocolate-covered jelly babies, and sticky buns and sausage rolls, in a long line across the counter. "We'll leave our junk food *here*," she said, moving a potted plant out of the way. "And now we'll go up to my room."

Shay's room was on the top floor. All the time we're going up the stairs I'm, like, looking over my shoulder in case her mum, the Vampire, might suddenly appear.

"It's OK," said Shay. "I told you, she hardly ever gets out of her coffin till five o'clock. They shrivel in the light, vampires do."

I whispered, "W-where is her coffin?"

Shay cackled and said, "In there!" pointing at a room on the second floor. "Better tiptoe or she might wake up and come and sink her fangs into us!"

I scurried like a frightened mouse up the last flight of stairs. As I scurried I couldn't help noticing how neat and clean everything was. At home we live in a state of what Mum calls "clutter". There's toys everywhere, clothes everywhere. Stuff waiting to be ironed, stuff waiting to be put away. Shoes. Socks. Dad's breakfast tray. It just all mounts up. Plus there's a big stain on the carpet where I tripped over with a bowl of soup (which I was taking in to Dad), and another, smaller stain where Sammy dropped his bread and jam and then went and trod it in, not to mention marks on the wall made by grubby fingers (mainly those belonging to the Terrible Two) and this thick oily dust, all black and treacly, that leaks in from outside and is very bad, Mum says, for Dad's emphysema and Lisa's chest. (It's why she snuffles all the time.)

There wasn't any black dust in Shay's house. There wasn't any dust at all. No stains on the carpet, no marks on the wall. No shoes or socks or piles of clothes. It was just *sooo* beautiful! It's how I shall keep my house, when I have one. It's how I *try* to keep my bit of bedroom, but without very much success, cos it's impossible to stop Kez and Lisa from trespassing.

As we reached the top landing, I hissed, "How does your mum keep it all so nice?"

I felt really ashamed when I compared what Shay's place was like with how it was at home. I didn't blame Mum for all the mess; I knew she didn't have time to keep dusting and cleaning and tidying up. But I still felt ashamed, and wondered what Shay must have thought.

"Do you help?" I said.

Shay said no. "Mrs Kelly does it."

I said, "Who's Mrs Kelly?"

"Person that comes in and cleans," said Shay. "Quick!" She grabbed me and pushed me ahead of her through the door. "Before the Vampire gets wind of us!"

I was quite astonished at the state of Shay's room. On the door there was this big angry notice: **PRIVATE. KEEP OUT. THIS MEANS YOU.** But I didn't think there was any need to have a notice; just one quick look would be enough to frighten people off. It was like a tip! It was even worse than my bit of bedroom when the Terrible Two had been on the rampage. It looked like someone had emptied bin bags full of rubbish in there. Totally *in-de-SCRIBABLE*. But if I had to – describe it, I mean – I'd say:

Tops, bottoms, shoes, socks, knickers

Coke bottles, water bottles, sweet wrappers

Knives, forks, spoons

Books, bags, papers

Pens, pencils

Magazines

CDs

And just general *junk*.

Loads of it, absolutely everywhere.

"You coming in, or what?" said Shay.

I slithered past a saucepan containing the shrivelled remains of what looked like spaghetti and waded across the floor through a sea of clothes.

"Don't worry about that lot." Shay kicked them, contemptuously, out of the way. "Sit down!"

I stared round, helplessly. Sit down where??? Every available bit of space was covered.

"Here!" Shay swept a hand across the bed and a pile of papers went flying up into the air like a flock of pigeons, then slowly settled back down again, all out of order. If, that is, they'd ever been in any order. Mine always are, but that's because I hate not being able to find stuff. It upset me, seeing so much mess and muddle.

"How do you know where anything is?" I said.

Shay said, "Don't wanna know where anything is."

"But how do you *find* things?"

"Don't wanna find things. If I wanna find things—" she stuck her toe in the middle of the papers and stirred them up again, "I put 'em somewhere. All this is just muck."

It *was* muck. I didn't know how she could live like that!

"I thought you said your mum had someone that came and did the cleaning?"

"Mrs Kelly. Yeah."

"So why doesn't she come and do your room?"

"Cos she's not allowed. No one's allowed. Not without permission." Shay marched over and yanked open the door. She jabbed a finger at the angry notice. "See? See what it says? **PRIVATE! KEEP OUT!**"

"Even your mum?" I said.

"My mum? What'd she wanna come in for?"

"Well... I don't know! Put clothes away? My mum's always coming into our room."

"Your mum's different," said Shay.

Or maybe, I thought, it was Shay's mum that was different. My mum was normal! Most people's mums went into their bedrooms. Millie's mum did. Mariam's mum did. Whoever heard of a mum being told to keep out?

"Wanna hear some music?" said Shay. She picked a CD off the floor. "What sorta music d'you like?"

"Um... anything, really," I said.

Shay unearthed a CD player from beneath a pile of clothes and slid the disc in. A weird wailing and banging filled the room.

"Yay! Freaky!" Shay jumped on to the bed, and off again. "That's cool! That's my kind of sound!"

It was pretty loud.

"Won't it wake your mum?" I said, nervously.

"Who cares?" Shay danced about the room, trampling on all the litter, some of which went *crack!* or *scrunch!* beneath her feet. I thought, this is gross! I was just so surprised at Shay, of all people.

"Ooh! Look at you!" Shay skipped round me, laughing and scrunching. "You look like a prune!" And she sucked in her cheeks so that her lips practically disappeared inside her mouth, which made me feel that I was being sour and small-minded. I was glad I hadn't admitted to her that last Christmas I'd actually asked  Mum and Dad if I could have a filing cabinet, one of those metal ones with drawers, *and a key*, so that I could put all my things away nicely in different-coloured files, with proper labels, in alphabetical order, so Kez and Lisa couldn't get at them. I had this feeling that she'd utterly despise me. (I didn't get the filing cabinet, anyway; Mum said they were too expensive and that in any case there wasn't any room.)

"Wanna see what I keep in here?" said Shay. She pulled open a drawer, where normally, I should think, people would put knickers and socks and pairs of tights, and dumped the contents on the bed beside me. I gasped; I couldn't help it. It was full of jewellery!

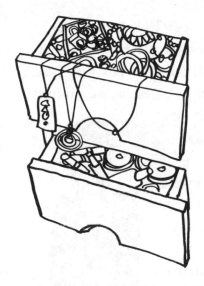

Bracelets and chains, rings, necklaces, hair slides, all winking and glittering.

"And in *here*—" she yanked out a second drawer, "I got make-up."

I could feel my eyes boggling. I had never seen so many pots and tubs and tubes and jars.

"I call it my collection," said Shay.

I remembered what she'd said about her mum being a beauty consultant. I thought perhaps that was where she'd got it from, but scornfully she said, "Nah! Got it myself, didn't I? There's loads of other stuff I could show you. I got—"

And then she stopped, and I felt this little shiver run through me. Someone was calling up the stairs.

"Shay!"

Could it be the Vampire?

Shay ran out on to the landing. "What d'you want?"

"I wanted t— Oh! Hallo. Who's this?"

Curiosity had made me a little bit brave. I'd gone pattering out behind Shay. I just couldn't resist! Shay scowled and said, "Someone from school."

"And doesn't someone from school have a name?"

I squeaked, "I'm Ruth Spicer."

"Well, hallo there, Ruth Spicer! I'm Shay's mum."

I could see why Shay called her the Vampire. Unlike Shay, who was dark-skinned, her mum was very pale, like a water lily. She just had no colour at all, and was so amazingly slender that she looked like the long white stem of a plant. She'd made up her eyes with thick black stuff on the lashes and purple on the eyelids, while her mouth and fingernails were deep blood red. I wasn't sure that I'd like her for a mum, but she was kind of fascinating, in a weird sort of way.

"Are you staying for tea?" she said.

"Yes, she is," said Shay. "I've got all the stuff."

"I saw." The Vampire tightened her blood red lips. She was obviously not pleased about something, but whether it was me staying to tea, or Shay not telling her that I was staying to tea, or something else entirely, I couldn't quite work out. "I presume," she said, "that that was what you wanted?"

"What?" said Shay.

"For me to see!"

"Dunno what you're talking about."

"Oh, come on! Everything all nicely laid out so I couldn't miss it?"

"I just laid it out ready," said Shay.

Slowly, her mum shook her head. "You do these things on purpose, don't you? Your one aim in life is to rile me. Well, all right! Go ahead, stuff yourself with artificial muck. Why should I bother?"

"You shouldn't," said Shay.

"No, well, I'm not going to. I'm off down the gym, now, then I'm meeting up with Boo and Ellie. I probably won't be back till late, but your father should be here well before then. He said he'd be home by eight. OK? Nice to meet you, Ruth. Have fun!"

"She really *hates* me eating junk food," said Shay, as we returned to her bedroom. "It drives her whacko!" She sounded quite jubilant about it, so that I began to think maybe her mum was right, and it really was her aim in life. "You don't have to look like that, prune face! She already is a whacko. Can't you tell?" She made her eyes go crossed and stuck out her tongue and waggled her fingers either side of her head. "Totally bonkers! Wanna try on some of my jewellery?"

I hesitated. I was worried by the thought of her dad not getting home till eight o'clock, because Mum was expecting me ages before then. I said apologetically to Shay that maybe I'd better leave now, while it was still light.

"I know it's silly," I said, though I didn't really think it was, "but my mum gets all fussed if I'm out late on my own."

"Won't be on your own," said Shay. "I'll come with you."

"But how will you get back?"

"Same as I did last week. Told you the Vampire wasn't the worrying sort. She doesn't care what I do – apart from eating junk food!"

I was beginning to think that Shay lived in a very peculiar sort of family. I couldn't imagine my mum and dad not caring what I did. *Or* going out and leaving me in the flat by myself. I'm always wishing that I could have a room of my own and enjoy a bit of peace and quiet, but I'd absolutely hate it if the whole flat was empty. I think, actually, I'd be a bit scared. Shay obviously wasn't scared, but maybe that was because she was used to it. It just didn't seem to bother her.

After we'd tried on some of her jewellery, and listened to another CD that she discovered by almost treading on it, we went down to the kitchen to eat our junk food. I suppose it was junk food. Shay said it was, though it seemed just ordinary to me. When we'd finished eating, I said that I'd have to go or Mum would start frothing, so Shay came with me all the way across town. I did feel a bit guilty seeing her go off again by herself, and thought that if anything happened to her it would be all my fault, but she really didn't seem to mind.

Mum opened the front door. She said, "Ah, there you are! Not before time. Did they bring you back?"

I said yes, because after all Shay *had* brought me back, and Mum then said, "I hope they saw you up in the lift?" to which I made a fluffy sort of mumbling sound.

"I hope they did!" said Mum, following me into the kitchen. "That lift's not safe this time of night – anyone could get in there with you. So what was it like? What's her mum like?"

I wasn't going to say that Shay's mum was a vampire and a whacko. I had more sense than that! I said, "She's very thin – she looks like a model." Mum sniffed and said that she could probably afford to.

"I suppose the place is dead posh?"

"Yes, but it's not as cosy as ours."

I said it partly cos I knew that it would please Mum, and partly cos it was true. Shay's place wasn't cosy, any more than Shay herself was. But I still felt flattered that she'd invited me!

# seven

The next week was half term. I didn't think, probably, that Shay would want to bother seeing me at half term, so when Millie called round and asked if I'd like to sleep over her place one night, I was quite pleased.

It was ages since Millie and I had done anything together. I could tell that Mum was pleased, too. She likes Millie and I don't think, really, that she did like Shay. She always said that she was "too knowing". I've never actually understood this, as I wouldn't have thought it would be possible to be *too* knowing. I'd have thought the more you knew, the better. But Mum obviously felt it was a bad thing, maybe because she thought Shay knew things she ought not to know, like grown-up type things, whereas Millie (Mum said) was "natural and unspoilt". I dunno! Just because Millie lived round the corner and wore the sort of clothes that Mum considered "suitable". She didn't consider Shay's clothes suitable. It really irritated her, Shay going round in designer labels. She kept on and on about it.

"Totally ridiculous! A girl that age."

So when I asked if it was OK for me to spend the night with Millie she said yes without any hesitation, even though she'd been hinting that it would be nice, now it was half term, if I could stay in and keep an eye on the kids for a change, while she went out. Dad would still have been there, cos Dad hasn't left the flat for I don't know how long, but Mum would never leave him on his own all evening with Sammy and the Terrible Two. I knew she'd been looking forward to having some time off and I thought perhaps I was being selfish, wanting to go to Millie's. But Mum seemed really keen.

"Maybe you'll get back together again. I'd far rather you had Millie as a friend than that Shay."

It was fun, being round at Millie's. For a little while it was almost like we were back at Juniors again, giggling together and sharing secrets. But Mariam had been with us then; it didn't seem the same without her.

It had always been the three of us. Millie said she'd called round Mariam's place and hadn't been able to get any reply.

"Someone said they'd moved."

I said, "*All* of them?"

"It's what they said."

"I thought it was just Mariam! So she could go to another school."

"I'm just telling you what I was told," said Millie.

I twizzled my toes under the duvet. (We were lying in bed at the time.) "Wish I could go to another school! Don't you? Wouldn't you like to go somewhere else? If you could choose."

"Dunno." Millie shrugged. "Krapfilled's OK."

"I think it's horrible," I said.

"That's cos you don't join in."

"Nobody ever asks me!" I said.

"So whose fault's that?" Millie rolled over to look at me. She propped herself on an elbow. "You go round making like you're so *supeeeeeerior—*"

I was indignant. "I do not!"

"You do. You just don't realise you're doing it."

I couldn't think what to say to that. I muttered that I didn't *feel* superior.

"It's the way you come across," said Millie. "Specially now you're hanging out with that Shayanne Sugar. She's really freaky!"

"She's my friend," I said.

"Yeah? Sooner you than me!"

Growing desperate, I said, "I only started going round with Shay cos there wasn't anyone else. Cos you and Mariam were both in gangs. I'd heaps rather you and me could still be friends!"

"We can be," said Millie. "Out of school."

"Why not in school?"

"You know why not in school!"

"Because of *gangs*," I said. "I hate gangs! I just hate them!"

"Well, there you go," said Millie.

I knew, then, that me and Millie could never get back together again. We could never be proper best friends.

"Gangs make people stupid," I said. "They make people do things they don't want to do. They make them all *follow my leader*. I couldn't ever belong to a gang!"

"You know your trouble?" said Millie. "You just don't try. You go to a new place, you gotta learn to fit in. Otherwise you'll just be, like, an outsider all the time."

It's what I was: an outsider. But at least I had Shay!

"How about we meet up again tomorrow?" said Millie, as she walked back with me through the estate the next day. "I'll call round... eleven o'clock. We'll do something. OK?"

I said OK, thinking that even just seeing her out of school was better than not seeing her at all, but then, quite suddenly, the following morning when I was least expecting it, I got this phone call from Shay.

"Hi, Spice! What you up to?"

I said, "Nothing very much."

"Me neither. Wanna meet? Shopping centre, same place as before? See you in half an hour. Don't be late!"

I forgot all about Millie. I said to Dad that I was going to meet someone in the shopping centre, and was about to go whizzing off when the Terrible Two started up, wanting to come with me. I told them that they couldn't.

"I'm meeting a friend."

"You're meeting *her*! You're meeting that girl!"

I said, "What *girl*?"

"That Shay person!"

I said, "So what if I am?"

"Mum doesn't like you seeing her," said Lisa, all virtuous.

"No, an' you're s'pposed to be looking after us," whined Kez.

"You never take us anywhere!"

"Who'd want to?" I said. I slammed the front door behind me and scooted off to the lift before Dad could find enough breath to tell me I couldn't go.

It wasn't till I got off the bus at the shopping centre and saw the hands of the big clock pointing to eleven that I remembered... Millie was supposed to be calling round! For just a moment I felt a pang of guilt, but then I reminded myself that Millie wasn't really, properly, my friend any more. When we were in school she hardly ever spoke to me. What kind of friend was that? Shay was the one who was my friend. She was the one who looked out for me and made it OK for me to do my homework and not get bullied or picked on if it was read out in class. I didn't care any more about Millie. She didn't stick up for me. Let her go round with her stupid gang, if that was what she wanted.

On my way in to the centre I passed a girl from school. Varya. She was with her mum – well, I suppose it was her mum. She smiled at me and said hallo, and I said hallo back, and as I did so I suddenly realised that it was the *very first time* I'd ever spoken to her. She mostly kept to herself and for some reason nobody ever bothered her. I'd always thought she seemed quite an interesting sort of person, but she didn't speak very much English and I was too shy to go and talk to her because how would we manage to communicate? But that day in the shopping centre she was, like, really friendly, like really pleased to see me, and her mum was, too, smiling and nodding as we passed, so that I went on my way feeling quite bubbly.

Shay was already there and waiting for me. I broke into a trot when I saw her.

"Sorry I'm late!"

"You're not late. I was early. *She* brought me."

"The Va—" Hastily, I corrected myself. "Your mum?"

"*The Vampire*. Yeah! She dropped me off. What shall we do? Wanna go and mooch round Sander's?"

Sander's is this big department store, which is brilliant for mooching as parts of it are like street markets with racks and racks of clothes, and one entire floor which is called The Bazaar, where you can find just about anything you could ever dream of. Shay said, "Let's go to Jewellery." She led the way and I followed. Sander's is *so* enormous that left to myself I would most probably panic and get lost, but Shay obviously knew her way around.

"Jewellery's my favourite," she said. "This is where I always come."

It's really beautiful in the jewellery department. There's counter after counter, piled high, everything all winking and flashing in a thousand different colours, like an Aladdin's cave. We wandered round, touching things and picking things up and trying on bracelets and chains. Shay found some earrings that she fancied. They were in the shape of parrots, swinging on a perch: bright red and blue and emerald green. They would've looked stupid on me as I have this rather ridiculous face, very small and squashed, but on Shay I could see they would be totally brilliant. I urged her to get them, and she was obviously tempted. She held them up by her ears and said, "What d'you reckon?"

"I think you should buy them," I said.

"Mm... dunno! I'll think about it." She put the parrots back and reached out for something else. "Hey, look! These would suit you!"

She'd found some tiny little earrings in the shape of flowers. I agreed that they were sweet, but I couldn't imagine ever wearing them.

"So what would you get," said Shay, "if you were going to get something?"

What I'd always, always wanted was a silver chain. I said this to Shay and she cried, "Let's look!"

There were so many silver chains that it was really difficult to decide which one I should go for, but in the end I settled on one which had a tiny little pixie figure hanging from it.

"That's Cornish, that is," said Shay. "Cornish pixie. That's a good luck charm! Is that what you'd get?"

I said yes, but of course I couldn't get it as I didn't have any money. But it was fun just looking. I mean, it didn't make me discontented or anything.

After we'd done a bit more mooching, Shay said we should go up to the self-service and get something to eat and drink. I quickly said that I wasn't hungry, but Shay said, "That's all right, I'll pay for it." Like she knew I didn't have any money and wanted to spare me the embarrassment of being forced to admit it. I didn't argue, cos it would've been rude when she'd made the offer. She bought us a Coke each, and a packet of crisps, and gave the lady at the till a five pound note. The lady asked if she had "the odd 2p" but Shay said she hadn't.

"See?" She opened her purse and shook it upside down. "This is all I've got."

I said, "I can give you 2p," feeling glad that I could make a contribution, even just a small one.

"I've got loads more money at home," said Shay. "I've got money in the building society. I can take it out whenever I want. It's just that I don't bring much with me cos of muggers."

I giggled at that. I couldn't imagine anyone being bold enough to mug Shay!

"Just let anyone try it," she said. "I'd bash 'em to a pulp! But I don't need the hassle, you know?"

After our crisps and Coke we went back out into the shopping centre and mooched round a few more shops, until Shay suddenly stopped and said there was something she'd got to do.

"Just wait there." She pointed at a seat, and I obediently sat down. "I'll only be a few minutes. Don't move! OK?"

I said OK. I didn't mind sitting there, watching people walk past, though I did wonder where Shay had rushed off to in such a hurry, and what she was going to do. She'd only been gone about two seconds when a girl came up to me and said, "Was that Shay Sugar I saw you with?"

I said yes, and she scrunched up her face into an expression of... well! Like if you saw a scorpion scuttling across the pavement. *Look out there's a scorpion* kind of thing.

"D'you know her?" I said.

"She used to go to my school."

"Oh. She goes to my school now," I said.

"Is she a friend of yours?"

I nodded. The girl went, "Hm!" I began to feel a bit uneasy; this girl didn't seem to care for Shay very much. "I'd watch out, if I were you," she said.

"Why?" I crinkled my nose, which I happen to know (cos I've done it in front of a mirror) looks really silly, but I can't seem to help it. It's a *mannerism*. "Why have I got to watch out?"

"I just would, that's all."

My nose went crinkle, crinkle again. I can actually, sometimes, be quite stubborn. According to Mum I can. I said, "But *why*?"

540

"Cos she'll make you do things."

"What things?"

"Things you don't want to do."

"I don't do anything I don't want to do!"

"That's what you think," said the girl.

I wondered why she was saying this to me. She didn't look like the sort of person who would spread malicious gossip. What I mean is, she was blonde and prettyish and had blue eyes. People with blue eyes always look like they're soft and gentle. But of course you never can tell. Looks can be deceiving.

Shay came back at that moment. She and the girl looked at each other, and both together they said, "Hi!"

"How's your new school?" said the girl.

"OK. How's St Margaret's?"

"A lot quieter without you there."

"Everywhere's a lot quieter without me," said Shay. "Must be *sooo* boring."

"Some people like it that way."

"Yeah? Some people are just mindless blobs."

"That's your opinion," said the girl.

"Course it is! Wouldn't quote anyone else's, would I?"

The girl said, "Who knows?"

"I do," said Shay.

So then the girl, like, gave up. She just went "Huh!" and stalked off in what I think is called a dudgeon, though I'm not actually sure what a dudgeon is.

It's indignation! I just looked it up. I think it's a good word and I'm going to start using it. *Dudgeon.*

"She's so stupid, that girl," said Shay. She put her arm round my waist, in a companionable fashion. "I'll walk you to the bus stop."

When I got home, Mum was there as it was her afternoon off. She was looking like a big black thundercloud. What had I done now???

"Where have you been?" she said.

"In the shopping centre."

"For *four solid hours*?"

"Dad knew where I was! I told him."

"And what about Millie? Did you tell Millie? You didn't, did you?" I shook my head. "Ruth, it's not good enough! You can't let people down like this."

"I'm sorry," I mumbled. "I forgot."

"That's no excuse! How do you think she felt, turning up on the doorstep and Lisa telling her you'd gone out? I suppose you were with that Shay?"

"She's my friend," I said.

"So's Millie – and she's been your friend for far longer!"

I protested that Millie wasn't properly my friend. Not any more.

"Why not?" said Mum.

"I told you," I said. "She's in this gang. She doesn't even talk to me when we're at school. If it wasn't for Shay, nobody would talk to me!"

"Why aren't you in a gang?" said Lisa.

"Cos I don't want to be!"

"I would. I'd be in the *best* gang. I—"

"Oh, shut up!" I said. I took off my coat and slung it over the back of a chair. As I did so, something fell out of the pocket. Something shiny. Lisa immediately pounced.

"What's this?"

"Yes, what it is it?" said Mum.

Lisa squealed, and held it up. "Ooh, pretty!"

It was the silver chain I'd picked out. How had it got in my pocket?

"Where did you get that from?" said Mum.

Quickly, I said, "Shay gave it to me."

She must have done; it was the only explanation. She

must have rushed off to the building society to take some money out, cos I knew she didn't have any more on her, then rushed back into Sander's and bought the chain. Then she must have slipped it in my pocket when I wasn't looking. It must have been when she put her arm round me. I'd thought at the time that it was an unusual thing for Shay to do. We didn't have a touchy-feely sort of relationship at all; not like I'd had with Millie. Me and Millie were always going round with our arms linked. Mum used to laugh at us and say it was like we were joined at the hip. But with Shay it had felt a bit uncomfortable, to tell the truth. Why couldn't she just have said, straight out, "I've bought you something?" Maybe she'd though I wouldn't take it off her.

Mum was holding out her hand. "Lisa, let me have a look at that. Are you telling me, that Shay actually bought this for you?"

I said yes. I mean, how else could it have got there? I hadn't taken it!

"It's a Cornish pixie," I said. "It's a good luck charm."

"Hm…" Mum was examining it, closely. "Well, it's not top quality. It can't have cost that much. All the same—" She handed it back to me. "She really shouldn't be buying you things."

"It's all right," I said. "She's got loads of money! She's got a *building society* account."

"Oh, I'm sure she has," said Mum. "But in future, just say no. OK? You don't have to be rude about it, just say your mum doesn't want you accepting things. And, Ruth—" She crooked a finger at me. "Just pick up that telephone and call Millie. I want to hear you apologise."

# eight

When we went back to school after half term, I told Shay thank you for my chain. Shay said, "You've got to wear it all the time, it'll bring you good luck."

"I can't wear it to school," I said, shocked. The very thought! Wearing my precious chain to Krapfilled High!

"I'd wear my earrings," said Shay, "except they'd probably make me take them off."

"You got them?" I said. "You got your earrings?"

"Thought I might as well. Seemed silly not to. But I don't reckon they'd let me go round with parrots in my ears... don't s'ppose they'd mind a chain, though."

"But someone might steal it!"

"Not with me around."

"No, it's too beautiful," I said. "It's the most beautiful thing I've ever had and I shall cherish it always. But Mum—" I added this bit reluctantly. "Mum says you mustn't go spending your money on me."

Shay gave one of her cackles of laughter. "Tell your mum she doesn't have to worry!"

"She really means it. I don't think she'd let me take anything else. She nearly made me give my chain back."

"That'd be daft. What'd she wanna do that for?"

I shook my head. I sort of understood how Mum felt, but I didn't want to say anything that might sound ungracious.

"It's what being friends is all about," said Shay. "I don't see why I can't give you stuff if I want."

"Cos I can't give you stuff," I said. "I haven't got anything!"

Shay said what did that matter? "It's not important!"

"It is to me," I said. "I'd like to give you something."

"Yeah?" She considered me a moment, through narrowed eyes, like she was trying to decide whether I was serious. "Maybe, in that case..."

"What?"

"We'll see what we can do."

She wouldn't say any more, so I was left not knowing what she meant. I kept trying to think of anything at all I might have that Shay would like, but I couldn't. All my stuff was old, and chipped, and tatty. Most of it had come from jumble sales. The only really valuable object I possessed was my silver chain. *Silvery* chain. I knew it wasn't real silver, but it was still my most treasured possession.

I now went round with Shay all the time at school. It was just something that seemed to have happened. Karina had drifted away, and hardly ever spoke to me. Millie never had spoken much, and since half term she wasn't speaking to me at all. She'd been quite huffy when I rang her. I knew that I was the one who was in the wrong, which was why I was willing to say sorry, but I wasn't the one who'd broken our friendship by going and joining a gang, so I really didn't think she had any right to take offence. Not when I'd *apologised*. And to tell me I was disloyal, going out with Shay instead of with her, that was just, like, totally unfair. I wouldn't ever have hung out with Shay if Millie and me had still been friends.

"I've got to hang out with *someone*," I said. "If it weren't for Shay, I'd be on my own!"

"She's got you right where she wants you," said Millie. "She's only gotta call and you go running!"

We didn't actually have a bust-up, cos I just hate,

hate, HATE quarrelling with people, but the telephone call became very frosty, so that I could almost hear the ice crackling as we talked. And now she wasn't just not speaking to me, she wasn't even looking at me any more. Mum seemed to think it was all my fault. She said, "All this talk about gangs! We had gangs at my school. It didn't stop us being friends."

Mum didn't understand, and it was no use trying to explain. She had no idea what it was like, at Krapfilled High. She said, "You're so impressionable! You're far too easy to manipulate. That Shay has just mesmerised you."

Everyone seemed to have it in for Shay and I didn't know why. Karina sidled up to me one day, looking all sly and secretive and practically on the point of bursting with self-importance. She obviously had something she was dying to tell me, but I still remembered the early days, when she'd dripped poison in my ears, like about Mr Kirk beating his wife and Brett Thomas being on drugs, so I turned and walked away from her, hoping she'd get the message. She didn't, of course, or if she did, she ignored it. She really was one of those people it's impossible to snub.

"Hey!" She poked at me, from behind. I turned, rather irritably.

"What?"

"D'you want to hear something?"

I said, "Not particularly."

"I think you ought to," Karina said.

"Why?"

"Cos you ought to. It's something you ought to know. It's about your *friend*... Shay*anne*."

I should have told her to just shut up, or go away, but I'm not very good at being rude to people. Shay used to say that I was too polite. "It won't get you anywhere." It is true, I think, that there are times when you have to be a bit blunt. I did try! I said, "I don't listen to gossip," and marched off across the playground. But with Karina you would most likely have to bash her over the head with a brick before she took any notice.

"It's not gossip!" She came scuttling after me, like a big spider, all eager to spit venom, or whatever spiders do. "It's the honest truth! Did you know—" She lowered her voice to a squeak. "*Your friend* was chucked out of both the schools she used to go to?"

Sniffily, pretending like mad, I said, "That's supposed to be news?"

Karina's face fell. "She told you?"

"Like you said, she's *my friend*."

"I bet she didn't tell you why she was chucked out!" I hesitated.

"She didn't, did she? D'you want me to?"

I tried to say no, but I wasn't quick enough. Karina just went rushing on.

"She *did* things. I can't tell you what things, but they were *bad* things. *Really* bad things. Now there aren't any more posh schools that will have her, which is why she's ended up here."

Karina looked at me, triumphantly. I said, "How do you know about it?"

"Cos I do. I know things."

It was true, Karina did know things. She made it her business to pry into other people's affairs and "know things" about them. She'll probably grow up to be a professional blackmailer.

"I just thought I ought to warn you," she said, smugly. "I wouldn't want you getting into trouble, or anything. Cos that's what she does... she gets people

551

into trouble. *You* think she's all lovely and sticking up for you, but what she's really doing is—"

"Stop it!" I said and I stamped my foot. I was so angry! "I don't want to hear. Shay is my *friend*."

I ran off as fast as I could. Karina's voice came shrieking after me: "You'll be sorry! You're making a big mistake!"

I tried to put out of my mind the things that Karina had told me. And the things that the girl in the shopping mall had said. *And* the uncomfortable feelings I'd had, once or twice. Shay was my friend and I owed her everything. I was doing my homework in the library, I was getting good marks – nearly all As! – and no one was bullying me or getting on my case. I wasn't going to listen to malicious gossip. Cos it *was* gossip, no matter what Karina chose to call it. It was gossip, and it was mean.

Sometimes, if Shay wasn't around, or even if she was, me and Varya would smile at each other and nod, just to be friendly. We still didn't actually talk, but I kept thinking of things that I might say to her, like "How did you get on with your maths homework last night?" or "Ugh! Yuck! Double PE this afternoon." Unfortunately, at the last minute, I'd either get stupidly tongue-tied or a teacher would appear and bellow at everyone to "Stop that confounded racket!" But I was determined that sooner or later I *would* try and start up a conversation.

It was like since meeting Shay I was getting something I'd never had before – confidence.

Like Julia and Jenice had a go at me one morning; they took advantage of Shay not being there.

"Look what the Geek is wearing!"

"That is just *so* cool!"

And then they both went off into these loud guffaws, like something out of a comic strip. If it had happened at the beginning of term I'd have been *mortified*. Well, I still was mortified to tell the truth, cos I knew I looked really stupid. My school shoes had got big holes in them and my trainers were falling to pieces, and Mum had said I'd better wear my wellies "just for today, as it's raining".

She'd promised to get me some new shoes for tomorrow, but tomorrow was too late. I wished I could have stayed at home! I couldn't, because Mum wouldn't let me, and suddenly I just felt so *angry*, I turned and shouted. I shouted, "SHUT UP, you

pair of blithering morons! You haven't got a brain between you!"

Julia said, "Ooh, blithering morons!" and Jenice gave a little titter, but after that, to my huge surprise, they left me in peace. I think they were just so taken aback that I'd dared to say anything. I was, too! But it did feel good.

One Saturday, a couple of weeks later, Shay suggested we go and have a look at the Elysian Fields, which was this huge out-of-town shopping centre that had just opened. It sounded like a really fun place, but I couldn't think how we'd get there. Shay said no problem, she'd get her dad to take us. "The Invisible Man", as she called him.

"We can get the bus back, there's one that goes all the way to my place. Then you could stay and have tea. Ask your mum!"

Mum wasn't all that keen, as I'd known she wouldn't be, but she said she supposed she'd have to agree to it if that was what I really wanted.

"But don't you let her go buying you things! And I

need you to be back no later than six. Is that understood?"

I solemnly promised, on both counts, and Shay said she'd call round with the Invisible Man and pick me up. Mum insisted on coming all the way downstairs, "just to make sure". When I said, "Make sure of what?" she muttered something about "Seeing you off". I knew that really she was just curious about Shay's dad. I was quite curious myself, and also a bit nervous, as I had no idea what he could be like.

He was sitting at the wheel of this big red car which Mum said afterwards was a Merc, meaning Mercedes.

(I don't know anything about cars, I can't tell one from another.) He was creamy-skinned, like Shay ("Foreign extraction," said Mum), with glossy hair, very thick and black. He didn't look like a dad, he looked like a movie star. I was quite in awe of him, and I think Mum was, too, as she didn't say any of the things she'd said she was going to say, like "I've told Ruth she has to be home no later than six o'clock" and

"Would you please make sure to give her a lift back?" All she said was, "How do you do?" and "It's nice of you to drive them." I didn't say anything at all, but just slid into the back seat next to Shay.

We drove all the way to the shopping centre in total silence. Shay looked out of the window, her dad drove the car, and I chewed my fingernails, which is something I haven't done since I was quite tiny. It was really weird. (I don't mean me chewing my fingernails, I mean nobody speaking.) When we arrived, Shay and I got out, her dad said, "OK, you know how to get back," and that was that.

Like I said, weeeeeird!

"He's the quiet sort," said Shay. "He never says much. Not unless he's having a fight with the Vampire."

"They *fight*?" I said.

"Yeah. Don't yours?"

"They sometimes have words," I said, "but they don't actually fight."

Shay seemed to think that that was rather weird. She seemed to think that all parents fought.

"Let's forget about them," she said. "C'mon! Let's go up the escalator... we'll start at the top and work our way down."

Which is what we did. It was like being in an enchanted town! I reckon you could stay there all day and not get bored. It would take about *two weeks* to actually see everything.

"I need a snack," said Shay, after we'd been wandering in and out of shops and up and down escalators for a couple of hours. "Let's go in the Chocolate Shop and have a hot chocolate. It's all right, I'll pay! Your mum can't object to me just buying you something to drink."

In the Chocolate Shop they had real hand-made chocolates decorated with tiny rosebuds and violets. So sweet! I felt my mouth watering as I looked at them, but I didn't have any money to buy any and I couldn't have asked Shay. But she must have noticed me looking, cos after we'd finished our mugs of chocolate and left the shop she suddenly put her hand in her pocket and brought something out and said, "Close your eyes and open your mouth." And when I did, she popped a chocolate into it!

"*Oh*." I munched, ecstatically.

"Good?" said Shay.

"Mm!"

"Have another."

She had a whole packet of them! I said, "How did you—"

"Just eat," said Shay. "Don't ask."

"But h—"

"I took them."

I said, "T-took them?"

"Took them! *Helped myself.*"

She meant that she'd stolen them. That she'd *shoplifted*. The bottom fell out of my stomach with a great clunk. I think my mouth must have fallen open, as Shay gave one of her cackles and said, "Are you shocked?"

I was – horribly. All of a sudden, I was thinking about my chain. And about the earrings. And the drawers full of make-up and jewellery.

"Honestly," said Shay, "you should see your face!" She pulled down the corners of her mouth and sucked in her cheeks. I felt like saying, "But it's *stealing*." Only I couldn't, cos it sounded too goody-goody.

"Stop looking so disapproving! It's only a bit of fun. It's like a kind of game... seeing what you can get away with. I'm pretty good at it! I can get away with almost anything."

She was actually boasting about it. I couldn't believe it! Me and Millie had once gone sneaking into Woolworth's and nicked a handful of lollipops, but that was when we were about *six*. Well, eight, maybe. But we'd known that it was wrong and I think we'd both been secretly a bit ashamed of ourselves. At any rate, we'd never done it again. Shay had obviously been at it for ages.

"Oh, come on, Spice, lighten up! It's not like I'm mugging old ladies for their life savings. I'm not hurting anyone! I never lift anything valuable. Not like real diamonds or anything. Just stuff that takes my fancy. I do it for *fun*. Yeah?"

I couldn't speak. I just didn't know what to say.

"C'mon!" Shay linked her arm through mine. "Let's go and look in the music shop."

I didn't enjoy the music shop. I was on tenterhooks the whole time, in case something else took Shay's fancy and she put it in her pocket and marched out without paying.

All the really expensive stuff, like the DVDs and full-price CDs, were in those plastic cases that have to be removed before you can leave the shop or they'll set the alarm bells ringing. I relaxed a bit round those, cos I didn't think even

Shay would risk setting off alarm bells. But then we came to the bargain section, where they didn't bother with plastic cases, and I started to prickle and shake all over again as I watched Shay picking up bunches of CDs and shuffling them like cards.

"That's a fab one." She flashed a CD in front of me. I tried not to look, but she insisted. "Techno Freaks. They're brilliant! They're my favourite band."

"You'd better put it down," I said. "People are watching."

"So what?" said Shay, but to my great relief she put the CD back with the others and said, "OK! Let's go."

I'd thought once we were outside we'd be safe. Shay bought a couple of pop ices from a kiosk and we perched on a low wall, side by side, licking at them, and slowly I began to breathe a bit easier. But then Shay said, "Remember what you said the other day?"

I said, "What was that?"

"About wanting to give me something?" said Shay.

I felt my blood begin to grow chill.

"Y-yes," I said.

"Did you really mean it?"

I swallowed. "Y-yes," I said.

"OK, so if you really mean it... if you really, really mean it..."

I waited, in a kind of numb horror, for what she was going to say.

"I'd like you to get me that CD!"

I felt my face grow slowly crimson.

"Techno Freaks. The one I showed you. Yeah?"

"I haven't any money," I whispered.

"You don't need money! I told you, you just go in and take it... easy-peasy! I do it all the time."

I stood there, my heart hammering.

"What's the problem?" said Shay. "What are you waiting for?"

"I... I can't!" I said.

"Why can't you?"

"I just can't!"

"I thought you said you really, really wanted to get me something?"

I hung my head. My face was pulsating like a big hot tomato, but my hands were all clammy with sweat.

"Isn't that what you said?"

"Yes."

"So why won't you do it?"

"B-because—"

"Because what? Because you're scared?"

"Because it's stealing!" The words finally came blurting out of me.

"Oh! Shock horror! It's *stealing!*" Shay gave a loud squawk and threw up her hands. A woman passing by turned to stare, but Shay didn't seem to see. Or maybe she just didn't care? "These people make millions! How's it going to hurt them, just nicking one little CD? They probably wouldn't even notice it had gone!"

I couldn't think what to say to this. All I could think was that it was *wrong*.

"Do you want me to come with you," said Shay, "and hold your hand—"

"No! I'm not going to do it!"

"You mean you're not going to get me anything?"

"Not like that," I mumbled.

"So how are you going to do it, then?"

"I don't know! I'll... save up my pocket money, or something."

"Huh!"

"I will. I promise! I'll get you something."

"Not sure I want anything now."

"Oh, please!" I sprang after her, as she turned and began to walk away. "Shay, please!" I tugged at her sleeve. "I'll get you something really nice, something you'll really like. I'll get you the CD, the one you want—"

"It'll be too late by then. I'll have got it for myself, thank you very much. And *I* won't bother saving up for it! Or do you mean—" She suddenly whipped round, to face me. "Do you mean you're going to go and get it for me right now, after all?"

I felt myself start to shake. It would've been so much easier to say yes! To go back into the shop and slip the CD into my pocket and have Shay happy with me again.

"*Well?*"

"I can't!" My voice came out in a self-pitying bleat. Shay's face darkened.

"So what you said was just a load of rubbish, about really, really, *really* wanting to get me something."

"It wasn't! It wasn't rubbish!" I felt a flicker of anger, somewhere deep inside me. "I do really, really want to get you something, but not like this!"

"Like *what*?"

"Stealing. I don't care what you say! It's wrong to steal and I don't think you should to be doing it!"

"Why not, if I enjoy it?"

"Cos it's *beneath* you," I said.

She stopped. "What d'you mean, it's beneath me?"

"It's beneath you! It's a mindless blob sort of thing to do!" I hadn't know this was what I was going to say, but as soon as I'd said it I knew that it was right. "Mindless blobs go out and steal cos they can't think of anything else to do. You're not a mindless blob! You're oceans better than they are."

"That's what you think," muttered Shay.

"It's what I know. You can do anything you want! You don't need to go out and nick things. It's *unworthy*," I said.

"Wow! That's telling it like it is," said Shay. She was trying to make a joke of it, but I could see that I'd got through to her.

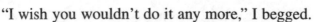

"I wish you wouldn't do it any more," I begged.

I trembled a bit as I said it, cos Shay could be quite a frightening sort of person. I really hated the thought of her being cross with me, maybe even stalking off and leaving me on my own, not wanting to be friends any more. But I knew I couldn't back down, not even if I was shaking like a leaf.

I think Shay was quite surprised; I don't think she'd ever imagined that I'd stand up to her. She looked at me for a moment through half-closed eyes, like she was trying to decide whether to be cold and cutting or just walk off; then suddenly she gave another of her cackles and said, "All right, then! Just for you."

I said, "F-for me?"

"Just for you... I'll stop doing it!"

I said, "You will?" I was stunned. I felt like I'd won the lottery! "You really mean it?"

"Watch my lips... what did I say? *Just-for-you*. I wouldn't stop doing it for anyone else, but I'm sick of you nagging at me!"

I said, "I wasn't nagging!"

"Course you were. Nag, nag, nag. Ooh, it's naughty! Ooh, it's stealing! And I still haven't got my CD."

"I'll get it for you, I'll save up for it!"

"Yeah, yeah, yeah." Shay waved a hand. "Don't bother, I don't really want it. I was just, like, testing you. Trying to see if you'd do it. It's probably just as well you didn't, you'd be bound to get caught."

"Yes, I would. I'd be shaking like a jelly."

"Dunno what I'm gonna do for kicks in future, mind you. Have to take up finger painting or something."

Greatly daring, I said, "You could always learn how to use a vacuum cleaner and tidy your room up."

"See what I mean?" said Shay. "Nag, nag, nag! I pity your husband if you ever get married... you'll drive him bonkers!"

For the first time, as we went back on the bus together, I felt that Shay and me were real proper friends, like I'd been with Millie. We were giggling together and sharing jokes, and I knew it was because I'd found the courage to stand  up to her. The girl who'd spoken to me that time in the shopping mall had said that Shay would "make me do things." I'd told her that I didn't do anything I didn't want to do and I hadn't! So I was quite proud of myself and felt that Shay respected me.

When we got off the bus she said, "Let's go and get some junk food for tea." I knew she was only getting junk food to annoy her mum, but I didn't say anything as I thought I'd probably said enough already. She'd promised to stop nicking stuff and that was the most important.

We went to a little corner shop that had one of those notices on the door: ONLY TWO SCHOOL CHILDREN AT A TIME. Shay said, "That's cos they steal things."

"Only if they're mindless blobs," I said.

"Yeah, right," said Shay.

We were in the shop, trying to decide what to buy, when I noticed that the old woman behind the counter was watching us. It made me uncomfortable, though I don't know why, since we weren't doing anything we shouldn't have been.

"How about this?" Shay picked up a packet of Starbursts. "And crisps! We gotta have crisps."

She was just reaching out for a bag of prawn cocktail when the old woman came over to us and snapped, "What are you two up to?" She must have had a *really* suspicious nature.

"Nothing," said Shay.

"Don't give me that! I saw you, trying to filch those crisps. I'm just about sick of you kids! You in particular." She snatched the bag from Shay and slapped it back on the shelf. "You've been in here before, haven't you?"

"So what if I have?" said Shay.

"I'll give you 'what if I have', my girl! And I'll have those back, as well!" She wrenched the Starbursts out of Shay's hand. "Nasty thieving brats, the pair of you!"

"Excuse me," I said. I was just so furious! What right had this horrible old woman to accuse us of stealing her rotten junky food? "We were going to *pay* for those!"

"Pull the other one," said the old woman. She gave me a shove. "And get out of my shop! You show your faces in here again and I'll have the law on you."

I screamed, "But we haven't *done* anything!"

It was Shay who grabbed me by the arm and pulled me away. I was really surprised that she hadn't answered back; I was the one practically beside myself with indignation.

"She hasn't any right to treat us like that! You can't go round accusing people of stealing when they haven't done anything. There's laws against doing that!"

I went on about it all the way back to Shay's place. It was so unfair – and especially to Shay. I couldn't understand why she wasn't more angry about it.

"I'd be *fuming*," I said.

"You *are* fuming," said Shay. "You're fuming enough for both of us." And then, in this very calm, laid-back sort of voice, she said that when she was really angry – "I mean really, *really*" – she didn't waste her energy shouting and banging around.

"I go away quietly and I plan things," she said. "That's what I'm gonna do now... I'm gonna go away all quietly and I'm gonna plan things. You'll see!"

# Secret Writings of
# Shayanne Sugar

That old witch in the newspaper shop is gonna GET IT.
She is gonna be WORKED OVER. She is gonna be
DONE. I mean it!

She's got some cheek, accusing me of stealing. I
might have done before, but I wasn't THIS TIME. I was
actually gonna pay the old witch. Well, that's it. She's
cooked her goose. Good and proper! Nobody, but
NOBODY, messes with this baby and gets away with
it. She has made one BIG MISTAKE.

Actually, I must have been mad. It was Spice's
fault, she was the one talked me into it. "It's
STEALING," she goes, all pathetic. So what do I do? I
go and promise that I won't ever do it again, miss! I'm
really sorry, miss! Please forgive me, miss! Dunno
what came over me. I shoulda told her to get lost.

She's nothing to me! Why should I care what she thinks, stupid old Matchsticks. I don't care what ANYONE thinks. She's got some cheek, telling me I'm like a mindless blob. Never thought she'd have the guts. First one that ever has! Gotta give it to her. Still doesn't explain why I let her get to me. Must be going soft inna head. TEMPORARY INSANITY. Yeah, and see where it's got me. Some old witch has the nerve to actually threaten me with the police!!!! ME. When I wasn't DOING anything.

Well, that's it. She's asked for it. She is gonna be HUNG OUT TO DRY.

And Spice is gonna help me do it...

# nine

I was so excited when Shay rang me, Sunday morning, to say why didn't I stay over at her place next weekend. It was Lisa who answered the phone. She yelled, "Ruth-it's-for-you-it's-that-girl!" The way she said it, *that girl*, it was like Shay had crawled out of a garbage dump. She'd picked it up from Mum. She knew Mum didn't approve, so now she didn't, either. It was totally mindless and it made me cross, especially since me and Shay had become real, true and proper friends. What right had my snotty little sister to be so high and mighty? I'd have ticked her off except I was just so thrilled at the prospect of actually being with Shay for a whole weekend.

"I'll even clear a bit of space in my bedroom," she said. "Just for you... cos we're friends!"

I immediately rushed off to ask Mum. To begin with my heart was in my mouth as I thought she was going to say no. I just couldn't bear it if she said no! It was Dad who came to my rescue. He said, "Oh, come on, Lynn! What harm can it do?"

"There's just something about that girl," said Mum. "I don't trust her."

Needless to say, Lisa was standing there with her ears going tick tock. I knew she was taking it all in and that later on she'd repeat it to me, parrot fashion.

"That girl... we don't trust her!"

Without having the faintest idea *why*. I don't think Mum ought to say these sort of things in front of Lisa; she's too young and stupid.

Anyway, Dad stuck up for me and in the end Mum gave in. She said all right, I could go, even though she wasn't happy about it.

"But since she seems to be the only friend you have—"

"She's my *best* friend," I said.

"Well, just be careful," said Mum.

What did she mean, *be careful*? What was there to be careful about? It didn't make any sense.

"Don't let her lead you astray."

Mum thought I was such a pushover I'd do whatever Shay asked me to do. Little did she know that I was the one who'd got Shay to turn over a new leaf! I'd stood up to her. I wasn't anywhere near as weak and feeble as Mum made me out to be.

On Saturday afternoon I met Shay in the shopping centre and we went into Marks & Spencer and bought stuff for tea. Mum never goes into Marks & Spencer, she says we can't afford it, but Shay said I had to have the best, "Cos you're my friend... and look, I'm paying for it! See? It'd be just as easy not to, but I'm doing it for you... cos you're my *friend*."

She'd cleared a bit of space in her bedroom, too, just like she'd promised. It wasn't very much space, and I thought that most probably all she'd done was just kick stuff out of the way, but at least there was a sort of path across the middle of the carpet.

Shay said that we'd have to sleep in the same bed, "Cos I haven't got a sleeping bag and you don't want to go in the spare room all by yourself, do you?"

I agreed that I didn't. The whole point of a sleepover is to be together, so you can lie there all nice and cosy in the darkness, giggling and swapping secrets. I said this to Shay and she said, "Well, this is it. This is what I said to the Vampire. *She* thought you were going to sleep in the spare room."

"Where is she?" I said. "Is she…" I giggled, "…in her coffin?"

"Nah, she's gone off for the weekend. Took her coffin with her. *He's* here. The Invisible Man. D'you wanna see him?"

I giggled again. I was getting used to the way Shay referred to her mum and dad.

"Don't see how I can, if he's invisible!"

"Yeah, good point," said Shay. "Let's have some music."

We spent the afternoon listening to various CDs that Shay dug out from the mounds of books and clothes and magazines that littered the floor, then went downstairs to eat our Marks & Spencer's tea. Shay's dad looked round the door as we were in the middle of it and said, "Oh, hallo… um… Rosie?"

"Ruth," snapped Shay.

"Ruth. Hallo!"

I said hallo back, turning a bit pink. I don't know why I found it so embarrassing, being in the same room as Shay's dad, but he just looked so totally un-dadlike. If she'd have said he was a movie star or a famous tennis player, I wouldn't have been surprised.

"I'm off out," he said. "I'll be back about elevenish. You OK here by yourselves?"

"What if I said no?" said Shay.

Her dad blinked. "Well, I guess I'd have to have a re-think. But there are two of you, so you won't be lonely. Just don't answer the door. Usual precautions. Oh, and you've got my mobile number if you need it. OK?"

Shay's dad went breezing out, leaving us on our own.

"What would happen if I wasn't here?" I asked.

"What d'you mean?" said Shay.

"Like... would he still go out and leave you?"

"They always go out on a Saturday. Both of 'em."

"Doesn't it bother you?"

"Nah! Why should it?"

"It'd bother me," I said.

"I'm used to it. They've always done it. Even when I was tiny. They never really wanted a kid in the first place."

"How d'you know?" I said.

"Cos she told me."

"Your mum? She *told* you?"

"Yeah. She said I was lucky she didn't have an abortion and get rid of me."

I could feel my eyes growing huge as saucepan lids. I couldn't believe what I was hearing!

"Welcome to the real world," said Shay. "Let's go and watch a video."

We watched videos and played computer games all evening, until suddenly, at about eleven o'clock, Shay jumped up and said, "Right! Time to go out."

I said, "*Out?* But it's dark!"

"Yeah? So what? I often go out in the dark. C'mon! There's something we gotta do."

"What?" I hurried anxiously after her as she went out into the hall. "What have we got to do?"

"Tell you when we get there. Here!" She flung my coat at me. "I just gotta fetch something. Won't be a sec."

She went down the stairs into the kitchen and came back up with a plastic carrier bag.

"OK! Let's go."

I was quite nervous, being out so late. I'm *never* out that late, not even with Mum. I mean, we just never really go anywhere; we can't, because of Dad. I kept telling myself that Shay did it all the time, so it had to be all right. But I knew that it wasn't. Not really. I knew that Mum would be horrified if she ever found out.

"W-where exactly are we going?" I said.

"Just into town a bit. Back to the shop."

I said, "What shop?"

"Shop where the old witch accused us of stealing."

I felt a row of prickles go tingling down my spine. "W-won't they be closed?" I said.

"Hope so," said Shay. She cackled. "Better had be!"

"So w-what are we going there for?"

"Gonna teach her a lesson is what we're going there for. It's all right! You don't have to *do* anything. Just be there."

I desperately didn't want to be there. Whatever it was that Shay was planning to do, I didn't want any part of it! But I was too scared to turn round and walk away, all by myself. For one thing, I wasn't sure I could remember how to get back to Shay's place, and even if I did get back, I didn't have a key.

Reluctantly, I trailed after Shay. The shop was on a corner. The shutter was pulled down over the door, and wire mesh screens were over the windows. All the other shops nearby were closed, and the street was empty.

Shay said, "Good! You stay here and keep a look-out. I'm going down the side. If you see anyone coming, you gotta let me know. OK?"

I nodded, miserably.

"Look, we're *friends*," said Shay. "It's what friends do... they watch out for each other. It's all I'm asking... just watch out for me."

She made it sound like I'd be really letting her down if I didn't do it.

"Anyone comes, you tell me. Yeah?"

I said, "Yes, but wh—"

"Don't ask! It's best you don't know. You're already an accomplice, of course—" I felt my legs begin to wobble. "But you can always say you didn't know what was going on. If anyone asks, that is. But no one's going to ask. Are they? Cos you're gonna keep a look-out! Here, just hang on to the bag."

Shay took something from it, then thrust it at me and disappeared down the side, leaving me to stand shivering on the corner. It wasn't really cold, but my kneecaps were bounding and my teeth kept clattering. I think it was because I was just so terrified.

Cars passed, but no people. A police car came down the road and slowed up as it approached. I did my best to look brave and confident, like I was just standing there waiting for someone, and to my relief it drove on. I was so busy watching it, making sure it didn't turn round and come back, that I didn't notice a street door opening at the side of the shop. A man came out, followed by a woman. I nearly died of fright! It was the old witch woman that had accused us of stealing. She didn't look quite as ancient as she had in the shop – and the man didn't look ancient at all. He was big and burly, like a rugby player. I gave a panic-stricken squeak and dashed off round the side.

"Someone's coming!"

Shay immediately stopped whatever it was she was doing and ran for it. I made to run after her, but the rugby player had me in his grasp.

"What the—"

I squealed and wriggled, but he just held on even tighter.

"Is this you?" He gestured furiously at the side wall of the shop. Someone had spray-canned all over it – **DEATH AND DESTRUCTION** – in big letters, plus lots of really creepy drawings of skulls and crossbones and hangman's nooses.

The old witch woman had appeared.

"You're one of those kids," she said. "I recognise you! What's in that bag? What have you got in there?" She snatched it away from me. "I thought as much!"

Triumphantly, she brought out a can of spray paint. Black, the same as the stuff on the wall. "Caught you red-handed, my pretty! Just as well my son's a fast mover... thought you'd get away with it, didn't you?"

"I don't reckon she was the one actually did it." The man still had a grip on me; his fingers were really biting into my arm. "I reckon she was just the lookout."

"No!" I shook my head. "It was just me!"

I don't know why I said that, except that Shay had obviously managed to escape and I didn't want to get her into trouble. After all, the old witch *had* falsely accused her.

"I did it by myself," I said.

They obviously weren't sure whether to believe me. The man said, "Are you telling the truth?"

"Yes! It was me on my own!"

A new voice broke in. "Don't believe her! She wouldn't dare!"

I spun round. It was Shay! She'd come back! The man immediately pounced on her.

"I knew it! I knew there was another of 'em!"

"You don't have to break my arm," said Shay.

"I'll do more than break your arm, you little vandal,

I'll— *Ow!*" He jumped back, with a curse, as Shay kicked out. "You little brat!"

"I told you, you don't have to break my arm! I'm not going anywhere. Wouldn't have come back if I was planning on going anywhere."

I don't know why she had come back. She could have got away quite easily – no one need ever have known. I wouldn't have told on her, no matter what they did to me. I really wouldn't! I was her friend. Friends don't betray each other. But oh, at the time, I was just so relieved!

The old woman's son wanted to turn us over to the police, but the old witch woman said no.

"Not that they don't deserve it, but I know this one." She pointed at Shay. "I know her mum and dad – they come into the shop quite often. Nice, respectable people. I think we'll go and see what they have to say."

"They're not there," said Shay.

"Well, let's just go and check that out, shall we?"

"You're wasting your time. She's away and he's out with his girlfriend."

But he wasn't. When we got back to Shay's place, her dad was there and already had a face like thunder.

"Where in God's name have you been? What do you think you're doing, going out at this time of night?"

"Vandalising my property," said the witch woman, "that's what they're doing!"

Shay's dad was horribly angry. I mean, like, really,

*really* angry. Cold and cutting, and his lips going into a thin line.

"What is the *matter* with you?" He took Shay by the shoulders and shook her. "Do you do this just to spite us? Don't you have everything you could possibly want? Everything that money could buy? Dear God! How many more times?"

Shay just stood, saying nothing. Needless to say, I said nothing, either. I couldn't have, even if anyone had wanted me to. My teeth were clattering and I felt like I was about to be sick.

Shay's dad had started to shout. "Are you some kind of delinquent? Do we have to have you put away?"

"Yeah, get someone else to deal with the mess," said Shay.

Honestly! I don't know how she dared. Her dad drew a deep breath, like he was trying very hard to control himself, and turned to the witch woman. Stiffly, he told her that of course he'd see that all the graffiti was removed from her wall and he thanked her for not going to the police. She said, "Well, my son wanted me to, but seeing as I know you... I thought maybe you'd rather deal with it yourself." Shay's dad said grimly that he most certainly would.

"You can rest assured of that." And he gave Shay this really black look as he said it, so I knew she was going to be in big, BIG trouble. And so was I. Being an accomplice is just as bad as actually committing the crime; we'd both have been locked up if the old woman's son had had his way. I would've died if that had happened! I'd have been so ashamed. I was ashamed enough as it was, cos I'd never done anything like that in my life before. I'd never done anything criminal at all, except for stealing the lollipops in

Woolworths, but that was when I was tiny. And that was just, like, being naughty. Spraying skulls and crossbones on the side of someone's wall, that was *serious*.

Shay's dad told us to "Wait in there, both of you, while I get something to compensate this good woman," and he pushed us quite roughly into the front room and shut the door. He was *angry*.

I whispered, "What's going to happen?"

Shay shrugged her shoulders. "Dunno. Who cares? You don't have to be involved! It's not like you did anything."

"But I was an ac-complice," I said.

"Yeah, but you didn't know what was going on. I'll tell 'em! Don't worry."

"But w-what about you?"

"Doesn't matter about me. I can look after myself."

"You shouldn't have come back!" I said.

"Had to," said Shay. "Couldn't leave you on your own." And then she said such a curious thing, she said, "Wouldn't have done it for anyone else. Just for you. cos you're different."

I shall always remember Shay saying that. I wished I'd asked her how! "*How* am I different?" At the time I was too worried sick even to think of it. Shay honestly didn't seem in the least bit bothered, but I was petrified. I've never been so scared in all my life! Shay couldn't understand it. She said, "Oh, come on, Spice, you didn't *do* anything. What are you scared of?"

What I was scared of was what Mum and Dad were going to say. Shay still couldn't understand it. She said, "Don't see why they should say anything. Don't have to know, do they? Who's gonna tell 'em? Not me!"

"But I c-can't let you take all the blame," I said.

"Why not?"

"Well, because... because we're friends!"

"It's because we're *friends*," said Shay, "that I'm gonna keep you out of it. It's what friends do... they look after each other. Anyway, it's not gonna help me any, you getting into trouble. Prob'ly just make it worse."

So then I thought that perhaps she was right, and Mum and Dad need never know, and this cheered me up a bit and made me feel stronger, until Shay's dad reappeared and snapped, "Right, young woman!" He meant *me*. "Let's get you back home."

"She's staying over," said Shay.

"Not any more, she's not. She's going home, and you and I are going to have a serious talk. Come along! The pair of you."

"Don't see why I have to go," said Shay.

"You'll do as you're told! Get a move on."

"I don't want to," said Shay. "I want to stay where I am."

"You really think I'd be fool enough to go off and

leave you here to get up to heaven knows what?"

"Yeah, why not?" said Shay. "It's what you usually do."

"What I may have done in the past, my girl, and what's going to happen in the future, are two entirely different things. Leave you here and risk getting back to find the place burnt to a cinder? No, thank you! I know what you're capable of. Now, shift yourself!"

We drove home in total silence. Shay was in such a sulk she didn't even say goodbye to me. Her dad asked me if I wanted him to see me to my front door, but although I was scared of using the lift at that time of night, I was even more scared of him coming with me and talking to Mum, so I said that I'd be all right. He said, "You sure?" and I said "Yes!" and shot out of the car before he could change his mind.

It was nearly midnight when I rang the bell. Mum and Dad would be in bed; they might even be asleep. But I couldn't stand outside all night! I rang and rang, and then called out through the letter box, "Mum, it's me!" If I hadn't called she might never have come, cos everyone's, like, really nervous once it gets dark. A lot of mugging and stuff goes on. Even though I'd called out, Mum still only opened the door a tiny crack and kept the chain on. And then she saw that it really was me, and she went "*Ruth?*" and took the chain off and quickly pulled me inside. "What are you doing here? I thought you were staying over! You haven't quarrelled, have you? They didn't let you come home by yourself?"

"N-no," I said. "Sh-shay's dad brought me."

"But why? Ruth! *Why*? What's going on?"

That was when I burst into tears and told her the whole story.

"I knew it," said Mum. "I knew something like this would happen. Didn't I say all along?

There was just something about that girl?"

"It wasn't her fault," I sobbed. "The woman accused her!"

"That's no excuse. And now look what you've done! You've got your dad up."

Dad had appeared at the end of the passage. "What is it?" he said. "What's all the rumpus?"

"It's all right," said Mum. "It's just Ruth come back. Get to bed, now," she told me. "We'll talk about it in the morning."

"Not in front of Lisa!" I begged.

Mum agreed, not in front of Lisa. It was a bit of a comfort, but only a little bit.

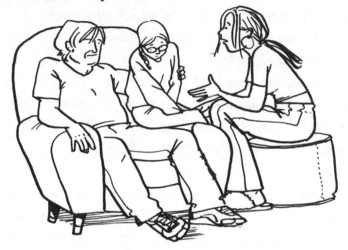

Next morning, Mum shut the girls and Sammy away and we had our talk. Me and Mum and Dad. Mum said that she obviously couldn't stop me speaking to Shay at school, "But I don't want you seeing her out of school any more. I don't even want you ringing her. I don't want you having anything to do with her! Do you understand?"

I nodded, miserably.

"I want you to promise me," said Mum. "On your honour!"

I had to promise; what else could I do?

"It's for your own good," said Mum. "A girl like that, she's a really bad influence. It bothers me that you'll still be with her at school."

Mum needn't have worried. Shay didn't come into school on Monday; she wasn't there all the rest of the week. Jenice Berry, who bunked off whenever she felt like it, said that she'd seen her hanging about in the shopping centre. And then, the following week, she came up to me and said, "Well, have I got news for *you*! Your friend Shayanne Sugar's gone and got herself nicked." Karina, who was there at my elbow, immediately squealed, "What for? What was she doing?"

"*Stealing.*" Jenice said it with relish; you could tell she was really enjoying herself. "In HMV. I was in there and I saw her being taken away. I don't reckon she'll be back!"

She never was. That night when I was brought home in disgrace was the last time I ever saw her. I did so long to know what had happened to her! I begged Mum to let me ring her, but Mum stood firm.

"It's best you just forget her," she said.

But how could I? I'll never forget Shay, as long as I live! When I'm grown up, and have passed all my exams, and have become a doctor working in a hospital – cos that *is* what I'm going to do – it will be all thanks to Shay. If it hadn't been for her, I'd just have given up.

I've puzzled and puzzled why she ever bothered with me. I can still remember, right at the beginning, when she told me that maths was not her favourite subject, and I said how it wasn't mine, either, and she said, "Well, that's one thing we have in common." But we didn't really have *anything* in common. Not really. Not even maths! Shay was good at maths. She was good at lots of things, but it was like she had this auto-destruct button inside her which she just couldn't resist pressing. If ever it looked like she might be going to do something people would approve of, where they might say "Well done!" or "Good work!" she immediately had to go and press the button – **BOOM!** – so it all blew up in her face. Like if one week she got an A for her homework it seemed the following week she'd just have to get a D, or even an E. Or even, sometimes, no mark at all, when she'd filled the pages with her big angry scribble.

Shay could have got As practically all the time if she'd wanted, and I could never understand why she didn't. I think now that maybe she didn't understand, either, or that she did understand but there just wasn't anything she could do about it, and that's why she got so cross whenever I tried asking her. And cross when I let people like Julia get to me. It was like I had to use *my* brain to make up for her not using hers. It wasn't that she didn't *want* to use hers; she just couldn't let herself. Maybe it was her way of getting back at her mum and dad for the way they treated her. That's the only thing I can think of.

I tried explaining all this to Mum. I so desperately

didn't want Mum to think badly of Shay! I told her about Shay's mum and dad, and how they used to go away and leave her on her own, sometimes for days and days. Mum was quite shocked. "I didn't know that," she said. "That's terrible!" And then she suddenly hugged me, which is something that Mum doesn't do all that often; I mean, she just doesn't have the time. She said, "Oh, Ruth, I know things haven't been easy for you, but we'll try to make them better. We'll get things sorted! It's not fair, putting all the burden on you, just because you're the oldest."

I don't know why Mum felt she had to apologise. It's not her fault if Dad's sick and can't work and I was born first. I told her this. I said, "I'd rather have you as a mum than have a mum like Shay's!" I think that made her happy cos she kissed me – which is something else she doesn't have time to do, usually – and said, "You're a good girl! I'll make it up to you. I promise! I won't let the others interfere when you want to do your homework."

She doesn't, either! She shoos them away and tells them to "*Be quiet*. Your sister's working." Ooh, it makes such a difference! They creep off as meek as mice and it means that I'm able to *concentrate*. I still go to the library sometimes, though. I've joined a homework club, which is fun, as you get to meet lots of people. The kids at school, they've mostly stopped bothering me. Just now and again the two Js try it on, like it's a sort of habit they can't break, but nobody takes much notice of them any more. Including me! The other day that horrible boy, Brett Thomas, told them to belt up. He shouted, "Knock it off, I'm sick of it!" Maybe he's not quite as horrible as I thought he was.

Actually, nothing is – as horrible, I mean. Things are getting better all the time! I had a long talk with Varya, the day we went back for the autumn term.
I've discovered that she's really nice. Her English has hugely improved, it's almost as good as mine! This is because I'm helping her. We hang out together and I give her lessons. Mum and Dad have put in for a new flat from the Council, one with more rooms, and if we get it, which Mum seems to think we might, I could have a room all to myself! Hooray! Varya could then come and stay with me and that would be neat, as I've already been to stay with her twice. I'd really love to invite her back.

One morning, about a week ago, a card came through the letter-box with my name on it. It was from Shay! Mum didn't try keeping it from me. She said, "Here, it's for you. I haven't read it." It didn't
really say very much; just a few words, in Shay's big bold writing. But at least she'd written!

**Wotcher, Spice! They've got me banged up, boo hoo! Think I'm too dangerous to be let out with all you law-abiding lot. Hope you're working hard and giving the blobs what for. YOU'D BETTER BE. See ya! – S.**

I asked Mum if I could write back to her. There wasn't any address, but I thought that if I sent a letter to her home, her mum and dad might forward it. Mum was reluctant at first, but then she relented, and so that's what I'm going to do. She might not reply, but at any rate I'll have tried. Even Mum has softened. She said the other day, "That poor girl! She never stood a chance."

I thought to myself that without Shay I'd never have stood a chance. I know now that I can look after myself. I can survive! I'm not a scaredy cat any longer. If someone like *Joolyer* gives me any trouble – well! She'd better just watch out, cos she'll get trouble back. You have to be prepared to stand up for yourself; Shay taught me that.

I shall never stop thinking about Shay, and wondering how she is. I know it's true that she used people, and that I let myself be bullied by her. But I did speak up in the end! I didn't go stealing when she wanted me to. And even though she tried to trick me, that last night, when she sprayed the graffiti, she did come back for me. She didn't have to; she could just have run away. I wouldn't ever have told on her! The thumbscrew and the rack wouldn't have got her name out of me. She only came back because in spite of everything, she was my friend.

She *was* my friend – I don't care what anyone says!

# Gone Missing

"We both ought to get out," I said.
Honey hooked her hair back over her ears. I
remember her eyes went all big and apprehensive.
"You mean—"
"Leave home!"
"Like... run away?"

Hi – I'm Jade and this is what happened when I ran away
from home with my best friend Honey. I was arguing with
my parents and Honey was having a miserable time with
her mum, so it seemed like a good idea at the time. I
thought we'd just get to London and everything would be
great. It was what to do next that was the problem...

978 0 00 715619 7

www.harpercollinschildrensbooks.co.uk

# Boys Beware

Everyone at school is just so envious of us!
Meg Hennessy couldn't believe that
we are truly independent.
"All on your own?" she kept saying.
"You're living completely on your own?"

Hi there. I'm Emily and my stepsister (and hugest best
friend!) is called Tash. We're into boys in a BIG WAY.
Mum and Dad are going away for a couple of months,
leaving us in our own flat in Aunty Jay's house, and we're
going to have the most fun ever!

978 0 00 716138 7

# Passion Flower

Of course, Mum shouldn't have
thrown the frying pan at Dad.
The day after she threw it,
Dad left home...

Stand back! Family Disaster Area! After the Frying Pan
Incident, it looks like me and the Afterthought are going
to be part of a single-parent family. Personally, I'm on Mum's
side but the Afterthought is Dad's number one fan. Typical.
Still, Dad's got us for the whole summer and things are
looking promising: no rules, no hassle, no worries.
But things never turn out the way you think.

978 0 00 715619 7

www.harpercollinschildrensbooks.co.uk

www.jeanure.com

# Pumpkin Pie

This is the story of a drop-dead gorgeous girl
called Pumpkin, who has long blonde hair
and a figure to die for.
I wish!

It's my sister Petal who has the figure to die for. I'm the
one in the middle... the plump one. The other's the boy
genius, my brainy little brother, Pip. Then there's Mum,
who's a high flier and hardly ever around; and Dad, who's
a chef. Dad really loves to see me eat! I used to love to
eat, too. I never wanted food to turn into my enemy,
but when Dad started calling me *Plumpkin* I didn't
feel I had any choice...

978 0 00 714392 3

www.harpercollinschildrensbooks.co.uk

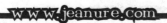

# Boys on the Brain

"What are you doing?" I said.
"I am trying," panted Mum,
"to – get- out – of – these – jeans!"

Hi there. I'm Cresta and that's my mum – thirty-three
going on eighteen. Me and my friend Charlie have great
plans: finish school, get the grades and conquer the
world! We've taken a vow – No Boys before uni, but it's
not easy with the gorgeous Carlito and Alistair around…
And how on *earth* can I put up with a mother who has
boys on the brain?

978 0 00 711373 0

www.harpercollinschildrensbooks.co.uk

# Fruit and Nutcase

## "Hi, this is Mandy Small telling her life story."

I may have trouble writing, but I have no trouble at all
talking! My teacher, Cat, suggested I record my life on
tape so here goes…

I live with my dad, who looks like Elvis, and my mum,
whose idea of a special meal is burnt toast. Sometimes I
feel like I'm the grownup and they're the kids.

But now everything's crashing about my ears, and Dad's
too, as he's just put his foot through the floorboards. I'm
trying really hard not to become a total fruit and
nutcase…

978 0 00 712153 9

# The Secret life of
# Sally Tomato

A is for armpit,
Which smells when you're hot,
Specially great hairy ones,
They smell A LOT.

Hi! Salvatore d'Amato here – call me Sal if you must –
and I am not writing a diary! I'm writing the best alphabet
ever. An alphabet of Dire and Disgusting Ditties.

I'm up to two letters a week, and I reckon it will take me
the rest of term to complete my masterpiece. By then I
plan to have achieved my Number One aim in life – to
find a girlfriend. After all, I'm already twelve, so I can't
afford to wait much longer…

978 0 00 675150 4

www.harpercollinschildrensbooks.co.uk